THRESHOLD

THRESHOLD

TRACEY SHEARER

TWILIGHT
SPARKS
PRESS LLC

ISBN 978-1-7330030-2-5

Cover art © 2022 by Jessica Petersen
Book Design by Jessica Petersen

Printed in the United States of America

Published by Twilight Sparks Press LLC

To my mentors and guides, including my incredible Finder Fairies, thank you for helping me grow even stronger and to shine even brighter on this magical journey . . .

CHAPTER 1

USING HER GIFT HAD ALWAYS FELT LIKE DYING—THAT shuddering gasp of pain, and then the beautiful release into surrender, into acceptance. Or at least that's what Beth Marshall imagined dying would feel like. When she could destroy her inner walls, call off the guards, and finally just *be*.

But last she checked, she was still very much alive and not enjoying her new gig one bit. Using her gift to find things for RAVEN, the black-ops military group she'd attacked not too long ago, sucked balls.

The gray walls of the military training center—along with the RAVEN peanut gallery who had come to watch her perform—faded into the background while she concentrated on calling her energy even further into her body.

The initial chill dissolved under the warm rush sinking into her bones. The air shimmered in front of her as if the stars had been captured from the night sky and held there just for her.

She reached her hands toward the glimmer. The flecks of light solidified into what always reminded Beth of a frozen lake, a cold mirror of a colder sky.

She tapped against the icy surface with her finger, directly in the center, and it began to clear.

A drop of red swam underneath the ice, twisting and turning like blood dissolving in water. A shape started to take form. She saw a folder in a man's hand. The title sharpened:

WAKEFIELD INITIATIVE 351

It's what she'd been asked to find. She didn't know what the initiative was, but she imagined it was nothing good if RAVEN wanted it.

Her reflection looked back at her—cold and remote, which fit her dead black eyes perfectly. They'd started shifting to black when she used her gift during her time in juvie. Not a surprise, considering what she'd had to do in there to survive.

"Look at her eyes," one of the RAVEN operatives muttered.

Another whispered, "She looks like a demon."

Beth laughed, still staring at the frozen lake in front of her that no one else could see. "My friend, Sammy, would agree with you."

Did she just say friend? Well, they've known each other for over twenty years now, even if most of them had been crappy ones. And when they'd performed their blood sister ritual with their friend, Kate, they'd been bonded together, whether they liked it or not.

If either of them found out she was helping RAVEN, they'd lose their shit. Right now, she was supposed to be taking a wilderness survival class. Flimsy excuse at best to hide her time at RAVEN, but they seemed to buy it.

"Sometime this century, Marshall," Jensen said. Her RAVEN handler wasn't one for patience.

She glanced at him. "Has anyone told you to moisturize? It'll help with those frown lines."

Jensen didn't say anything. He just gritted his teeth.

But she'd delayed long enough. It was time to get this done. A thick silver cord rose in front of her, coming from her body. Not really from her body, more like from the energy surrounding her when she used her gifts. Ever since she was a little girl, when the cord appeared, that's when she knew she was going to find something.

The silver cord swayed this way and that, as if sensing her hesitation. She wasn't seeking something for one of her reality show audience members, to help them find peace, achieve closure. This would be helping RAVEN.

The enemy.

But a deal was a deal.

The cord stilled, suddenly sure in purpose. With the quickness of a viper, it struck, hitting the icy lake, going through it, and pulling Beth with it, yanking her from her body.

A beautiful sunlit garden filled her vision. There were three young children playing with a ball to her right. A gray-haired man sat in a chair in front of her with armed guards flanking him. The folder sat in his lap.

The breeze blew strands of her hair against her cheeks, tickling them. That was new. She'd never felt physical sensations before while using her abilities. Being part of the Triumvirate with Kate and Sam seemed to have shifted things for her. All of them were growing stronger.

She focused back on the man. His fingers traced the title on the folder, the tips trembling against the words. Tears perched on his sunken cheeks. She tasted the salt of them in the air.

His words were a whisper in her mind.

"What have I done?"

Beth hurtled into her body again. She stumbled a few steps back but managed to not land on her ass.

Her gift's elegant way of telling her she'd seen enough.

"What did you see?" Jensen asked.

She hesitated. The last time she'd found something for RAVEN, two people had died—more blood on her hands.

He gripped her arm, almost hurting her, but Beth had faced much, much worse.

"I'll tell you, but you have to spare his grandkids."

There was a flicker of some emotion in Jensen's face, but it was gone before she could identify it.

He loosened his grip. "You really despise us, don't you?"

Beth fought the urge to rub her arm, knowing she'd probably bruise tomorrow. "Your word that your operatives won't harm the children."

"You don't have any leverage here." Jensen's words lacked conviction at their core.

Beth just stared at him, enjoying the tightening of his jaw. "We both know you can't force me or torture me to use my gift. It won't work if you do, so if you want me to find anything else for you, you'll agree about the kids."

"You have my word," a voice said behind them. "The children will not be harmed by RAVEN operatives."

Major Oliver Wilson walked forward from the back of the room. Beth hadn't heard him come in. In the short time she'd known him, he was one of the few who could sneak up on her. She didn't like that.

But then again, his creepy father ran the Scottish arm of RAVEN, so Ollie had probably been raised early in the family tradition of stealth and secrets.

Beth stared at him for a few moments. His dark red hair was tidy as usual, but the circles under his eyes spoke of uneasy nights.

"There's an old man," Beth said. "He's got the file. He's in Italy." She paused, weighing whether or not to tell them about the guards. But the kids could get caught in the crossfire. "He's got guards. I saw four, but there could be more."

Beth held out her hand, and Jensen gave her his tablet. She pulled up a map of Italy and closed her eyes, letting what she'd seen fill her again. She tapped the screen to move further south. Then expanded it for more details.

Her gift didn't spit out addresses, but she got pretty darn close. "There," she pointed at a location on the map. "Give or take a few miles." She handed the tablet back to him. "That's where you'll find him." She fixed him with a hard stare. "And his grandkids, who aren't to be harmed."

Jensen shook his head. "Whatever you think of RAVEN, we don't kill children. What we do *saves* lives."

Someone drank the Kool-Aid deep. She ignored him and turned to Ollie.

Ollie nodded to Jensen. "Brief the operatives on the ground accordingly."

They saluted the Major and filed out, leaving Beth and Ollie alone.

They stared at each other.

"You look tired," Beth finally said. "You need to get more sleep."

"Sleep" was their code word for a meeting.

Ollie shook his head. "If only I could. My schedule is too tight right now."

No meeting. Crap. She'd agreed to this deal with RAVEN to protect Sam, Kate, and the others, but there was another reason. With Ollie's help, she was going to take his father down, and with it, the faction within RAVEN who fueled the experimentations, kidnappings, and extortions.

"We'll let you know when the next assignment comes up." Ollie nodded to her, then turned his back and headed out the door.

Taking down RAVEN was going to take longer than she'd hoped, which meant Sam and Kate would have more time to push against her inner walls. They'd already made some progress against her defenses since she'd come to Scotland a short while ago, but she couldn't let them get all the way in.

Because if she did, they'd have the power to hurt her again, really hurt her. She hadn't given anyone that power over her since getting out of juvie. Since leaving her parents behind.

She'd had enough pain to last a lifetime and then some.

The walls inside her needed some repair, but they'd hold— they'd stand.

They had to.

CHAPTER 2

BETH SCANNED THE FRONT PAGE OF *THE ROSEBRIDGE PRESS* while Kate bustled around the B&B's kitchen, making breakfast. She shifted in her seat at the table and read the missing person story for the second time. Something hummed against her senses, almost like when she was going to be asked to find something.

Kate walked over and set a heaping plate of crispy bacon on the table. Her long red hair was dusted with bits of powdered sugar, and the apron she wore said, *"A party without cake is just a meeting. —Julia Child."*

"Dig in," Kate announced with a smile. "French toast is up next." She hummed to herself, walking back to the stove.

Beth turned to Sam sitting at the table with her. She lowered her voice. "Is Kate having problems with Logan?"

Sam looked up from the pages of her current manuscript and shook her head. "Not that I know of," she whispered back. She tucked a strand of blond hair behind her ear. "They're getting along really well from what she's said."

Sam looked like one of the heroines in her romance novels. Long blonde hair with a natural wave that even the rain didn't dare mess with and green eyes the color of Brussels sprouts. Beth hated Brussels sprouts.

Beth kept her voice low. "Then why is she making such a huge breakfast when it's just the three of us? This has stress-cooking all over it."

Sam smiled, her eyes crinkling. "I think she's happy. She's also doing her usual mother hen thing, taking care of everyone through food. It's just on overdrive right now."

Kate suddenly turned away from the stove. "I heard that." Her stern look dissolved into one of pure bliss. "I *am* happy. It's incredible. Logan is *so* amazing. He seems to know just what I mean when I tell him to—"

Beth held up her hand. "It's already bad enough hearing Sam gush about the ghostly nasties she can do with Robert in the bedroom." Sam glared at her, but Beth ignored her. "If you turn into Miss Mary Sunshine too, I might have to shoot myself."

Kate slid another slice of French toast onto the skillet. "Well, we wouldn't want that. Then Sam would be stuck talking to you as a ghost, and we know how awful that would be."

Sam guffawed, clapping her hands. "Touché, Kate. Touché."

Beth grabbed a piece of bacon and took a bite. It helped to hide her smile. It wouldn't do to have either of them thinking she enjoyed this banter, which she didn't.

"You could always move out if we bother you so much." Sam poured some orange juice into her glass. "It's not like there isn't another B&B around." Sam watched Beth closely, no doubt to gauge her reaction.

Beth had considered getting a room in town, but she didn't trust RAVEN. Deal or no deal, they might come sniffing around, and she wasn't going to let anything happen to Kate or her daughters, Emily and Patty.

"Why pay for a room when Kate will let me stay for free?" Beth shrugged. "Once my crew gets here, we'll rent a house." She saw a protest looming on Kate's face. "We'll have a lot of equipment, and our filming schedule will be crazy. I wouldn't want to disrupt the kids."

Kate frowned, but didn't say anything.

"Did you see the missing person story in the paper?" Beth said. "That should be pretty unusual around here, right? I mean, it's not like we're in L.A."

Kate's B&B was in the tiny town of Rosebridge in Scotland. Except for the serial killings weeks ago—which Sam, Kate, and Beth managed to stop—this wasn't usually a hotbed of crime.

Sam nodded. "I saw it. I've been waiting for their ghost to come to me, but nothing yet."

"Maybe they don't want to talk to you," Beth said, letting the usual bite fill her words. Things were getting a little too cozy between them. "And you might not be the only game in town."

Kate put a plate of French toast on the table. "Or they may not be dead." She shot Beth an admonishing look. Ever the peacemaker.

"I suppose that could be true about there being another

necromancer in town," Sam admitted after a moment. "I don't know how the whole necromancer thing works." She flashed a smile at Kate. "And they might still be alive. We can hope."

No snarky comment back?

No rising to the bait?

Keeping Sam at arm's-length would be a whole lot easier if she'd go back to treating Beth like crap. If she ignored her like she used to.

Kate grabbed a jar of jam and a small glass bowl filled with something white and put them on the table. She sat between Sam and Beth.

"I hate seeing you like this. You two used to be inseparable when we were kids." Kate looked back and forth between them.

"We're not kids anymore." Beth stabbed a piece of French toast, her fork hitting the plate with a loud *clink*.

"But we're all getting closer," Kate continued to push. "You can't deny it. Not after everything that happened with bringing Robert back to life and at RAVEN."

"This—" Beth gestured with her fork in between Sam and herself and included Kate, too. "—is temporary. Once I leave, it'll go back to how it was."

Sam frowned. "I hope not."

"I agree with Sam." Kate stared at Beth. "And I'm going to do everything in my power to make sure that it doesn't go back to how it was. We're sisters again."

Beth didn't say anything. Kate wouldn't listen anyway. Once she got something in her head, there was no stopping her.

But they'd never be sisters, even with the ritual they'd performed as kids.

Sam pointed at the jar. "Is that your homemade orange marmalade?"

Kate slid it toward her. "I remember how much you loved orange marmalade with your French toast, though I'm sure mine isn't as good as your mom's." Sam kissed Kate on the cheek and gave her a side hug.

Kate touched Beth's wrist. "I didn't forget about you. Or your favorite." She pushed the small glass bowl toward Beth.

Now that it was closer, the scent of vanilla yogurt with a hint of sweetness reached her nose. It mixed so well with the aroma of the French toast.

"I never realized it before, Red, but your kitchen has the same feel as Mrs. Hamilton's house," Beth said. It was where she used to go after Sam patched her up. The one place she had felt safe.

The scars on Beth's back itched. She hunched her shoulders like she used to, to cover the one that showed on her neck from her father's last beating.

With an effort of will, she straightened, angry at herself for falling back into the old habit. Anyway, her messy bob had grown a bit longer. Long enough to hide the evidence of her torture.

"You're right, Beth. No wonder I love being here so much." Sam's eyes were bright with tears. "Sorry. The memories are hard sometimes."

Kate smiled at both of them. "Your mom always made it

feel like home," she said. "I'm glad I've been able to do that for both of you."

If Beth wasn't careful, they'll be braiding each others' hair next and planning a slumber party. She had to get this conversation off the sentimental highway.

Beth cut her French toast into pieces. "You haven't seen your mom since the night we saved Robert?" She looked at Sam.

"No. Not my dad's ghost either. I haven't figured out how to get in touch with them."

"Especially since it's technically against the rules." Kate eyed the ceiling, and Beth knew she was thinking of the Universe.

They were all wrapped up in the tendrils of fate. Sammy said they were bound together by chains when they'd become the Triumvirate.

And Beth knew if she wasn't careful, she'd drag Sam and Kate both down with her.

Beth shoved a yogurt-dipped piece of delectable French toast into her mouth.

"You look like you did when you were eleven," Kate said with a smile. She doused her French toast with maple syrup.

"I miss those days." Sam's voice was low. She held her mug in both her hands, tightly. "Before things became more complicated than they already were."

Beth took a sip of coffee. "You mean when we were getting into trouble hunting ghosts, having visions, and finding things some people wished we hadn't?"

She still wondered how things might've been different if she hadn't reacted the way she did at the Hamiltons' funeral.

And if Bronson, Sam's butler, hadn't called the police on Beth, landing her in juvie.

"Our adventures weren't all bad," Kate said. "Not enough for that frown, Beth."

Sam leaned back in her chair. "She's thinking of Bronson."

"I hate that you can read me." Beth hadn't meant to say the words out loud.

"And I hate that you can't forgive me." Sam got up and walked to the counter to grab the half-and-half.

Kate shook her head. "Isn't it time you both finally got over—"

The front door opened, cutting off Kate's words. Beth's hand went to her Kershaw knife. Her aim had gotten even better with the training sessions RAVEN had made her take part in.

But it was just Logan at the door.

Beth slid her knife back into her boot sheath, trying to ignore her disappointment. "You gave him a key?"

Kate nodded. "Of course, I gave him a key." She met Logan halfway and dissolved into his arms.

Sam arched an eyebrow at Beth. "You've never given anyone a key before, have you?"

"Don't get all judgy with me. I bet you haven't either." Beth crossed her arms. "And you don't have to with Robert since he can pop in and out of Entwine."

"Sorry to interrupt, ladies," Logan said. "Are Patty and Emily here?"

"They're at Riley's," Kate replied. "Apparently he has a money spider living on his porch, so they're taking pictures for school."

Logan looked relieved. "It's about Alison Clark."

Beth sat up straight. "The missing person?"

He ran a hand through his short brown hair. "We've found her body. And I need your help."

In addition to being Kate's new boyfriend, Logan was the Detective Chief Constable in Rosebridge and damn good at his job. There must be a reason why he needed their help.

"She didn't die of natural causes, did she?" Beth asked, already knowing the answer.

Logan shook his head. "She was murdered."

The initial humming against Beth's senses became a jarring, painful push.

If this was the start of another serial killer spree, she was flying everyone out of Scotland, kicking and screaming if she had to.

She grabbed a plate, put French toast and bacon on it, and set it next to her.

"Have a seat, Logan, and tell us what we can do."

B ETH STOOD NEAR THE PATCH OF GROUND WHERE THEY'D found the body. Where they'd found Alison Clark. The clearing at the edge of Caleb's woods was beautiful, with most of the trees still retaining their autumn leaves. The sun dipped at the edge of the horizon now, burning red. Like blood.

The earthy scent of peat smoke filled Beth's lungs. She could use a good fire and a glass of something strong.

It was just the three of them and Logan. The other constables were at the road nearby, in view of where Alison had been killed. The nearest house was ten minutes away. Logan said they'd canvassed all the neighbors, but no one had seen anything suspicious.

Logan shared that Alison liked to take walks, and it was common knowledge this was on her usual path.

Another strike against living in such a small town. If everyone knew your habits, they knew the best time and place to kill you.

Beth turned and walked toward where the woods grew thicker. Had the killer waited for Alison here?

A quick cracking of a twig snapped her attention to the left. In the approaching twilight, it was hard to tell if the shadow she saw was a person or an animal. The shape moved away, silently, the the forest swallowing it up.

She rushed to follow, but quickly found her way impassable, the trees dense without a clear path through.

If that figure was a person, they knew this forest well enough to navigate it efficiently and quietly, which probably meant it was an animal after all. She was just jumpy.

"Your first time?"

She whirled around to find Michael Forbes. She expected to see his usual look—part teasing, part know-it-all—but his expression was simply concerned.

He should've looked smaller against the tall trees, but he was still an imposing presence—all leg, broad shoulders, and blond hotness. Even though he'd cut his hair shorter. She'd liked it a little long and shaggy. It made him look dangerous.

Why Sam invited him to the crime scene, she wasn't sure. Sam said he could sense things others couldn't, but Beth didn't buy it. There wasn't anyone here needing to be patched up or healed, or have their emotions manipulated, so he didn't belong.

And she wasn't upset about him not responding to any of her texts over the past few weeks.

Not. One. Bit.

"My first time at what?" she asked.

"At a crime scene."

"I've been to a few in L.A. when my show took me there."

Michael nodded. "You must be missing the spotlight." There was no hint of snark in his tone, but she felt it anyway.

"Lacey and Quinn will be here soon so we can film a few episodes locally." She crossed her arms. "Aren't you missing your surgical spotlight in New York?"

He smiled. "If that's your roundabout way of asking if I'm still on sabbatical, yes, I am."

"It wasn't."

It was, but he didn't know that. Or did he? If Sam was right about him sensing things, she'd need to be careful.

Michael sobered. "Well, I can't leave until I know why RAVEN isn't coming after my family and why they've left our town alone." He gazed off into the trees. "They wouldn't have just let us go. Something's up."

Logan joined them, his breath misting in white puffs in the cold, late afternoon air. "I've been wondering the same thing too. I'm thankful, don't get me wrong, but it's too convenient."

Definitely time to get them off the RAVEN track.

"Has Sam picked up on any ghosts?" Beth asked.

Logan shook his head. "At least I know my brother couldn't have done this. He's in prison."

Beth wrapped her scarf in an extra loop around her neck. "Stop beating yourself up over having a serial killer in your family. I have a fucked-up family, too. Shit happens. It's not your fault."

Both Michael and Logan looked surprised.

She could be supportive.

Sometimes.

"Who found the body?" Beth asked.

"It was Mrs. Fitzsimmons out walking her dog. When we got here, we found Alison on her back, fully clothed, ground undisturbed, like she had just fallen asleep there." He hesitated.

"What?" Michael asked.

Logan hunched, shoving his hands into his pockets, and turning toward the last light of day. The colors lit his face in orange and crimson. "I told this to Sam and Kate, too, but it still raises the hair on my arms to think about it."

Beth didn't say anything. She just waited. Michael did, too.

"The expression on her face was nothing I've ever seen before, and I saw my brother's victims." A haunted look crept into Logan's eyes. "Her face was frozen in terror. Like fear had killed her, slowly and painfully through every pore of her body. I know it doesn't make any sense."

The wind rustled the leaves and slipped inside Beth's wool

coat with an icy breath. She shivered. "We deal with things that don't make sense, Logan. That's what Sam, Kate, and I do. I can't speak for them, but I'll help you find who did this."

"I will, too." Michael clasped Logan's shoulder. "Something is definitely off."

Logan smiled. "Thank you both. I've got this feeling we're not dealing with the usual here. My mother used to call it my fae wings bristling, though Sheila at the office likes to use the term 'Spidey-sense.' But whatever it is, it's on extra alert."

Beth looked at the ground as if it could tell her what had happened. "I agree with you, Logan. Something's up. Something big." The feeling from this morning hadn't gone away. She wondered if she was going to be compelled to find something again, like Ray's pipe.

Usually, she needed someone to ask her to find an object in order for her abilities to activate, but with the poltergeist's pipe, she'd been forced to find it. Forced by some unseen entity. It had brought her to Scotland, reuniting her again with Sam and Kate, and to form the Triumvirate.

She cast a wary look upwards. Was she really the Universe's bitch just like she accused Sammy of being?

Kate and Sam joined them.

Kate's navy fleece cap fought a losing battle with her hair. The breeze had turned strong, whipping red strands this way and that. "I think it's RAVEN," she said.

Beth instantly stiffened, but then fought to relax her shoulders. "Why would you say that?"

Sam looked sheepish. "Ever since I made my Bargain with

the Universe to save Robert," she said, "I've started sensing when people have gifts. I think it might have to do with the ghostly energy I've been given as payment." She took off her glove, and blue sparks danced at the edges of her fingertips.

"And you felt something?" Beth asked.

Sam nodded. "A faint blip only, but I think she used her abilities here. Maybe to try to fight off her attacker."

Michael nodded. "I sense the remnants of her emotions. There was fear, but also a healthy dose of anger. She fought."

"Since when do you pick up emotions?" Beth narrowed her gaze. "I thought you just affected emotions through touch."

"I'm an onion, Beth. Layers."

She snorted. "You're definitely something, all right."

"I agree with Kate about RAVEN," Michael said. "Someone with gifts dying under unusual circumstances? They could've used one of their soldiers with abilities to kill Alison."

Beth kept her voice casual. "Their method is leverage and kidnapping, not murder."

Kate moved closer to Logan, and he put his arm around her. "True," Kate agreed. "But we know that Oliver and Mackenzie's dad, the General, isn't above killing. He's been calling the shots for RAVEN for years. And maybe their usual tricks weren't working on Alison, so they removed her from the chess board."

Beth shook her head. "I'm no fan of RAVEN, but this doesn't feel like them. Logan's wings are bristling, and I'm with him on this."

Kate gave Logan the eye. "Wings?"

He shrugged. "Fae wings—what my mother called my extra

sense of things. I don't think we know enough yet to form any theories that will hold weight."

"Excellent point, Logan," Beth said, happy they were moving away from the RAVEN topic. She was afraid she'd let something slip about her arrangement with them if she wasn't careful.

Sam's gaze, however, remained on Beth. Nothing seemed to get by her. It was like she saw your ghost while you were still alive. And now Michael was going to be in the mix, sensing things that should be hidden.

"Alison still hasn't approached me, even though this is a murder," Sam said after a moment. "While there could be another necromancer around, something just doesn't feel right."

Beth tilted her head. "I wonder where Alison is?"

The leaves shook above them as if they had the answer of the wayward ghost's whereabouts.

Sam's gaze was worried. "I'll check with Beatrice. If anyone can discover where a ghost may be hiding, it'll be her."

"Be careful, Sam." The words were out of Beth's mouth before she realized she'd spoken.

Where had that come from? Sammy didn't have to worry about any danger coming from ghosts, especially now that she had embraced her necromancer role more fully. But something spurred the warning. What?

"I will." Sam smiled. "Are you getting soft on me, Marshall?"

Kate snorted. "Not likely."

"You wound me, Red," Beth drawled. "I might just care." She laughed softly. "Well, mostly because we need to catch this killer, and we can't have one of the members of TOP down for the count."

Sam walked over and bumped her shoulder. "Come on, let's get out of here before you start telling us how much we matter to you."

Kate hurried to Beth's other side and bumped her, too, though it was mid-arm because of Kate's height. "Yeah, how much you lurrrrrrve us."

Beth swallowed a laugh, pretending to cough. "Oh, please." She tried to outdistance them, but they kept up with her all the way to the car, being absolutely ridiculous.

If she wasn't careful, she might admit how nice it was not being alone.

Another good reason to focus on solving this murder.

Life was too messy.

Death was something she could understand.

CHAPTER 3

SAM AND ROBERT SAT AT THE DINING ROOM TABLE, WAITING for Beatrice to appear with an update. Beatrice was Robert's family maid and had essentially raised Robert after his mother had died. With her contacts in Entwine, Sam hoped she'd found something out about Alison.

Sam looked at Robert. He'd cut his hair again, but not too short. She loved the waves and the piece which always managed to fall over one eye. His olive-toned skin had darkened just a bit with his time in the gardens. He loved helping Kate's girls with their flower project. She remembered how she'd thought he was a dream when he'd come to her for help in clearing his family name. He'd been her first ghost in years.

And the first man she'd truly loved.

"I am sure Beatrice will have some news of Alison's ghost." Robert patted Sam's hand, and she put her hand over his.

"I have no doubt she'll do her best."

"But?"

"But, I have a bad feeling that there's something darker

happening here." She didn't hesitate to tell him her worries. She still couldn't believe how lucky she was to have him in her life. Centuries and death had separated them, but they'd managed to find each other.

All because of the Bargain she made with the Universe to never turn her back on her gifts again as a necromancer. Though the forest and Caleb called her "*the* Necromancer," she knew there were others.

Maybe there were assigned districts or something? What was her district?

"Whatever darkness approaches," Robert said, "we will face it together." He kissed her temple, shooting warmth throughout her.

Her phone buzzed. Sam picked it up from the table. It said *Unknown Caller*. Probably a telemarketer.

The ghostly essence in her hand flared with blue light, up her fingers and around the phone.

Dread filled her. She stared at the screen until the call went to voicemail.

"What is happening?" Robert asked.

Sam swallowed, her throat suddenly dry. "I don't know."

Her phone rang again, and she almost dropped it. Same caller.

She needed to answer it. If nothing else, to discover what could cause this reaction from the essence she held in her body. Sam put the call on speaker.

"Hello?"

Her voice sounded tentative, but she couldn't shake the

dread still sending a chill through her body.

"Hello, Sam."

The voice was a man's. She didn't recognize it.

"Who is this?"

"I'm a necromancer, just like you. And hello, Robert."

Sam froze. How did he know Robert was sitting here?

If he was a necromancer, that meant . . .

She scanned the room quickly for ghosts. She sensed three of them, but they hadn't materialized, so she wasn't sure who they were.

Sam leaned in close and whispered in Robert's ear, "Find Beatrice. Ghost spies."

Robert took his ring off and disappeared into Entwine, the ghostly realm in between the world of the living and what lay beyond.

Sam picked up the phone, holding it to her ear. The ghostly essence tickled her cheek. "What do you want?"

"I've been wanting to meet you for some time. We have a lot in common, Sam."

Her ghostly lie detector remained green. If he was truly a necromancer, she should be able to tell if he was lying. It worked on anyone connected to Entwine. At least, so far.

"Such as?"

A soft laugh, almost endearing, came through the connection. "They haven't told you yet why you're so special, have they? Why the Universe was willing to bring a ghost back to life, all to get you to sign on the dotted line again?"

Sloane had alluded to the fact that Sam was different from

other necromancers, but it couldn't be anything that amazing, could it?

Heaviness filled the air. A ghost was materializing. Beatrice appeared. Her maid's cap and apron were askew. She gave Sam a sharp shake of her head, her face filled with frustration.

"We'll talk again soon, Sam." The line went dead. She put the phone down, and the blue ghostly essence surrounding it flared bright red for a moment. A flicker reached for Sam's fingers. She pulled away instinctively. Then the red essence dissipated, leaving behind flecks of what looked like ash.

Sam stared at the phone for a long moment. What the hell was going on?

Beatrice tucked her red curls back under her cap. "My team chased them, but they got away."

Robert appeared, out of breath. "They were too fast." He slipped his ring back on. "Did you discover who the man was?"

Sam shook her head. "But I'll hear from him again, whoever he is." She looked at Beatrice. "Any news on Alison?"

Beatrice shook her head. "I looked in all the hiding spaces I know and even called in a few favors to the outlying areas that I dare not venture to again."

Sam sat up straighter. "Outlying areas of Entwine?"

Beatrice nodded. "The edges that brush up against your realm and others. The Veil. They can be dangerous parts if you don't have enough essence to sustain you."

Like the ghostly essence Sam received as payments from the ghosts. Iron could deplete it, as could poltergeists. If the essence was drained away, the ghost was destroyed.

"We do not want you endangering yourself." Robert stood and took Beatrice's hands. Sam didn't know how he was able to touch ghosts still, but she was happy he could.

Beatrice smiled, her face softening as it always did when she looked at Robert. "Don't worry yourself, my lord. I went to the Veil in my early years in Entwine, but I've steered clear since. However, it can be an effective hiding place for ghosts. The Wardens can't detect you clearly there."

Sam stood and began to pace. It helped her think. "Even if Alison didn't seek me out, she should still be in Entwine. There is always unfinished business with murder."

"I agree." Beatrice pursed her lips. "I even asked Darrin if the Runners had hidden her away for some Warden business, but he denied it." She crossed her arms. "And I believe him. He's got a tell when he lies." She hesitated. "But when I asked him if another necromancer could be around, he got shifty."

Sam walked over to one of the windows and looked out at the slanted afternoon sunlight hitting the tops of the trees in the B&B's forest.

"That call I just got was from a supposed necromancer."

Beatrice stiffened. "What?"

Sam turned around. "That can't be a coincidence."

"So could this other necromancer have already helped Alison to move on?" Robert asked.

Sam thought about the red essence that had tried to devour hers at the end of the call.

It had reached for her, as if it was hungry.

"I don't know," she replied. "He could also be on the

Wardens' payroll, making sure I don't talk to Alison."

Robert rubbed his jaw. "From what we know of the Wardens, this would not be beyond them. Especially if they did not wish Alison's ghost to tell you something they wanted kept secret."

"It's not unheard of," Beatrice admitted. "Some necromancers can be bought, for a price."

Sam walked back over to them. "Do you think it's worth asking Caleb about Alison and a potential other necromancer? He might have other avenues of information, just in case Sloane doesn't come clean." Though she was starting to trust the Warden, Sloane always had her own agenda.

Robert nodded. "We do not want another killer on the loose in Rosebridge. It would be worth taking advantage of all our resources."

"And he can't demand anything if he doesn't have any information," Beatrice added. "But you know how Caleb acts like he has more than he does. Best be careful he doesn't put a shine on a worn-out, old shoe."

"We'll be on our guard," Sam said.

"Thank you for your assistance, Beatrice." Robert hugged her. "We will let you know if we uncover any more clues."

Beatrice smiled, but then gave them a worried look. "Be careful, you two. If the Wardens are involved, they won't appreciate you snooping around."

Hearing her echo Beth's warning to be careful sent a tiny shiver down Sam's arms.

Just what did happen to the ghost of Alison Clark?

Beth's steps through the forest were loud, courtesy of the dry leaves on the ground. She suspected Caleb might have coaxed some of the trees to shed their leaves close to his own tree. A bit of an early warning system.

The night was chilly, but still. No wind.

She hoped either his trees had seen something when Alison died or that he knew where her ghost was. But Caleb had a way of not exactly giving you what you wanted.

"You didn't have to come," Sam said, walking beside Beth with Robert. "Robert and I have handled Caleb before."

Beth held up her gloved hands. "I just wanted to meet Caleb officially. You know, beyond the let's-stop-Graham-in-the-forest-before-he-kills-us craziness."

"I am thankful you are here," Robert said.

"You are?" Beth asked.

"Yes. I have not had the time to get to know you." Robert's face glowed in the moonlight. The clouds had cleared earlier. "You grew up in the same village as Samantha?"

"That village has over twenty thousand people." Beth laughed at the surprised look on his face. She stepped over a few branches and managed not to soak her boots in a deep puddle in their path. "But yes, I did live in Kingston. I was at a different school until the 3rd grade. I met Sammy and Kate when my parents moved us."

"I remember the first time I saw you," Sam said with a hint

of a smile on her face. "You stared everyone down in the class like you were daring them to challenge you, but I saw the trembling in your arms."

Beth remembered that day too. Everyone gaping at her because of who her parents were. Even though they were new to Kingston, their reputation had followed them.

Beth wanted to shove her hands in her pockets, but concentrated on letting them continue to hang by her side. "You and Red smiled at me." Beth cast her a quick glance. "You two were the only ones."

Robert smiled, and it warmed his entire face. "Which is why I suspect you all became fast friends. Each an outcast in your own way."

"I knew you'd be my friend that first day." Sam's voice was soft. Beth strained to hear it over their loud footsteps.

Beth stopped and looked at her. "I always thought I just grew on you—like a fungus."

Sam and Robert stopped too. They were almost at Caleb's tree. Just a few more minutes.

"Nope. I knew in that moment." Sam walked over and took her hand. Beth inhaled quickly, surprised she didn't want to immediately pull away.

"Why?" Beth didn't like the vulnerability in her voice, but she couldn't help it. She had wanted to know for a long time why someone as annoyingly noble as Sam would have wanted her as a friend.

Sam squeezed her hand, and then dropped it. "Because I knew what it was like to be bullied and treated as a disease.

And you weren't letting it stop you, letting *them* stop you. I respected that. I still do."

Beth couldn't ignore the warmth circling in her chest at Sam's words. "More likely you just wanted someone crazy enough to go ghost hunting with you." She playfully hit Sam's arm and began walking again. "You were always dragging me into dangerous situations."

Robert caught up with Beth. "Such as? Samantha has not shared those childhood adventures with me yet."

"We did get into a lot of scrapes," Sam admitted. "Not all of them my doing, I might add." She shook her head. "Our gifts always seemed to put us in danger, but with you and Kate, I always felt like I could do anything."

Beth couldn't stop her grin. "Me too. And those adventures are not mine to share, Robert. But ask Sam to regale you about the witch's lair we discovered when we were nine. I still have the scar on my arm to remind me."

Robert looked appropriately horrified, and Sam and Beth laughed together.

For a moment, they were girls again. Bound together. Ready to take on anything.

Dangerous. This was too dangerous.

Beth tried to pull her usual cloak of uncaring around her, but it was difficult with the rips made by Sam, Kate, the girls, and even Michael. It was getting harder and harder to stay protected.

"Is that his tree?" Beth pointed at the large beech just ahead.

Robert nodded. "Just a few more steps and we will be there."

They stopped in front of the tree. The white bark glowed in the moonlight, revealing a green sap running underneath the surface. Long limbs made it a few feet before dropping to the ground and continuing to grow. It reminded Beth of a landlocked octopus.

"Back again, Necromancer?" a dry voice said. "I see you've brought the Seeker."

Caleb stepped out from behind his tree. He always reminded Beth a bit of the Scarecrow from *The Wizard of Oz*, made up of bits of things. His skin was pale, like the bark from his tree, but his veins matched the sap she saw beneath. White hair tufted from his scalp. Just how much ghost and how much tree was he? If he even was a ghost. Duncan seemed to believe he was the Green Man.

He continued to look a bit younger each time she saw him. They suspected something had changed after the night Sam brought Robert back to life, but Beth knew Caleb would never come clean about it.

Sam bowed slightly toward Caleb. "Thank you for seeing us. We come seeking some information."

Caleb scratched his jaw, his brownish nails flaking off flecks of wood with the motion. "I figured you'd be by."

"Your crows?" Beth asked.

"They might have mentioned something." Caleb smiled. His teeth, if you could call them teeth, looked whiter than before.

Robert also bowed, mimicking Sam. "Do you know who the killer of Alison Clark is?"

Straight to the point and no small talk. Beth was impressed.

The smile slid quickly from Caleb's face. "My trees have been struck mute where the poor lass was murdered." He placed a hand on one of his tree's branches. Beth couldn't tell if it was to gain comfort or to give it.

"You mean your trees in the clearing where she was killed can't tell you what they saw?"

That feeling in her gut and Logan's bristling wings had been right. Something big had happened. Something big enough to silence the trees.

Caleb gave Beth a quick nod. "In the natural course of things, some trees slumber, yet others are awake. Each tree sees things in their own way. As Sam found out, even though Graham had killed several women in these woods, the trees couldn't give me a name, just vague images." He clenched his jaw. "But to cause trees to go completely silent . . . there are very few beings who could accomplish that atrocity. Vivian has agreed to assist me in my attempt to reawaken them." When he said his daughter's name, the light came back into his eyes. "But I don't know if it will be enough."

"I am truly sorry about your trees," Sam said, "and I do hope you can heal them, but you didn't answer Robert's question. Do you have any idea of who killed Alison? I know you have sources beyond your trees."

Caleb shot her a sharp look. "I have my suspicions. But are you here to bargain over my thoughts of who might have done this, or over what I know of the lass' ghost?" He rubbed his hands together. Small green shoots sprang from his knuckles. "I understand Beatrice has been of no help in locating Alison."

Beth put a hand on her hip. "Do you *actually* know anything about her ghost?"

Caleb frowned. "Are you certain you're not related to Beatrice? You certainly have her prickly side."

Beth matched his frown. Robert and Sam stayed silent.

The forest ghost lifted an eyebrow, sending a shimmer of dust into the moonlit air. "I know exactly where Alison's ghost is."

"My ghost lie detector is green," Sam said. "He's telling the truth."

"What do you want for the intel?" Beth asked. They'd talked about what to offer him on the way over, but no one knew exactly what Caleb would want. They were at his mercy, and from the crafty gleam that entered his eyes, he knew it.

Caleb appeared to consider his options. "Healing trees is a delicate thing. Vivian and I could use the help of Kate and her daughters."

His request made sense. Kate was a protector of the forest now, and her daughters both seemed to have connections to the trees, even the soil they grew in. But he could have just asked them, which meant there might be an element of danger Kate might not agree to.

"We can't guarantee their help," Beth said. "And when it comes to the girls, that decision is always Kate's. But we can guarantee we'll ask them and let them know how serious this is."

Caleb pursed his lips, but didn't argue. He looked at the trees around him, and a sadness softened the lines in his face.

Beth stepped toward the ghost. "I know what it's like to lose a connection like what you have with the trees—something that holds you firm, something that holds you strong. If Kate can help, I know she will. And if the girls can, too, they will."

Caleb's eyes glistened with something almost like tears, but the fluid was thicker. "You do know that indeed, Seeker. Yours has not been an easy path." His gaze flickered where her turtleneck covered the scar on her neck. "Well then, we have a deal."

"Tell us where Alison's ghost is," Beth said.

Caleb lifted his hands toward the skies. "She's part of the Universe now."

Sam looked up, following his gaze. "What does that mean?"

"If you do not know where her ghost is, Caleb, there is no point pretending," Robert said. He looked disappointed.

But Beth knew exactly what Caleb meant. She didn't believe the potential necromancer, who'd cold-called Sam, had hidden Alison away or helped her move on.

He had done something much worse.

Beth gazed at Caleb. "Could a necromancer destroy a ghost?"

Caleb nodded, looking grim. "They are one of the few beings who can."

Sam became as white as Caleb's beech tree. She kept shaking her head, making no sound.

Beth met Caleb's stare. "Alison's ghost has been destroyed. Completely destroyed."

CHAPTER 4

MICHAEL LOOKED AROUND THE TABLE AT THE GATHERING of their town's protectors, also known as his family.

Well, some of his family was missing. His mother was in town, checking in with some new arrivals. And his twin sisters, Aggie and Izzy, were still abroad, chasing rumors of an artifact that would help Izzy gain better control of her abilities.

The meeting was called to discuss what extra protection the town might need in the aftermath of the RAVEN rescue. Michael was certain RAVEN knew that Benning Brook was filled with people who had abilities—abilities they could exploit. Yet nothing had happened for weeks.

What had stayed RAVEN's hand?

Even with a fire going, there was still a chill in the air in the downstairs study. Deep grooves scarred the long white oak table here and there. His father refused to get a new table. It was where the Covenant had been created, and so it would stay.

"I hope this isn't going to take long," Michael said. "I have to be back at the hospital in a couple of hours." He was still on sabbatical, but was helping out at the local hospital while he was here.

"I've already come up with a solution," Lennox said, "so the meeting should be quick."

His eldest brother sat back in his chair, rubbing a long bruise on his forearm. When Michael looked closer, it appeared to be a ring of bruises encircling his left arm. Lennox loved boxing at the local gym and had come home with bruises before, but never in that shape. Michael couldn't imagine what made that type of injury. Or who.

"Everyone will have their opportunity to come up with their own solutions and weigh in on yours, son." Their father, Alec, kept his gaze on Lennox. "Everyone."

Lennox shrugged. "Of course, Da."

Glenna tapped Michael's shoulder. With her love of over-sized sweaters and sweet, elf-like face, she looked much younger than twenty-five. "Can you pass the biscuits?"

Michael dutifully handed her the plate of biscuits their mother had provided before bowing out of the meeting. Chocolate chip was Glenna's favorite.

"Thanks." She took two for herself and stashed away two more in her pocket.

Michael eyed said pocket.

"They're for Mackenzie," she whispered.

Mackenzie's father ran the RAVEN facility and had experimented on her for years before Sam and Robert rescued her. Michael understood how it felt to be used by your family, and he wasn't surprised she'd retreated from everyone after she got out. Everyone except for Glenna. He loved seeing his sister so happy, though he was still a bit worried. Glenna was dangerous enough when angered, given her ability to control electricity, but Mackenzie could fold someone in half with just the power of her mind.

He hoped they never got into a serious fight with each other.

The thought of fighting immediately brought Beth to mind. She'd been magnificent when they rescued his brother from RAVEN. He'd tried to avoid her, avoid whatever was building between them, but he had to admit it had been nice to see her the other day, even given the sad circumstances. He missed her—and sparring with her, both verbally and physically.

"What's making you smile, brother?" Duncan asked from across the table.

Duncan had barely healed from his wounds he'd suffered during the escape from RAVEN, but the color was finally returning to his face.

"Not you, if that's what you're asking," Michael replied.

Glenna grinned. "I bet it's about Beth. He's smitten."

"I've thought so, too." Duncan laughed.

"My love life is none of your business." Michael tried to give them a stern look, but couldn't hold it against the power of their smiles.

"Now then, children, let's behave." A smile twitched on Lennox's normally somber face.

For a moment, Michael almost forgot why he left his home, why he stayed away for the past seven years.

"I can't express how much it means to me to see all of you

like this." Their father looked suspiciously like he might have a tear in his eye.

Lennox shook his head. "Don't get all mushy, Da. Michael will leave again as soon as he can." He looked at Michael. "Won't you?" His words had a taunting lilt to them.

"I'll leave once I know Benning Brook and my family are safe from RAVEN."

Lennox opened his mouth, but their father spoke before he got a word out. "Thank you, Michael. Your mother and I appreciate you being here and helping us with the Covenant."

Due to the Covenant, an agreement signed long ago by the Forbeses, they were responsible for the safety of their town. But protecting the town also meant killing anyone who threatened to reveal its existence. Though it was a last resort to keep their town safe, it was one of the reasons why Michael fled his home and never looked back.

Lennox slammed a wooden gavel against the table. "Let's call this meeting to order."

Glenna sent Lennox an exasperated look. "There's no need for that."

"He's overcompensating," Duncan whispered loudly.

"And wanted to change the subject," Glenna whispered back.

Their father turned to Lennox. "As long as there is breath in my body, son, I will call our meetings to order." His words weren't harsh, but they were firm. He held out his hand for the gavel.

Lennox handed it over, and then leaned back in his chair,

running a hand through his short, buzzed hair as if he didn't have a care in the world. But Michael didn't miss the frustration in his eyes.

His father laid the gavel on the table. "We all know why we're here. Benning Brook has survived for decades because of our diligence, safe from the prying eyes and technology of RAVEN." He met each of their gazes. "But we don't know if Ken Allen only betrayed Duncan to RAVEN, or if he indeed betrayed our town."

Glenna shook her head. "Mr. Allen might've been a bit unhinged, but he wouldn't have put his daughters in danger. Fi and Nora live in Benning Brook."

"I agree with Glenna." Duncan rubbed his knuckles against his beard. "I've known Ken all my life. He wouldn't have willingly given up my name without being tortured. But no amount of pain would have pushed him to harm his own family."

Michael frowned. "But he did try to cause an earthquake that would have swallowed up his house and his wife in it." Not to mention killing Michael's mom, Kate, Sam, and Duncan, who had been there trying to help.

"I agree that Ken wasn't himself," their father said. "But I don't believe he would have put his girls in danger. He was drunk and hurting badly when he almost caused the earthquake."

Lennox leaned forward. "Whether he sold us out or not," he said, "we should still act as if RAVEN might attack at any moment." He looked at Duncan. "How are the dampening stones holding up?"

"They're good," Duncan replied. "Nora is sequencing and

placing the new ones I received from Vivian." He gave Michael a wink. "Does Nora still have that massive crush on you from when she was a kid?"

"I wouldn't know." Michael took a biscuit and bit into it.

Glenna poured herself another cup of tea. "She does. When she heard he was back in town, it was all I could do to keep her from showing up at the Manor." She added some cream to her cup. "We didn't need anyone else getting caught up in the mix with our RAVEN mission."

Michael remembered Nora as a teenage—gawky and fascinated with medicine. She'd moved back home after her and Fi's father had disappeared. "I'm sure you're exaggerating."

Glenna didn't respond, just gave him a smile full of mischief.

"So, the dampening stones are good," Michael said, attempting to steer the conversation back on track. "What other defenses does the town have?"

"You'd already know if you'd held up your responsibility." Lennox's gaze was brimming with disapproval.

Their father lifted a hand. "I released Michael of his role. You know that, Lennox. There's no point in badgering him about it."

"In addition to the dampening stones, we have several other protections," Duncan said, clearly trying to make peace or get through the meeting more quickly. Either way, Michael approved.

Glenna nodded. "We've got a small team in town that patrols and checks the perimeters for suspicious activity. And we maintain and monitor the tunnels below the town, in case a quick escape is necessary. Each building has access to the tunnels."

"It's not enough." Lennox's words were quiet. Michael was used to his bluster, but not this. Everyone turned to look at Lennox. "If RAVEN does know about Benning Brook and attacks us, we'll lose." Lennox tapped the table, his eyes earnest. "If Kate hadn't had that glimpse of the near future at RAVEN, Glenna would be dead."

Their father paled. "Why did no one tell me this?"

"I didn't want to worry you," Glenna said. She twisted her hands in the bottom of her sweater, pulling it taut.

"And again, without Kate," Lennox continued, "we would all have died at the hands of RAVEN or been captured and experimented on."

Duncan shook his head. "No one asked you to come rescue me, Lennox."

"That's not the point, brother." Lennox stood. "I would have gladly died to save you. But we're talking about an entire town of people, including children, who are counting on us to keep them safe." Michael had never seen Lennox be this honest or vulnerable. He looked scared.

"I can't believe I'm saying this, but I agree with Lennox." Michael stood as well. "Kate can't see the future on demand, and it's dangerous if Duncan does it too often. If RAVEN attacks, we need measures beyond the patrols and tunnels."

"Sit, both of you." Their father lifted a hand toward each of them. They obeyed. "What did you have in mind?"

Lennox looked at him. "Vivian."

Disbelief shone on their father's face. "Now wait a minute,

son. She helped us with the dampening stones, but we have nothing to bargain with for that kind of boon."

"And she can't travel beyond the forest grounds," Duncan added.

Glenna shivered. "Plus, she's scary. And unpredictable."

"Her owls can travel beyond the forest. They're her eyes and ears," Lennox said. "She's connected to the roots that run under Benning Brook and Rosebridge."

Suddenly it clicked in Michael's mind. "Her vines gave you that bruise, didn't they?" He pointed at Lennox's arm.

Duncan paled, no doubt reliving his past encounter with Vivian.

Lennox lifted his chin. "What of it? I got what I needed."

"Which was?" Glenna asked, her eyes widening.

"Her agreement to help defend Benning Brook from RAVEN." Lennox's voice held a strong thread of pride. "She can open up sinkholes, impale with roots, and kill with vines."

A river of ice pushed through Michael's veins. "What did you promise her?"

Lennox's gaze locked with Michael's. "What I was willing to give. And I won't tell you, so there's no point in pushing." Lennox's eyes hardened. "And if you try to force it out of me with your powers, I *will* end you."

Clamps tightened around Michael's heart, making it skip a beat.

He was suddenly back on the dock, nine years old.

Watching Lennox drown.

"There's no need for that type of threat," their father said, but his voice was distant to Michael's ears. He knew he and Lennox would never be friends, not after what had happened in their past. But he'd thought something had shifted with Lennox after their mission to RAVEN.

Clearly that wasn't the case.

"I've sworn never to use my gifts to force anyone to do something against their will." Michael's words were the only sound in the room. Even the wind outside had quieted.

Glenna looked confused. She had never witnessed the things he'd done. Duncan, on the other hand, wouldn't meet his gaze, and his father had suddenly found the ceiling fascinating.

Lennox nodded. "I'm glad we understand each other." He glanced at their father. "Just know that I'm at peace with my decision." He leaned back in his chair. "And if RAVEN never attacks, there's no payment to be made."

"Does anyone have anything else to add?" their father asked, a hopeful note in his voice. "Or any other defenses to suggest?"

Duncan shook his head. "I have no doubt that Vivian will kill RAVEN."

"I'm sick to my stomach thinking about it." Glenna stood. "I need some air." She left the room quickly, leaving the door open.

"I've got to get back to the hospital," Michael said and followed in her wake, rushing through the house until he was outside.

Glenna was nowhere in sight.

He took in several deep lungfuls of cool air, still moist from the recent rain. It was a mistake to come back to Scotland. His family would always be a constant reminder of his failures.

He would honor his commitments, both to help the local hospital and to help find Alison's killer.

But as soon as those were finished, he'd be on the first flight home, RAVEN or not.

"WHAT EXACTLY DID YOU PROMISE I WOULD DO?" KATE asked. She filled the rest of the loaf pans with her pumpkin bread mixture. "And what the girls would do, too?"

She loved having Beth back in their lives, but Beth's judgement wasn't always the most sound. Case in point, not talking to Sam for over ten years.

Beth leaned against the kitchen island. From the wounded look on her face, she appeared to be trying to impersonate Sam's puppy dog eyes.

Kate waved a hand at her. "Keep your TV job where you can do multiple takes. You'll never pull off Sam."

Beth grabbed a peanut butter cookie from the plate on the counter, not seeming to be hurt at all. "I didn't promise Caleb that you would do anything. Just that I would ask."

"Uh-huh."

Beth held up her hands. "I told him the girls were your call. Scout's honor."

"You were never a Girl Scout."

"These are still my favorite." Beth took a bite of the cookie, getting crumbs on her crimson sweater. "Soooo good."

"You say that about every cookie I bake." The initial anger ebbed a bit in Kate.

She wasn't against having the girls help in the forest. If their recent challenges with facing down RAVEN and meeting Vivian had shown her anything, it was that her daughters belonged in this crazy paranormal world as much as she did.

And there was no way she would do to her kids what her adoptive parents did to he—make them doubt their abilities and their value, and act as if there was something wrong with them and their gifts.

However, she wanted to make sure she understood the risks of helping the trees before she asked the girls what they wanted to do.

Kate opened the stove, closing her eyes for a moment against the rush of heat on her face. She slid the loaf pans inside and turned back to Beth. The cookie had been devoured.

"Okay, I'll consider helping, but I need to talk to Caleb first." Kate took the kettle off the stove and poured hot water into the teapot. "Do you really think it was this mystery necromancer who destroyed Alison's ghost? I have to admit, it doesn't sound like anything RAVEN could pull off, not something *that* big. And if they were going to kill someone, they wouldn't need to stop the trees from speaking. There'd be no reason to conceal their evil from Caleb or the Wardens. Everyone already knows what's what when it comes to RAVEN."

Beth shook her head, sending the strands of her dark bob dancing against her jaw. "I'm with you on the RAVEN front— they didn't do this. And if it isn't this supposed necromancer

Sam talked to, it could be someone using iron. We saw what Sam's daggers did to Robert."

"You're right. He would have disappeared if it wasn't for us." Kate tilted her head pondering. "Do you think it could've been unintentional—I mean, the destroying-the-ghost part?"

"Could be." Beth grabbed some mugs and brought them to the table along with the plate of cookies. "From what Logan said, it looked as if she died from pure fear." She sank into one of the chairs. "Which makes me think supernatural baddie rather than homegrown human. And if so, then they might know what iron could do."

"I guess all we have are a lot of theories without any substance. Logan would be disappointed in us." Kate brought the teapot to the table and got the half-and-half from the fridge.

Beth laughed. "He would, which is why we're not floating any theories to him until we have more concrete facts." She gestured at the pictures on the wall by the pantry that Kate's girls had drawn. Some just had trees but several had Vivian and Caleb. "The kids really love the forest, don't they?"

"They do." Kate sat at the table. "Which is why Patty will be crushed to learn about what happened to the trees."

"She said the trees have stories they need to tell." Beth smiled softly. "If anyone can reach those trees and help them, it's Patty."

Her seven-year-old finally came out of her shell after her father's death a few years ago, and embracing her gifts was a big part of it.

Caleb, along with his daughter, Vivian, had been essential to

Patty's healing, if Kate was being honest. They'd accepted and understood Patty immediately. They'd helped Kate see just how both her daughters fit into this new world they'd discovered.

"I felt something strange, too," Kate admitted, "when we were where Alison died."

"What something?"

Kate thought back on the memory. She didn't realize it was anything important at the time. The whole place had felt like death, but she thought it was from the murder.

"It was like when your foot falls asleep," Kate said. "Before you start shaking it to get the blood flowing. It's just a dead lump, like something has been cut from you. That's how the forest felt. Cut off. Cold. Dead."

"You're connected to the forest now. It helped you save all of us back at RAVEN." Beth looked worried. "If more trees lose their voice, will that affect you?"

A chill slid down Kate's spine. "I have no idea. It's all new to me."

Beth poured the tea into their mugs, steam rising into the air. "Sorry. Didn't mean to worry you, but I've been thinking about it since Caleb told us last night."

"Will we ever have a quiet month?" Kate asked. "One without dead bodies, kidnappings, and mysteries?" She put a teaspoon of brown sugar into her mug. Then another. "When I have guests again soon, I can't just put my business aside to go traipsing off to save people constantly. Can't the world just stay safe for a bit?"

Beth raised an artfully shaped eyebrow. "First of all, I've never seen you traipse. You run headfirst into everything. Second of all, just hire a manager when things get up and running."

"Bronson's off in London looking for one now," Kate said—Sam's old butler was a godsend to her struggling B&B—and then she smiled. "But now I'm thinking I'm going to have to ask them a few extra questions in the interview. Do you have any problems with ghosts? No. Okay, how about murder? No. Oh good. Well, I'm the Oracle, and I might have visions which take me off to save lives. Are you okay with managing things while I'm gone?"

Beth let out a bark of laughter, bending over. Kate loved hearing her laugh. Really laugh. It didn't happen often, but Beth had changed since arriving to help in Scotland. More like she used to be before what happened with Sam.

"All you would need is Robert jumping in and out of Entwine to send them screaming from the house," Beth said, her face flushed from laughter. "Don't worry about it, Red. We'll find someone."

"We'll?" Kate tried not to let the surge of hope rise through her. "Are you staying in Scotland a bit longer than planned?"

Something flitted across Beth's face. Something dark. And then it was gone. "I still need to film a few episodes of my show. I also can't let Sammy take all the credit for helping you with the B&B once it's booming again."

Kate opened her mouth to pry more when the sound of footsteps pounding down the stairs reached her ears.

A few seconds later, her daughters burst into the kitchen. Emily's curly red hair was in its usual disarray. Patty's t-shirt had a fresh chocolate milk stain on it, and one of her braids had broken free from its bonds.

"What did I say about running in the house and down the stairs?" Kate's words brought them up short, skidding to a halt. "Remember the story of how Auntie Sam broke her arm falling down the stairs?"

"You didn't tell them she was pushed by a poltergeist?" Beth asked under her breath.

Kate gave her a tight shake of her head.

"Sorry, Mom," Emily said. Her nine-year-old had a drawing in her hand.

Patty danced from foot to foot. "I saw something, Mommy. It can't wait."

Kate reached out and both girls came to her. "You had a look-see?" That's what they called it when either Kate or Patty saw the future through a vision.

"I did." Now that they were closer, Kate saw a sheen of sweat on Patty's skin. "Something bad is going to happen in the forest."

Beth scooted her chair closer to the girls. "Like what?"

Patty's glance went to the window. "Someone is going to be hurt. And the trees, too."

"She drew this." Emily handed the paper to Beth. "It's bad."

Beth held it out between her and Kate.

The dark green strokes of crayon were unmistakable for the forest. Toward the bottom was a stick figure with a gray blanket over it. Its eyes were Xs, and there were black X marks on the trunk of each tree with red blobs at the end of each line.

The warmth fled from Kate's body the longer she looked.

"Who's that?" Kate asked, pointing to the figure.

Patty's face scrunched up. "It's a man, but I don't know who. He's going to be hurt."

Kate looked at Beth and knew what they were both thinking. If it was another victim, then the killings were only getting started.

"Could you tell if it was someone we know?" Beth asked. "Logan? Robert? Michael?" Her voice faltered on Michael's name. Interesting.

"It's not anyone *I* know," Patty said. "It felt different than when I saw Mommy in danger. Or Daddy."

Kate pointed to the Xs on the figure's eyes. "Does this mean they're dead?"

"Yes." Patty's voice quavered. "They were screaming before it happened."

Kate took her into her arms and hugged her, feeling the shivers run through her tiny body. "It's okay. You did the right thing by telling us."

Emily pointed at the X marks on the trees in the picture. "Patty said that the trees are going to be hurt, too." She looked scared but her voice was strong. "Not on the outside, but on the inside."

"The trees will be silenced," Beth whispered.

Patty stiffened in Kate's arms. She pulled away and looked at Beth. "How did you know?"

"Because it's already happened," Beth replied. She put the picture on the table behind them. "And now we know it'll happen again unless we can stop it."

The initial reservations Kate had about having the girls help the forest dissolved. If Patty had a vision about it, she needed to heal the wounded trees and prevent others from being hurt. For herself as much as for the forest.

Kate moved Patty to her lap and grabbed Emily's hand. "Caleb and Vivian want our help with the trees who have lost their voice."

"We have to do it," Emily said. "Caleb and Vivian and the forest are all part of our family now."

"Did you know our B&B is on forest grounds, too?" Kate had discovered it when she'd researched the land after becoming an anchor of Entwine. "I think that's what drew me here."

Emily smiled, showing off the small gap between her two front teeth. "I knew this place was special."

"Me, too," Patty said. "Together, we can save the trees, Mommy. I know we can."

She hugged them, bringing them in close, breathing in the scents of strawberry lip balm and dirt. They are so brave and caring. She was very lucky to be their mom.

"Tell Caleb we'll help," Kate said to Beth.

Hopefully, somehow, they could heal the trees and stop this next murder.

Her stomach clenched. And do it without the killer realizing it. Otherwise they might all be next on the list.

CHAPTER 5

"WE SHOULDN'T KEEP SLOANE WAITING," DARRIN SAID to Sam and Robert. The Runner had brought them into Entwine to see Sloane at Sam's bidding. She'd used Robert's ring to summon him.

That ring was the only thing that kept Robert from slipping away into Entwine. Even though the Universe had brought him back to life, they still didn't understand what that really meant. This was unknown territory.

Darrin was dressed as usual—black pants, black vest, and a gray shirt. Last time she saw him, his vest had been marked with the same symbols at the bottom as those on the silver cuffs around his wrists. However, now there were more Celtic symbols woven into the vest, stretching up toward his neck.

"Promotion from Sloane?" Sam asked, gesturing toward his vest.

Darrin didn't smile. "Something like that."

Sam didn't say anything further. Something was definitely bothering the Runner. She wondered if it was the loss of a friend he'd mentioned to her and Robert not too long ago. Grieving wasn't ever on a timeline.

"I didn't mean to delay us. I just wanted to see the archways again," Sam said.

She looked down from the platform which sat above a series of archways below. It always reminded her of a train station. Her favorite, so far, was the one that beamed sunshine and had butterflies around the edges.

But this time, her attention was drawn to one which looked Egyptian. It had curved, golden palm stems as the arches, reaching to a large scarab beetle at the top center. She wanted to explore all of them, the places where ghosts crossed over into different realms.

Robert touched her arm. "I realize how fascinating this all is, but Darrin is right. And we have a potential second murder to prevent." She turned to look at him. Worry had pinched his brow. "Sloane could hold the answers we seek."

Sam realized she'd been stalling. Last time they'd met with Sloane, they'd overheard a conversation, one that had surfaced into her mind the night of that strange phone call. Logan tried to trace it, but it came from a burner phone.

Caleb had confirmed her suspicions when he said a necromancer was one of the few beings who could destroy ghosts. Once she asks Sloane about it, there would be no turning back. She hoped she was wrong about her suspicions. "Let's go."

She followed Darrin and Robert further into Entwine. Gone were the paneled walls from her childhood home the Wardens had tried to fool her with the last time she was there.

The walls were now made of emerald green vines, constantly moving, sliding against each other with a soft *whooshing* sound. If Sam listened closely, it almost sounded like voices speaking in whispers.

Here and there, the vines would pause, making Celtic symbols that looked like the ones on Darrin's clothes and Sloane's jewelry. Then they would move again. Darrin had been right that they never stopped.

She wanted to study this more, too, but tamped down her curiosity. They needed answers.

They made it to Sloane's door quickly. Rather than the usual waiting or barging in, the door opened on its own. Well, not really on its own. Someone was leaving.

It was the man they'd seen last time. Very tall and thin, wearing a top hat. Seeing him from the front, he looked to be in his forties and extremely worried.

"Winston, wait." Sloane's voice stilled his steps. "I'll expect your report within the hour."

The man frowned, his gaze flicking to Sam and Robert. "Dark days are ahead for all of us." His voice was a whisper. He turned back to Sloane. "As you wish, Warden." Then his long legs took him swiftly from the room and down the corridor.

Sloane smiled and beckoned them forward. "Come in, I've been expecting you."

Winston's words echoed in Sam's mind. Robert looked equally as troubled. What did Winston mean specifically?

"Entwine to Sam, hellooooo."

Sloane's voice finally broke through Sam's haze of worry. She looked over at the Warden. She wasn't wearing a motorcycle jacket like last time. Today it was a long, burgundy tunic shot through with threads of gold and plum that appeared to move like the vines of Entwine. Black leggings and combat boots completed her ensemble.

Her dark hair remained the same, longer on the top but buzzed short on the sides. Sam wondered if it was to show off her completely pierced right ear. The same Celtic symbols sparkled on the metal studs decorating her ear from the lobe up to the top. Her left ear remained bare.

Sam walked into the study, followed by Robert. To her right, a curious foursome clustered in front of the fireplace, talking in whispers: a gladiator, a monk, a wisp of a girl, and an imposing woman with a blacksmith's apron.

"Begone," Sloane said, gesturing toward the fireplace. Though they all looked upset by her dismissal, they left without argument.

Robert gave Sloane a low bow. "As always, we are grateful for your time and attention to matters of our concern."

Sloane grinned. "I could listen to you talk all day, Robert. So polite." Her smile dimmed just a hair when she turned to look at Sam. "And though I'm happy to see you, too, I know I'm not going to like what *you* have to say."

"Then you already know of the murder?" Sam wasn't surprised she knew, just that she wasn't beating around the bush. Sloane wasn't always straight to the point.

The Warden didn't answer her question. "Follow me." She led them behind her desk to a large bookshelf to the right of the picture window, which always seemed to show a different time of day than when they had left. And different weather. This time, it was dead night through the glass.

Sloane gripped the spines of several books in a sequence, and the bookshelf moved inward, and then slid to the right, revealing a room. Sloane stood to the side and waved them in.

Sam and Robert hesitated. "Will this harm Robert or I in any way?"

"No," Sloane replied. "This is for all of our protection."

Sam's lie detector blazed green for the truth. She nodded to Robert, and they followed Sloane into the room. The soft *whoosh* of the bookshelf behind them ended in a solid *click* of concealment.

There was another window, this time showing a beautiful expanse of water and a dark, rocky beach. It reminded Sam of the Pacific Northwest coastline.

Two comfy-looking couches formed a V in front of the window. A small table sat between and already held drinks, along with a bottle of something that looked like cider. Sunlight poured through the window, bathing the wooden floors and the couches in golden light.

Sam heard a wind chime's low, peaceful tones echoing through the glass. She immediately felt calmer and saw the change in the Warden as well.

Sloane untied her boots and kicked them off to the side. She sat on one of the couches, feet tucked underneath her. "This is my private place. No prying ears for what we need to talk about." She closed her eyes and turned her face toward the sun.

Robert seemed mesmerized by the view through the window. The sunlight blazed through his hair, bringing out the red streaks. He turned to Sam and smiled.

She gave him a quick kiss and vowed to take him to a real beach in the near future, as long as they both survived this next disaster. She tugged on his hand, and they both sat on the couch opposite Sloane.

"I'm sorry to hear about what happened. Caleb filled me in," Sloane said. "Before Kate arrived in Scotland, there hadn't been a murder in Rosebridge for almost fifty years." She picked up the bottle of cider and took a long swig.

"Are you saying she's causing this?" Sam couldn't keep the shock from her voice.

Sloane shook her head. "No, nothing like that. Not directly anyway. It's just that energy, neither good nor bad, causes reactions, causes changes. Kate was a powerful force even before she tapped into her potential, and she's only scratched the surface there."

"Perhaps we should leave Scotland when this is all done," Robert said. "Return to your home in New York, Samantha. Lessen the energy of the Triumvirate."

The thought of leaving Scotland and Kate—and even Beth, for as long as she stayed—felt like someone had hollowed out Sam's chest and taken her heart with it. When had she become so attached to everything here in Scotland?

She looked at Robert. She knew when.

He had come into her life and changed everything. Without him, she wouldn't have had a chance at fixing her broken friendship with Kate and Beth. He made her see things differently, for the better. He made her realize that Scotland wasn't just the place of her parents' death, it was a place of love and magic, too.

Sloane just watched her, like she waited for her reply with more weight than necessary.

"We're not leaving. The energy will balance out." Sam sat back into the couch. It was as comfortable as it looked and warm from the sun. The heat soaked through her, easing some of her stiffness.

Robert passed her a drink. It was orange-colored with a salty rim. She sipped it. A peach margarita.

"Glad to hear you're staying," Sloane said. "Now, what are you hoping I can tell you about the murder?"

Sam took a long sip of her drink. Sloane was going to make them spell it out, à la Caleb. "We know that Alison's ghost was destroyed and that the trees around the site of the murder were silenced, hopefully only temporarily. That's not the work of a regular killer."

Sloane rolled the cider bottle this way and that, catching the sunlight. The liquid inside seemed to spark and glow as she moved it.

"It's not," Sloane replied.

Robert leaned forward. "Could a Warden have done this?"

"They could," Sloane conceded. "We all have the ability to destroy a ghost's essence, but to do so would condemn the Warden to the same fate." Her gaze shifted and locked onto Sam. "But you already suspect who did this, don't you?"

Sam nodded. "A rogue necromancer. *The* rogue necromancer we heard you speak about last time we were here."

"You're right."

Sam had believed it was true, but to hear the Warden say it made it real. Someone who was a necromancer, just like her, murdered a living person, and then killed their ghost. Even when she'd hated her gift, she'd never considered harming a ghost, even if she'd known she could.

"He's destroyed ghosts before, but never killed a living person." Sloane looked perplexed. "We're not sure why he would change his tactics suddenly."

"Could someone else have killed Alison? And perhaps this necromancer is responsible for the ghost's demise only?" Robert asked. Sam wondered the same thing.

Sloane gave him an approving nod. "It's not impossible, but it's very unlikely. Every ghost who enters Entwine is recorded. Alison never made it to Entwine, which means she was destroyed almost instantly after her death."

"There will be another murder unless we stop him," Sam said. "Patty had a vision. And more trees will lose their voices."

Robert looked at Sloane. "And he may have contacted Samantha."

Sloane flinched. "What? When? Were you hurt?"

Sam was touched by the true concern on Sloane's face. She might not understand the Warden's motives, but she did seem to be an ally.

"He called me, but didn't tell me his name." Sam willed the ghostly essence to her fingertips. "This essence was drawn to the phone. It covered it while we spoke and then it was destroyed."

Sloane's lips tightened. She got up and began to pace. "We'd hoped he wouldn't realize who you were. This is not good. Not good at all."

"Is Samantha in danger?" Robert asked.

The Warden paused and shot him a look. "No way to tell. He's unpredictable."

"I think it's time you tell us what you know," Sam said.

"He's masking his energy using essence. We haven't been able to track him," Sloane admitted.

"Why has he been killing ghosts?" Sam asked.

Sloane returned to the couch and sat again. "For the Brigh —that's the official name we use for ghostly essence," she added quickly. "It gives him power." She looked like she was about to say more, but then stopped herself.

"But what could he do with the power?" Robert asked.

"Anything."

The word was out of Sam's mouth before she'd realized it.

Sloane gazed at her with understanding. "Every necromancer has experienced its allure."

Sam remembered how it had felt in the forest when she'd received the essence from all the ghosts she had saved. Essence which she'd used to save Robert.

But for a moment, she'd felt drawn to use it for herself.

"At first, I thought it was because I'd never received ghostly essence before," Sam said. "That it was just a rush of something new and powerful."

"It hasn't stopped, has it?" Sloane asked. "The temptation."

Sam shook her head. "I don't even know what I'd do with it. But I feel like it wants to be used."

"It's because it's the essence of life at its core," Sloane said. "It wants to have purpose. It *needs* to have purpose." Her eyes met Sam's. "But your intention is the key—to heal, or to harm."

"Who is this rogue necromancer?" Robert asked.

Sloane looked at him. "You've met him before, Robert. In the Rinth."

Sam remembered Robert's stories of his time in the Rinth, a realm of purgatory, where Robert had wandered for years

Robert shook his head. "You do not mean the creature with a cloak the color of autumn leaves?" Fear shone in his eyes. Sam hoped it wasn't the same creature they would be facing.

"That was . . . someone else." Sloane's words harbored something deeper, but Sam knew not to push. Not when they were close to getting the information they needed on the other necromancer.

Robert's eyes cleared. "It is Connor then. Darrin's apprentice." He turned to Samantha. "When I met them for the first time, they told me what I needed to do to cross into your world, to find you so that you could help me."

"What makes you say it's Connor?" The Warden gave him a keen gaze.

"I sensed a sharp mind. He had confidence." Robert paused. "There was an air of power around him. I remember thinking Darrin had trained his apprentice well." He paused again. "And Darrin shared his pain over losing a friend not too long ago, which would make sense if Connor had turned from his path."

Sloane gave him an approving nod. "You're right on all counts, Robert. I still think Connor would have made an excellent Runner until the others made their mistake."

"What do you mean, they made a mistake?" Sam asked.

"You had buried your gift." Sloane leaned back into the couch. "Balance is needed in all things, which meant we needed another necromancer to take your place."

Sam shook her head. "Wait. You mean this is *my* fault?"

"It was not your fault, Samantha." Robert took her hand. "You had no idea there were others like you, let alone how your actions might affect the nature of things."

But she'd known the Universe gave her the gift of talking to ghosts. Her refusal of that gift had come with consequences she hadn't wanted to consider.

Sloane's eyes softened. "You are guilty of creating a power vacuum. And no matter how hard I . . . we tried, we couldn't get you to change your mind." Sloane stood and lifted her hand toward Sam. "Remember."

Her voice deepened, reminding Sam of how her own voice changed when she made a Bargain. Like she was speaking not for herself, but for something larger, something bigger.

Her temples felt the press of fingers, as if Sloane were touching her, but the Warden hadn't moved.

Memories flitted in and out of Sam's mind like blazing fireflies. Sloane had been there. For her first ghost, Zach. For when she was seven and helped their neighbor, Morris, when his wife had died. And when the school bus of children woke her in the night and sent her screaming into her parents' room.

Just a presence at the edge of her mind. Comforting. Unseen. Sloane snapped her fingers, and the warmth at Sam's temples faded, but the memories remained.

"You were there." Sam blinked back the sudden tears.

Sloane nodded. "You were my ward. I offered you the Contract, and you accepted it."

This meant she hadn't been alone at the mercy of the Universe. She'd had guidance.

"Why didn't I remember?"

"It's a Warden policy. We wipe those memories, as I was supposed to wipe mine." There was something in the Warden's voice. Not tears, but something close.

"You could not bear to lose your memories," Robert said. "Even if it meant your judgment might be clouded in the future. Something the Wardens would not have sanctioned."

"We're not supposed to form connections to anyone." Sloane seemed to have regained her composure. "But then again, I've never been a rule follower."

Sam stood and walked over to Sloane. "Thank you." She pulled the Warden into a hug. "You helped me when I was so scared," Sam whispered.

Sloane's arms tightened around her, and Sam felt what she'd felt in her memories—comfort, safety, love. She might have lost her parents, but Sloane had raised her, too.

"We'll keep your secret," Sam said, pulling back and releasing the Warden.

Sloane nodded, her eyes suspiciously bright. "Even with the power vacuum you created, they shouldn't have chosen someone so old. Necromancers are offered their Contract on their seventh birthday."

"I was five." Sam's voice was hollow. She still remembered the night the first ghost, Zach, came to her and the first Rule had floated into her mind.

Sloane nodded. "As we've danced around before, you're special, Sam. More special than the usual necromancer."

"How old was Connor?" Robert drew Sloane's attention away from Sam.

"Twenty," Sloane said. "I petitioned for more time, because I knew you'd come to your senses eventually. But I was overruled. We had other candidates, but none as skilled, and we needed a replacement before the Balance grew too unstable." She steepled her fingers, their tips touching just under her chin. "To be fair, if the Balance failed, we'd have faced something even worse than a rogue necromancer on the rampage, so I can't really fault them completely."

"Why would they not listen to your wise counsel," Robert asked, "and chosen someone else?"

Sloane shrugged. "I'm one of the newer Wardens, so I didn't have enough clout. But now they're seeing what I saw."

Robert stared at her. "And what is that?"

"Connor is damaged." Sloane's gaze narrowed on Sam. "And I fear with the failures of the other necromancers, it's going to be up to you, Sam."

"To stop him?" Sam asked.

The Warden's eyes darkened. "To kill him."

CHAPTER 6

THE SOLDIER STOPPED IN FRONT OF THE DOOR TO OLLIE'S office so quickly, Beth almost ran into his back. She caught herself just in time. That's what she got for letting her mind wander elsewhere. But she couldn't stop worrying about the murder and what kind of danger Sam and Kate might get themselves into. Especially now that she knew there could be another murder if they didn't act in time.

Hopefully Sammy could shake out some information from Sloane. The Warden seemed to have a soft spot for her. She needed to leverage that to her advantage.

Either way, Beth needed to take advantage of her own sources of information as well. Ollie had already asked to meet with her about a previous assignment, so it was a perfect cover. She'd ask him a few things so it would look good on anything that got recorded in his office. She wouldn't put it past them to record everything, everywhere.

Which meant the real discussion with Ollie would happen later, off the record, where they could talk freely about who could have destroyed a ghost's essence and harmed Caleb's trees.

The soldier put in his code, gave a retinal scan, and slid his card key into a slot. The door unlocked.

The card key was new. Those are easily hackable. There must be something else to them.

"Come in, Ms. Marshall." Ollie lifted his hand toward her from his desk. He was in uniform as usual. Everything neat and tidy.

She hadn't been in his office before and stopped just a few steps in. It wasn't like anything she expected in a cold military facility. Bookshelves of dark wood lined the walls and were filled with books of all kinds, from the look of it. Military books, historical tomes, 18th century art, cookbooks, and even some Stephen King novels.

Thankfully none of the books appeared to be Sam's novels so she didn't have to swallow her barf.

She could hear Kate's voice in her head telling her to let bygones be bygones. She was trying, though. She was.

Sort of.

The door clicked shut behind her, and she shifted her focus to the room again. A deep green plush rug covered most of the concrete flooring, and the color went beautifully with his writing desk. The desk had curved legs and feet with gold embossed leather on its surface. It looked like a Sligh original—if she wasn't mistaken—from France in the '70s. But it was higher than most she'd seen. Fit for a taller man's legs. Custom.

The four paintings on the back wall, behind the desk, were Degas and Morisot. She itched to know if they were original, to look at the brush strokes, but now was not the time.

If she'd known Ollie collected art, she would've added an original Degas to the pot as her RAVEN signing bonus. Maybe she could renegotiate?

"Does everything meet with your approval?"

The deep voice came from General James Nivens, Ollie's dad, also known as the SIC—Sociopath in Charge. He sat in one of the chocolate brown easy chairs in front of Ollie's desk.

Beth hadn't even noticed him, so intrigued by the artwork.

She'd only met him once, when they'd agreed to their deal. His dark hair held no red. Though he was clean shaven, his beard shadow was in full swing, making him look even more forbidding. His cool blue eyes, which studied her, were tilted at the edges, giving him a natural air of inquisitiveness.

She studied his posture. He was at ease, leaning back, no tightness in his face. Also, no thinly concealed glee or satisfaction, so most likely he hadn't figured out what her and Ollie were up to.

Fingers crossed.

"I'm surprised. I wouldn't think this office was up to military code, which is why I like it." Beth sat down in the other chair and leaned back, mimicking the General's posture.

"The General has some questions for you." Ollie's voice was normal, no sign of an edge to it. She knew he was smooth, but he definitely had skills that would even rival her dad's.

The General smiled, but it never moved further than his lips. "Tell us about Assignment 11."

Beth shrugged. "Not much to tell. I found the encrypted

flash drive in Russia in an underground facility outside of Moscow."

"Yes, we know all that," the General said. "However, based on the data from your first ten assignments, you found the flash drive much more quickly than before. And with more precision. Why?" He tilted his head, reminding Beth of a bird deciding if it should stab the juicy worm or leave it.

He was right. It had been quicker. It was actually getting easier with each assignment, like she was getting stronger somehow.

She felt her reach expanding, too. For the last ten years, her cap had been just under two centuries, unable to find anything older. But lately, something had shifted. It wouldn't surprise her if she was up to three hundred years now.

There was no way she would clue RAVEN in on it, though. Every time she showed up, she still wasn't certain if she'd be able to leave or not. They'd experimented on John Anderson until he almost died and would have done the same to Michael's brother, Duncan, before she rescued them.

"Ms. Marshall? My question?" There. A hint of impatience. Her answer was important to the General.

"Sorry, I was just thinking back to see if I had done anything differently." She shook her head. "But everything was the usual. However, it could've been because I was going after a dirtbag."

"Why would that make the job different?" The General exchanged a look with Ollie, but Ollie gave him a slight shake of his head.

Beth leaned forward. "I might not have a pure soul, but

what I've done doesn't compare with RAVEN's exploits." Ollie shifted in his seat but remained silent. The General just looked at her as if she was an amusing puppy. "Since I still have some morals," she continued, "it bothers me when I have to go after good people on behalf of RAVEN. So, when I went after the flash drive that would nail that Russian arms dealer to the wall, I didn't have a conflict. I wanted you to take him down."

The General looked bored. "And you truly believe that every assignment we've given you, except this one, was against good people?"

Beth opened her mouth to agree wholeheartedly, but then stopped. The truth was, she didn't know. She just assumed based on what she saw when she used her abilities.

"Are you saying you never go after innocents?" she shot back.

A spark lit in the General's eyes. "We both know no one is truly innocent, except for children. And every single one of *your* assignments has been an effort to save those good people you are so concerned about."

Beth snorted. Of course he believed his own propaganda. His words were meaningless. Convince her? Please.

Ollie leaned back in his chair. "It's true, Beth. Under my father's leadership, we've prevented atrocities from being committed."

She knew Ollie had to toe the company line in front of his father, but there was a thread of truth in his words. "So it's okay to torture, coerce, and experiment for the greater good. Is that the RAVEN motto?"

"You don't understand what we're up against." The General's

words were fast and harsh. Determination blazed from his face. The mask he wore had slipped. "Are you naive enough to think RAVEN is an anomaly?" He leaned forward. "Other countries and governments use many of the same methods we do, but many are much, much worse."

He believed what he said, that much she knew. Why he was trying to convince her didn't make sense.

The thought of other countries and governments with souped-up hit squads made her stomach roll. And she'd done her research. The legit part of RAVEN did come up with new vaccines and treatments that saved lives. She found the nice black and white lines she had when she thought about RAVEN had muddied a bit—gray seeping through.

But that didn't mean they weren't destroying lives, too.

"Are we good with Assignment 11?" she asked, needing to get out of there and get some air.

The General gave Ollie a nod.

"We're good," Ollie said.

"Before I leave, I have a question for both of you," Beth said. "What do you know about the murder of Alison Clark?"

Her eyes were on the General, and he didn't flinch in the slightest.

"Just what we've read in the news," the General responded. "Why? Is there more?"

Beth tilted her head. "Not sure. I've offered to help. The DCC is dating my friend, Kate Banberry."

She'd used the code phrase "not sure"—another term her and Ollie used for needing a meeting. They couldn't keep using "sleep" all the time without it looking suspicious.

Ollie didn't say anything, which meant the meeting was on.

"Are you fancying yourself a detective again, Ms. Marshall?" A shadow of a smile lifted the General's lips at the edges. "First Graham Dunning, and now a new mystery killer. Perhaps you're thinking of leaving the television world behind?"

Beth didn't miss the lure on the end of his line. He wanted to know her plans for the future. If his new toy would try to escape his grasp.

Beth snorted. "Leave TV? Not likely. I get paid way too much for that job."

"I know you don't think very highly of RAVEN," Ollie said. "But I can assure you, we wouldn't draw undue attention to ourselves with murder." He turned his gaze to his computer screen.

Dismissal.

Beth stood. "True. We would've never found the body if RAVEN had killed her."

Ollie's eyes flicked to hers briefly then back to his laptop again. "Is that all?"

"If you do find something about the murders, you know, through all your military intel and blackmailing gigs, I'd ask that you let me know." She paused. "It would help sweeten my motivation on the next assignment."

The General nodded. "We will, of course, share any information we feel would be vital to your investigation."

He turned away from her and began speaking with Ollie directly about some report. Dismissal times two.

She left Ollie's office and made her way to the east door without getting lost, a feat within the maze of bland corridors they had built in this place.

Slipping outside, the chilled air sent goosebumps across her skin. A thin line of reddish-purple on the horizon was the only sign of the setting sun.

She took in several deep breaths. RAVEN still needed to be taken down, but the good stuff they did needed to be kept. Oh man, did she just think "good" in association with RAVEN?

Her senses pricked, and she stiffened. No one was around her, so it wasn't her internal proximity alert. She scanned the grounds. Nothing. She looked at the trees in the distance.

There. On the other side of the fence, just past the training field, someone watched her from the treeline. She could only make out the shape, but when they turned and slipped back into the trees, she recognized the movement. It was the same thing she'd seen at Alison's murder scene. She'd dismissed it as an animal, but she was wrong.

She took off at a run.

CHAPTER 7

BETH STOOD AT THE EDGE OF THE TREES, LETTING HER heartbeat settle. After that run from the main RAVEN compound, the cool air was a wonderful welcome. Though once her body temperature regulated, she'd be chilled again.

The automatic lights came on along the RAVEN metal gate. She turned away quickly, but still found she had halos when she looked at the trees from the sudden change in light.

Being careful not to walk too close to the trees, Beth made her way up and down the treeline. She hoped the mystery person she'd seen would take the bait and attack her.

No such luck.

The lights had probably scared them off.

But maybe not.

Beth chose a tree with a thick trunk and put her back to it so that she faced the RAVEN fencing. The raised bark dug into her shoulders through her fleece jacket, as well as the moisture from the earlier rain.

Closing her eyes, she listened to the falling night. The leaves rustled slightly in the breeze. Peat smoke reached her nose along with the smell of decay—the plant variety, not flesh, thankfully.

Though she didn't hear anything out of the ordinary, the killer might have stopped, listening like she was. Maybe just out of sight.

Well, she couldn't stand here all night. Time to see if they'd left any clues. And maybe they'd be curious to see what she was doing, what she might find, and they'd come back. They'd make a mistake.

The sky was completely dark now. Stars visible, even with the RAVEN lights. She got out her knife, just in case, and flicked on the small flashlight she always carried with her. She carefully approached the muddy ground near the trees. She treaded carefully, searching for signs of a shoe print.

Nothing. Nothing. Raccoon print. Nothing.

There. Footprints next to an old oak tree further in.

Beth moved closer. It was just the front part of the shoes, almost like the killer walked on his toes. Based on the size, it looked like a man's shoe. But she had large feet, so she knew it could be a woman's, too. Given the close proximity to RAVEN, this could be a footprint left by one of the operatives. Not anything to warrant having Logan take a look.

A twig cracked, and she froze in place. A surge of adrenaline spiked through her. She turned off her flashlight, slipped it into her pocket, and moved to the right, behind a smaller tree.

"Don't trust RAVEN," a voice said, sounding both close and far away. Emotion colored the edges of his words. There was something familiar about the man's voice. She couldn't tell the age, but it wasn't a boy. There was authority in his tone.

"I don't trust RAVEN," she replied. "Even RAVEN knows that."

If she kept him talking, she might find out more and potentially take this sicko down right here, right now.

Or it could be a test. Ollie's dad wasn't her number one fan.

Maybe someone was going to pretend to be a RAVEN defector, trying to win her trust? It would be something she might have tried if the boot were on the other foot.

"If you don't trust RAVEN, then why are you working with them?" The voice had moved. It was behind her now. She fought not to whirl around and instead turned as quietly as she could. Her night vision was good, but she couldn't make out any shapes beyond the trees.

"They threatened my friends and other people I know." She breathed in, hoping to smell sweat, metal, soap, cologne . . . anything. But now it was just the scent of rain mixed with mud. "But again, everyone at RAVEN knows this. It's no secret I'm not there of my own free will. If you're spying for RAVEN, you're out of luck on getting any useful intel."

"I'm not with RAVEN." The voice paused. "Not anymore. Not for many years."

The slight sound of leaves being crushed underfoot, to the left.

For some reason she believed him, which made him the "killer" option once again.

Beth chose her steps carefully to avoid twigs and anything

else that could cause noise. She might be able to take him down if she could get close enough. He hadn't used a gun on Alison, so it wasn't likely he'd shoot her before she got near him.

And they didn't know for sure if it was a necromancer who killed Alison. Caleb had only mentioned the possibility. Plus, Sam was vulnerable to being killed—and she was a necromancer—so either way, it was worth a shot to take out the killer.

She remembered what Logan had said, that Alison had looked like she'd died of fear. Maybe she was crazy playing cat and mouse with a killer, but for some reason she didn't feel afraid.

But then again, she didn't care if she died. No one would mourn her.

A lie.

She didn't need her inner voice to pipe up to know it. Even if she didn't trust in Sammy's offer of friendship again, Kate would be devastated. And maybe the junior pipsqueaks would, too. An image of Emily and Patty at the kitchen table floated into her mind.

She gave her head a hard shake. Distractions. And even if they did mourn her, they'd get over it quickly enough.

"Are you all right?" The voice came again, sounding genuinely concerned. "I know you're still there."

"Why don't you tell me why you were at the scene of the crime, where Alison Clark was murdered?"

She stopped and listened again. There. An exhale. An exasperated one by the force of sound. "I was there to see you."

A few more steps toward the sound, and she stopped again. An outline of a head, there, caught in a stray bit of moonlight.

He was about three trees away.

She moved her knife to her left hand and eased out a throwing star from the satchel at her waist with her right. She'd only had a few weeks of shuriken practice, but she should be able to hit him, at least hard enough to distract him.

"I saw you working with RAVEN, and that only leads to disaster. I had to warn you," the voice said. "But you were there with the DCC and your friends." There was silence for a moment. "I'm so glad you have friends."

This guy was a pure nut-job.

One who obviously had fixated on her.

She had a clear shot of his legs. Her fingers tightened on the star, feeling the warmth she'd already given the metal. The flick from her wrist was fast, sending the star spinning through the air. On target.

He sprang to the nearest tree, scrambling easily up the trunk as if he were Emily's age. The star hit the wood with a solid *thunk*.

Dammit.

"I'm not your enemy, Beth."

She raced to the tree, knowing she was being stupid. He could throw a knife at her. Hell, he could have a bow and arrow for all she knew, but she wasn't going to let him slip away. If she could stop him from killing anyone else, she was going to.

"Heard my name at Alison's crime scene, huh?" Beth peered up into the tree, but she couldn't see anything but leaves. "Did you enjoy killing her? You won't find me as easy a target."

"I didn't kill her." The voice was at least two trees away now, to her right.

Who was this guy? The Scottish Spiderman?

"Tell me the truth, then, why were you really there at the crime scene?" She walked toward his voice. No need to run again. There was no way she'd match him with tree climbing, but she could get close enough to try another throw. She slid a star out of her satchel.

"Because I wanted to see you." The trees rustled in front of her. A shape hurtled from one tree to the next. At least she'd seen him this time.

"Do we know each other?" She couldn't help the question. The way he'd said the words held something within them. Sadness. Not exactly killer mentality.

Everything grew silent. The wind died. Even the gentle creaking of the trees ceased.

The hairs on the back of her neck hadn't just risen, they'd spiked to attention.

Something had changed. Something was different in the forest. It wasn't the stranger. It was something else.

She sensed a presence behind her and whirled around. It was the figure she'd been hunting. He grabbed her wrists. He was strong.

"Run," he hissed, and then pushed her back toward the tree line and the blazing bright RAVEN fence.

Beth stumbled but caught herself. She turned around. The man was gone. The forest had swallowed him. Just like it extinguished what little light there had been. The absolute blackness crawled toward her like a shadowy beast. The trees loomed above her, closing off the starry sky.

Something was coming.

She froze, unable to move, though her mind screamed at her to get the hell out of there. The root cellar from her childhood filled her mind, where she'd been punished. So dark. So cold.

The crickets cut off mid-chirp.

Move, Beth!

A woman's voice came from inside her.

Run!

This time there were more voices. All women. All shouting inside her head. Ghosts?

Her body finally broke out of its stasis. She turned and ran with everything she had. Her boots ate up the ground. Tree branches tore at her clothes, raked her back and shoulders like sharp talons pressing into her flesh. A touch of something icy circled her ankle, and she jumped the last few feet toward the lights, tumbling out of the forest and into a RAVEN patrol.

Jensen frowned at her, but didn't lower his gun trained on the trees behind her. "Go home. The woods can be a dangerous place."

The other soldiers scanned the forest, looking worried. Jensen hadn't grilled her on what she'd been doing out here, which wasn't like him. They knew something was up.

She took a deep breath and willed her control back in place.

"You don't have to tell me twice," she said casually and sauntered past Jensen, keeping close to the well-lit RAVEN fence.

She didn't want to be near any shadows. Not for a while.

Warmth crept down the back of her neck. She touched her skin, and her fingertips came away bloody. The trees had scratched her up. Had they been trying to urge her on, to save her?

Beth cast a quick glance over her shoulder. Jensen and the other soldiers were headed back to the front gate. She made her way quickly to her car.

She didn't know who the stranger was, but now she knew in her gut he wasn't Alison Clark's killer. He'd tried to save Beth from whatever that "Big Bad" was that she'd felt.

Beth glanced back over her shoulder, hoping he'd gotten out okay. Because if what she felt in those woods *was* Alison's killer, they'd need all the help they could get.

They were way out of their league.

SAM HELD UP HER HANDS. "WAIT A SECOND, I'M NOT GOING to kill anyone."

"So you'll let him continue his rampage unchecked?" Sloane asked. "Destroying ghosts and potentially killing more people?"

"Surely there is a compromise in the middle. A way to stop Connor without killing him," Robert said.

Sloane frowned. "We've tried everything."

"My guess is that all your attempts have been by force?" Sam fixed the Warden with a hard stare.

"We tried to dissuade him through Darrin. When that

failed, we sent a few of the other necromancers to reason with him."

"The other necromancers?" Sam still wondered who they were and if she'd get a chance to meet them.

The Warden nodded. "When he injured them so badly that one almost died, we pulled back."

Robert's face darkened. "And you seek to send Samantha up against this threat, knowing this?"

Sloane lifted a hand. "I know, I know. I wouldn't put Sam in danger, but it's not up to me."

Robert seemed mollified by her answer, but still not happy. "I learned the importance of diplomacy at my father's knee. Once you cross the line into action, into violence, you can never go back."

Sloane sipped on her cider. "You're preaching to the choir."

Robert shot her a questioning look, and Sam explained, "It means she agrees with you." Sam looked at Sloane. "So the rest of the Wardens wanted physical action taken against Connor?"

Sloane nodded. "When my efforts through Darrin failed, they escalated. I didn't have control of the Collective. Not enough votes."

"The Collective?" Sam sat back for a moment, her initial shock replaced by interest. The more she learned about the Wardens and how they operated, the better.

"It's the Warden voting body, so to speak. It's where all the decisions get made." Sloane stretched out her arms to catch the sunlight from the window. "Where policies are put together, sentences decided, and so forth."

Robert drained his drink. "Which means they overruled your intent to continue with nonviolent measures, and now you are grasping for options."

Sloane smiled. "Yes, something like that."

"Has anyone found out why he's doing what he's doing?" Sam asked. "Or even tried to find out?"

She wondered if Connor had always been this way, or had something caused his murderous streak?

"We tried, but he wouldn't talk to anyone I sent."

"So you know he's seeking power," Sam said, "but you don't know why or what he's planning to do with it."

Sloane had the grace to look sheepish. Sam had expected more out of the Wardens. They'd created this problem, and yet they had no idea why it happened.

Robert raised an eyebrow at Sloane. "There is a reason you are asking Samantha to kill Connor rather than the Collective banding together and accomplishing the deed themselves."

Sloane flinched just slightly. Robert had scored a hit.

"We can't utilize Brigh like a necromancer can," Sloane admitted. "He has become too powerful for Wardens to fight."

Sam leaned her elbows on her knees. "That tracks with why you sent necromancers against him, but why would I succeed where others have failed?"

Sloane let out a long breath. "Connor has that special something like you, Sam. Not as much, but he's got it. And he's figured out how to use it to his benefit."

"It?" Robert asked.

Sloane got up and padded over to a desk in the corner that

Sam hadn't noticed until now. "Part of what makes Sam so special and desirable as a necromancer is her ability to hold onto ghostly energy."

"I thought that was just part of being a necromancer," Sam said.

Sloane grabbed a book and brought it back to them. The title read *Necromancy: Levels and Expectations.*

"Scoot over," she said to Sam, and she immediately did so. There was no way she was passing up an opportunity to learn more about who she was. Sloane flipped open the book and pointed to a footnote at the bottom of the page:

> Level 17 (subset): Siphoners. These candidates' bodies have the ability to siphon Brigh easily and, more importantly, hold onto it beyond the usual lifecycle of payment. The prolonged presence of ghostly essence in a necromancer hasn't been measured beyond the usual healing and increased lifespan due to these candidates being so rare. But the ability to amass Brigh could pose a threat to the Collective and to Entwine itself. Or perhaps these Siphoners could become Entwine's greatest ally.

"It sounds like the Wardens aren't sure if a Siphoner would be a savior or a destroyer," Sam mused. She looked down at her hands. Could she bring destruction to Entwine?

Robert took Sam's hand in his, no doubt sensing where

her thoughts had tumbled to. He looked at Sloane. "So other necromancers do not keep the energy when they get payment from the ghosts they help?"

"No. They use it to keep their bodies and minds healthy, to survive injury, and even to heal others, but the essence doesn't stay. If they don't use it, it eventually leaves their body and returns to Entwine."

"If I'm like Connor, am I upsetting the Balance by holding onto this? Could that destroy Entwine just by itself?"

Sloane shook her head. "The ghosts give you their energy freely in the exchange of the Bargain, so that has always kept things balanced. Connor isn't using the Bargain. Plus, he's taking every last bit of their essence when he destroys a ghost. *He's* the one upsetting the Balance."

"Have there been many others before me?" Sam asked.

Sloane gazed at them. "Very few. We had no way of knowing Connor would turn out to be one, too, though we should have suspected it."

"What does that mean?" Sam sensed Sloane hadn't meant for that to slip.

Sloane closed the book with a loud bang. "I'm not at liberty to say." She got up and put the book on her desk again.

"But you are a breaker of rules," Robert argued.

Sloane gave him a smile. "Nice try, but I can't. Hey, at least I told you I couldn't rather than just lying to you. That's worth something, isn't it?"

Sam found it was. She'd accept honesty, even if they didn't get the answers they wanted. "Logan is on the case, and we know Connor will try to kill again," she said. "So can you give us any idea of how to track him? You mentioned he was using the essence to block your attempts to find him."

"Even though our efforts have failed, I think you two might have better luck," Sloane said. "Robert's ring might help you. It was made with ghostly essence."

Robert took his ring from his pocket. "And that will be enough for us to succeed when all your other attempts have failed?"

"I'm not saying you will, but there's always been a special connection between you two, even before Sam brought you back to life. And you still stand firmly in both Entwine and the living world." She shrugged. "Just saying, you might want to give it a shot. And though I hate to end this, I do need to get back to work. Keep me posted."

Sam stood, as did Robert. They needed to get back to the B&B anyway and let Kate and Beth know what they'd found out. "What does Connor look like? So we can have some warning if we see him."

Sloane walked over to her desk and came back with several pictures. One was a young boy and girl together, smiling like they shared a secret. Another was a picture of them with their parents, Sam assumed. The final one was of a young man who looked about nineteen or twenty.

Robert looked at the last picture and nodded. "That is Connor, but in person his eyes are different colors. One is blue while the other is brown. And his hair was a bit longer when I saw him last."

Sam mulled that over. Pretty distinctive. He'd probably change his appearance to blend in, which meant he could look like anyone. She would do the same in his shoes.

"So, if we find Connor, will you help?" Sam asked Sloane.

Sloane nodded. "I will."

Green light on her lie detector.

"If I can subdue him and stop him," Sam said, "can he be contained somehow?"

Robert brightened. "Yes, in a prison where he would pay for his crimes."

"We have such a place," Sloane admitted. "It's on one of the lower levels of Entwine. But we'd need to fully drain him of any ghostly energy before we could transport him there. Otherwise, we'd never hold him."

Sam walked over to the entrance that would lead them back to Sloane's study. "TOP was already committed to stopping the murderer, but we won't be killing him."

The Warden hit a hidden switch that opened the door. "I don't want to see Connor die either."

She was telling the truth yet again. Even though Sam felt closer to Sloane after recovering her memories, she knew Sloane still had others to answer to. Sloane might want to save Connor, but would she if the other Wardens demanded his death?

Beth eyed Michael's front door. Well, the door of the Forbeses' manor, Michael's temporary home. She looked at her wrist. Her Fitbit showed 12:15pm. She hoped he was home for lunch and hadn't gone out with his family.

Though it was dangerous seeing him again, especially if he could sense she was hiding things. If he knew she was working for RAVEN, he'd throw her in their dungeon.

If they had a dungeon.

She stepped back and eyed the semi-castle again.

Yep, they had a dungeon.

The door cracked open, startling her out of her reverie.

"Are you trying to stare the door into submission?" Michael asked. He opened the door fully and leaned against the doorjamb, all six-foot-something looking entirely too attractive in jeans and a cream-colored sweater.

Then he straightened, his gaze lingering on her red leather jacket, moving down to her boyfriend jeans and black leather boots. "Wow. You look amazing."

"I know."

He laughed softly. "What brings you to my door?" Then he sobered. "Was there a break in the case?"

"No." She shoved her hands into her jacket pockets. "You offered to help with the murder, but I think we're going to need everyone's help."

"Everyone?"

"Your souped-up fam."

"Even Lennox?"

Beth nodded. "Especially your obnoxious brother who can manipulate metal."

Michael staggered on his feet, clutching his chest. "Is the

world suddenly going to end? Beth Marshall asking for help?"

"I ask for help." She clenched her hands into fists, and then released them.

"Since when?"

"You're in a mood. This was a mistake." She turned and made it two steps before she felt a firm grip on her arm.

Beth let him stop her. She even allowed him to turn her around.

He smiled, bringing out green flecks in his eyes. "Hey, we used to have fun jabbing at each other. You know, friendly banter. Everything okay?"

Friendly banter? Had he put her in the "friendzone?"

Well, they weren't really more than that.

She willed her top lip not to curl.

"We're good," she said. "You just never answered my texts, which was pretty rude after we stormed RAVEN together."

And she hadn't meant to mention the texts. Or lack of response thereof.

Dammit. He messed with her brain.

Michael rubbed his jaw. "I'm sorry, Beth. Things have been hectic with helping out at the local hospital and making sure Duncan recovered after the attack at RAVEN."

She didn't need his powers to know he was hiding something. "Whatever." She shrugged. "Like I said, we're good. Even if you are a dick sometimes. I bet you didn't even read my texts."

"A dick?" He looked as if he was trying to be mad but couldn't help smiling. "You're right, I should've definitely replied back to your sparring requests. Especially to the one where you mentioned you wanted to 'beat shit up' and asked if Lennox had any punching bags."

The smile reached her lips before she could stop it. So he *had* read her texts. And hell, everyone was entitled to secrets, she had a truckload of her own.

"Yeah, you should have replied. What's wrong with you?" She punched his arm. "No one is too busy for sparring."

He smiled back, and suddenly it was . . . okay again.

"Come inside and you can tell me how the Family Forbes can help."

She followed him inside the manor. It was just as she remembered it—posh, elegant, and so not her.

Glenna came around the corner, face glowing. "Mackenzie and I found a flat that looks amazing online. We're going to go check it out."

"Beth wanted to ask for our help with something," Michael said.

Glenna gave her a smile. "Whatever you need, I'm down for it."

"But you don't even know what I'm asking," Beth said.

"It doesn't matter." Glenna put on some gloves. "We owe you, Sam, and especially Kate for saving Duncan and me. Not to mention Lennox."

"Let's not mention Lennox," Michael said drily.

Glenna gave him a kiss on the cheek. "He'll agree, too, no questions asked." She frowned slightly. "Though you may want to have Kate ask him. He respects her the most out of TOP."

Well, she did rewind time itself to save all their asses, so Beth didn't blame him.

Glenna's phone buzzed. "That'll be Mackenzie. I've got to run."

Michael gave her a hug. "I hope the flat has a big soak tub."

She winked at him. "You know it. I need my bath time." She looked at Beth. "Remember to let me know if you need any help with your show when your crew gets here. Don't forget, I'm killer with electronics."

Beth laughed. "I will." It was fitting that someone who could control electricity had become an electrical engineer. She had to remember to tell Lacey about her.

As Glenna grabbed her coat and disappeared out the door, Beth heard singing somewhere distant in the house. Very off-key, but sung with conviction.

Michael sighed. "My parents are in the kitchen trying out new recipes."

"And your brothers?"

"They're down at the stables."

"Duncan's not riding, is he?" She'd managed to save Duncan at RAVEN, but he'd been wounded pretty badly.

"No. He's just taking care of the horses. And Lennox is there in case Duncan overdoes it."

"Hmmm, Lennox doesn't seem like the caring type."

Michael hesitated a moment and then gestured down the hall.

"The sitting room already has a fire going." He led her into the room she'd remembered from all their meetings before the RAVEN mission. The heat hit her as soon as she walked across the threshold. It helped ease some of the chill that had remained in her bones after last night. Whatever had been with her in the forest was bad news.

"Would you like any refreshments?" A man's voice said from behind her. Beth turned her jump into a sidestep. Was Bronson teaching ninja butler tactics to everyone?

Michael eyed her with concern. "Nothing with caffeine, Percy. How about some herbal tea and the lemon cake my mother made?"

The butler nodded. "Very good, sir."

Beth eased into the chair next to the fire. She kept her jacket on. She wasn't planning on staying long. Give him the details, see how the family could help, and then she'd jet.

"What's going on?" Michael sat down in the chair across from her. "I've never seen you skittish." His gaze fixed on her neck. "Are those scratches?" He reached toward her, but she took his hand and pushed it away.

"They're from my time in the forest last night. They're shallow. No biggie."

"Which forest?"

"The one near RAVEN."

Michael gave her a concerned look. "What were you doing there? It's dangerous to be that close to the facility."

"I was careful." She clasped her hands in front of her. "I was scouting the area when I saw someone who looked like the same person I saw when Logan brought us to the crime scene."

Michael leaned back in his chair. "And of course you

charged into the forest by yourself, without any backup, trying to apprehend a killer."

Beth bristled. "I've done it before and been pretty successful."

He just stared at her.

"Okay. It probably wasn't my best moment, but I didn't realize there would be extra supernatural shit going on. I thought it was your usual serial killer."

Michael's gaze grew even more icy. "Do you hear what you're saying?"

Beth stood. "If I did get killed for being stupid, who would care?"

He stood, too. "How can you even ask that? Sam loves you, even if you won't acknowledge it. Kate would be crushed if anything happened to you. Emily and Patty would have to go through losing someone important in their life again. And that's not even getting to Fi, who you've managed to tuck under your wing to teach the ways of the Force."

Fi had helped them in the attack at RAVEN. Her skills at seeing through walls, bodies, really anything had been a necessity. RAVEN might have killed Fi's dad. Beth still hadn't been able to find out for sure.

Beth sank into the easy chair. "Fi's coming along very well in her knife skills."

Michael sat as well. "She's been telling Glenna and MacKenzie all about it."

Percy came back in with a tray filled with lemon cake, a teapot, cream, and cups. He put it down carefully on the table, and then retreated. Beth watched Michael cut the cake. She should keep Michael and his family out of this. It was too dangerous. Yet she'd come here. Why?

She stared at Michael. Because he made her feel safe. After the RAVEN attack, seeing him hold his own had changed things in her mind. He could kick ass with the best of them.

It was hard always carrying the load. The responsibility.

How would it feel to have someone else to share the burden?

How would it be to have a partner?

"So what's the verdict after all that internal debate?" His tone was dry. "Your head hasn't exploded yet, so that's a good sign." He handed her a cup of tea. From the smell it was chamomile.

She gritted her teeth. "You are so frustrating. I'm back to thinking this was a mistake."

A hint of a smile quirked his lips. "The cream cheese icing my mother makes is incredible. It has a secret ingredient she might be willing to share with Kate. I mean, if you thought it may be good enough to help with the B&B's recovery."

"I see what you're doing here."

"I'm sure I don't know what you mean." The innocence in his voice was dancing on top of contained laughter.

Michael didn't need to use his powers to influence emotions. He was naturally good at it. "Then I guess it's my duty to test out this so-called incredible icing."

"For Kate." Michael handed her a plate.

"For Kate." She stabbed her cake with a fork.

Michael took a sip of tea. "Tell me what's got you more scared than the usual serial killer."

She savored the burst of lemon on her tongue cooled by the

icing. This was pretty awesome cake if she was being honest. And her standards were much higher than they used to be after living with Kate for weeks.

But it was time to spill it. At least what she could.

"There was something evil in the woods."

Michael put down his cup. "Like supernatural-type evil?"

Beth nodded. "Like kill-you-with-a-look evil."

"Crap."

"Yup."

She had Michael's full attention now. "I didn't see anything to suggest a supernatural element when we were at the crime scene, except for any powers Alison might have had."

Beth held the cup in between her hands. "The trees were silenced, and Alison's ghost is gone. Obliterated."

"What?" Michael shook his head slowly. "How do you know all this?"

"Caleb told us."

"What was his price?"

"That Kate and the girls try to help save the trees."

"You've certainly been busy." He sounded a bit miffed. "I could have helped earlier if you'd asked me."

"I'm asking you now," Beth said, injecting a hopeful note. "Because what I felt in the forest last night is beyond normal supernatural shit."

"Define 'normal.'"

Beth took another bite of cake and chewed it slowly, thinking of how to explain.

"I've got abilities, you have them, and so forth. Our stuff has a limited effect. One person, a few people at the most."

Michael nodded. "So if that's a level . . ."

"Five."

"Okay, a level five. Then say John Anderson being able to move things with his mind would be?"

"A seven. And Fi's dad with his earthquake skills would be an eight in my book."

Michael tilted his head. "And the thing you felt in the woods?"

Beth lifted her hand above her head. "A fifteen. The entire forest was affected. The trees were scared. Even I sensed it and I don't have a connection like Kate and Patty do." She paused. "It felt like I was going to be swallowed whole."

Michael touched her knee. "It's good you came to me. I'll ask my father to check the Archives and see if we can find out any information about what this is."

Beth put her hand over his. "Thank you."

He hadn't freaked out, and he even accepted the fact that she'd run into the forest on her own. Yet he kept challenging her, keeping her on her toes. He was the first man in a long time who seemed to understand her.

She pulled her hand back and took a sip of tea. For just a moment, she let her potential what-ifs be. No squashing. No pounding. No obliterating.

Kate would be so proud of her. Sam would, too, if Beth ever shared something like that with her. For the first time, she felt herself take a step out from under her parents' toxic shadow.

Not that anything was going to happen with Michael. They

lived on opposite coasts. Two separate worlds, and all that rigamarole.

But it was progress, nonetheless.

Her phone buzzed. She took it out of her jacket pocket.

It was a text from Logan.

We found another body.

CHAPTER 8

KATE HELD PATTY'S HAND WHILE EMILY WALKED AHEAD of them, following a crow who half-hopped, half-flew toward the place where Alison had been killed.

She wanted to turn around and take the girls home. Taking children to visit the scene of a murder is not something any good mom should normally do, but both girls were determined to save the trees. She'd promised to support her daughters in this new world they were part of now, and she kept her promises, no matter how scary.

As soon as she'd stepped into the forest, she'd felt the same pull she had the other day. Now that she was an anchor of Entwine, things had changed.

That was the understatement of the week.

Things had exploded.

When they'd fought against RAVEN, she'd used the power of the forest to help her wrangle the fabric of Time to do her bidding in order to save everyone.

Emily had been right. The forest was her home now, too.

Kate felt it with each breeze that shook the leaves. The trees were part of their family, and they'd been hurt.

Patty squeezed her hand painfully. "We're almost there, Mommy. I can feel it."

"What does it feel like?" Emily turned around. The tie Vivian had given her shone in Em's red hair, holding a loose ponytail. Caleb's daughter had told Emily it was made by a vine containing her magic. All Kate knew was that it was stronger than anything she'd ever felt. She was glad the forest deity was on their side.

Her youngest gazed off into the distance, the skin around her eyes crinkling. "It feels like the echo of a scream. Sharp at the edges, but hollow in the center."

The crows ahead of them cawed, and the message was clear. *Follow.*

Another few moments and Kate didn't need Caleb's presence to know they'd arrived. It was what she'd told Beth before, like a piece of her had gone numb. The trees were gone, yet still standing.

The forest ghost frowned deeply. Kate sensed the pain running through him.

"I'm so sorry, Caleb," she said. "I'm only feeling a shadow of what you must be suffering."

Caleb gave her a short nod. "In all my years, a tree has never been silenced this way." He walked over to one of the trees and touched its bark. "We've suffered through drought, disease, and mankind using our wood, but this is much, much worse."

Patty slipped her hand free of Kate's and walked over to

Caleb. She also placed her hand on the tree. Her eyes closed, and for a moment, the only sound was the creaking of the upper branches.

"They're still there," she said in a quick rush. Her excited gaze met Kate's, then Caleb's. "I couldn't tell until I got closer, but they hid. Deep within the earth for protection."

Caleb's eyes glistened. "I thought I had imagined it. I hoped I hadn't. But knowing you felt it too, lass, changes everything."

Emily placed her palms to the ground. "How do we get them back, so they can speak again?"

Patty's face scrunched. Kate knew she was thinking. "We first need protection. They won't come back unless they know it's safe. And *all* the trees need to be protected."

Kate looked at Caleb. "Patty had a vision of another murder coming and more trees being silenced just like these. It's going to happen again unless we stop it."

Caleb pursed his lips. "I had hoped this was an isolated incident. A fluke. But if it was deliberate with the trees, then that's a different story. I've reinforced the protections in this forest, but I fear it might not be enough."

"Maybe we should let the trees hide for a bit longer where they're safe," Kate said, "until we figure out what did this?"

Caleb shook his head. "The longer they stay separated, spirit from tree, the harder it will be for them to come back."

The crows in the tree branches cawed.

Emily looked grave. "The crows say the trees will die if they don't come back."

Kate didn't know when her daughter had learned crow. Last

she'd heard, Vivian was teaching her how to speak to tawny owls.

"And if the trees die?" Kate asked.

"The forest is weakened." Caleb's gaze swept over the trees. "And it will be an opening in the protection around this anchor point of Entwine. The Threshold will be vulnerable. An opening that could be exploited by you-know-who."

"Voldemort?" Emily asked.

Caleb looked confused.

Kate jumped in. "No. He means that nasty organization we stopped a little bit ago."

Emily looked like she knew more than she should, but she didn't say anything.

"It means we have to figure out a way to protect the trees from another attack." Kate looked at Caleb. "What are our options?"

"How 'bout asking the Wardens?" Emily leapt on top of a fallen log. "They sound really powerful."

Caleb frowned. "They'd help if they could. Weakening the barriers to Entwine isn't good for them either. But they have no power to affect the forest."

Patty turned away from the tree she'd been touching and looked at Caleb. "We need your cousin."

"Which one?" Caleb already looked worried.

Kate wasn't surprised he had cousins. They'd just recently discovered he had a daughter. Who knew how large his family was—or how powerful?

"He's got horns like a deer." Patty put the back of her hands against her forehead and wiggled her fingers above her head.

"You mean antlers, silly," Emily replied.

Kate shot a sharp look at Patty and then Emily. "Have either of you *seen* this cousin?"

If Caleb was introducing them to his family without Kate's knowledge, they were going to have words.

Emily shook her head but Patty nodded. "In the trees' memories. He came to this forest a long time ago to help Caleb. He's a forest god."

Caleb grumbled. "One of several, but Patty is right. He'd be able to save the trees if we worked together, but I hesitate to involve him."

"Why?" Kate asked, not liking the frown on Caleb's face.

Caleb began to pace. "I know the one thing that can get him to agree, and it's a dangerous thing."

"If my girls come to harm—"

"It's not that," Caleb interrupted her. "He would never harm someone else's child. That's one good thing you can count on with him out of very few good ones. But I'm not sure about Morag."

Emily gave him a sharp look. "Who's Morag?"

"She's the love of my cousin, Karnon." Caleb flicked his gaze to Kate. "He's also known as Cernunnos, the god of the hunt."

"And this Morag is bad news?" Kate asked.

Caleb nodded. "Very bad, even as a ghost. She's strategic, smart, and sneaky. A very bad influence on my cousin." He rubbed his jaw. "And unfortunately, she's the only leverage we have to get his agreement to save the trees."

"But he loves the trees," Patty piped up. She looked confused. "He's helped them before."

Caleb walked over to her and touched her shoulder. "Very true, little one, but we're getting close to Winter Solstice, and Karnon's powers wane during this time until he is reborn. To help us now could put him in peril from his enemies, especially since he would be vulnerable outside of his own lands."

"And I was sure my butterscotch cookies would definitely do the trick," Kate joked. She didn't like seeing the worry in Emily and Patty's eyes. "My cookies charmed Vivian right away."

Caleb laughed. More like cackled, really. "True, but she has a soft heart underneath her bark."

Kate had seen it too. Vivian truly loved Emily and Patty.

"We'll ask Darrin to help Sam find this Morag." Sam couldn't dial-up specific ghosts—they always needed Darrin for that.

Caleb shook his head slowly and lowered his voice. "That's only part of it, I'm afraid. The Wardens keep Morag under lock and key behind the Veil, so to speak. To release her, even for a short time, would be against their Rules."

This was getting worse and worse the more Caleb spoke. Kate looked at the trees behind him—the ones who'd lost their voices.

"Would the Wardens agree to let Sam go behind the Veil, knowing it would save the trees and help Entwine?" Kate asked.

"They might," Caleb acknowledged. "But they're slow to decide. Our best chance is to get Sloane's approval. Then Darrin would be free to help."

Caleb was uneasy, and it wasn't just because of the thought

of Morag—Kate could tell by the nervous way he tapped his fingers on his thigh.

"Will this be dangerous to Sam?"

Caleb tilted his head. "Not if she uses her daggers to harness ghostly essence. They should shield her."

She didn't miss that he said "should" not "would."

Kate looked at the trees around them. "And if we don't restore their voices, even if the rest of the forest is left alone, what will happen?"

"We have to help the trees, Mommy." Patty pulled on Kate's shirt hem.

"I'm not saying we won't, pumpkin," Kate replied. "We just should know the full consequences to any decision."

Caleb placed his hand on the tree trunk closest to him. "If we can't save them, even if they don't come under attack, there's no telling what could happen to the rest of the forest after they die. Grief and sorrow are powerful things in all of nature."

Kate knew that all too well. Their family had suffered from the loss of Paul, both as a husband and a father. It had taken them years to heal.

"We'll talk to Sam," she said to Caleb. "But we also need to know if your cousin is willing to help."

"I'll put in my portal request. Karnon has to approve my access to his lands."

It made sense in a weird sort of way. She supposed gods, or whatever Caleb was, wouldn't just call each other up on the phone.

"If he's going to help our forest, I want to be there for the meeting, so include me in your request. And Logan." Kate met his gaze and held it, daring him to tell her no.

But Caleb just nodded. "As is your right."

"I want to go, too," Emily said.

Patty was already jumping up and down in excitement.

"You can meet him later when he comes to help the trees." Kate gazed at their crestfallen faces. "But you can help me tell Auntie Sam about her mission."

They brightened somewhat.

"I want to tell Auntie Sam," Emily declared. "And I'm going to draw her a picture so she can see the Veil. What does it look like, Caleb?"

"I'm going to draw a picture, too," Patty declared.

The girls gathered around Caleb while he described the Veil. Their voices became a buzz in Kate's ears.

The one thing Caleb hadn't brought up, and neither did Kate, was the one question they needed answered.

Who had done this to the trees?

If they didn't find the answer to that, then the entire forest would continue to be at risk.

She rubbed her eyes. One crisis at a time.

Her phone buzzed. She read a series of texts from Beth.

Logan found another body. Forest by RAVEN.

I'll swing by and pick you up.

Can't reach Sam.

Logan says it's someone we know.

SEEING THE WOODS AGAIN, THIS TIME IN DAYLIGHT, DIDN'T make them feel any less creepy to Beth. Kate had already run up ahead to join Logan. He was inside the forest somewhere.

"I don't know if it's worse or better that Logan prepared us, telling us that someone we know died," Michael said. He'd insisted on coming with her as soon as she'd told him about the text.

"It's better." She put her hand on his arm. "But I still need a minute. I already know it happened when I was here last night. When I felt what I felt."

Michael gazed at her for a moment. "We don't know if the victim was killed by the same means. This could be a random murder."

Beth snorted. "We both know it's not."

"RAVEN is right there." Michael gestured at the facility. "They could have killed whoever Logan found."

"But they wouldn't have left the body. RAVEN is too smart for that."

Michael seemed like he was about to argue, but then turned away to look at the forest. "You never told me what led you to the woods last night."

Beth couldn't very well tell him she'd been at RAVEN—after her meeting with Ollie—when she saw the potential killer. She'd been trying to think of an excuse the entire way over but came up with a fat lot of nothing. So she needed to just wing it.

"Kate initially thought it was RAVEN," she said. "It was a long shot, but I figured I would check out the forest around their compound."

"What were you hoping to find?"

"I wasn't sure what I was looking for." The breeze sent a cold prickling through her hair and scalp. "I can't sense the tree stuff like Kate can, but if RAVEN had someone whose abilities could affect trees, maybe they had done something I *could* see." She shoved her hands in her pockets. "Anyone can kill, but what happened with the trees was something more."

"True." He seemed to buy her bullshit this time. His face grew serious the more he stared at the forest. "Something did happen here." He lifted his hand. "There's a cold, dead spot to the right, inside the forest."

"Have you always been able to sense stuff like this? Death?"

Michael glanced at her. "I've always been able to pick up emotions without touching people, but I didn't realize it would extend to nature."

Well, one secret out of the bag. She knew he had more.

Logan emerged from the tree line and waved them over. Kate was by his side. The constables and the medical examiner headed to their cars, passing by Michael and Beth.

When Beth got closer to Logan and Kate, she found Kate looking pissed.

"Logan wouldn't let me see the body," Kate said. "He wants to show all of us at once."

Beth crossed her arms, steeling herself.

The DCC looked grim. "You'll understand once you see the

victim. And I sent my team to wait by their cars until we're done."

"I need to see who was killed. *Now.*" Kate pushed past him and ran deeper into the woods.

"Hold up, Kate!" Logan shouted.

"I'll go after her." Beth took off at a sprint.

Kate had disappeared from view quickly, but Beth heard her thrashing through the forest.

Beth heard Logan and Michael running behind her, but she spotted Kate first.

Kate skidded to a halt in between two oak trees. "Oh my God. No."

Beth reached her seconds later, in a small clearing that reminded Beth a lot of where Alison had been killed.

A stranger being murdered is horrible, but when it's someone you know, there's no explanation of the feeling that tears through you. Not only for the loss, but for knowing that their last moments were terrifying.

The body in front of them lay contorted. Nothing like the neat, almost sleeping arrangement of Alison's form. He'd physically fought his attacker, and he'd fought hard.

Perhaps RAVEN was behind this after all?

Because the last time Beth had seen the victim was when they'd rescued him from that very facility just a few weeks ago.

It was John Anderson.

He had a gray jacket on, just like Patty's vision.

And his face was frozen in fear, just like Alison's.

Had he been fighting for his life already while Beth ran from the Big Bad? Her heartbeat sped up, and the trees around her began to fuzz out.

Had he seen her? Maybe called to her for help and she hadn't heard?

How was she going to tell Dr. Withers he'd died after everything they'd done together to save him?

Her vision checkerboarded, the edges folding in on themselves. She was going to faint. Oh man, and she'd probably impale herself on something pointy on the way down.

Michael's arms caught her and leaned her back against a tree, easing her down to sit. His face filled her vision. "Put your head down between your knees." He helped her. "Breathe in through your nose and out through your mouth."

She followed his instructions, and her vision cleared. She lifted her head and found a relieved Michael smiling at her. He slipped a piece of gum into her hand.

"It's peppermint. It will help with any nausea."

Beth unwrapped it and popped the gum into her mouth. A few chews, and she felt semi-normal again. "Thanks, Doc."

"Are you okay?" Kate asked. She looked like she wanted to hug Beth, but Michael was in the way.

Beth nodded. "It just hit me that I'd been in the woods at that same time. Maybe I could've saved John."

"Or maybe you could have been an extra victim," Michael said. "We don't know what we're up against."

Kate put her hands on her hips. "What the hell were you doing in these woods last night? There's a killer on the loose, Beth. A killer who almost got you. Who got poor John." The anger fled from her face, replaced by grief. "He was my responsibility. I was supposed to save him."

Beth got to her feet slowly, and then took Kate's hands in hers. "You did save him at RAVEN. That was your vision, Kate. Not this. This was unnatural."

"You didn't have a vision about his death here. You weren't supposed to prevent it." Michael's voice was soothing and calm.

"But Patty did," Kate said. "She's not bound the same way I am to prevent what she sees, but she saw this." She shook her head slowly. "I just didn't think it would happen outside of Caleb's forest. We failed."

Logan put his arm around her, snuggling her close. "We won't fail again."

Beth appreciated his vote of confidence, but until they knew more, there would be other bodies. She knew in her gut that the killings were just starting.

"What I'm wondering is how the hell did someone get the drop on John?" Beth asked. "He could have stopped any weapon before it reached him, including any attacker."

Even weak from being experimented on, John had halted bullets midair, flung soldiers across the room, and helped them get free of RAVEN with his telekinesis powers.

"Which means he either didn't see his attacker, or it didn't matter." Michael gazed around at the forest as if the trees would provide the answer.

"Like Alison Clark, we don't know what killed him. Unlike Alison, we don't know why he was here, so close to the facility that experimented on him." Logan flipped open his small notebook. "The medical examiner couldn't find any evidence of a weapon. No bullet holes, no knife marks, no evidence of strangulation or even that he was tied up or confined at any point. Of course, we'll do a more thorough examination, but I think we all know it'll be the same as Alison."

"He looks petrified, like she did," Kate said.

Guilt pushed against her defenses but Beth held it back. She couldn't lose it again. "He does," Beth agreed. "Whoever the killer is, they're not using conventional means to kill."

Kate hugged herself. "The trees have been silenced here, as well. I recognize the feeling now."

"It's like a cold spot in the middle of a warm lake." Michael's eyes looked haunted. He pointed at the five trees closest to John's body. "Those are the ones that are affected. And the trees next to them feel . . ."

"Like they're in shock," Kate finished his sentence. "If this keeps happening, we could lose entire forests."

Beth scanned the trees. "This is too far away to be part of Caleb's forest, right?"

Kate nodded. "True, but all the forests here are connected deep down. It's how I was able to pull on the energy from my forest when we were inside RAVEN." Her eyes were already filling again. "These trees helped pass on the energy to save us. I couldn't have done it without them."

"Maybe Sammy found out some helpful intel from the Wardens, and that's why she's been gone so long." Beth tried for a chipper tone but failed.

Kate walked over to one of the trees and placed her palm

against the trunk. "You watched him die, didn't you?" Several tears rolled down her face. "I should have helped him. Why didn't I have another vision?"

Logan joined her. "You can't save everyone, Kate. I've had to accept that in my line of work."

"But I'm the Oracle," Kate's voice rose. She tore the knit cap from her head and flung it up into the sky. She looked up at the clouds and shouted. "What's the point, Universe? What. Is. The. Point?"

Mayday, mayday. Kate was imploding. Beth grabbed her, pulling her into her arms. Kate fought for a second, but ultimately hugged her back, her entire body shuddering.

"There is no point, Kate," Beth said. "That's what I've been trying to tell you and Sammy. The Universe does what it wants."

"It's not fair," Kate mumbled against her coat.

"I know. I know." Beth rubbed her back. "It'll be okay. We've got you. We're the Triumvirate of Potency after all."

"It's Triumvirate of Pluthar." She felt Kate smile.

"Are you sure? Maybe it's the Triumvirate of Pluckiness?"

"I love you."

"I love you, too, Red." Beth released Kate and stepped back. "Anything more we should see here, Logan?"

The DCC shook his head. "No. But if any of the remaining tests or evidence produces anything of value, I'll let you know."

Kate gave him a quick kiss, and then they left him behind, heading back to Beth's car.

"I hope Sam gets back soon," Kate said. "She's going to have to go beyond the Veil to find Caleb's cousin's first love so we can get him to agree to save the trees, including these. Oh, and apparently his first love is dangerous."

"I'm lost," Michael said.

"Me too," Beth replied.

"I'll fill everyone in back at the B&B," Kate said, opening the car door and getting in. "Just another day in Crazytown." She closed the door with a loud *thunk*.

"I'm worried, Michael. About Kate, about the killings, about all of it." Beth looked at him. "I don't want you to get hurt. Or your family. Maybe you should stay out of this."

Michael touched her shoulder. "What Glenna said is true. We owe you."

"Don't die, okay?"

He kissed her cheek, lips lingering for a moment. They were so warm against the cold air. "Same goes for you."

Her heart scrambled into a pounding beat. She gazed into his eyes, finding strength there that she could hold onto.

The walls inside her trembled, and a few bricks fell.

He held open the driver's door for her, and she slipped inside.

She was in trouble.

CHAPTER 9

WHEN BETH PULLED UP TO THE B&B, SAM AND ROBERT opened the front door to greet them. "We just got back from Entwine," Sam said. "I saw your text about the body."

Kate closed the car door. "We were just out there." She looked back over her shoulder at Michael. "Stay for dinner. We've got a lot to chat about."

Michael smiled at Kate. "I love the 'Kitchen Debrief' sessions."

"It's not a thing," Beth said, locking the car.

"It's a thing," Michael countered.

Beth frowned. "It's happened a few times. We're not that predictable."

"It's a thing, isn't it, Robert?" Michael asked.

Robert looked torn between agreeing with Michael and defending Beth's assurance. Typical. "I am unable to disagree. However, I have come to find these regular sessions extremely helpful when we are faced with a deadly foe."

"Nice save." Sam kissed him on the cheek. "Let's get inside.

We have about an hour before Patty and Emily get home, and what I have to share is something we don't want them to hear."

They filed inside. Kate grabbed a bottle of red and a bottle of white wine while Robert helped her with the glasses.

"I think we can all use a drink," Kate said. "I'll start dinner when the girls get back. It's spaghetti, so it'll be quick."

Beth cleared away the crayons and construction paper from the main table, and everyone sat down.

"Who was the victim of the second murder?" Sam asked.

Sam poured wine for everyone while Beth caught her up on the scene. Kate remained mostly silent, but still looked like she wanted to hit something hard.

She even spilled more details about her RAVEN forest visit the night before. Well, she gave them the heavily redacted version, leaving out her mystery Scottish Spiderman, working for RAVEN, and the voices in her head. But she was honest about the creepy feeling in the forest.

Robert tilted his head. "John was indeed a formidable adversary, but if what Samantha and I discovered is indeed true, it is no wonder he died."

"Spill it, Sammy." Beth took a sip of wine.

Sam stared at Beth and then Kate. "Sloane told us it's a rogue necromancer."

"A rogue necromancer?" Michael asked. "What does that mean?"

"It means someone who does not abide by the Rules of the Universe," Robert said. "Nor the laws of the Wardens."

"Why would a necromancer kill people?" Kate looked over

at Sam. "You deal in ghosts, not in the living. You don't have any new special powers over the living, do you?" She squinted at Sam as if trying to see said powers herself.

Sam shook her head. "Nope. I can sense if people have abilities now, but nothing I do can affect people who aren't dead."

Robert shook his head. "That is not entirely true, Samantha. Your daggers felled a RAVEN guard most effectively. You did it not by iron alone, but by the essence you wielded."

"True," Sam agreed, "but I'm using a tool, the daggers. I'm not zapping people with Brigh. That's the official term the Wardens use for ghostly essence."

Beth looked at Sam's fingertips, even now sparking blue. "Have you tried zapping anyone?"

"Let's not. I've had enough violence for one day," Kate said. She brought over some rolls and butter to the table. They had a rich cheesy smell to them.

"Who's the necromancer, Sammy?" Beth asked.

Sam looked grim. "Connor. They don't know for certain it's him, but Sloane was pretty sure. He's been destroying ghosts and using their essence for power for a while now."

Michael blanched. "How is that possible?"

Sam looked uncomfortable. "He's a Siphoner like I am. Sloane finally told us what my special sauce is. Apparently, not only can I siphon ghostly energy easily, but I can hold onto it too. Longer than the other necromancers, except for Connor."

Kate looked worried. "Are you going to turn evil from all that energy you're holding onto?"

"We don't know that's what's causing his murder spree,

Red," Beth said. "And Ms. Goody Two Shoes here could never turn evil." She said it playfully, but Sam just frowned at her.

Michael leaned forward. "I wonder what you can do with that energy. Have you tried healing yourself?"

Beth took out her Kershaw knife. "I can give you a shallow slice and see you do your stuff."

"I'm not going to turn evil," Sam said. "And no one is cutting anyone."

Michael looked a little disappointed. Probably the doctor in him wanting to experiment to see if his hunch was right.

Beth almost smiled at him but decided to just put her knife away.

Kate slathered some butter on one of the rolls. "Okay, so Sam gets energy from ghosts during a Bargain, but she doesn't destroy them. Connor, on the other hand, is taking their entire lifeforce." She lifted the roll to her mouth but paused. "which means he's more powerful than you are, Sam."

"I believe we should also share that Sloane has indicated Connor might be tetched in the head." Robert touched the side of his temple.

"Well, shit." Beth leaned back in her chair. "It's bad enough he's using this Brigh for power, but he's also potentially crazy."

"We don't know if Sloane was exaggerating," Sam said. "The Wardens messed up in a big way with Connor, offering him the Contract to become a necromancer at an older age than usual, so they might be trying to justify killing him."

Kate shook her head. "They want you to do it, don't they?"

"Yes. No. I mean, I already told Sloane I wouldn't do it. That *we* wouldn't do it."

Not surprising. Sam hadn't wanted to kill Graham, even when he'd tried to kill them all.

"Can you juice up your haunted daggers to take him down?" Beth asked.

"They're not haunted." Sam sounded unsure. "And I don't know."

"You need to find out just what those things can do," Beth said. "We can't lose anyone else." She shook her head slowly. "If I hadn't run, I might have given John a fighting chance."

"You don't know that," Sam said. "And if you hadn't run, you might have died. Then we'd have no chance of stopping Connor." She looked down into her wine glass. "I'm afraid we're going to need TOP to have any chance of stopping him."

The old Sam would have jumped on the opportunity to take Beth down a peg, to make her feel like shit. But it had been weeks since she'd seen the old Sam. She found she secretly hoped this new version stayed, even if it meant leaving her would be harder. Well, provided they all survived this Necromancer Apocalypse coming up.

Beth got up and leaned against the side of the fridge. "So there's a virtual smorgasbord of ghosts in Entwine. Why take the risk of killing people to get their ghosts?"

"He is not just killing people," Michael said. "He killed people with gifts. Would that create a larger amount of essence in their ghostly form? Or perhaps more powerful essence?"

Kate put down her wine glass and looked at Sam. "Have you noticed a difference in the essence that you collect from the various ghosts you've helped?"

Sam stared off into space. "Some have felt more buzzy than others, more charged, but I never made the connection. It could be tied to their gifts."

"It would also not surprise me that Sloane did not share this insight with us," Robert said. "Though I feel the Warden is invested in our well-being, she is still bound by the Warden's rules to a point."

"They might not want necromancers knowing that intel," Beth said. "Because I could see some of them only helping ghosts of people who had gifts. More bang for their buck."

"And disparity continues even in the afterlife," Kate sighed.

"I fear there is much we are not seeing as of yet, even with this new insight we have gleaned," Robert said. "Such as why now? Why has Connor started killing the living *now* when he could have done so from the very beginning, as Beth surmised?"

"And why here?" Michael's eyes narrowed. "Killing where he must know another necromancer lives. Unless he wants to get caught?"

Robert tilted his head. "He did reach out to Samantha, so perhaps that is why he is here."

Kate looked around the table. "That could be part of it, Robert, but we've got a steady feeding ground of supernaturals if you think of the people RAVEN has in their ranks, including those they're still experimenting on. And Benning Brook is close by." She shook her head. "Someone will have to be with Emily and Patty at all times, just in case."

Sam nodded. "I'm sure Aggie and Stu will help, too. We'll

all help," she said, and Kate smiled at her, but worry still pulled her mouth tight.

"What's his endgame?" Beth had been mulling this over since she'd seen John. "What I felt in the forest last night was pure evil. Whatever Connor has planned, it's not going to be good for anyone but him."

There was a rap at the front door.

Everyone jumped except Robert. Thankfully no wine glasses gave their lives as a result.

Kate shook her head. "The girls must have forgotten their key again. But it's perfect timing. We can tell you about Caleb's cousin and the trees."

Beth hopped up. "I'll let them in. I could use some hugs from those two after what we've been talking about."

She made her way to the front door. "Okay, you know the entrance fee," Beth said through the door. "Who's giving me a hug first?" Then she opened it to peek around the corner.

She stiffened.

Her grip fell from the door.

It slid wide open with a moaning creak.

"I'll be happy to pay the entry price."

The man who stood in front of her looked older than the last time she'd seen him. His short black hair had gray flecks throughout, though it remained as thick as Beth's. Wrinkles had stolen more acreage on his face than before, but he still looked every inch the snake charmer who had conned so many out of their money.

His face had the open quality of someone who was honest,

but his eyes still gleamed with the promise of lies, abuse, and danger.

Her father had found her.

CHAPTER 10

THAT AWFUL GARLIC BREATH SMELL SHE REMEMBERED FROM childhood wafted over her.

"What the hell are you doing here?" Beth's words barely choked out of her tight throat.

"Shouldn't your first question be how we got out of jail early on parole, Tiffany?"

The innocent tone and expression had worked so well on his marks, but Beth knew the real menace underneath. She wasn't going to bother correcting him on her name, reminding him she'd legally changed it, opting to use her middle name instead. It would only fuel him to use it more.

He couldn't be here when the girls got back, but she couldn't push him away too quickly. Otherwise, he'd know there was something more than her revulsion fueling her.

Beth crossed her arms. "How you got out of jail early on parole? My guess is that you had leverage over someone who got it done."

A slight pull around his eyes. Bingo. They'd leaned on

someone and been released. She'd hoped for more years so she could finish her exit strategy.

The one where she disappeared from everyone, so her parents couldn't find her.

"You always were too smart for your own good." Her father smoothed back his hair in a gesture she remembered from childhood. He'd always been a vain bastard.

"Spill it. Why are you here?" She stepped outside into the chilly night air, causing him to back up. Beth tried to close the door behind her, but it was caught on something.

On Michael's hand. He opened the door, and everyone joined her outside.

Sam, Kate, Robert, and Michael.

Shit.

The more her father saw, the more he'd make connections that he could use to his advantage. Nothing escaped his perusal. She'd learned that the hard way.

"It's nice to see you again, Sam and Kate," her father said. "My time in prison showed me how wrong I had been all those years ago. I'm truly sorry for any pain I had caused."

"State why you're here, and then leave," Michael said. His voice was as cool as an iceberg.

"I see you have a new boyfriend." Her father scrutinized Michael in the span of a heartbeat, and she knew he'd already gleaned much of the information he'd need for a con. But he didn't realize Michael could pick up on his emotions.

There would be no fooling Michael Forbes.

That thought alone brought a smile to her face.

Her father frowned. "I see I should have called first. I didn't realize I was interrupting."

"You'll always be interrupting, Mr. Marshall." Sam stepped forward to flank Beth.

Kate took up position on her other side. "This is my property, and you're not welcome here. If I see you on my grounds again, I will call the constables."

Her father hesitated, not moving.

Robert stalked forward. "I can assure you, we will physically remove you from this residence by force if necessary. Though I am certain no one wants matters to come to that resolution."

The threat in his voice was crystal clear.

Beth felt like her heart wanted to explode and expand at the same time. It pounded painfully against her chest.

Everyone was standing up for her. Even Robert and Michael who only knew pieces of her past.

And they were now condemning themselves to whatever her father had in store for them.

She couldn't let it get that far.

"Come on, Harvey." She'd stopped calling him "Dad" years ago. "We can talk over there." She pointed to the end of the driveway. It was out of earshot, but still within eyesight. As much as she wanted to see Robert and Michael toss her father from the grounds, no need to poke her criminal psycho dad any further than necessary. And she did need to find out what he wanted so she could get rid of him as quickly as possible.

"Thank you." Her father dipped his head, but she didn't miss the angry look on his face. He'd wanted to control this, control her, like he used to, but her team had kiboshed his plans.

It felt incredible to have a team. Even if it was only short-lived.

Beth led the way down the driveway.

Her father kept up. "Nice setup you've got here."

"It's not a setup. Let's not waste time on small talk we know neither of us means." She stopped at the edge of the driveway. Everyone was still by the front door, watching.

As were the crows on the nearby trees. Caleb would get an earful tonight.

Her father frowned again, deeper this time. "If you were ten, I'd take a lash to you for your attitude."

The scar on her neck suddenly itched. She fought not to scratch it.

"Do you have anything to say or not?"

Her father gave her a look she'd never seen before. Approval. "You're stronger than you used to be."

She just stared at him, knowing he wouldn't delay much longer, not when money was on the line. And blackmail should be what he was after. She was counting on it.

"Your mother and I need money." His tone held unshed tears. Fake. But he still had the touch. "You could give it to us as a dutiful daughter."

Beth shook her head. "Considering how I stole for you and Gloria for years, I think the 'dutiful daughter' jar is overflowing."

"If we end up struggling to make ends meet," he continued, "we might have to resort to other means of making money." He paused as if what he was going to say next pained him. "Given your show being in the top five of your time slot and your viewers clamoring for your Scottish episodes to be filmed, I'm sure your network wouldn't want the news of your past getting out. If they find out you came from a, let's say, grifter family, they might not feel your miraculous finds are legitimate."

And there it was, as expected.

"The network will understand."

He nodded. "They might. You are a moneymaker for them. But your audience is another story. Especially if people start coming forward saying that you paid them for the 'information' on their lost objects so you could look like you had abilities."

This piece she hadn't expected. But it made sense her parents had kept their web of lowlifes who would do them a solid if needed.

"You're something else, Harvey." She made sure to let a bit of admiration color her tone, knowing he loved to feel clever. And in this case, he really had been. Even though she had already anticipated some of this, she was a bit impressed by the depths they would sink to.

"Just looking out for you, Tiff. I know how unforgiving people can be when someone's checkered past is revealed. Look at what happened to your mother and me."

He smiled, and for a moment, just a brief one, she remembered some of the good times growing up. When he was pleased with something she'd done. When she'd felt almost, just almost, loved. She'd been starved for those moments. Still was.

But not from *him* any longer.

"You killed someone." Beth pointed a finger at him. "At

least the one person I know about. Our pasts are not the same. Not even close."

"We never intended to kill Randolph. He wasn't supposed to be home during our visit." He pursed his lips.

Visit. His quaint way of referring to their break-in at the house of a local politician when they lived in New York.

"Are you going to give us the money, or does this need to become unpleasant?" Harvey asked.

She'd resisted enough to be believable. At least she hoped so. Money didn't mean what it used to.

And if she were their meal ticket, then they wouldn't dare harm anyone she cared about. She could keep everyone safe.

She gave him what she hoped was a resigned look. "If I do this, I never want to see you again. We can handle everything electronically. That *has* to be part of the deal."

Triumph flashed across his face before he covered it with a practiced art.

"That can be arranged. We'll set up regular payments to an offshore account."

She lifted her hands. "Of course, you will. I bet you already have the account set up."

"You know your mom. Always likes to be prepared."

"Fine. If it gets you out of my life, at least physically, it's worth it."

"You haven't even asked how much."

"I bet Gloria has already hacked into my accounts to find out how much I can afford to give and then add ten percent more." She frowned at him. "Enough to bleed me, but not enough to kill. I've seen this game before, if you remember."

Her father laughed softly. "That's right. The local cops were such easy pickings when you were growing up."

"Where is Gloria, by the way?" she asked. If she managed to get rid of her dad, she didn't want her mom popping up at the B&B too.

There. Just the slightest tick in his jaw.

Something was up. Trouble in criminal paradise?

"Your mother is fine and well in London. We thought it would be best if I came alone. This way, if you were prepared to do the smart thing, we could keep this under the news radar."

A sound of a car engine rumbled through the air. Someone was coming to the B&B. Her stomach plummeted. It had to be Aggie dropping off the girls.

If Beth tried to hustle her dad off the grounds now, it would only pique his interest, and she didn't want him to focus on the girls. She'd gotten the deal she could live with, that they *all* could live with.

Cool. She had to play it super cool. It's not like her dad wouldn't know Kate had kids. They'd have done their research. She just had to present an indifferent front.

Aggie turned off the engine and the car doors opened, releasing Patty and Emily, who flew at the B&B at a full run. But both girls stopped short when they saw Beth and her father.

From the worried look on Patty's face, Beth wondered if the kid had seen her father in a vision, or just sensed he was bad news.

Aggie walked up behind the girls. Gone was the kind

caretaker Beth was used to. The woman who stared at her father was all business. Wary.

She walked past the girls and stopped, effectively blocking them from Harvey's view. The girls ran to Kate.

"And who do we have here?" Aggie asked.

Beth could have kissed her for the distraction. "Harvey," she replied. "He was just leaving."

Aggie nodded, her long gray hair catching the moonlight. "Harvey Marshall, of course. Your wife has been poking around the firewalls of the B&B. Please let her know she's wasting her time."

Beth knew Aggie was a hacker—she'd helped with their RAVEN mission—but Beth hadn't realized just how good she was. Keeping Beth's mom out was no easy feat.

She looked at her father. "We done here?"

"I remember you at their ages," her father said, looking at where the girls had disappeared into the house.

Anger and fear surged through Beth, pounding at her control. "I remember being their ages, too." She let her words burn in the air. He'd expect her anger. "But luckily, Kate doesn't beat them into submission, so I have high hopes neither one of them will grow up to be a fucked up mess like me."

Aggie didn't flinch. Just gazed between Beth and Harvey. Beth didn't care what she heard at this point. Everyone needed to realize just how dangerous he was.

"A mess? Look at how successful you've become. You wouldn't have gotten there without the lessons we taught you." He smiled at Aggie. "Tough love worked wonders on our girl."

Beth shook her head. "Don't try to dress it up as anything other than abuse and torture. Have Gloria text me the routing information and amount. Goodbye." Her voice was steady and stronger than she'd expected.

She turned around and walked back to the cluster of Sam, Michael, and Robert by the door.

When she reached them, she heard the sound of a car engine blazing to life behind her. She turned slightly to see Aggie watching until her father's car disappeared down the drive.

Now she just had to see if her parents would take the low-hanging fruit.

If they didn't—if they threatened anyone she loved—she'd stop them.

No matter what it took.

CHAPTER 11

MICHAEL EASED BACK IN HIS CHAIR, FEELING LIKE HE'D gained ten pounds from the meal. He'd known Kate was more than baked goods, but that spaghetti was incredible. Something about the sauce. She should really sell it as a take away item when the B&B got back up and running.

No one said anything about Beth's father during dinner. They really couldn't with the girls there. But Michael felt the curiosity coming off of Emily in waves. That one would be tempted to go "investigate" if she thought Auntie Beth needed her help.

Which would be dangerous.

Thankfully, they'd both gone up to bed without any protest for more information. But he didn't doubt they'd pepper Beth with questions later.

Even if Michael hadn't known that Beth's parents had abused her, her father would have instantly put him on alert. There'd been a mixture of emotions swirling in Beth's father. Worry was one of the main ones, but that was understandable since he'd shown up unannounced with a blackmail scheme. At least that's what Michael had assumed it was. Then there was envy, along with a dash of deviousness.

But the one emotion that concerned Michael the most was the rage.

It boiled just under the surface of the other emotions he sensed. It was vast. And ugly. Just what had happened to cause her father to direct so much rage at Beth? Or had her father always been like that?

He glanced over at Sam and Robert. They were looking at the pictures the girls had drawn on that Kate had pinned to the walls.

"They'll make wonderful parents," he said to Beth, who sat beside him at the table, keeping his voice quiet.

Beth nodded. "I know. Sammy always manages to get everything she wants. Even if they have to adopt, because the I'm-now-suddenly-alive-and-not-a-ghost sperm doesn't work like it should, they'll raise incredible kids." She pushed at the remaining spaghetti on her plate. "It's not fair."

"Some would say your fame isn't fair."

"Hey, I worked hard for what I have." She dropped her fork. "I made sacrifices."

Michael smiled. "I'm just trying to give you some perspective. Sam gave up her freedom to the Universe to have Robert in her life. She sacrificed, too."

Beth pursed her lips. "Did Kate put you up to this? I'm working on being nicer to Sammy, but don't push it."

He found he wanted to push it. He wanted to dig deep and

discover what made Beth Marshall tick. But that was danger-ous territory.

He needed to keep things light. "Kate didn't put me up to anything." He bumped her shoulder with his. "I just like to poke at you."

"You might not like how hard I poke back."

"I can take it."

A hint of a smile softened her lips. "I can't figure you out, Forbes."

"I can't figure you out, either, Marshall."

"Oh really?" She leaned in a bit closer. "And here I thought your powers would strip me naked in front of you."

Her words had the desired effect, as he knew she'd intended. He'd been imagining how it would feel to be skin-on-skin for weeks now.

Had she been doing the same, or was she just toying with him?

Was that heat in her eyes?

Those gorgeous brown eyes with rims of amber.

He should look away.

Banter about something easy and casual.

"What's wrong, doctor?" Beth whispered, a hint of teasing, with something darker in her tone.

His gaze brushed across her lips. He imagined how they'd feel crushed under his.

"Keep it in your pants, you two." Kate's voice doused Michael like a tub of ice cold water, and Beth jerked, knocking her fork onto the floor with a loud *clatter*.

"We're not," Michael sputtered. "There's no pants issue here."

Sam laughed, walking over. Robert gazed around the room, clearly uncomfortable.

Kate sighed. "Apparently you're just as deluded at Beth when it comes to emotions."

"Oh, like you were all on board the Logan train," Beth snapped.

"That was different."

"We saw how gone you two were over each other," Beth said. "But noooo, you weren't interested in Logan that way. You couldn't let yourself be interested."

Kate laughed. "Beth has an honorary degree from the Kate Banberry School of Deflection."

"I think Michael and Beth are perfect for each other." Sam clapped her hands together.

Beth stood. "Don't think you're matchmaking anyone, Sammy. I choose my men, and Michael isn't on the menu."

Michael kept his seat. Said pants were a bit too tight at the moment, and he wasn't going to give Kate the satisfaction of being right. "What she said. Well, reverse, but you know what I mean."

Robert finally looked at them, a bit of mischief in his eyes. "Remember what they say about those who argue too much."

"Protest too much," Sam corrected.

If Sam and Kate were seeing their attraction, this was going farther than Michael had intended. He needed to be careful.

Beth took their plates to the sink. "So do you want to hear

about my parents, or do you want to keep the teasing up?"

Kate looked torn but Sam sighed. "You two are just so cute, we couldn't help it. But, yes, we want to hear about your parents."

Cute? Indignation helped to cool things off rapidly. He gave Sam what he imagined was a harsh look, but she just smiled sweetly at him.

"So you had no idea they'd been paroled?" Michael asked, turning toward Beth.

She flashed him a thankful look. "Nope. They must have more people on their payroll than I thought." She wiped her hands on a towel and joined them back at the table. "Including my contact within the prison, who was supposed to let me know if anything changed."

"I wondered about that," Kate said, grabbing a plastic container. "I figured you had set up some sort of early warning system." She popped the lid open, and the scent of cinnamon and vanilla wafted up.

Sam pulled out a chair and sat at the table. "Can parolees leave the country, or can we get him sent back to jail just for being here?"

Beth grabbed two cookies and handed one to Michael. "Their crimes were confined to New York State, so they didn't get into the feds' territory. Which means they're allowed to leave the country with approval. I checked on that initially, just in case they made their last parole hearing. But none of my contacts at the airports pinged me."

Michael nodded. "Which means they might have flown by

private jet." He took a bite of the snickerdoodle. No wonder this had worked as an offering to Vivian.

"And someone scrubbed their flight plan," Kate added.

"I covered multiple states, just in case they drove and then flew to throw me off the scent." Beth frowned. "They probably anticipated that and drove out further. Or Gloria hacked in and changed the commercial records."

"Your mom could do that?" Sam asked

"That and more," Beth said.

"Are they trying to blackmail you?" Kate asked softly.

Beth nodded. "I expected it and I'm willing to pay. The network already knows about my past—I told them years ago—but my dad is threatening to discredit me by having audience members lie, saying that I paid them off for information for the show. But that's not why I'm agreeing to it."

"You're protecting Emily and Patty." Michael said what they all were thinking. Beth couldn't hide how much she loved those girls.

"And all of you. My parents are dangerous people. If they think hurting any of you will get them more money, they will. I'm trying to keep them focused on me being their cash cow."

Sam fisted her hands. "I wanted to punch your dad so badly when I saw him. The times I patched you up after the beatings. He deserves to be beaten until he screams."

Beth gave her a small smile. "Thanks, Sammy. I'm with you there. If only I had been strong enough to turn them in earlier. To stop stealing for them." The last words were soft.

"You were just a kid," Kate said gently. "And braver than all of us to get through what you did without being completely fucked up."

Sam nodded. "Yeah, you're only partially fucked up." Her words were kind, and he knew she was trying to get Beth to laugh, just a little. But Beth looked down, playing with cookie crumbs on the tablecloth. He didn't have to use his abilities to know she was fighting tears.

Michael reached out and took her hand. He couldn't help it. The need to comfort her couldn't be stopped. "I've got plenty of would've, could've, should'ves in my past," he said. "But I've tried to accept that I made the best decisions I could at the time. Give yourself a little grace there, Marshall."

She squeezed his hand so hard it hurt, but he didn't pull away. "Thanks," she whispered, and then looked up at him—the tears making her eyes shine in the kitchen light.

It was like looking in a mirror. The self-blame warring with fragile hope, all wrapped up in a drowning swirl of fear and pain. He wanted to kiss her. Not out of attraction or lust, though there was still plenty of both within him. But to show her he saw her—*really saw her*—and the darkness within. The same darkness he had.

He didn't think Sam and Kate could really understand as hard as they might try. But he did. There was no point in denying it any longer. He cared for Beth Marshall—deeply.

Now the real question was—what was he going to do about it?

CHAPTER 12

"TELL ME AGAIN WHAT CALEB SAID ABOUT THE VEIL," Sam asked Kate. She'd convinced her to come with her to Scottish Glamour, the local apothecary shop run by their friend, Yasmin. It had a healthy dose of mystical treasures—and hopefully the perfect gift to cheer Beth up.

Kate turned away from a shelf sagging under the weight of tarot cards and gems and herbs. "He said you have to go through it in order to reach his cousin's first love and bring her back with you so he can have a chat with her. I'm assuming you'd have to take her back, as well." She picked up a deck of tarot cards with a Viking theme. "What about these for Beth?"

"Beth would just see bad omens in everything," Sam said. "Think along the lines of healing crystals."

Sam navigated around the small tables heaped with books to reach Kate. The usual smell of sage and rosemary filled the place. There wasn't really a card that said, "Sorry your abusive parents got out of prison early," but they could get her a little reminder that she wasn't alone in all this.

"We should probably keep our voices down when we talk about the Veil," Sam said in a whisper when she reached Kate. "There are a few other customers in here."

Kate rose on her tippy-toes, craning her neck to see over a statue of Aphrodite. "Where?"

Sam tilted her head so she didn't have to point. "Ethyl from the bakery is by the candles, and Aggie is perusing the incense with Stu."

Kate brightened. "Oh, I'm going to say 'hi' to them real quick. I'll be right back." Kate put the deck down and made her way through the maze of the store to reach the B&B caretakers. Sam watched her red hair bobbing in and out of sight.

Kate had told Aggie and Stu last night about the serial killer potentially being a rogue necromancer targeting people with gifts, like Yasmin. No doubt, Stu was worried about his niece. Everyone needed to be worried until they could find Connor and stop him.

The flute sounds coming from the speakers on either side of the back counter died to be replaced by the usual rhythmic drumming Sam always associated with the shop. It was primal, yet somehow grounding.

Yasmin came out of the back room where she gave her readings. Her usually dark, flowing hair was in a messy bun. It was complete with hair sticks that had figures of the Buddha on the ends. Black leggings, a long, red tunic, and tall boots completed her ensemble. Her baby, just a few weeks old, was snuggled up tight to her chest in a crimson baby sling.

A man followed Yasmin out of the back room. Sam didn't

recognize him. He was just a bit taller than Logan with dark brown hair and eyes.

He didn't look exactly like the pictures Sloane had shown her of Connor, but he had the same oval-shaped face. They expected he would be disguising himself, so Sam reached out with her senses. No hint of any gifts or any ghostly essence. Sam's shoulders released, relaxing down.

Yasmin waved goodbye to the stranger and made her way over to Sam.

"It is so good to see you." Yasmin touched her arm. "How is your new book?"

"On hold until we catch the serial killer."

Yasmin grew serious. "The rogue necromancer. Do you think that TOP can stop him?"

"We've got to." Sam took a deep breath in and let it out slowly. "If we don't, the Wardens will figure out some way to kill him."

Yasmin gave her an encouraging smile. "If anyone can do it, it's you."

Sam laughed softly. "Thanks for the vote of confidence. But in all seriousness, you should be extra careful. Don't go any-where alone."

"I'll be okay." Yasmin patted the pocket of her tunic. "I've got backup if necessary."

Sam didn't want to ask what that "backup" was. Yasmin's gift, though not as powerful as Kate's, was always timely in a practical sense. She knew who needed what item and when. Maybe it was an emergency beeper that would summon the police? Or summon Stu? He was ex-military after all.

Kate popped out from behind a collection of masks. Sam scrambled back, knocking over several books on astrology.

"Hey, Yasmin." Kate went to give her a hug, and then stopped when she saw the baby. "He gets cuter every time I see him."

Yasmin snuggled her son. "It helps, especially when he's waking us up for feedings in the middle of the night." Her words were filled with love and exasperation.

"I remember those times well," Kate said. "Oh, Ethyl needs your help deciding on a candle color."

Yasmin shook her head. "She's trying a love spell again. Until next time, my friends, be safe." Sam heard her muttering as she navigated the route to candles.

"What were you two talking about?" Kate raised an eyebrow.

Sam leaned in and whispered. "The serial killer. I told her to be careful. You know, the usual."

"It is our usual." Kate sighed. "So, what do you think about the Veil—piece of cake or Temple of Doom?"

"Probably somewhere in between." Sam picked up one of the pins on a nearby table. "Beatrice told me the Veil is extremely dangerous to ghosts. I don't know how I'll make it through, even with Darrin's help, let alone bring a ghost to and from without them coming to harm."

"Caleb said you could do it with your daggers, though this Morag you're supposed to get sounds like bad news." Kate scooped up a pin with the Tree of Life on. "Ooh, I'm getting this for Patty. Now I just have to find a crow one for Emily."

"We're here shopping for Beth." Sam reminded her.

Kate laughed. "You're shopping for Beth. I already know how to cheer her up with baked goods. Pumpkin pie. One of her favorites."

Sam couldn't argue. Beth was a sucker for Kate's treats.

"Did Caleb share how I could go through the Veil with my daggers?"

"Nope." She looked thoughtful. "Which must mean you'll either know how, or Darrin can help."

The air grew thick around Sam. "Incoming," she whispered to Kate. She wondered who it could be. She had scanned for ghosts before they entered, just in case Connor had spies here, but found nothing.

The hazy outline of a figure appeared, and then the black dress became clearer, along with a perfectly tailored jacket. Her heart-shaped face was next, gray hair lying in waves against her head. Then her piercing blue eyes with a disapproving gaze that Sam had grown accustomed to.

Imogene Clarissa MacCallum.

"What are you doing here at Scottish Glamour?" Sam asked. "You usually haunt your family antique store down the street."

"Poor manners as usual." Imogene clucked her tongue. "You owe me a Bargain, Necromancer, so a cordial 'hello' or inquiry about my health would have been more proper." She examined her nails. "And I don't 'haunt.' I resent that terminology."

Sam didn't know what to say for a moment.

"Is it Imogene?" Kate asked. Her whisper was almost an actual whisper. She'd been practicing.

It helped to break Sam out of her surprise. "I apologize, Imogene. If you'll follow me to the back corner of the store, it will be easier for us to speak."

The back corner, with its large volume of inspirational plaques, was thankfully deserted. Kate touched her arm lightly, no doubt to hear the conversation. When either Kate or Beth touched Sam now, they could hear ghosts through her.

Sam turned to Imogene. "I haven't forgotten about the Bargain I owe you, but as I'm sure you know, there's a necromancer who is killing people and ghosts."

Beatrice had spread the news throughout Entwine as a warning.

A brush of fear swept through Imogene's gaze. "Which is why I came to talk to you. Like with Graham Dunning before, the killings must end. Balance must be restored." She flicked a bit of something from her jacket.

"Do you know where he is?" Sam asked.

Imogene shook her head. "Connor hides himself well, but I can help you with your Veil quest."

How did she know about going through the Veil? Kate had told Sam to keep things quiet, especially about who they were going to retrieve, and she had. And Imogene hadn't been in the shop when they'd been talking earlier. But the ghost had proven herself to be resourceful in the past. She probably had a team like Beatrice did.

"How can you help us on our quest?" Kate asked,

Imogene raised an eyebrow at Kate, as if noticing her for the first time. "I'm surprised any of Beatrice's relations would rise to the stature of the Oracle." She crinkled her nose like she'd smelled something rotten.

A slight shift in the air. Not heavy, but a ghost was coming.

"I can manage my own reputation quite handily," Beatrice said, appearing next to Imogene. "And I'd thank you to leave Kate out of any of your machinations, unless you want to find yourself scrubbing out the Wardens' latrines."

Imogene scowled so deeply, Sam thought her face was going to cave in on itself.

If Imogene was offering help and information on how to get through the Veil, Sam didn't want to lose that chance. "It's wonderful to see you, Beatrice," Sam said. "Imogene knows how to get through the Veil safely."

"You just use a Runner." Beatrice placed a hand on her hip.

Imogene mimicked her stance. "What about the ghostly essence being sucked from her body? And would the Runner bring a ghost through without being under direct orders of a Warden?"

Beatrice frowned. "I have someone in mind."

Imogene sniffed. "Your questionable contacts aside, even with a willing Runner, Sam needs ghostly essence to make the return trip." Imogene hadn't mentioned anything about who they were retrieving. Sam felt a little of her anxiety ease.

"Sam will just use her daggers," Beatrice replied.

The burgeoning look of triumph flagged a bit on Imogene's face. "I wasn't aware everyone knew about the daggers."

Beatrice lifted her chin. "I'm not 'everyone.'"

Imogene looked at Sam. "Be careful that your rogue

colleague doesn't find out about the daggers. He would be even more dangerous with those to wield."

The daggers would never work for him, but Sam wasn't going to give powerful information away. When she had summoned the spirits of the daggers—or whatever they were—during the RAVEN attack, she'd felt the bond. They were hers to use, and hers alone.

And since then, they'd been silent.

"The thing I've been struggling with," Beatrice said, "is how to get Sam in and out fast enough. The longer she's behind the Veil, the more ghostly essence she'll have to use to survive. If she runs out . . ."

Kate looked ill. "I didn't know that's what Caleb meant by dangerous."

"If there's not a safe way for me to go through the Veil and come back, we'll have to find another way to get that help for the trees."

"I might know of a way to provide you safe passage through the Veil," Imogene said.

They waited for her to speak, but she obviously was using the moment for dramatic effect.

Sam took a step closer to Imogene. "If I die trying to go through the Veil or up against the rogue necromancer, you don't get your Bargain."

Imogene pursed her lips. "Fine. The Oracle can stop time and hold it in place while you travel through the Veil."

"I can't stop time." Kate looked embarrassed.

"It pains me to say so, but you can." Imogene raked her gaze over Kate. "I knew a previous Oracle. He could manipulate time as he chose."

"A previous—"

Sam held up her hand, cutting Kate off. She could talk to Imogene all she wanted to once they got through this.

"Stopping time could work." Sam glanced at Beatrice who grudgingly nodded. "Thank you for this information, Imogene. I will honor my promise as soon as we restore the Balance."

Imogene nodded and simply disappeared. No threats. No jabs. Very unusual.

"Didn't Robert almost pass out taking you through Entwine?" Kate asked. "How's he going to manage both of us?"

Beatrice tutted at Kate. "Sam can use Robert's ring to make the journey herself. Then Robert can take Kate."

Sam turned back to Beatrice. "What do you mean, use the ring?"

A sly look came into Beatrice's eyes. "I heard Sloane speaking with Darrin. The ring is in tune with Entwine. If someone living puts it on, they'll be transported to Entwine."

"But it keeps Robert here. It does the opposite for him," Sam said.

"Because Robert already has energy from Entwine inside him. Like meets like and cancels each other out."

"Okay, so I go with the ring and Robert takes Kate. Is he up for that? Kate's right that he barely got me through."

"Robert has been practicing." Beatrice glowed with pride. "With several of Caleb's crows—with their full permission, mind you. And his stamina has been increasing, as well."

"I want to go to Entwine," Kate said. "I really do. But I've never stopped time before."

Beatrice smiled at Kate. "Like Robert, you just need a little practice." She looked at Sam. "I'll check the patrol schedules to see when you should go." Beatrice scrunched her nose. "If it's Morag you're getting, Caleb must be calling on Karnon."

"That's him." Kate nodded.

"He's even more squirrelly than Caleb," Beatrice said. "He's an old god and powerful. Be careful not to anger him. Caleb blusters, but Karnon will burn the flesh from your bones."

Sam felt her lunch roll around in her stomach. "Awesome. This is sounding better and better the more we talk about it." She looked at Kate. "Are you sure we have to save the trees?"

Kate crossed her arms, and Sam sighed.

"Fine. Let's head home so you can start learning how to stop time."

BETH PUSHED AGAINST ONE OF THE POSTS ON THE RAVEN training field, stretching out her pecs. She'd already done a quick run to loosen up. Now she just needed to stretch before she started throwing shuriken. If she didn't, she'd pay for it later.

The crisp air felt wonderful in her lungs. The sunshine had taken the extreme chill off the day. She could even smell the sweetness of the grass near the trees to her left.

She hoped Ollie had some intel on the killings and on Connor. She also hoped the practice would clear her thoughts. It should be her criminal father spinning in her mind, but instead it was Michael.

Their flirtation in the kitchen had been fun and light. Just the way she usually liked things. But then he'd had to go and ruin it all by looking at her the way he did when he'd taken her hand.

She'd seen something in his gaze she'd never thought to find—acceptance. Not a hint of I-want-to-get-in-your-pants. It was full on deep. As if she'd been naked in front of him and he was cool with it, scars and all.

She wanted to see him again. To see if she'd imagined it. Because against her better judgement, she couldn't deny she felt something for Michael Forbes. And she didn't know what to do about it.

The eastern door to the facility closed with a loud *clang* in the distance, startling her out of her thoughts. She saw Ollie heading toward her. They'd been training on shuriken for the past week, but she'd been practicing on her own whenever she could and apologizing to the trees in the back of Kate's B&B.

A minute later, Ollie joined her. "You ready?" he asked. He slipped off his jacket and put it on a nearby bench. Gone was his usual uniform. He looked like someone she might meet at the gym. Unassuming. And that made him very good at what he did.

"Quick question before we start."

"Shoot."

"Why did you sign me up for combat training?" she asked.

"I love learning how to use new weapons, but this doesn't have anything to do with finding things for RAVEN."

He shrugged. "I didn't. My father requested it."

"He's expecting me in the field eventually, isn't he?" Beth asked.

"I've told you how it works here," Ollie said. "It's strictly need-to-know. If I hear anything, I'll tell you."

She wasn't going to get any more intel out of him on the subject. She took out her satchel filled with the various shuriken they'd been using.

Ollie walked over and looked at her choices. "You don't need this one. It's too big." He tapped on the one Lacey had mailed to her. "Shuriken are a distraction, not the main attraction, remember?"

"I've done my research. You can kill with these."

"True, but I wouldn't count on that outcome." Ollie pointed to where she kept her Kershaw knife. "That's your better bet. Distract them with the shuriken, throw them off balance, get in close, and then kill them."

"Have you killed someone before?" Beth had been wondering just how deep Ollie was embedded in his dad's ways.

"I have." He looked off into the distance for a moment before meeting her gaze again. "Each time has been to save someone, but it doesn't make the burden any easier to bear. You?"

She shook her head. "Almost, but not yet."

"Not yet?"

"Given what we've been up against over the short time I've

been in Scotland, I think I'll be faced with that eventually."

"Can I give you some advice?"

"Sure."

Ollie's jaw clenched. "Once you've decided there is no other choice, don't hesitate. I've lost too many soldiers to that hesitation."

"I'm sorry your old man put you through what he did," she said. She hadn't forgotten what Kate had seen when she'd touched one of Ollie's old toys. He was a survivor, like she was.

A hint of light chased away the darkness in his eyes. "Same to you." He pointed at her shuriken again. "You'll throw the smaller ones faster."

"I bet I can throw the big one pretty fast."

He smiled. "Oh yeah? Let's see." He took out one of his favorites. She knew that because he never came to training without it. It reminded her of a Halloween ghost with four waves around the center: one for the head, one for the feet and two for the arms.

It was about half the size of hers.

They took position in front of each of the wooden posts.

"Ready?" she asked. She took a deep breath and centered herself—left leg in front of her, not in a lunge, but slightly bent. Her weapon was in her right hand, ready to throw like a frisbee.

"I'll set the alarm." He touched his watch, and Beth knew the beep would go off anywhere from 5 seconds to 15 seconds from now.

The post filled her vision. Ollie fell away. RAVEN disappeared. Then the alarm's sharp beep shot adrenaline through her, but she had learned how to harness that rush. It didn't control her, it fueled her.

Her star flew from her grip. Strong. Sure. The solid *thunk* of impact.

Seconds after Ollie's.

Dammit. She hated when he was right. Okay, she hated when anyone else was right.

He grinned at her while he pulled his star free, but he didn't say "I told you so," which gave him some points in her book.

She wrenched her star out of the post and joined him by his stash of weapons.

"That one looks kinda big." She pointed at one that had six arms, all ending in razor sharp edges.

"It's still manageable with the torque I can generate in my throw. Now, what did you need to talk to me about? I'm assuming the killings?" He kept his voice low. The odds of them being overheard out in the field were slim, but they were both still careful.

"We know who it is."

He slipped another star free and handed it to her. "Try this one."

They each resumed their positions and threw again.

This time she almost beat him.

"It's a rogue necromancer. Sam got the 411 from her sources, so we believe it's legit. Also, fair warning, he might be a little cray-cray."

Ollie retrieved his star and dropped it back on his cloth. "I walked in on the end of a phone call my father had. I think he might know something about this."

"Do you think your dad knows him?"

Ollie shook his head. "I don't know. We usually steer clear of necromancers. They're too unpredictable, and we don't want the Wardens to get involved in what we're doing here."

It made sense. They could poach supernaturals all day long without anyone stopping them, but if they pissed off a necromancer, or even harmed one, they'd be up shit's creek.

"You must have pissed your pants when you saw Sam in your facility."

Ollie laughed. "I used it to convince my dad to take the deal with you. Even associating with a necromancer gives you a bit more protection against him and the Society." He sobered. "Though I wouldn't count on it saving any of you if things go sideways."

"Noted." Beth never had any illusions that a deal with RAVEN would do any more than delay the inevitable. Ollie's dad was well connected, which is why RAVEN let the Society, a smaller faction within RAVEN, run things their way in the U.K. No one would bat an eye if there was more bloodshed.

"I can tell you Alison Clark wasn't being targeted by my dad." He gestured toward the posts. "And we don't know why John was in our forest." Dead end there. "You haven't really worked on your overhand throw for a while," Ollie said.

"Because I don't like it."

"But you should be competent in both methods in case you're in a tight spot. Plus, I find I get more penetration power when I throw overhand." Ollie met her gaze. "Which could come in handy in case you're going up against, I don't know, a rogue necromancer?"

"Fine," Beth grumbled. "Show me again. Alison had gifts, though, didn't she?"

Ollie nodded. "Small time. She made the Registry, but that's about it."

"Registry?"

"The list we use to keep track of potential recruits." Ollie held up one of his shuriken. "You can hold it in one of two ways, but I'll show you the grip I like best. You press your thumb and forefinger against both sides, and then rest the back into the webbing between your thumb and forefinger."

He took up a balanced stance, one foot further out in front of the other in the lunge position he'd taught Beth. Rocking back and forth a few times, he suddenly threw the shuriken at the post.

The *thunk* was more resounding than with their other throws. Beth jogged over to look. It was halfway into the wood.

"Wow. That *is* deeper."

Ollie joined her and dug it out with a bit of effort. "Both methods are effective, but you don't know what position your arms might be in when you go to throw, so it could save your life to know both."

"You've made your point." She smiled. "Literally."

He laughed again. "You're my most surly student."

"I'll take that as a compliment." Beth grew serious. "Were you still after John Anderson before he was killed?"

"No. That was part of your deal. We monitored him but we left him alone."

Beth perked up. "Monitored him?"

Ollie nodded. "Just like we still monitor Duncan and Mackenzie." His face grew wistful, and Beth imagined he was worried for his sister. Beth didn't think Mackenzie had reached out at all since their escape from RAVEN.

"I'm going to try the throw." Beth walked back over to her post. Ollie followed and helped her get the right grip on the shuriken.

"Be careful that you don't squeeze too hard, otherwise you'll cut into your hand where it's resting."

"Got it. So, does RAVEN have anything that could help us with a necromancer?"

Ollie stood back, giving her room. "Don't bring your arm completely down on your throw or else you'll hit the ground with the shuriken, not the post. I'll check out our storage. I remember something from a few years back that might help. If I find anything, I'll bury it by the tree where you found the footprints the other night."

Beth wasn't surprised he knew what she'd been doing before Jensen showed up in the forest. Nothing got past Ollie. Or RAVEN.

"Did your surveillance that night catch anyone?"

Ollie shook his head. "Just you. Did you have something to share?"

"Nope."

So the mysterious stranger she'd talked to in the forest had stayed off of RAVEN's radar. He had mentioned he'd worked for them in the past.

Ollie lifted his chin. "Are you going to stall any longer or can we see just how bad your throw is?"

She ignored him and breathed in and out, centering herself. Once again, Ollie, RAVEN, everything fell away. All she saw was the post in front of her and all she felt was the metal in her hand.

Steady. Flick your wrist sharply before you release.

Beth froze and looked around. It was that same woman's voice she'd heard in the forest.

She should really talk to Sam about it. Maybe she had a guardian ghost?

"Did you say something?" she asked Ollie, just in case.

"Nope. Are you hearing things?"

She shook her head. "Just my inner voice telling me how crazy this whole situation is."

Ollie smiled. "They must know my inner voice." He pointed at the post. "Try again."

Beth took a deep breath and tried to center herself again. It took longer this time, but she got there.

Her eyes focused on the post. Everything else zoned out.

No voices. Nothing. She waited a few beats more.

And then threw the shuriken, putting the sharp flick on the end as the voice had instructed.

The metal flew true, hitting the post dead center. Even from a distance, Beth knew it had sunk deep, just like Ollie's had.

Your father taught me to throw. He'd be so proud to see this.

Beth spun around, nearly going down, suddenly unsteady.

"Who is that? Who are you?" she whispered, controlling her urge to shout it into the sky. That would be something RAVEN couldn't ignore.

Ollie was by her side in an instant. His hand on her arm steadied her, giving her something to ground herself with.

The voice had mentioned her father. He couldn't throw a shuriken if his life depended on it.

"You heard it again?" Ollie asked.

Beth nodded. "I'm either losing my mind, I've got a ghost pal, or my powers are shifting again." She began to gather up her things. "I hope you find something in the RAVEN storage."

"If I do, it'll be ready for you tonight." He began to pack up.

She needed to get out of there before that voice piped up again. She'd come back after nightfall to check the tree. RAVEN would still see her in the woods, but it would be harder to track her every movement in the dark.

Just what was going on with that phantom voice? She needed to talk to Sam.

And figure out an excuse to see Michael again.

CHAPTER 13

MICHAEL WATCHED HIS FATHER PUT IN HIS CODE, unlocking the room in their manor which held the Archives. He hoped they would find something to help them against Connor.

"You should really have more security than that," Michael said. "Anyone would be able to break that code."

Beth was rubbing off on him.

His father's smile held mischief at the edges. "True, but only a Forbes can step across the threshold."

He held out his hand for his cane. Michael gave it to him. He should be walking freely in a few weeks. The knife wound was mostly healed but his ankle would take a bit longer.

He could have died.

Michael fought against the guilt that gnawed at his resolve. If he had been here, it wouldn't have stopped his father from being injured. Alec Forbes would always put the town first in front of his own life. He believed in the Covenant.

But maybe Michael could have found a better way, a safer

way, to protect whomever RAVEN had targeted that led to his father being injured.

"You're thinking, 'How is it possible that only a member of our family can pass?'" His dad tapped his temple. "Let's just say, we know a witch who was extremely grateful to the Forbes family for rescuing her brother from a cult."

Michael couldn't tell if his father was teasing him, but he sounded serious. "A witch?"

Alec walked into the room, leaving Michael behind. "A good friend of your mother's, I might add. They were in debate club together."

The older he got, the more Michael realized he didn't know his parents quite as well as he thought.

Michael followed his father. "And what happens if someone other than a Forbes enters the Archives?"

"They wouldn't make it more than a few steps in." His father's face grew serious. "It's only happened once since you've been gone. Not a RAVEN operative, mind you. Just an overly curious town member."

Which meant there was no way Michael could bring Sam, Kate, or Beth down here, no matter how much they might beg.

The room holding the Archives was on the basement level and butted up against the ground on one side. It helped to keep the cool temperature needed to preserve the documents. Michael remembered that much from his initial training, when everyone thought he would take over this role from his father. There were still dehumidifiers in place in the main room to keep the moisture low, and the lighting was just a dim glow.

What was new were the shelves built into the walls, and on those shelves were boxes filled with books and documents.

His father noticed his gaze. "The file cabinets were cumbersome. It made more sense to build the shelves, which made it easier to find things as well." He pointed at the small labels on the shelves. Michael moved closer to take a look. All the labels in this main room were from the 1900s and later. "Lennox actually came up with the idea."

"Lennox?"

"He took over helping me with the Archives once you left."

"He barely sits still to eat." Michael didn't hide the disbelief in his voice.

"Your brother has had to take on many of your former responsibilities." His father gave him a shrewd stare. "You would be wise to be grateful your absence has not harmed the protection of the Covenant."

"Meaning if my absence had impacted your plans, you would have tried to force me to return home?" Michael already felt the heat of anger building. "I know you think you're all powerful, but even that you wouldn't be able to manage."

His father gestured to his stomach, where the healing stab wound was, and then to his injured right ankle. "I know quite well that I'm not all powerful and haven't been for some time, even with this." He lifted his fingers and moved them in the air, igniting flames between them. He closed his hands and the flames died.

Michael felt another twinge of guilt. This time, though, he couldn't banish it. Lennox, Duncan, and the rest of his family were fulfilling their duties and putting their lives on the line for the town they'd sworn to protect.

"I needed to know there was someone I could pass these duties onto," his father said, "and Lennox stepped up. He did it to spare Duncan, though he'll never admit it."

"Lennox, the white knight," Michael said under his breath and realized, with sudden clarity, he sounded just like Beth when she spoke about Sam. He rubbed his jaw. "I'm sorry, Dad, it's just difficult being home."

And painful. And sad.

His father gripped his shoulder. "I know, son. All I'm trying to say is that not everyone has the luxury of escaping their family duties to pursue their dreams. Lennox doesn't want to be here anymore than you did, but he knows this is bigger than him. We have a responsibility."

"To the Covenant, to the town," Michael repeated the dutiful refrain he'd heard often enough growing up.

"Yes. Your mother and I thought you would be the one to carry on after I'm gone. Your gifts would have been helpful in keeping the peace and in sensing when someone might be tempted to tell our secrets to RAVEN."

"I am more than my gifts." Michael realized his hands were clenched. He tried to relax them. "You and Mom saw me as something to plug a hole, something to smooth over a rough patch. What *I* wanted never mattered." He hadn't planned on having this talk with his parents until he was leaving to go back home to the States. That way, he could have escaped the fallout. But the words couldn't be held back any longer.

His father stared at him for several long moments. "Is that what you really believe to be true?" His tone was neutral.

Michael had vowed to never use his abilities on his family again, so he couldn't tell what his father was feeling.

"I do."

Michael found himself standing up straighter, bracing himself for the inevitable fight that always came whenever he went against his family.

His father's eyes softened. "I'm sorry, son. That was never our intention." He shook his head slowly and walked over to one of the chairs and eased himself gently down. "Another one of our failures."

Michael stood there for a moment. This was unheard of territory. His father had never expressed anything but steely resolve. He finally grabbed another chair and sat next to him.

"You're not dying, are you?" Michael looked at him more closely. "Is that what's causing this change?"

"You mean my admission of fault?" His father laughed quietly. "I'm not dying son, not yet, but I'm feeling age catching up with me."

"You're just barely sixty-two. That's the new forty."

Though he dealt with death being a doctor, he wasn't ready for his parents to die yet. Then again, when was anyone ready for that?

"I appreciate your pep talk, but I need to take ownership of what your mother and I did to your childhood." He took Michael's hand. His grip still felt strong. A bit of tension eased in Michael's chest. "We used you, you're right. We had a household of headstrong, gifted children, and we were under water."

"I know you were doing the best you could." His therapist had helped him see that, but it still didn't take away the hurt.

"Did you know your mother was able to access your gifts when she was pregnant with you? It's not uncommon, but it never happened with your older siblings." His father's eyes grew unfocused. "I remember the first time she stopped a fight between Lennox and Agnes. She was about two months pregnant at that point. We realized then just how special you would be."

"You forced me to use my gifts before I even knew how to handle them." Michael let go of his father's hand. "I've hurt people with my lack of control."

His father gave him a stern look. "I'll accept our role in some of that, but no one forced you to do what you did to Lennox."

Michael looked down at the floor, studying the minute cracks in the concrete. "You're right. I was wrong to react as I did, even after Lennox . . . but I believe if I'd been allowed to develop and hone my gifts the way everyone else did, things might have turned out differently."

"I'll give you that." His father tilted his head. "You were an alarm silencer. You gave us immediate peace, and we didn't show the restraint we should have. We were desperate."

Michael looked at him. "It couldn't have been that bad."

"It was." He twirled his cane in his hands. "We were able to handle the ghostly errors of Agnes and Isabelle for the most part. There was another medium in town who was able to intervene. But Owen couldn't control his ability, no matter how hard we tried. He caused a sinkhole that killed your Aunt Leona."

Michael felt the blood drain from his face. They'd never spoken of how she'd died. It had always been hush-hush. Now he knew why.

Owen had run from the family the first chance he got.

Michael understood about regrets from childhood. He needed to reach out to Owen when this necromancer hunt was all over.

"And Duncan?"

"He didn't have his first vision until you were several years old, so he helped us manage what we could."

Michael noticed his father hadn't mentioned Lennox, which meant he was probably the worst one of all. He had to ask. "What about Lennox?"

His father's face grew even more serious. "When Lennox became angry, he heated all metal nearby. We'd refused him something small, I can't even remember now what it was, but he lashed out with his powers, and your mother's necklace, earrings, and rings burned so hot they melted, taking a good portion of her skin with it." He took a ragged breath. "I can still smell the blood mixed with her charred flesh. We had to keep him locked away in the attic for a week until we could remove as much loose metal as we could from the house. And from our clothing."

Michael's mind spun, imagining how things must have been for his parents. They'd had Lennox when they were barely twenty. They'd been out of their element from the beginning.

"Why did you keep having kids after Lennox?"

His father's face softened. "Agnes and Izzy weren't planned. Don't worry, they already know that. They spoke to the ghost of the doctor who'd delivered them. And their gifts were manageable, so we thought Lennox was the exception. We felt safe to have Owen. And his gifts didn't show up until after we had Duncan."

"If only you could have seen the future." But it was probably good they didn't have that gift in the family yet, otherwise he wouldn't have been born.

His father shook his head. "I don't regret having any of you."

Michael's head spun trying to process everything he'd just learned. "I didn't realize how bad things were," Michael finally said.

"We didn't want you to know. Your brothers and sisters have blocked much of it out. The doctors said it was a coping mechanism. I don't know how much they truly remember." His father sighed. "Mind you, we went to every doctor, every specialist—gifted or not—to find some way to help our family."

Michael leaned back in his chair. "And then mom gets pregnant with me, and suddenly there is calm for the first time."

His father nodded. "Not only calm, but the chance to help your siblings truly learn to control their gifts. We had done everything we could, but we couldn't curb their emotions long enough to make any significant headway."

"Which is why you both pushed me to use my gifts as soon as I understood what they were. Because Mom wasn't able to use them anymore once I was born."

Michael didn't want to understand the fear they must have faced, the extreme guilt over not being able to help their children. If he did, then he wouldn't be able to hold onto the anger that had been his constant companion for years.

But he already felt that anger seeping away.

"We'd managed to make good progress for seven months while she was pregnant with you. Enough that we could hold things together until you could use your powers on your own."

"Then when Glenna came, everything was already in place."

His father gave him an approving smile. "You helped her manage her gifts easily and early. She didn't have to go through what the others did and for that, your mother and I will always be in your debt."

Michael tried to process what he'd just learned. It was going to take a while for him to fully wrap his head around things, but he found knowing the past had already changed the way he saw his siblings.

And helped explain some things, too.

"I still don't approve of how you used me." Michael held up his hand when his father tried to speak. "But I understand more why it happened. And you and Mom were trying to figure things out, too."

His father cleared his throat. "I love you, son." Michael heard the hint of tears in his tone.

Michael looked at the man he'd tried so hard to make proud, the man who he had despised for so many years. More wrinkles had flourished around his eyes, and the gray had won out over the brown in his hair. But he realized now that he hadn't seen what had always been there in his eyes.

Love.

Michael would have done better in his place, no doubt in his mind, but he could have easily made some of the same mistakes.

His wall inside was already missing several bricks at the top thanks to Sam, Kate, and especially Beth.

While he stared at his father, several more bricks, further down, shuddered and pulled themselves free.

He'd never forget what they did, but he was finally able to forgive them.

"I love you too, dad."

His father smiled and wiped his eyes. "Let's look for what you came for. If our town ever faced a rogue necromancer before, it'll be in the Archives."

Michael followed his father into the back room, feeling lighter than he had in years.

"ARE YOU SURE YOU WANT ME TO KEEP SHOOTING NERF darts at you?" Logan asked Kate as he reloaded the chamber of the Nerf Strongarm blaster.

"Yes," Kate replied. She'd asked him to come over to help her with the "stop time" experiments. They'd started in the B&B's gardens, but when that resulted in zilch, they moved into Caleb's forest, in case she needed to be closer to the trees to access her powers. But so far, all she'd managed to do was get pummeled by Nerf darts. They didn't hurt her physically, but her confidence was severely bruised.

No matter what she'd tried, she couldn't stop time. No way. No how.

Logan put the Nerf blaster down and walked over to her.

"Hey, this is something new, a new skill you're trying to learn." He took her Nerf blaster gently from her hands and laid it on the ground. "No one expects you to master it immediately." He pulled her into his arms.

Kate snuggled into his chest. "Beth does."

"Well, Beth's been known to be unreasonable in her expectations."

She pulled away and looked up into his face. "What if I can't do it?"

Logan smiled, bringing out a dimple. "Then we'll figure out another way to keep Sam safe."

"How are you so sure?"

He squeezed her. "Because I love you, and I believe in TOP."

She'd fought so long against falling in love with Logan. Partially because she didn't feel she deserved it. Even now, she couldn't believe she'd been given a second chance at love.

"I love you, too." She put her hands on his chest, feeling the strong beat of his heart underneath her palms. "Thank you for believing in me. Even when I'm all out of confidence."

Logan shook his head. "You have accomplished things that others would have failed at, that others would have been too scared to try. It's not hard to believe in you."

Kate laughed. "I keep feeling like the Hallmark movie

cameras are on us and a director is going to yell, 'Cut!'"

He laughed too. "You *are* their biggest fan. Well, behind Beth, though she'd never admit it."

"I do like the R-rated stuff, too. You know, for variety."

"You are one for variety, that I do know." He kissed her nose.

"You missed your mark, kind sir." She pointed to her lips.

He slid his hands to her hips and pulled her closer. "Apologies, my lady."

And then her phone chimed.

"The girls?" Logan asked.

She pulled out her phone from her pocket. "They're home from school an hour early." Kate gave him a quick kiss. "Sorry."

He touched her cheek. "Don't be. There will be plenty of other opportunities, especially once Connor is handled." He brightened. "Maybe the girls can help you stop time."

Kate texted them where they were—the forest outside the gardens. Moments later, the sound of laughter and running feet echoed through the air. Emily came flying out of the garden and into the woods at a full run with Patty hot on her heels.

"Nerf war!" Emily yelled. She grabbed the Nerf blaster by Kate's feet and immediately took aim at Logan, firing away. He grabbed his Nerf blaster and returned fire. Patty alternated between screams and laughter, occasionally shouting out warfare tips.

Kate loved watching Logan and Emily play together. He'd become a part of their lives as if he'd always been there.

Logan fell to the ground in a death scene echoing classic

William Shatner. Emily rushed over and put her foot on his stomach. "I take this territory for my own." She surveyed the forest with a look worthy of any conqueror.

"We're going to have to tell Miss Vivian," Patty declared. "She's teaching us how to be strong rulers."

They'd gone to see Vivian, Caleb's daughter, more often than what had been agreed to, but only because the girls loved being with her. Kate had come with them the first few times to make sure things felt legit and safe. Beth and Sam had taken shifts as well.

Emily helped Logan to his feet. "And I'm going to learn how to talk to badgers next."

"So you've mastered tawny owl and crow, have you?" Kate asked.

Emily nodded. "Miss Vivian says I have a natural ability for languages, though I can't speak to the forest like Pats can."

Patty slipped her arm around Emily's waist. "That's why we make a great team. I've got the plants, and you have the animals."

Kate grabbed them both into a hug. Just a few months ago, they were so different. Both still struggling to process their father's death, even though it had been almost two years. Kate knew it was because she hadn't fully moved on yet either.

But things had changed once Beth and Sam came back into their lives.

"What were you trying to do, Mom?" Emily asked. "With the Nerf blasters."

"Yeah, why are you in the forest?" Patty chimed in.

Logan crouched by Patty. "Your mom is trying to stop time."

Patty's eyes widened. "Really?"

Kate nodded. "I slowed down time at RAVEN and even had it rewind a few times, but I'm not sure how to stop it."

"I might be able to help you with that." Vivian suddenly appeared between two trees and stepped into the clearing.

Kate noticed her usual autumn-themed dress had shifted to the coming winter. Mistletoe and red berries were woven around the bodice. Cascading down from her waist was a mixture of holly and ivy. Frost clung to the holly's sharp points, sparkling in the light. Underneath, there was still the same blackness of decay her other dress had held, but it made all the other colors seem brighter.

"I'll take any help I can get," Kate said, finally pulling her attention away from Vivian's dress. "But I didn't bring any snickerdoodles with me." That had been one of the offerings she'd given Vivian the last time they needed her help.

Vivian swept aside her long black hair with a pale hand. "That won't be necessary. A blood sacrifice will do."

Kate laughed. A few weeks ago, she would have freaked out, but she'd come to realize this goddess had a sense of humor. And Caleb was right about her big heart underneath all that prickly mistletoe.

"I'm all out of Band-Aids to patch up a wound," Kate said. "Would apple tarts later this week do?"

Vivian smiled, and it was like the sun had come out from the clouds. "I can work with that."

A tawny owl landed on the tree next to Vivian, and she

turned to it. "I don't think Kate would make a worm pie for you, dear Chester, but I can ask." Her smile grew, making her tri-colored eyes glow in the shadows already creeping into the forest as the afternoon light faded.

"Ick," Patty said, her face scrunching up.

"Ooh, can you, Mom?" Emily asked.

Kate smiled at the enthusiasm in her daughter's voice. "I'll look into it," she promised.

Patty took Logan by the hand and led him over to Vivian. "This is Mr. Logan. He's a constable and really brave. We love him." She looked at Logan. "And this is Miss Vivian. She's Mr. Caleb's daughter and has been teaching Emily and me all about the forest."

Logan nodded, looking a bit gobsmacked. "I see. It's very nice to meet you, Vivian." He bowed in a perfect imitation of Robert.

To Kate's surprise, Vivian grasped Logan's shoulders and pulled him into a hug. The sharp holly must have hurt his legs, even through his jeans, but Kate didn't hear any sound of pain.

"I knew your mother, Meira," Vivian said and then released him.

Logan stumbled back but regained his footing quickly and his composure. "You did?"

Kate remembered Logan telling her of how his mother had believed in fairies and the Fae. It had been her well-worn copy of *The History of Rosebridge* that had helped Kate approach Vivian for the first time without getting everyone killed.

Vivian's smile grew wistful, and flowers sprung up around

her and Logan. Deep purple blooms swayed in the breeze. "She would visit me often as a girl, sneaking away from home to give me treats. Then later, after she married your father."

"She never told me." Logan's words were soft.

Vivian cupped his cheek. "You look like her. She was the kindest human I have ever known. And she came to me at a time when I had almost lost myself." Vivian searched his face. "Know that I tried to save her, but she refused to go against your father."

A tear ran down Logan's cheek. It hit Vivian's hand and disappeared into her skin. "I should have done something."

Vivian dropped her hand, her gaze fierce. "You were seven. There was nothing you could have done. But if I hadn't been bound to the forest, I would have." She paused, and her eyes grazed across the girls, listening in rapt attention. "Let us say I would have helped her be free of your father. Forever." She gave him a slight bow, just the dipping of her head. "I am in her debt and, thus, in yours still. You may call on me for one boon, and I will comply."

"Thank you," Logan mumbled. "I . . . thank you." He cleared his throat. "If it would be all right, I would love to come with the girls for one of their lessons sometime. And maybe you could tell me more about my mother?"

Vivian nodded. "It would be my honor."

"What's a boon?" Patty asked loudly.

"It's a gift," Emily answered. "If Mr. Logan needs help, Miss Vivian said she'll give it."

Kate rubbed her hands together. They needed to be ready to

go to the Veil once Beatrice gave the word, which meant she needed to figure this out quickly.

"All righty then. Acquaintances made, boons promised, now how can you help me with stopping time?"

Vivian stalked forward. The grass where she had stepped blackened, but then sprung back to life. "Time has a natural progression. From what my father told me, you rewound it, suffering severe . . ." She looked at the girls again. "It made you very tired."

Kate nodded, thankful for her discretion. The girls knew the basics, but not that Kate had almost died.

"Have you stopped time before?" Vivian asked.

"Nope. I had some aftereffects after being tired," Kate said. "Time played through the same events a few times until I changed the outcome, but I never stopped time itself."

Vivian's brow furrowed. "It sounds like a loop of sorts, much like the lifecycle I can move plants through. Did you see the Time Stream itself?"

Kate nodded. "I saw it before all the looping happened."

Chester hooted, and then made a sound like a cry.

"Yes, my friend," Vivian said. "I believe you are right." She looked at Kate. "It appears you took some of the Time Stream with you," Vivian said. "That's why you were able to create the loops."

"Well, I did walk into the middle of it."

Vivian looked ill. "You did what?"

"It was the only way to split the time streams for Beth and Sam. Plus, I had to shove my powers into them so they could see their own futures and save themselves." She thought a bit more about what she did at the Time Stream. "I did hold the future in my hand for a few seconds."

"Then you did stop time?" Logan asked.

Vivian shook her head, still looking a little green. "The future hasn't happened yet, so there's essentially nothing to stop. It's the same with the past. In order to stop time, you would do so in the present."

Chester hooted again, and Emily looked at Kate. "Chester said what you did was unheard of—splitting the time streams."

"I had no other choice."

"You're more powerful than I realized." Vivian had found her balance again. The gaze she gave Kate was one of intense consideration. Like she was measuring Kate's threat capacity.

Kate caught herself tugging on her sweater—much like Beatrice pulling on her apron—and dropped her hands. "I accept that I'm the Oracle, but it's not like I know what I'm doing. My gifts have always been a bit unreliable."

Vivian shook her head. "They're unreliable because you still don't fully believe you're capable." Her gazes softened. "I know of your adoptive parents and their treatment of you. Don't let that stop you from becoming everything you can be."

"How did you know about my parents?" Only a few people knew about the psychological torture her adoptive parents had put her through and Vivian and Caleb hadn't been part of that select crowd.

Vivian shrugged. "My father watched over you from afar."

Kate's mind swam, thoughts jostling against each other.

How did Caleb know? But more importantly, Vivian was right. Part of her reluctance, of her hesitation with owning her powers, was because of her adoptive parents.

Even now, years later, they were still holding her back.

It wasn't something she'd be able to let go of in an instant, but it was something she could chip away at.

"Thank you," she said to Vivian and wiped her eyes.

Vivian just smiled.

"Are you okay, Mommy?" Patty took her hand.

Kate nodded. "I'm getting there, baby." She squeezed Patty's hand, and then released it. "Can you help me stop time, Vivian?"

Vivian nodded. "I will try."

Patty shook her head. "Do or do not. There is no try."

Logan laughed. "She does love her *Star Wars* nights with Robert and Sam."

"I think Dr. Who is much better than Obi Wan. He's a Time Lord." Emily lifted her chin. She walked over to Kate and gave her the toy Tardis. "You might need this again, Mom."

"You're probably right." Kate slipped it into her pocket already filled with tissues, gum, and baggies. The Tardis had helped her to slow the stream last time. She'd take any help she could get.

Vivian looked at Kate. "Are you ready?"

Kate nodded. "Let's stop time."

CHAPTER 14

SAM HELD ROBERT'S RING UP IN FRONT OF HER AND concentrated on connecting to the energy of Entwine like Sloane had suggested.

She'd been at it for the past half hour trying to see if they could track Connor.

And . . . nothing. Again. It was just a lump of metal in her fingers.

"Maybe you need to try it?" She handed the thick, silver ring back to Robert. Even the Celtic symbols carved inside seemed flat and dead, no glow at all.

They sat together in Kate's garden on some folding chairs Robert had brought out from the shed. The afternoon sun was starting to fade.

Beatrice walked over to them. "Still clear. I've doubled the patrols." Which meant Connor couldn't spy on them, at least not through ghostly means. "And I'm working out rotations so we can also keep watch at the Forbeses' Manor."

Caleb's crows kept watch on the grounds, as well, just in

case Connor decided to make an appearance in person. They weren't taking any chances.

Robert held the ring and closed his eyes. A deep furrow carved a line in between his eyebrows. After about a minute he shook his head. "I sense the energy Sloane spoke of, but only at its surface. Maybe we need to combine our efforts?"

Sam considered his words. "I should have a connection to Connor on a necromancer level."

"And I have actually been in his presence."

"I'm willing to give anything a try at this point."

She'd only met John Anderson that one time at RAVEN, but without him, more would have died. He'd been an innocent in all this when RAVEN had captured him. And because of Connor, he had been obliterated completely.

He'd deserved so much more. The killings had to stop.

Robert held out his hand, the ring in his palm. Sam put her hand over his, cocooning the ring in between them.

"Show us where Connor is," Sam whispered. "Say it with me, Robert. Let's focus our intention. Picture him in your mind."

"Show us where Connor is," he repeated, and it became a quiet chant. A plea to Entwine. A glow began around Robert's hand. It was the ghostly essence she'd always seen in him—blue with flecks of gold. His connection to Entwine, still there. The essence she held in her body rose through her skin to meet his.

His eyes opened wide. "The last time this happened was when I was a ghost."

Sam nodded. "When we were first together. But it hasn't

happened since. I thought it was because you'd been brought back to life."

His essence joined with hers, twining together around their hands. Warmth radiated from their hands and traveled up her arm. It didn't burn, though. It was comforting. Like coming home.

Robert reached out with his free hand and cupped her cheek. "It appears there is still so much to learn about what we share, you and I."

She leaned into his touch. "You are mine." She said the words she'd said that night when they'd finally joined together.

"As you are mine."

That same popping sound they'd heard that night came again as if swallowing and recording their words.

"Let us say it again, our need," Robert whispered.

Together they repeated their earlier plea. "Show us where Connor is." The essence around them blazed bright and then pulsed like a heartbeat. Then suddenly, a single strand branched off and shot through the air. It went back toward Kate's B&B, passed it, and headed straight for Rosebridge.

"It's leading us to Connor. I feel it." Sam looked at their hands. "But if we break the connection, we'll lose him."

Beatrice gave her a sharp nod. "I'll have it tracked." She disappeared. Sam was thankful for the hundredth time that Beatrice had her Entwine connections.

"What will you do when we find him?" Robert asked. "Do you plan on telling Sloane?"

"Not yet. I want to see if we can talk to him first." Sam

shook her head. "Even if Sloane doesn't intend for lethal means to be used, she could get overruled again."

"Fair point," Robert conceded. "But once we have his location, we should alert the others."

There was no way Sam would tell Beth. She knew she'd want to kill Connor. And Kate was off trying to figure out how to stop time. Besides, Kate had no offensive powers. At least Sam had her daggers, even if they weren't talking to her.

"I wonder how long it will take Beatrice?" She wanted to get up and pace, but they couldn't break their connection.

Robert rubbed his thumb against hers. "She will do everything she can to trace the trail quickly. I feel your worry through whatever this is." He looked at the essence buzzing around their hands.

"You can?"

He nodded. "It is like I am you, yet still myself."

"I'm going to try." Anything to stop herself from wondering where Beatrice was.

Sam concentrated on Robert, on his strength, on the steady rise and fall of his chest. Her worry dissipated immediately. It was replaced by a surety, a calmness that filled her body. She suddenly felt taller in her seat.

"What are you feeling?" Robert asked.

Sam shook her head, losing her grip on the serenity she'd felt, but at least the worry had dropped in intensity.

Beatrice appeared, looking concerned. "We found him."

"Where is he?" Robert asked.

"MacCallum & Sons."

Sam's chest tightened. That was where Imogene usually was. Had he found out she'd helped them?

"Come on." Sam sprung to her feet and gave Robert back his ring.

"I will go on ahead." Robert slipped his ring into his pocket. "But worry not, I will merely observe until you arrive." He disappeared into Entwine.

Sam ran for her car. If anything had happened to Imogene, she'd never forgive herself.

BETH WALKED INTO THE BUSTLING BAKERY AND WAVED AT Ethyl, the owner. "I'll be over with your usual when I get a moment," Ethyl called out.

Beth nodded. She could already taste the chocolate croissant and the latte with a shot of hazelnut syrup. This was one of the few things she liked about small towns. She could have a "usual" that people remembered.

The tables were all filled but Michael had snagged one by the large window looking out onto the sun-drenched street. Clouds were starting to gather with glimpses of sun still managing to poke through.

He'd asked her to meet him here. He'd said there was news from the Archives which might help.

Of course, he could have given her the information over the phone. Just like she could have explained why she needed the Forbeses' help with a call, even with FaceTime.

But it seemed they were both making excuses to see each other. Could it be he'd realized what she finally had—that they were both interested in each other?

He turned to her approach, and his eyes widened.

"You're stunning." He stood and ran a hand through his blond hair.

She'd made sure to wear her favorite jeans, tall, brown suede boots, and a black tank top that gave a healthy glimpse of her goods, plus the red leather jacket Michael had liked so much. Everything was on point.

"You look pretty good yourself, Forbes."

But then again, he always looked delectable. His white shirt was unbuttoned just enough to make her want to pop the rest and listen to them hit the ground. His long legs looked even better in jeans. She wanted him to turn around so she could admire his ass, but there wasn't really a good way to work that into the conversation.

She sat, and he did the same. Beth eyed his food and beverage choices. A huge apple danish and a steaming mug of coffee. Black.

"Thanks for coming," he said.

She nodded. "You have deets from the Archives?"

"I do." He leaned in closer over the small table. "But I didn't think about the chance that Connor might have ghostly spies here." His voice was low.

"Excellent point. Sam's still back at the B&B, so she won't be able to scope anything. She was busy trying to find our friend when I left." She reached over and broke off a piece of his danish. "So, should we try to play charades where I guess the information?"

Michael smiled at her. "While charades would be entertaining, I thought we could just talk." He took a sip of his coffee. "Unless you have someplace you need to be."

RAVEN had texted her to come by, and she still needed to retrieve any potential help Ollie had left in the RAVEN forest to use against Connor.

But all that could wait.

She popped the danish into her mouth. It wasn't as good as the chocolate croissant, but close.

"I can spare some time," she said and decided to ask something that she really wanted to know the answer to. "So what happened between you and Lennox that made him hate you?"

Michael stiffened. "How about starting off with a safer subject? Like the weather."

She shrugged. "Small talk is for pussies."

He leaned back in his chair. "What happened between Lennox and I is complicated."

"Any life worth living is complicated, Michael."

"I could go for an easy, normal life sometimes." He rubbed his eyes.

"You and I aren't cut out for normal."

Beth glanced back at the busy front counter. Her order would still be a while.

She snagged another piece of danish.

"We're not, huh?"

"Nope." She picked up his mug and had a sip. "This definitely needs cream, but at least you had the good sense to douse it in sugar."

He took the mug gently from her hands and poured in cream. "Here."

"But it's your coffee."

"It's okay." He smiled at her, and she just stared at him.

The men in her life had never been caring. And none of them would have done something as small as ruin their own coffee so she could drink it.

"Has Harvey contacted you again?" he asked.

She let him change the subject. He'd made his offering. She took a long sip of the now exquisite creamed coffee.

"No. But Gloria sent me the wiring information to set up the payments. She's nothing if not efficient." She couldn't keep the bitterness from her voice.

"We've both had parents who treated us as commodities." Michael took a bite of his danish.

So he was willing to open up a bit about his family, but not about Lennox. Interesting.

"You came back here to not only check on your dad, but to make peace with them."

He flashed her a surprised look. "You're pretty intuitive."

"Well, we con artists have to be," she replied. "At least that's what you accused me of when we first met."

He looked sheepish. "And I was an ass."

Ethyl brought over her croissant and latte. "Sorry, Beth. The tourist crowd today is keeping us hopping."

"No worries," Beth said. "I had his coffee to tide me over."

"And his danish, too, I see." Ethyl looked at both of them and gave Michael a knowing smile before she walked away.

"What was that about?" he asked.

Beth took a long sip of her latte and pushed Michael's coffee back to him. "We are two amazingly hot people, and she probably sensed the energy between us."

There. She'd tossed out a line, finally. Well, she didn't exactly say she liked him, but this way, if he wasn't interested, he could play it off and she wouldn't look foolish.

Gah. What was she twelve?

He stared at her for a long moment. She felt him wrestling with something. He obviously wasn't interested and was trying to figure out how to politely disengage.

"So, about Glenna's new—"

"I've been thinking about that energy you mentioned," he interrupted her. "Whatever this is that's between us."

She leaned her arm on the table, palm face down. "Go on."

"We're both adults." His gaze swept over her, making her toes tingle.

"We most definitely are." Desire spiked through her. "What did you have in mind, Forbes?"

He mimicked her pose, his fingertips just touching hers on the table. "I could think of several things."

The chatter around them, the sounds from the front counter faded away.

"Me too," Beth said. "Though I kinda hate to give Sam and Kate the satisfaction of being right. But then again, it's not like we'd be a real couple." She slid her hand closer and he took it.

The spikes of desire turned into warm swirls of caramel sliding through her body.

"It could just be something fun," Michael said. "Besides, it can't really be anything more. I'm going back to New York after my sabbatical, and you'll be heading to Los Angeles after your episodes are filmed."

"And if we keep it a secret, then Sam and Kate can't gloat."

He lifted her hand to his lips. "Sounds delicious." He kissed her knuckles.

And then nibbled on them.

Her breath quickened.

She wanted those lips in other places—right now.

She pulled her hand free and wrapped up her croissant in a napkin to stick it in her purse for later.

"Perfect. Let's go."

"What, *now?*" He looked shocked and aroused at the same time.

"You were the one nibbling on my hand and giving me those eyes."

He didn't argue any further, just followed her quickly out of the bakery.

"Where are we going?" he asked, stopping to the side of the front door.

"Your place." She couldn't bring him back to the B&B, they both knew that.

He shook his head. "My family is there."

"One of the cottages?"

"Duncan's having friends over at his place, and the other

two are in different stages of renovation."

She glanced over at the small alleyway just a few feet away in between the stores. "We could have a little fun in there. Not full on sex but a least a make-out sesh."

"But people might see us." He started to fidget.

She laughed. "I didn't take you as the shy type."

He frowned at her. "I know some of these people. They're not strangers."

"And I'm on television. No one's going to bat an eye if they see us kissing each other."

He looked so horrified that she wanted to laugh again. But she knew how to persuade him because it was something that would work on her: a challenge.

Beth crossed her arms. "I understand now. You're not that great of a kisser."

"Excuse me?"

"I get it." She shook her head slowly. "Gorgeous and lacking at the same time."

He leaned in close, his breath hot on her face. "I'll show you kissing."

Michael pulled her into the alleyway.

One of his hands wrapped around her waist, sliding her closer. The other moved up her neck to her cheek with a light touch until he cupped her jaw. The heated look he gave her almost buckled her knees.

Then his lips met hers. Nothing tender. Nothing gentle. Just urgent. Her mouth opened under his. He tasted like apple danish. He pulled her deeper into the shadow of the alley. She wrapped her arms around his waist, pulling him to her until there wasn't any space between them.

His hand moved from her face to her chest, fingers dipping into her tank top and finally into her bra. She pulled back from the kiss to moan.

His lips brushed against her ear, sending shivers down her spine. "I can't wait to taste you." He ran his tongue along the top of her ear and she almost came on the spot. "All of you."

The sound of a screeching car broke through her lusty haze. They both turned toward the sound as Sam's car came to a stop in front of the bakery. She got out of the car and ran past them at full speed.

Neither of them said anything. Beth fixed her top and took chase, Michael following behind.

Something was happening, and it wasn't good.

Beth prayed it wasn't another dead body.

CHAPTER 15

"I HAVE AN EFFECT ON THE PLANTS AROUND ME," VIVIAN told Kate. She crouched and lifted a finger toward a drooping flower. It perked up, regaining its old bloom. Then she spun her finger, and the flower lost its glow, withering again.

Another lift of her finger, and the flower bloomed once more and stayed there.

"Are you moving the timeline of the flower?" Kate asked.

"Excellent question. Yes," Vivian replied. "Not time itself around the flower, but time within the flower, keeping to its natural progression."

"Okay, so how do you do what you do?" Kate stepped closer.

Vivian stood and strands of her hair, shot through with leaves, lifted in the breeze. "I don't see the Time Stream. That's your gift. But I sense it within the flower. My intent, plus my movement, guides the progression."

"And how you feel, too," Patty added. "When you're upset, plants die."

"But she always brings them back to life," Emily insisted.

"I'm not saying she doesn't," Patty shot back.

Emily frowned. "You said plants die. Miss Vivian isn't a murderer."

Vivian held up her hands, and the girls quieted instantly. "I don't actually kill plants, I merely wither them when I'm upset. And if they are dead already, I can't bring them back to life. That's beyond my realm of power."

The girls hung on her every word. Kate needed to get things back on track before this became a teachable moment for her daughters on how to wither plants. "I use my hands, too, a bit," she said, "like you did with the flower. And my intent. And my heart, too, now that you mention it. So, there aren't any real instructions?"

"Did you need instructions to have visions?" Vivian asked.

"No."

"And did you have instructions to access the Time Stream the first time? And to know how to do what you did to help Sam and Beth?"

Kate crossed her arms. "Well, no, but it would have been nice to have. And if you don't have any instructions, then are you just here as my forest pep squad?"

Vivian raised an eyebrow, and the nearest tree bloomed fresh leaves along one branch.

"Not exactly just your pep squad, as you call it." Vivian ducked her head, but not before Kate saw her grin. "I can provide more than just encouragement. If you'll let me, I can help guide you once you connect with the Time Stream."

"Oh." Kate uncrossed her arms. "That would be great,

actually, though I'm a bit nervous about trying to find the Time Stream again."

"Don't be." Vivian lifted a hand toward the sky. "You are part of Time itself. You were not chosen by chance."

"Mom's a Time Lord." Emily fist pumped the air. "I knew it!"

Vivian laughed softly. "She's even better than that." She fixed Kate with a strong gaze. "Because if she listens closely enough, she'll be able to talk to Time itself. In fact, I think you have already done so with a few of its messengers, haven't you?"

As if summoned by Vivian's words, the memory of the death vision filled Kate's mind—when she'd talked to it and welcomed it to reveal itself. Was that a messenger of Time? Were all her visions brought by messengers?

Vivian studied her. "How did you get to the stream last time?"

Kate sighed. "Blood, as usual." She held out her hand. "Logan, do you have your knife?" She really needed to get one of her own at the rate they were going.

Logan joined them and handed over his pocketknife. "I made sure to clean it just in case." Kate was both horrified that he'd thought they'd be spilling blood tonight and appreciative of his Boy Scout nature. She cut the tip of her finger and squeezed some blood onto her hand over the golden leaf brand Caleb had given her when she'd become an Anchor of Entwine.

It absorbed the blood and blazed bright gold.

Vivian was by her side. Kate hadn't seen her move. She took Kate's cut finger and squeezed out some more blood, catching it on the tip of her own finger.

"You'll need this for our connection," Vivian said. She took the blood and smeared it on the flower brand she'd given Kate and the girls on her left hand, which connected them to Vivian's domain.

"How will we know—"

The rest of Kate's words were cut off. Even though she was in the same forest, Logan and her girls had disappeared.

Vivian's grip on her arm steadied her. "They're fine and safe. Chester is keeping watch along with my father while we're away. And technically, our bodies are still there."

Kate touched her pocket, feeling the toy Tardis' hard shape through the fabric. "I think this is what happened last time. I just didn't realize it was astral projecting."

Vivian nodded. "Eventually, you'll be able to call Time to you in the physical realm. But for now, you're still testing your abilities."

"How do I summon the Time Stream here?"

Vivian dropped her grip on Kate's arm and pointed to the right. "You already did."

Kate looked over. The Time Stream glimmered just past the trees. They walked over to the stream. It was just as beautiful as the first time she saw it. The flowing waters glowed, holding the past, present, and future within.

"I've never seen Time before," Vivian said, words hushed, wonder lighting her face. "Not outside of the living things in the forest."

Kate took a few steps closer. She saw people within the water, lives playing out in front of her. She saw more clearly this time, or maybe she was just prepared for it.

The present dropped off to the left, like an escalator, as it fell into the past. Though the past disappeared into the shadows, she realized she could easily grab it if needed, for it was still part of the stream. To her right, the future flowed forward, stretching from the present.

"What do you see when you gaze upon it?" Vivian asked.

"The same thing you see."

"I don't think so."

"Why? What do you see?" Kate asked.

"A beautiful stream humming with life." Vivian stretched out a hand toward it. "I know there is more. More that is beyond my grasp."

"So I *am* a Time Lord, and you were just keeping it a secret from the girls?" Kate waggled her eyebrows at Vivian.

Vivian laughed. "I'm not quite sure what you are. There hasn't been a Triumverate of Pluthar made up of your particular talents—yours, Sam's, and Beth's. And no oracle I've ever known has had the strong connection to Time that you do." She looked thoughtful. "Though my father predicted it."

"He's a sneaky bast . . . one," Kate amended quickly.

"He is."

"You know I'm going to grill him about how he kept tabs on me as a kid."

Vivian nodded. "I would expect no less. And I'll enjoy witnessing such grilling."

Kate could almost forget Vivian was a forest goddess, one

who could kill so easily. Right now, she felt like a friend sharing a joke about her dad.

They stood in silence for a few moments, staring at the stream. Vivian didn't pressure Kate to get a move on, like Beth would've done. Or tried to give her the "You can do it" speech that Sam would have.

It was really . . . nice.

Kate squared her shoulders. "As the first step, I need to slow down the stream, which I've done before." She pulled the Tardis from her pocket. "With this." She held it to her lips and whispered, "Slow the stream for this present moment, in the forest, for me, Emily, Patty, Logan, and Vivian. Well, I don't know if Vivian counts. She's a goddess, so a time whammy probably won't affect her."

In front of her, the stream's rushing slowed to a more languid flow.

Vivian inhaled sharply. "I feel it. There's a change."

Kate walked closer to the stream. She knew it was larger than what she was seeing—larger than what her human mind could comprehend. She couldn't build a dam to stop time. Even if she could, the pressure of time backing up would be dangerous.

Oh God, could she break time?

No one taught her how to be an oracle.

She was probably screwing it all up.

Vivian placed her hand on Kate's shoulder, her scurrying mind instantly quieted. "Focus your thoughts. Ground yourself."

Vivian was right. Grounding herself was what gave her

clarity last time. She took a deep breath and imagined herself as a tree with roots tunneling through the dirt until they reached the earth's core. Warm energy bubbled up through her.

She stretched out her arms, feeling her leaves rustle in the wind.

She was the forest, and it would support her, give her stability and calm.

"To stop Time is to hold it," Vivian said. "How would Kate Banberry hold Time?"

To Kate, Time was a fluid, like water. It would slip through her fingers.

"I need a container."

"*You* can be the container."

Kate's head immediately started shaking. "I wouldn't even know where to begin."

Vivian exhaled slowly. Kate didn't miss the disappointment on her face. "What kind of container would you need?"

"A jar, a bucket, a bottle," Kate rattled off. "Something with a lid to hold it safe." Then her brain clicked. "Wait a second. I've got just the thing."

She rustled around in her pocket and grabbed a zippered baggie that had a few crackers still in it. Kate dumped out the crackers and ate them quickly. Then she tried to get the rest of the crumbs out of the bag.

Vivian frowned. "Are you serious?"

"Baggies have come to my rescue more times than I can count."

Vivian just rubbed her temple like she had a headache.

Kate stared at the Stream. "Hey, Time and your messengers. I could use a little help here."

A chill touched her ankles. Much like what she felt at the beginning of a vision. Words floated up into her mind, and she spoke them aloud. "Bring forth those I seek."

She stretched her hand toward the Stream. It shifted and made space, bringing forth Patty, Logan, and Emily's faces from the depths. Their images rippled along the surface. The stream's flow remained sluggish.

More words came to her.

"Capture this moment in time and hold it."

Kate fisted her right hand, just like she'd done when she held the future at RAVEN.

A glowing ball of Time lifted free from the Stream, holding Patty, Logan, and Emily inside. Kate put the baggie underneath it, and then moved the plastic up to capture it.

Zippity-doo-dah, and the baggie was sealed.

"I did it!" Kate exclaimed. "Thanks, Time and company."

Vivian looked embarrassed but also a bit impressed. "Let's see if you truly did it. We must return." She held out her hand to Kate.

Once they touched, they were suddenly back again, in the forest, with Patty, Logan, and Emily. They were all frozen. The girls were in midair, clearly jumping with some sort of cheer. Logan watched them carefully as if to catch them if they fell.

Kate held up the plastic bag filled with glowing Time. "I bet this is the first ever Time Baggie."

Vivian chuckled and then caught herself. "I am sure you are

right. You chose a solution specific to you, one that resonated, and Time provided you with the words."

Kate eyed the baggie. "Can I let this go now?"

Vivian nodded. "Yes. I wouldn't suggest holding onto a piece of Time for too long. Futures that might have been could be lost as time rushes to catch up to what was missed. Lives irreparably changed forever." She raised her eyebrows. "Because of your 'Time Baggie.'"

Kate almost dropped the baggie, but held onto it for dear life. "How long is too long?" Her voice squeaked.

"You'll know. The pressure will begin to build within you. Painfully so."

"I better get it back to the stream, then."

She reached into her pocket to fish out Logan's pocketknife again for the requisite spilling of blood but froze when the Time Stream appeared at her feet.

Vivian crossed her arms. "See. Once you start believing in your abilities, you won't need props or blood."

Kate frowned at her. She hated the I-told-you-sos.

She opened up the baggie and dumped the contents back into the Stream.

With a loud snap, everything whirred back to life around them.

Emily and Patty jumping and shouting a cheer, which sounded like, "Go, Mom, go! Make Time slow," as Logan watched them and clapped in time.

Just what could she do if she let herself truly believe?

Sam reached MacCallum & Sons and rushed inside, finding it packed with tourists—several of whom turned and looked at her quizzically.

She didn't want to cause a panic. Who knew how many Connor could kill?

She tried to calm her pounding heartbeat and look casual. She spied Robert in the corner by the figurines of frogs and hurried over.

He gripped her shoulders and leaned in as if he were about to kiss her.

"The item we seek does not appear to be in the shop. However, I am unable to see through that door while within Entwine," he whispered, moving his eyes to her left.

She looked and found a door to the side of one of the glass showcases marked "Storeroom."

Sam kissed him lightly on the lips to complete the charade, and then pulled back.

She reached out with her senses and found three ghosts in the store who hadn't materialized. When she turned her gifts to the Storeroom door, she couldn't pick up anything.

She imagined this is what Superman must have felt when faced with a lead-lined door.

They needed to keep things cryptic in case those ghosts were spying for Connor.

At least the ghosts couldn't harm her, so they didn't present a threat other than warning Connor she was on his trail.

"Any sign of our *old* friend?" she asked.

He shook his head. "No. I was saddened I did not receive my usual welcome when I arrived."

No Imogene then.

Please don't let him be killing Imogene behind that door, she sent up as a silent prayer to the Universe.

Either Connor was in the Storeroom, or he wanted them to think so. Whatever the case, she had to get in there, but she needed a distraction.

The Storeroom was near one of the cases. She couldn't just saunter past everyone and hope it wasn't locked. This could be her chance to catch Connor and talk to him. Stop him.

Robert's glance moved past her to the front door. Surprise lit in his eyes.

"Hey, you two," Beth said.

Sam spun around. Beth and Michael stood there, looking flushed.

"What are you doing here?" Sam asked.

Beth scanned the store. "Chasing you. We saw you pull up. We were at the bakery."

"Having a danish and coffee," Michael supplied.

Beth was more dressed up than Sam had seen her, and Michael looked like he was missing a button on his shirt. Something was definitely off with those two, but now was not the time to find out what.

Sam moved closer and lowered her voice. "The new item we were chatting about earlier might be here." She tilted her head slightly toward the Storeroom door. "And I'm feeling there could be some spiritual guidance to be found nearby."

Understanding dawned in Beth's eyes. "So, what's your play?"

"I think you should tell the tourists here about your upcoming episodes," Sam said. "Build some excitement."

Beth gave her a wink. "Come on, Forbes. Let's go be captivating."

They walked to the main counter, and Michael exclaimed, "Aren't you Beth Marshall?"

Sam heard someone squeal. Phones were lifted in the air taking pictures. The tourists and clerks moved away from the case by the Storeroom. Beth's megawatt smile locked in place. She began to regale everyone about the new episodes she had planned.

"Be careful," Robert whispered to Sam.

Sam walked to the door. Now that she was closer, she saw a thin red line of essence running along the doorframe. Unease spread through her, raising goosebumps along her skin. It was that same feeling she'd had when the red essence had blazed along her iPhone.

But she was an expert on not taking on ghosts' emotions. She quickly constructed a barrier within her mind, and the dread diminished to a bare whisper.

She reached for the handle, and the essence moved suddenly, like a snake, and struck her hand.

The pain was sharp, but she swallowed her cry. The essence left a blackened bruise in its wake. Her hand throbbed, aching.

The blackness began to spread under her skin, reaching out for her fingers.

Sloane had said ghostly essence could heal. Sam willed her own essence into her hand. It bubbled up through her skin like a wash of cool water, tumbling against the darkness. The blue essence flared brightly and burned away the black, and then extinguished, taking her pain with it.

Sam lifted her hand closer. No trace of any injury.

She looked quickly around, but no one was paying attention to her except for Robert, who gave her an approving nod.

Sam concentrated and coated her hand in her ghostly essence. She reached for the door handle again. The red essence struck, but it couldn't penetrate the shield she'd built.

The door opened easily.

Sam looked inside. It was tidy and well-ordered. Metal shelves lined the walls to her left and right. In the back stood a large table with boxes on it. A chemical smell lingered in the air, like disinfectant. She closed the door behind her.

She tried to sense any ghosts in the room, but her radar was still off, like it was being jammed.

"Imogene, are you here?" Sam whispered.

Nothing.

"Connor?" Sam tried.

Again nothing.

She took out her daggers and walked further into the room.

Hey, daggers, I might be going up against another necromancer. I could use your help.

Her attempt to spark the daggers into a conversation was

an epic fail. They remained cool in her hands. No sign of life.

She made it to the back of the Storeroom without anything jumping out at her and found another door behind the shelves to the right. No red essence.

Sam opened it.

And found Imogene.

The ghost was bound with glowing ropes of some kind. And gagged. Boxes and pieces of broken furniture were stacked up against the walls. Imogene tried to speak, but Sam couldn't understand her.

"Is Connor here?" Sam asked.

Imogene shook her head.

Sam let out the breath she'd been holding.

"Beatrice, can you hear me? Robert?" One of them might be able to free Imogene of her bonds since Sam couldn't touch her.

No response. It appeared the red essence kept other ghosts out.

There was another way, but it was risky.

"I'm going to get you out of here," Sam said. "But you'll need to hold very, very still." Even if her daggers weren't speaking to her, they could still do what they'd been forged to do—absorb ghostly essence.

Imogene's eyes widened. She shook her head frantically.

"Stop, Imogene," Sam pleaded. "It's going to be okay. My dagger will only cut through your bonds."

The ghost wasn't listening. She backed into the farthest corner of the small room.

It sounded like she was pleading with Sam not to kill her

from what she could make out of the panicked garbles coming from behind her gag.

If Imogene couldn't calm herself, Sam *would* likely kill her. She needed Imogene to listen to her, to really hear her. There was one voice that might break through the ghost's fear.

Sam summoned the voice she used for Bargains. It immediately came, rising through her throat in a warm rush.

"Stop. Be still."

Imogene immediately froze.

Kate had always described it as if Sam wasn't speaking alone. That there were other voices within her that came through. Sam always wondered if that was the Universe or something else.

She walked over to Imogene. Fear shone bright in the ghost's eyes, but Imogene didn't move a muscle.

"Calm yourself."

Imogene let out a long breath, and her gaze was suddenly steady. Sam slid her dagger up under the bonds around Imogene's hands. Where the dagger touched the ghostly bonds, they disintegrated, the energy disappearing through the dagger's surface.

Imogene shook off the tatters around her wrists and pulled the gag free from her mouth. "Thank you." Her words were soft. Not the usual biting tone Sam was used to.

Sam let her own voice return. "What happened?"

Imogene ran her hands over her hair, putting any loose strands back in place. "He captured me before I could flee into Entwine. That perverted essence of his is deadly." She shivered.

"He said he was going to punish me for helping." She met Sam's gaze. "He wants Entwine weakened, and he knows Caleb can't bring the trees back on his own."

"He said that?"

Imogene nodded. "I think he didn't care what he said because I wouldn't be here to tell anyone." Her gaze grew in intensity. "But then he was warned you were tracking him."

Of course, there had been a chance Connor would find out, but it still pissed Sam off. She understood why the ghosts might be helping—they feared him—but it wasn't going to make their job of stopping him any easier.

"Don't take this the wrong way, Imogene, but I'm surprised he didn't destroy you anyway." Sam shook her head slowly. "Even if I had arrived in time, it's not like I could take him on power-to-power. I saw what just a sliver of his essence can do." She rubbed her right hand where the bruise had been.

Imogene pulled on her black jacket, straightening the pearl buttons. "He said I was a good faith offering, though it's not like we're close, Necromancer. You owe me a Bargain, that's it."

It was true. Sam didn't have any great affection for Imogene. It wasn't like she was Beatrice or Ray or any of Graham's victims. But she knew what he was trying to prove to her.

"He's trying to show me he doesn't have to be a killer."

Imogene huffed. "One pardon does not make a saint."

"Very true." Sam walked back into the main storeroom and the door leading into the store. She turned back to Imogene. "Can you warn the other ghosts, the ones not working with Connor, to stay within Entwine? I don't want them to get hurt."

Imogene graced her with a thin smile. "You are very different from other necromancers that I've met."

"How so?" Sam asked.

"You actually care."

Imogene disappeared. Hopefully to Entwine, where she'd be safe. But her words repeated in Sam's mind.

She couldn't let Connor continue. If he could capture Imogene, he could do that to any ghost.

Sam looked over the door back to the showroom. The red essence around the edges was gone. She opened it up a crack and peeked outside. The coast was still clear.

She joined Robert.

"Is he gone?" Robert asked.

Sam nodded. "We need to find a way to protect Beatrice and the others from Connor."

Robert's face lost its color. "Did he hurt Imogene?"

"No, but he could have. Eventually, the good will he's trying to foster between him and I is going to wear thin, and no ghost will be safe."

CHAPTER 16

LUCKILY, SUNSET WAS EARLY THESE DAYS—ONE OF THE reasons late fall was Beth's favorite season.

She had no doubt the RAVEN cameras were watching her as she approached the forest, but she had a good reason for being there. Helping Logan to find the killer was her cover story, and they might have missed some valuable clues.

No one would know she was really there to pick up whatever Ollie might have left her from RAVEN storage. She hoped it was something that could make the difference in the fight against Connor.

She made it to the old oak tree where she'd found the footprints of her Scottish Spiderman. There. To the left, in the shadow of the tree, the ground was disturbed. She crouched and used her knife to quickly dig up the dirt.

Whatever it was that Ollie had left her, it was small and wrapped in plastic, along with a piece of paper inside. She took a step into the forest and behind one of the trees. Unless RAVEN had cameras hooked up to the trees themselves, she should be safe from their view.

She cut open the plastic wrap with her knife. It looked like a crystal of some sort. Dark, too, but she couldn't see the color in the shadows. Shaped like a Christmas tree, it was about the size of a lipstick case with bits of crystal forming what looked like branches.

Beth took it out of its wrapping and felt a warm rush spread from her fingers into her hand. Whatever this was, it was powerful.

She looked at the note. It was typed. Ollie was being extra careful, just in case someone else found this. She didn't blame him. She was just able to make out the words in the dim lighting:

> *This Moldavite piece was retrieved a little over*
> *a hundred years ago from a necromancer. Only*
> *reference mentions the disruption of energy.*

She wrapped the crystal tree back up along with the note, slipping both into her pocket. It might or might not help, but the bigger question was how she was going to get it to Sammy without revealing it came from RAVEN?

It was peaceful to just stand there in the forest. Everything quiet, just the occasional rustling of branches in the light wind.

Being back made her thoughts turn to John Anderson. If she had known he was there, she would have tried to save him.

She needed to let the cameras catch her again, so RAVEN didn't become too suspicious. She slid her knife back into its sheath and walked along the tree line, slowly. In the distance, she saw the lights of Rosebridge. They were all getting together for dinner tonight at the B&B to—hopefully—celebrate Kate being able to stop time.

In Los Angeles, Beth's dinners were prepared by her personal chef. Her usual companion was her laptop or phone. Ever since coming to Scotland, she'd had more meals with human beings than she'd had in years in L.A. Kate's face filled her mind, laughing yet somehow always knowing when to be serious. Sam was next. The sadness in her green eyes was gone, banished by Robert. When Sam held her head a certain way, she looked just like her mom.

Beth hugged her arms to herself. She missed Mrs. Hamilton so much. She'd promised to help Beth to escape her parents, legally. But before she could make good on that promise, the car crash had taken her life—and the last of Beth's hope with it.

Tears filled her eyes, blurring the lights of Rosebridge. She really should stop blaming Sam for surviving that crash, but it was hard to let go of the things that brought comfort over the years, even if it was cold comfort.

She placed her hand against one of the tree trunks. "Got any life advice for me, Mr. Tree . . . or Ms. Tree?" Her words were low. "Or maybe Gender-Neutral Tree?"

A sharp crack of a twig pulled her out of her reverie. She saw a shape in the shadows, in between a cluster of trees.

It wasn't the necromancer. There was no instant fear flowing through the forest.

"You stepped on that twig on purpose." It wasn't a question.

Whomever it was had snuck up on her without a sound. They were good.

"I did." The voice matched her Scottish Spiderman. "I didn't want to frighten you like last time."

Beth laughed. "I wasn't frightened by you. It was the necromancer who almost made me piss my pants."

A laugh floated out from the darkness. It was warm. "You've got your mother's spunk."

"You must not know my mother well." Beth frowned. "I'd call her a lot of things, but spunky isn't one of them."

She didn't like that this stranger felt familiar. Did he know her parents? Was he maybe one of their cronies? Now that her father had showed up, anything was possible.

"Why don't you come out into the light, so I can see you?" she asked.

"You know why I can't."

So he didn't want to be seen by RAVEN. That didn't narrow anything down. There were a lot of people who wouldn't want to be on their radar.

"Well, I'm not going to sit here talking to a shadow all night. When you're ready to let me see you, ping me. I'm sure you know my number since you seem to know so much about me."

She turned and started to walk back toward the lighted gate. Kate would call her foolish for giving him her back, but he'd had multiple opportunities to attack her and hadn't done so . . . yet. Plus, he didn't frighten her. She'd been honest when she'd told him that.

There was a rustling and she sensed him moving closer. "If

you come into the clearing, then we can talk. We'll be away from RAVEN's prying eyes."

Beth stopped. "'Come into my parlor,' said the spider to the fly," she said softly. "Ah, no. I know you're not the serial killer, but you could still be a nasty piece of work—especially if you know my parents."

She started to walk away again.

"Wait. What if I could tell you about your mother?"

Beth shook her head. "I know all I want to know about that witch and you can tell her I said that."

"I'm not a spy for them."

"Which is what a spy would say."

"They're not really your parents."

Beth's stride froze. She glanced back over her shoulder. "What are you trying to sell now?"

There was a long sigh from the shadows. "You were adopted. Neither Harvey nor Gloria are your birth parents.

A chill crept through her. What was he talking about? This was too elaborate a con for her father to play. And he'd already gotten her agreement on the blackmail. And none of their cohorts would go this route, undermining her parents.

"Prove it." Beth turned around.

"I will if you come into the clearing."

Beth looked back at the lights of Rosebridge. She needed to know if what he said was true. And if not, what was his angle? Michael's words floated into her mind. He'd accused her of being stupid by rushing into the woods alone. And he was right.

Even though it was temporary, she had a team now. One

that stood up to Harvey without hesitation. And a member of the team whose kiss she still couldn't get out of her mind.

She took out her phone and texted Sam, Kate, and Michael.

At RAVEN woods.

No Connor.

If I'm not home in two hours, come find me.

Beth slid her phone into her pocket. She thought about taking out her gun, but given how fast this guy moved, she'd most likely hit a tree. And Caleb would never forgive her if that happened.

Hell, she wouldn't forgive herself now that she knew they felt things. Knife it was. The handle felt warm in her hand.

Legs steady, adrenaline banked for use, she stepped into the shadows.

CHAPTER 17

BETH WALKED THROUGH THE TREES, FOLLOWING THE SOUND of the stranger's footsteps. They reached a clearing in under two minutes. The moonlight was strong there, but clouds had begun to gather overhead. She still had the ability to escape, if needed. They were close enough to the RAVEN fence and their cameras.

Her stranger turned around, and Beth finally got a chance to see what he looked like. She placed him at around six feet without his boots. Slim, but muscled, like a bicyclist. Dark hair to the nape of his neck. Dark eyes, most likely brown, and decent cheekbones, though he had a long scar running over his left one.

The age was hard. He looked in his forties, but she had a feeling he was older. Not by the way he moved, but by the look in his eyes.

She kept a good distance between them. There was no telling what weapons he might have.

"Okay, I'm here." She kept a good grip on her knife but let

her other arm hang loose. "What's this drivel about me being adopted?"

He gestured to a fallen log. "Do you mind if I sit? I've been searching the woods all day for signs of the killer."

"Sure, take a load off."

He went to the far end of the log and sat down. Behind the it would make a good place to conceal a weapon. Beth walked around to the other side of the log and scoped things out. It looked clear.

She sat on the other end and sheathed her knife. She took out a shuriken instead and held it in her right hand, ready to throw.

The man smiled, his teeth white in the moonlight. "I'm not going to hurt you, Beth."

"Talk."

His smile died quickly. "I met your mother when she was barely twenty."

"My supposed bio mother, right?"

He nodded. "I'll give you proof when we're done talking."

"First, what's your name?"

"You won't find my records online. I've done what I can to keep off the grid." He lowered his voice. "My name is Evan Frasier."

She'd indulge his story for a bit, see if he tripped himself up.

"Go on, Evan. Tell me how you met my mother."

She couldn't deny there had always been a part of her that had hoped Harvey and Gloria weren't her parents. That maybe, just maybe, she wasn't inherently fucked up in her genes.

Evan leaned forward, elbows on his knees. "When I first saw your mother, she was a prisoner of RAVEN."

"What the fuck?" Beth lifted her hand up.

He nodded. "Oliver didn't tell you because he didn't know. His father kept her in a separate wing of the complex. It's not on any schematics, but you'll find it past the O wing. It's where they kept all the prisoners who were valued."

There was no way Beth could get anywhere inside RAVEN without someone seeing. This info didn't help one little bit, even if it were true.

"What did you do for RAVEN?"

Evan looked uneasy. "I was a guard, but not of the facility. They called me in when they had subjects who needed special handling."

"Did you hurt her?" Pain jabbed her hand and she realized she'd gripped her shuriken too hard. Blood dripped from her palm, but she didn't let go of her weapon.

He shook his head. "By the time I met her, the experiments had been halted. They'd kidnapped her to try to harness her abilities, but they couldn't. She was a Seeker, like you are."

"Go on."

"She fought them initially, but finally gave in to protect her sole remaining relative. A brother." Evan stared at her. "The man who adopted you."

Beth's mind spun. "Wait, Harvey's my uncle?"

"He is."

"Go back, rewind. How did *I* come into this?"

"I helped your mother escape, and together, we ran."

There was something in his voice, in the way the edges of his face softened.

"You were in love with her, weren't you?"

"I was. I still am." He cleared his throat. "We couldn't leave Scotland because they would have found us. so we hid in the forest. Then a few days later, a ghost visited us. But I realized afterwards it was a god."

She knew it had to have been Caleb. He'd never let on he knew her mother. But then again, information was power. He wouldn't willingly share it.

Evan continued, "He offered to hide us in his lands. I don't know how he did it, but he did. We built a cabin there." His gaze softened. "And we had you."

Did he just say he was her father?

Beth shook her head. She wanted to believe this—having a kick-ass father would be epic—but she had absolutely no proof except his word.

He's telling the truth.

That woman's voice again. The same one she'd heard before.

Beth stood. "Okay, voice from beyond, just who the hell are you?"

Evan looked at her with alarm in his eyes.

She waved her hand at him. "Don't sweat it. We deal with ghosts all the time."

"You have a ghost talking to you?"

"I think it's a ghost. I don't have Sam's abilities, but for some reason I can hear this one."

"When did this first start happening?" Evan asked.

"The night I met you." Beth looked around as if she'd somehow see the ghost. "She told me to run."

Evan laughed. Beth heard the edge of tears in the sound. "Of course. It's got to be Melody. It's your mother."

Tell your father he looks tired. He needs to get more sleep.

"I am not telling anyone anything," Beth said, "until I have some proof. For all I know, this is some twisted game." She hated the look of disappointment on Evan's face. "I want to believe. I do." She shook her head slowly. "I *really* do. But I've seen too many cons to trust this outright."

She sat back down and slid her shuriken away. Regardless of whether or not he was telling the truth, she wasn't afraid of him, not really.

He frowned. "I didn't realize about the abuse until it was too late. By the time I was able to reach you again, you had just gotten out of Port Ewen Correctional."

"You tried to find me?" She realized she really wanted to know the answer to this—more than she should. He was a stranger after all. And potentially a liar.

"After I brought you to your aunt and uncle for adoption, I came back here because I didn't want to lead RAVEN to your new home. They found me when I returned to Scotland." Evan's hands fisted, but he released them quickly. "RAVEN planned to kill me after I wouldn't give up your location."

"Did they torture you?"

Evan nodded. "For a few years. Then they forced me into service again as a punishment. I was finally able to escape years later, and Caleb hid me once again."

"How did my mom die? Did RAVEN kill her?"

"No." Evan moved a bit closer to Beth. She found she didn't want to move away. "Your mom died of an aneurysm in her brain." Evan's voice was gruff. "It was sudden, and she wasn't in any pain. You were just two years old."

"What did you name me?" Beth asked.

Diana.

"Diana."

Both the voice and Evan said the name at the same time.

You were our miracle.

Beth still had doubts. If it wasn't her bio mom, then it was someone who was scheming with Evan to deceive her. But to what end? What could they want?

"Elizabeth was your middle name," Evan said. "After my mother, though she was always called Beth. It was part of the agreement that Harvey would keep Beth in your name." He looked sheepish. "Sorry you got saddled with Tiffany."

His hand slipped into his jacket. Beth stiffened for an instant out of habit. But he didn't pull out any weapon, just several pictures. He held them out to her.

Beth stared at them for a moment. "What are those?"

"Take them."

She didn't move for a long moment.

Don't be afraid.

"I'm not afraid," Beth said sharply to the phantom voice. She stood and walked closer to Evan. She reached out her hand. The four pictures trembled in her fingers.

She laid the faded pictures out on the fallen log. They still could've been photoshopped fakes. But as soon as she saw the woman's face, she knew. Somewhere deep inside there was a spark of recognition.

"Mom," she whispered, touching her finger to the picture.

She had Beth's eyes and the shape of her face. Even her smile was Beth's, when she allowed herself to smile. She also had light brown hair and a sprinkling of freckles across her nose. Those Beth didn't get.

Beth looked at Evan. The hair and cheekbones had come from him.

The next picture was her mom and Beth, hugging, all smiles and joy.

The tears came quick and sudden. Beth didn't even realize she was crying until a drop hit the pictures. She quickly wiped it away.

Then came a picture of her and Evan. He was lifting her over his head, and she had her arms outstretched like she was flying. The happiness was undeniable on both their faces.

She'd been loved.

Through blurry vision, she looked at the last picture.

It was Evan, Beth, and her mom. They held Beth, one arm each around her, but it was the look they shared between them that pulled at something deep within her.

The love there was unmistakable. That love she'd been searching for. A love that said, "I don't care what happens, you're my ride or die."

There was no mistaking that it was Evan in the pictures.

She'd ask for a DNA sample to prove he was her father, but

there was no doubt he'd loved her and her mother.

Beth handed the photos back to him but he shook his head.

"Keep them. I have copies."

She slid them into her jacket pocket. She wanted to look at them again—to keep looking at them—but she needed answers.

"Why did you give me up?" she finally asked.

Evan wiped his cheek with the back of his hand. His eyes were red. Seemed she might have gotten the don't-show-emotions-easily gene from him, too.

"RAVEN hadn't given up on finding your mom and I. I figured they would never suspect I'd give you to her family. That would be too obvious. And your mom loved her brother deeply. We had talked about what to do if anything would happen to one of us."

"But you could have kept me. Stayed in Caleb's forest."

Her life could have been so different.

"The forest wasn't safe any longer." Evan looked grim. "There had been an attack on Entwine . . . well, on the Threshold."

"The Threshold?"

"It's the entrance to Entwine, a gateway of sorts. Protecting it had weakened Caleb severely, which meant he didn't have the reserves to shield us any longer."

"And you didn't have family you could have given me to?"

"None that I would be able to leave you with without it being obvious I had done so." He looked as frustrated as she felt. "Your aunt and uncle had been trying to have children. When I gave them to you, it was with the promise that they would move immediately, so that your adoption would be concealed. A new town, new faces. No one would know that you weren't theirs."

Intellectually, what they did made sense. Especially if her father had been faced with trying to raise her alone and keep RAVEN off their scent.

"You gave me to monsters." She didn't bother to keep the bite out of her words. Even if he hadn't intended to, Evan had made her life a living hell. And it wasn't her mother's fault, even if she had wanted her to go to her brother. She'd died and had no say in the matter.

But he had.

"I'm sorry, Beth, I truly am. I messed up. There is no excuse for what happened to you." He shook his head. "What Harvey put you through, it's all my fault."

"It *is* your fault." She just stared at him for a few moments. He didn't squirm. He seemed ready to take whatever she threw at him as punishment. "But the real villain here is Harvey. No one made him hurt me. He made those choices all on his own."

"I'm still sorry, Beth. And if you let me, I'll spend the rest of my life making it up to you." He held out his hand to her.

She didn't take it. "Pictures or not, I still don't trust you."

"I would expect nothing less from my daughter."

"But I do know how you could start making it up to me."

He raised an eyebrow. "Name it."

Beth took out the plastic-wrapped Moldavite tree Ollie had given her. "If everything checks out with the DNA test and my friends ask you, you were the one who gave this to me."

Evan quickly nodded his head. "What is it?" he asked.

Beth looked down at the crystal, immediately warm again in her hand, even through the plastic. "I'm hoping it helps us in some way against Connor. I better fill you in on the necromancer we're facing."

A flicker of surprise raced across his face, but it was gone in an instant. "I'll do everything I can to help."

Beth felt tears threatening again while she looked at this man who might be her father. A father eager to help, not hurt.

She sent up a quick prayer to the Universe that everything he said was true. The Universe owed her big time. And this would be a great time to pay up.

CHAPTER 18

BETH HAD BARELY OPENED THE DOOR WHEN SHE HEARD Kate's voice call out, "That better be you, Beth, because I just took the chicken out of the oven, and it'll be too dry if I let it sit to go and save your butt."

The kids must've been in the kitchen. Otherwise Kate would have said "ass."

"It's me. I'm here." She hung her jacket and scarf on the hooks by the door.

This is what it felt like to be missed. If she wasn't careful, she was going to get all teary-eyed and shit again.

Beth felt a little nervous. She knew they'd be doubtful about her potential adoption, as they should be. As she should be. But those pictures had weakened some of her immediate protests.

Or maybe it was just because finding out she was adopted would be an answer to a long ago wish. A wish of a young girl before the hope had been beaten out of her.

The DNA proof would decide it all. She patted the samples in her pocket that Evan had given her.

Beth walked into the kitchen, inhaling the delicious scents of baked chicken, pilaf, and potatoes au gratin, if she wasn't mistaken. Sam, Robert, and Michael were helping Emily with a puzzle at one table. They waved at her. Michael gave her a warm look that sent atomic butterflies racing through her stomach. Logan and Patty were coloring a picture of what looked like a Disney Princess. Neither of them looked up because they were arguing over which purple would be the best for the sash.

Fi walked forward and handed Beth a glass of red wine. "Michael had me come," Fi said. "He wanted to tell me about Connor, so I could get the word out in town. Warn people."

Fi still had her nose ring in. Her white blonde hair with purple tips at the end now brushed just past her shoulders. Thankfully she wasn't showing her bra tonight. She was a good kid, but definitely needed some fashion tips.

Beth clinked her glass with Fi's and took a healthy sip. "Have you been practicing the throwing techniques I taught you?"

Fi nodded. "I'm still having a bit of trouble with the aim. I almost hit Tavis in the privates." She laughed behind her hand.

Beth remembered him from the pub. He'd definitely been head over heels for Fi. And obviously still was. "You know you're supposed to practice with non-living targets, right?"

"Yeah, I was just having some fun." The mischievous gleam was obvious even under the rivers of black eyeliner. She reminded Beth of herself at that age. Early twenties and testing her limits.

"Where are my table setters?" Kate asked.

Emily and Patty leapt from their seats and Logan followed

them. He handed them plates from the cabinet, and they carried them out to the tables. Beth helped put away the crayons and papers. They'd be a little cramped tonight, but they'd manage. It was probably best to wait until the kids were in bed before she spilled about Evan, and what Ollie had given her.

The dinner was pleasant. Fun even, especially when they played a few rounds of twenty questions with the girls. The prizes were the bite-sized brownies Kate had made. Beth helped Kate clean up the plates while Robert took the girls upstairs for story time. They were already cracking huge yawns, so it wouldn't take much. Their adventures in the forest with Miss Vivian and Kate had apparently worn them out. Plus, the Nerf fight, which Emily had proudly announced she'd won.

Kate put on a pot of coffee and a kettle for tea. "I hope everyone has room for my berry cobbler."

Michael patted his stomach. "I'm not sure how I can fit it, but your berry cobbler will be worth it."

"How do you stay so slim, eating here like you do?" Fi asked.

Beth had wondered the same thing. She'd had to up her workouts in order to keep the extra pounds in check. She supposed she could say "no" to Kate's cooking, but life was short. She was going to enjoy the hell out of that berry cobbler.

"There's a YMCA in the next town over," Michael replied. "I swim before work."

"Would your contact who helped us before with DNA be willing to do it again?" Beth asked Michael.

"Sure. What do you need?"

"I'll grab it. Hold on." She went out to the hallway to collect the samples from her jacket. She left the Moldavite tree in her jacket for now. She'd show it to Sam the next time they were alone. She didn't want to get everyone's hopes up, just in case it was a dud.

She handed Michael a large baggie with two smaller plastic baggies inside. One was a cheek swab safe within its plastic casing. The other was a strand of hair.

Michael looked surprised. "Who are these from?"

"Potentially my biological parents."

She waited for her words to sink in.

"So, not from Harvey and Gloria, I take it?" Michael asked.

Beth shook her head. "I met my potential Bio Dad tonight, Evan Frasier. According to him, Harvey is my uncle by blood."

Sam cocked her head. "And this Evan Frasier just magically appeared here in Scotland to do what? Reunite with you again?"

"And why now after all these years?" Kate narrowed her gaze on Beth. Beth appreciated the skepticism in their voices. It did sound far-fetched.

Logan shot her a sharp look and took out his notebook. "I'll run a background check on him. See what I can find." He scribbled something down.

"He said he's stayed off the grid to avoid RAVEN, so I'm not sure what you'll find."

Robert walked into the kitchen. "The girls are fast asleep. I barely made it through the first page, and their eyes were already closed." He studied the room. "I fear I have missed something vital."

"Yup." She bounced on the balls of her feet. She hoped

with everything she had that what Evan told her was true. "Sit down, and I'll tell you all what happened."

Robert's raised eyebrows were the only indication of surprise. He did as she asked.

Kate gave her a wistful smile. "I haven't seen you this excited since I lent you my cap gun when we were nine."

Kate and Fi handled the coffee, tea, and cobbler, while Beth told them about seeing Evan for the first time the night John had died. And then again tonight when he had shown up at the forest by RAVEN. She told everyone she had gone back to look for any clues they might have missed.

They seemed to have bought why she had gone back, but Sam had that I-smell-something-funny look on her face. She probably knew Beth was lying, but didn't call her out on it.

"He also told me that there's an entrance to Entwine in Caleb's forest." Beth hoped this might dull their detective senses, giving them the full truth and all that.

Michael nodded. "The Threshold. It's in our Archives. It's one of the few access points to Entwine, and it has suffered regular attacks for years."

Kate held up her hand. "Threshold-shmeshold. I'm still pissed you ran into the forest after a potential serial killer the first time. And then you did it again not even knowing who this guy was."

"Hey, I texted you," Beth said.

Kate frowned. "So we could find your dead body? How thoughtful."

"I'm trying, okay?" Beth protested. "I'm not used to this,

having people who care." Oh crap. She hadn't meant to say that last part. Now the mush would begin.

Kate's face immediately softened. "It's because I love you so much that I worry. We care about you, *all of us*."

"We do," Sam said. "Even when you make it so difficult."

But she found herself staring at Michael, wanting to know his response. He smiled. "We all care about you, Beth. Even when you steal someone's apple danish."

She laughed. The tightness in her chest dissipated. "It's your fault for having such a large danish."

Fi looked between them and grinned. "Is that an old-time term for having a big—"

"Thanks for your help with the DNA results, Michael," Beth interrupted her.

"Even if this Evan has hidden his digital footprint," Logan said, "his family might not have. We know his mom's name was Elizabeth, so that could help." His smiled just slightly. "Let's find out what we can. I wouldn't want you to be duped."

She couldn't disagree with his plan, and it was nice that he was worried for her—that they all were.

Sam leaned back in her chair. "I'm still trying to wrap my head around it. RAVEN experimented on your mom while your dad was her guard. They fell in love, escaped, and had you." She raised an eyebrow. "If we give Evan the benefit of the doubt."

"And your name was Diana," Kate said. "Like Wonder Woman."

Michael laughed. "After seeing you in action, I think it fits."

"Evan and your mother were very brave," Robert said, "if this all is found to be true."

Beth nodded. "I'm almost afraid to believe it, because if it is, then it means there's . . ." What it might mean felt too big, too much.

Kate grabbed her hand. "It's okay. Whatever you need to say, we're here for you."

Beth looked around the table. They'd all moved further past her defenses than she'd realized. She cared what they thought. Which meant they could hurt her once they abandoned her, like everyone eventually did. But she needed to get this out. Damn the consequences.

"It means there's a chance I didn't come from garbage. That *I'm* not garbage." Her words echoed the fierce hope she felt in her heart.

Sam grabbed both Beth and Kate's hands. The current that hummed between them was immediate. Though it still felt like chains to Beth, they were thinner, less heavy. "You're going to be okay no matter the results." Sam squeezed their hands.

Michael touched her shoulder lightly. "If everything does check out, I'll be really glad you finally found out the truth. Did he tell you why he approached you now?"

Because she was working for RAVEN. "He said he'd been keeping tabs on me since I came back to Scotland, trying to figure out how to approach me. But when the new murders started to happen, he wanted to reach out."

"Does he know Harvey is here in Scotland?" Robert asked.

Beth shook her head. "No idea."

Fi held her mug in both hands and took a long sip. "If he is your dad, spend as much time as you can with him. The last words I ever spoke to my Da were in anger."

"We don't know Ken is dead, Fi." Michael's words didn't seem to comfort her, but Beth wasn't surprised. The odds were very good that RAVEN had killed him after he gave up Duncan and the rest of their town.

But who knows? She hadn't seen him, but she didn't have access to all of the facility.

Beth leaned back in her chair. "All right, now that we know Connor doesn't want us saving the trees, we definitely have to save them. So, what's the next step? Sammy and Kate do the dance of the seven veils?"

Kate shot her a look. "Hardy har har. But yes, we need to go behind the Veil and grab Morag." She looked at Logan. "Caleb said we're good to go on the trip to see Karnon tomorrow morning. He received his portal approval."

Logan nodded. "I'll take a sick day. We don't have any leads I can officially follow up on regarding the murders, and I can't exactly tell my team we're looking for a necromancer."

Kate leaned over and gave him a sound smack on the lips. "You're the best, do you know that?"

"Well, I do now." Logan grabbed her, pulling Kate onto his lap.

"Get a room," Fi and Beth said at the same time and then laughed.

Beth felt lighter than she had in years. In ever.

Knowing that her parents might not be her bio parents

didn't erase what they'd done, but it also meant she might not have to be bound by it.

If she hadn't been born bad, then maybe she had a chance to shine up her blackened soul.

THE FOREST WAS QUIET THIS MORNING. KATE HEARD JUST A few bird calls and the creaking of the woods in the wind. And their footsteps.

At least Kate and Logan's footsteps. Caleb made no noise whatsoever. But then again, he *was* the forest.

"Where's the portal to Karnon's lands that you mentioned?" Kate asked.

"Not far from here," Caleb replied.

Logan helped Kate over a fallen tree in their path. "Do you trust him?" he asked Caleb.

Caleb frowned. "When it comes to his word, yes. He will not go back on an agreement or a bargain. But he always has his own agenda. At least Morag is a ghost, though she still has the power to influence him. Their love has lasted centuries, even through death."

"She sounds pretty incredible," Kate said.

"She is." Caleb grunted. He seemed like he was going to say more, but didn't.

They finally stopped at the edge of Caleb's forest. There was an old tree, cracked down the middle, but still holding together somehow. Its branches were gray and twisted. No leaves, no sign of life any longer. There was a touch of smoke in the air.

Kate inhaled deeply. It was definitely smoke. "Did someone burn the tree?"

Caleb shook his head. "The trees in my forest have been spelled not to burn by fire."

"But it seems dead." Kate reached out with her senses, just a bare brush toward the tree. The energy from that light touch hit her so hard, she stumbled back into Logan's arms.

Not only was the tree definitely not dead, there was an incredible power all the way down to its roots. They stretched under the ground, gripping the earth with a hold so strong, Kate was sure it could withstand a hurricane.

The ground underneath Kate's feet pulsed once, then twice, then three times, until it took on a regular rhythm, like a heartbeat. Logan looked at her with surprise, and she knew he felt it, too.

Caleb placed a hand on her shoulder. "Reavis just likes to appear dead. It dissuades the usual passerby. But he is a guardian, holding portals into various lands."

Kate moved out of Logan's grip, sure on her feet once more. She bowed toward the tree. "Thank you in advance for your help, oh great guardian of the portals."

A deep, rumbling laugh filled the woods. The smoke smell dissipated, replaced with a fruity pleasant aroma. She couldn't place the odor, but it made her smile.

You've chosen your newest anchor well, Caleb. The voice came from the tree.

Caleb smiled. "And she's the Oracle to boot. I couldn't go

wrong, Reavis." More laughter rumbled from the tree, and Reavis' branches shook.

"Pleased to meet you, Reavis," Kate said. "Thank you again for helping us. We're trying to save the trees in Caleb's forest and the ones connected underground."

Reavis' branches stilled. *We heard their screams. The entire forest did.*

Kate's stomach rolled when she thought of the poor trees and what they'd witnessed. Connor had harmed so many already.

"How do we use the portal?" she asked.

Caleb gave her an approving look. "It'll take power and blood. I'll give you some of my power, and you'll share some of your blood. This way neither of us will be completely drained."

Logan already had his pocketknife out. "You should just keep this for now," he said to Kate. "At the rate you're going."

She kissed his cheek. "Thanks, babe." She looked at Caleb. "Do we have to do it in unison or anything?"

Caleb nodded. "When I touch the branch, cut your hand and drip the blood into the ground. Though Reavis knows what we seek, I have to say the exact words to activate the portal."

Kate poised the knife over her palm. "Ready."

He turned to the tree. "We seek the way to the Horned God, to Cernunnos, to Karnon, the Protector of the Forest and the Bringer of Life." Caleb's words rang out clearly in the misty morning air.

Reavis shuddered, shifting his limbs. One branch moved until it stopped directly in front of Caleb. The message was clear. Caleb gave Kate a nod, and she cut her palm. He wrapped his fingers around the limb. She fisted her hand, dripping blood onto the ground.

She needed to remember to pack more Band-Aids, too. And some antibiotic. They really just needed a ritual care kit. Probably one for everyone.

Green leaves sprouted along the tree limb, and fresh grass grew where each drop of Kate's blood had hit.

Payment has been made.

A glow began in the center of the tree, yellow, as if the sun had been captured within it. And heat came through it as if whatever was on the other side was warmer than here. It reminded Kate of Vivian's tree, but this felt more powerful.

Caleb looked at both of them. "I'll go through first but follow quickly behind me or be stranded on this side until my return."

Kate grabbed a tissue from her pocket and pressed it to her wound. She looked at Logan. "Ready?" He nodded.

Caleb walked toward the glow and disappeared. Logan and Kate walked through next.

Kate expected to dissolve and end up on the other side, like the transporter in *Star Trek*, but everything moved in slow motion to her eyes. She was alone, and a vast expanse of darkness stretched out, lit only by what she assumed were other portals in the distance. Glowing orbs in the blackness. She tried to lift her hand, but it felt stuck in molasses, barely able to move.

A soft melody reached her ears, like someone humming.

"Kate!"

Logan's yell snapped her attention away from the music, and

suddenly she hurtled forward, landing in front of a wolf.

A wolf the size of a pony.

CHAPTER 19

Beth sat in the Rosebridge Library waiting for Sam to pick up the books she'd reserved, trying not to yawn. She hadn't slept well last night after learning about Evan. Michael said he'd rush the DNA tests through his contact, but it would still be another day or so before they got the results.

Kate had already been gone this morning, off to visit Caleb's cousin about the trees. And, of course, Beth had just had to see Harvey skulking around outside Scottish Glamour. While she'd hoped he'd left town, she'd expected he hadn't. But why would he be interested in Yasmin's shop? It didn't make sense. She wasn't rich, and Beth hadn't been in the store for anything since he'd arrived.

Her mind kept tumbling over the question of her bio mom's choice. Why hadn't her mom realized her brother was as cruel as he was? That it was a mistake to have him take her in?

But Harvey was a top-notch conman. Her mom could have easily been fooled, especially when love was involved.

Sam walked over to their table and dropped three large

books onto the surface with a loud *thunk*. Luckily the library was pretty deserted that morning. Otherwise, Beth imagined there would be a lot of shushing coming their way.

Beth picked up the books and looked at the covers: *The Energy From Beyond*, *Connections to the Afterlife*, and *Tapping Into the Essence of the Universe*.

"You think these will help?" Beth asked.

Sam slid into the chair across from her, cheeks altogether too pink and rosy. At least her blonde hair was back in a ponytail, so Beth didn't have to endure the walking shampoo commercial vibe.

"These three talk about ghostly energy, the essence I pick up." Sam lowered her voice at the end. "If we can get some ideas as to what Connor can use the energy for, we might be able to guess his next move. I've researched everything I can online, and nothing."

Beth flipped open one of the books. "At least you and lover boy were able to do that scrying spell to find Connor. That's something."

"It hasn't worked again since. It's like he's hiding his essence." Sam frowned. "And it's not a spell. I'm not a witch."

Beth's lips twitched.

Sam hit her arm. "Okay, only when you're around. You bring out the worst in me."

"I bring out the fire in you." Beth looked up at her. "Your life was boring without me, admit it." Sam didn't say anything, but Beth saw the smile she tried to hide.

Sam grabbed a book from the pile. "Speaking of lover boys,

when are you and Michael going to finally go out on a date?"

"Oh, please." Beth worked hard to school her face. Sam didn't know that her attempt to catch Connor had interrupted some sexy sexy time with Michael.

Sam raised an eyebrow. "Don't give me that look. The sexual tension is so thick between you two."

"I bring that out in guys." Beth gave her a wink. Sam wasn't buying it by the look on her face. "Even if I wanted to, what's the point? We're on different coasts and have different lives."

She was not going to be the one to get Sam and Kate's hopes up about her and Michael. They'd agreed to keep it a secret for this very reason. Well and to prevent their gloating, too. That was probably the biggest reason.

Sam flipped to the next chapter. "Have it your way." Then she looked up from the page at Beth. "I just hate seeing you lonely. I was lonely for too long. I know how awful it can be."

Lonely? She wasn't lonely. Not really.

Don't lie to yourself, Beth.

There it was. That woman's voice again.

Beth looked around the library. "Do you sense any ghosts here?"

Sam closed her eyes for a moment. "No, just the energy that you always have around you."

"You mean what you and Robert mentioned at RAVEN— those shapes near me? My aura?"

Maybe she had a ghost attached to her? Or multiple ghosts? But then why wouldn't Sam sense them?

Sam nodded. "Yup, that's it. It's like a buzzing against my

senses. Robert saw it more clearly. We can always ask him to have a look again." Her gaze narrowed. "Why are you asking this now? Is something going on?"

Beth looked past Sam at the dusty shelves. "I've heard a voice a few times now. A woman's voice. She sounds familiar. She makes comments like she knows Evan, and she just chimed in again on my internal dialogue no less."

"What did she say?"

Beth shrugged. "It doesn't matter. You don't think it could be Melody, do you?" Her words held too much hope, but she couldn't take them back. "Whoever it is, she definitely knows Evan."

Sam reached out and touched her arm lightly. "It might be. Maybe she's connected with you more closely than a usual ghost because of your gifts."

"Even if it is her, why am I hearing her now? How?"

Sam looked thoughtful. "I don't know. Maybe we're all still changing. I felt things shift when I brought Robert back to life and again when we saved Kate. Maybe we can pull on each other's abilities, just a little."

It made sense. And it made Beth feel a little less creeped out by it. She didn't mention the other voices to Sam. She'd only heard them in the forest and who knows how many people had died there.

"Thanks, Sammy. That helped."

Sam smiled. "Good." She looked back at her book.

"And I hope I can return the favor." Beth took the plastic-wrapped Moldavite tree from her pocket and put it on the table in between them. She'd been nervous about showing it to Sam because of the questions that would come up. She didn't know how much longer she could keep lying about RAVEN.

She'd almost left the crystal tree at home, but Sam needed to see this, just in case it was something they could use against Connor.

Sam stared at the plastic, and then her eyes widened. "I'm feeling waves of energy or something off that. What is it?"

"Be careful touching it. The shards that remind me of branches are sharp." Beth unwrapped the plastic and set the crystal tree on top of it. "I did some research on it last night. It's made of Moldavite, which is said to have come from a meteor over fifteen million years ago. Then there was something about the frequency it gives off, which it seems like you're sensing. And there's something called a Moldavite Flush. I felt it when I held it in my hands."

Sam reached out to take it. She lifted the crystal up and then hissed, moving it to her other hand. "You're right. I barely touched it and I cut myself."

The blood from Sam's finger shivered on one of the shards of crystal, and then the Moldavite absorbed it. The crystal glowed for a moment and then returned to its normal green.

Sam put it back down on the plastic and grabbed a tissue to put against the wound on her finger. "When it glowed, it felt like my whole body vibrated for a second."

Beth tilted her head. "I didn't feel anything. Evan said it had something to do with disrupting energy. Maybe it's affecting the ghostly essence inside you?"

"How did he get this?" Sam asked, and Beth felt her shoulders ease a bit. Sam had accepted it had come from Evan.

"He got it from the RAVEN storage room. He still has friends on the inside, and he heard this came from a necromancer in the past."

All true. It shouldn't ruffle Sam's radar. But there was no reason for her to worry. Sam's entire focus was on the crystal.

"Did Evan tell you anything else?"

Beth shook her head. "Nope. Just that."

Sam looked up from the crystal and met her gaze. "Thank him for me. I don't know what it does yet, but it's definitely powerful." She smiled softly. "I really hope he's your dad, Beth."

The warm look in Sam's eyes made Beth's throat tighten a bit. "I'm going to miss this a little," Beth said. "Talking without biting each other's heads off. Sharing stuff." The last words were said almost under her breath.

"Me too."

"Even after all the crap I've slung at you?" She didn't try to hide the surprise in her voice.

Sam nodded. "I don't know if we can rebuild what we had, but I miss these moments. It reminds me of when we were kids." Sam paused, seeming to struggle with what she wanted to say, but instead of speaking, she reached across the table and took Beth's hand.

Beth looked down at their hands. For a moment, they became their hands from when they were just girls—Sam's so pristine and Beth's usually bruised. Sam would hold her after Harvey had beaten her, while she cried. Sam had been her strength. Thinking of her had helped Beth get through some of the worst of the pain. But she didn't want to be hurt again, not by her best friend who she realized she still loved.

Beth pulled her hand away. "We can't fix the past. And soon I'll be out of your glorious, annoying hair."

"Is that what you want?"

She couldn't tell Sam exactly what she wanted—to have her friends back, to have a normal life, and to put Harvey and Gloria behind bars again.

Maybe even fall in love.

Beth shoved her hands into her jacket pockets. "It doesn't matter what I want. I don't get happy endings."

"That's not true."

Beth's phone buzzed. It was Michael, giving her a way out, an escape from the dangerous path of memory lane.

"I've got to go." Beth got to her feet. "Michael has a lead from the Archives on something that might help with Connor."

Sam gave her a knowing look. Beth turned her back on her before she could call her out, to put words to what she'd seen in Sam's eyes.

Sam knew she was running.

Running from the future she dreamed of and didn't deserve.

Running from the best friend who still had the power to gut her.

Running from the memories which reminded her of what she'd lost.

She feared she'd never run fast enough.

THE WOLF HAD AMUSEMENT IN ITS EYES. KATE WAS SURE she looked a sight, sprawled on the warm grass.

She sat back and took a deep breath in. The grass smelled sweet. Here and there, bees buzzed around flowers at the edges of the clearing. The sunlight baked into her back.

If they weren't on a mission to see a god, she would have settled back for a nap.

"And this is the Oracle." Caleb laughed without as much of the dry cackle he usually had. "Kate, this is Fornwith. He advises my cousin, Karnon."

Kate smiled. "Very pleased to meet you, Fornwith."

Logan held out his hand to her, and she let him lift her to her feet. She looked around at the trees. Mixed in with the green were leaves of gold. And not just the gold of autumn, but *gold* gold. She let go of Logan's hand and walked over to one of the gold leaves.

"Don't touch it," Caleb warned. "My cousin will know."

Kate frowned. "I wasn't going to steal it, just see if it was real or not."

"It's real, I can assure you," Fornwith said. The wolf gave Caleb a disapproving look. "One of these days, you need to visit without wanting something in return."

"How do you know I want something this time?" Caleb failed at sounding innocent.

Fornwith sniffed. "You never come here without an agenda."

Caleb didn't say anything. Kate knew he was probably remembering he said the very same thing about Karnon.

A resigned look flashed across the wolf's face. "He's waiting for you by the hot springs." Fornwith turned and padded away. Caleb followed him. Kate and Logan rushed to keep up.

"Do you have hot springs stashed somewhere in your forest?" Kate whispered to Caleb.

Caleb shook his head. "Karnon is older than I am, and he uses his magics for different things."

"Can we *get* a hot spring?" Kate asked, already thinking of how that would boost business for her struggling B&B.

Caleb frowned at her.

"Karnon is not an anchor of Entwine," Logan said to Caleb. "So he's not in constant protect-mode like you are. That's where most of your magic goes, isn't it?"

Fornwith looked back over his shoulder. "Logan is wise. Is he your advisor, Caleb?"

"He is not." Caleb gave Logan a considered look. "But perhaps he should be."

Logan stood up straighter, looking like a kid who had just received a gold star.

"Karnon can freely use his powers in many ways, most not benefitting anyone but himself." Caleb had a distasteful look on his face.

"You know he can hear you," the wolf said. "Like you *are* the forest in your realm, Karnon is the same here."

Caleb waved his hand at the wolf. "I didn't say anything I wouldn't have said to his face." Kate heard the mixture of love and wariness in Caleb's voice. He clearly cared for his cousin, but he was worried.

Logan scanned the forest as they walked, no doubt memorizing every detail, including their way back if they had to make a run for it.

Kate looked around, too, noting the depth of shadows in between the trees—darkness where even the bright sunlight couldn't penetrate.

Everything was beautiful, but her senses told her there was something more—perhaps something sinister.

"Are we safe here?" she asked Caleb in a whisper.

"Yes," Caleb replied. "My cousin cannot harm me or my companions, just as I am unable to harm him if he finds himself in my lands."

Kate felt the moisture in the air before they even came upon the springs. Beautiful, large, white rocks circled two pools of water, which bubbled and churned. Plumes of steam rose into the air. In the center of one pool, Kate saw something, like the tip of a branch, sticking up.

It moved.

She grabbed Logan's arm.

The branch rose out of the water. It wasn't a branch at all, but the most beautiful antlers she'd ever seen. They were a gorgeous dark bronze shot through with veins of gold. The very tips were blackened, though. They looked dead, if that were possible.

Then Karnon's head broke the surface of the water. Long blond hair fell past his shoulders in wet ropes. The strands reminded her of the color of his antlers, dark and light woven together. Karnon stepped free from the springs. He was absolutely beautiful.

And absolutely naked.

Fornwith nudged Kate's thigh. "He enjoys having an audience."

Kate nodded, not looking at the wolf. "He deserves one."

"You can stop staring, Kate." Logan's tone was dry.

"You know Beth and Sam will demand details. I'm doing my TOP duty."

A hand moved in front of her gaze. It was Logan's. She turned to look at him. "Sorry. It's just that you don't see a naked god every day."

Logan raised an eyebrow. "Just remember that when I gawk at a naked goddess."

Kate didn't like that idea. Not one bit. "You've made your point."

Logan smiled and kissed her temple. "Good."

Karnon dried off and slipped on some clothes, acting like he wasn't on display. The tunic had no sleeves, showing off his muscular arms. And the pants were tight. Verrrrry tight. Nothing left to the imagination. Hell, she didn't need imagination. She'd seen his goods.

Kate turned and looked at the trees.

"Is there something which makes you uncomfortable, Oracle?" Karnon's voice was buttery and rich. It tickled her skin. He sounded truly curious.

She turned back to him and found he was within arm's-length. She controlled her urge to back up. The eyes gazing at her were gold with a rim of bronze around the edges.

This close, Kate saw lines around the god's mouth, and deeper ones etched around his eyes when he smiled. Caleb had mentioned something about the cycles and Karnon getting closer to rebirth.

Being honest and being herself had worked well with Vivian. Might as well keep it up.

Kate gave him a small bow just in case. No need to piss off a god. "I love this man." She took Logan's hand. "And staring at you, no matter how delicious a sight, just didn't feel right."

Logan squeezed her hand, and Fornwith exchanged a considered look with Karnon.

"It is rare to hear the truth spill forth from a human's lips," Karnon said. "Caleb made a smart choice indeed choosing you as an anchor of Entwine." He frowned slightly. "One of very few wise decisions my cousin has made."

"Keep your opinions to yourself," Caleb said. "We're here on important business."

Karnon sighed. "Ah, yes. What is it you want this time, cousin?" He glanced at Kate and Logan. "Never just a friendly visit, a chance to sit and exchange the old stories."

Caleb harrumphed. "You always were overly dramatic, K."

Karnon winked at Kate, charm on high voltage. She almost swayed on her feet. "Always taking from me, cousin, never giving." He placed his palm against his chest.

"Fine. Anything to stop your antics." Caleb's tone could have sliced Kate's palm again. "I'll visit more."

"Without needing anything but my company?" Karnon asked.

"Agreed." Caleb pursed his lips.

Karnon laughed, and the sound rumbled through the forest, breezing through the leaves on the trees. "We will haggle over the number of visits later, but for now, let us discuss your quest. Follow me." He turned and led the way deeper into the forest with Fornwith at his side. They followed.

"He doesn't seem so scary," Kate said to Caleb quietly.

Caleb gave her a look she couldn't read. "He can be charming when he wants to be, but my cousin has a fickle temperament. Make no mistake, he can be dangerous if the mood takes him."

Logan nodded, face serious. "Noted."

Caleb exhaled. "But it doesn't mean he isn't family to me. Having Vivian in my life again made me realize how lonely I've been."

"I get it," Kate said. "In the end, we're not going to regret not working more, or getting degrees, or winning the race. We'll regret not spending more time with the people we love."

Caleb stopped and took her hand, startling her. Initially his skin felt uneven and scratchy, like bark, but once she clasped her fingers around his, it had smoothed out into something close to skin. "You and your girls brought my daughter back to me." Caleb squeezed her hand, and then let it go. "I will never be able to thank you enough for that."

Kate smiled up at him. "You're part of *our* family now, too. And family sticks together."

"Do not tarry," Karnon called out. They followed his voice

and found him in a large clearing. "I look forward to hearing what boon you will grant me, and I hope, for your sake, that it is deserving of this time I have granted you."

There was a sharp edge to his words. Not enough for full alarm, but after what Caleb had just told them, she hoped this worked.

Caleb met Kate's gaze. She nodded.

Showtime.

CHAPTER 20

KARNON GESTURED FOR THEM TO SIT ON THE BENCHES that Kate swore hadn't been there a moment before. "If you are hungry, please feast at my table."

The god lifted his hand, and a table appeared, laden with fruits, what looked like a roasted chicken, steaming soup, and mugs filled to the brim with a caramel-colored liquid.

Logan shook his head. "It's not wise to eat from a god's table. It can trap you here."

Caleb smiled. "Very true, Logan, for many gods. But Karnon is bound, as I am, by explicit bargains." He looked up at the brilliant blue sky. "The Universe doesn't allow us subterfuge when it comes to agreements with humans. It must be spelled out."

Kate filed that little nugget of info away. But that still didn't mean they couldn't mislead. From what she'd seen of Caleb and Vivian, gods might be gods, but they had human emotions. And weaknesses.

She knew in her kitchen to reject the offer of food was an

insult to the cook. While Karnon didn't make this feast, he offered it just the same.

Kate walked over to the table and picked up a cluster of green grapes. "These look delicious." They were perfect. Taut, firm skin and a beautiful fragrance that spoke of days in the sun while they ripened.

She felt Karnon's gaze on her—waiting, assessing.

Kate popped a grape into her mouth. The flavor was sweet, but tempered by the tartness of the skin. She chewed, swallowed, and turned back to Karnon.

"Thank you for your hospitality," Kate said. "Unfortunately, we don't have time to waste, so I'll let Caleb tell you what's been going on in his lands with the trees. It's bad."

Karnon sat up straight. "Your trees were harmed, cousin?"

Caleb nodded. "Several have gone silent."

Darkness gathered in Karnon's eyes. "Who is responsible for this crime?"

"A rogue necromancer," Caleb said. "He's killed humans and devoured their ghosts while the trees watched."

"Trees cannot run," Fornwith said, shaking his head slowly, "so they retreat into the land when faced with the horror of murder."

"But my brother killed someone in Caleb's woods," Logan said. "Why didn't that cause the trees there to suffer?"

Caleb lifted his chin. "It was one death in my forest, and your kin didn't destroy Ellie's ghost, just her living form."

"I never thought of trees witnessing horrible things," Kate said. "Until I moved here, and my daughter opened my eyes."

"Many humans still don't consider the effect they have on the land with their actions," Karnon said, his words biting. Dark flames began to lick along the length of his antlers. "Or the taint of their evil upon all living creatures in their realm."

Kate couldn't refute his words. Humans had done a number on the planet, and they still were. But there were others who were trying to protect it, too.

"Can you help them?" she asked. "Our trees?"

Karnon looked grim. "How many are suffering?"

"Ten in my forest, and another seven nearby," Caleb said.

The flames absorbed back into Karnon's antlers. "You are lucky it is so few, but the damage can spread." He looked at Caleb, then at Kate, and then at Logan. "The stain and horror can flood a tree's roots, bonding with its energy. Rot will follow. And spread. Even to trees who did not witness the acts."

His words leached the sun's warmth from Kate's skin. She couldn't bear to lose even one tree. And Patty might not recover if they lost them all. She'd already been through too much loss.

"Can you reverse the damage?" she asked.

Karnon nodded. "However, you have caught me toward the end of my journey when my energy is at its lowest until Re-birth. I cannot do this alone." He looked at Caleb. "And if I agree, know that I will need to immediately retreat to my lands afterwards to recover. I cannot help you with your necromancer problem. That will not be part of any agreement we broker."

Caleb nodded. "Understood. Vivian will help, and Kate's two daughters can assist, as well."

"Saving these trees is important, not only to prevent their

loss, but also to protect Entwine. However, someone needs to stop this necromancer," Fornwith said. His dark fur bristled. "The Balance must be restored."

Kate stood as tall as her five-foot-three frame allowed. "Leave that to the Triumvirate. We'll take care of him while you take care of the trees."

She didn't know how the hell they were going to accomplish taking down a necromancer, but they would figure it out somehow. They always did. Even if it was at the last minute with a solution pulled from their asses.

Karnon lifted his chin towards Caleb. "And what is your boon, cousin? You know it would take much for me to venture from my lands during the end cycle, even for your trees."

"Morag." Caleb said her name in a tone filled with reluctance.

Kate saw Fornwith stiffen. The look on his face wasn't a happy one.

Karnon stood. "But the artifact you provided me last time could only be used once to see my love."

"You're going to get the real thing this time," Caleb said. "We have a necromancer who can retrieve her."

"Through the Veil? But the necromancer will be killed."

"What?" Kate took a step forward. "No one said anything about Sam being in mortal danger."

Caleb frowned. "Usually, what K says is true, but Sam's daggers will protect her."

Karnon looked puzzled.

"They hold ghostly essence," Kate explained "A local ghost

told us that they would keep the essence safely, so it didn't go poof. And it'll shield Sam."

Karnon gave her a half-smile. "We definitely wouldn't want it to go 'poof' and take your necromancer with it." He turned to Caleb. "I have never heard of any such daggers capable of this feat."

"They are the only daggers of their kind," Caleb replied, but Kate sensed he knew more than he was sharing. Caleb gave Kate a shrewd look, no doubt seeing her wheels turning. "However, and more importantly, the Oracle will be key to their success to and from the Veil."

Once this whole necromancer problem was solved, Kate and Sam would tag team Caleb and get him to spill about her daggers.

Karnon bowed low toward Kate. "You do not know what this means, to have the chance to see Morag, even if it is for only a brief moment." His voice trembled at the end.

"I do know." Kate blinked back the sudden moisture in her eyes. "I had the opportunity to see someone I had loved dearly and lost. The peace I received, the closure, was immeasurable."

"I do not seek closure," Karnon said. "Our love is eternal. It is both a torture and the most exquisite pleasure to be in her presence once more."

Karnon's voice held such love and sadness. Kate hadn't realized she'd reached his side until she was there. She touched his arm lightly. It felt like a man's arm. Nothing godlike. Just human. "I'm so sorry for your pain," she said.

Karnon looked surprised, but then he covered her hand

with his. "You are brimming with kindness. I am thankful the power of Time is in your care."

He looked at Caleb. "I accept your boon." He released Kate's hand and stepped back from her. "And I will come back in the spring to help train your daughters in the ways of the forest. My cousin knows a fraction of what I'm able to teach."

"I know plenty," Caleb said.

"I have more experience, more years."

"But my experience is centered around the forests. Yours is not."

Logan joined her and slipped an arm around her waist. Kate leaned against him while they watched the two gods bicker.

Fornwith curled up in a patch of sun and closed his eyes.

"What did he mean about you having the power of Time in your care?" Logan asked.

"Not sure. I can futz around with it some, but nothing major." She looked at Logan. "There are other oracles, or there have been. Vivian mentioned something like that to me."

Logan shook his head. "Too many questions and not enough answers. The more I feel like I somehow understand your world, the more I realize I know so little."

"You're an honorary member of the we-make-it-up-as-we-go club." She kissed his chin.

He looked down at her. "I'm a constable. We plan. We don't make it up on the fly."

"Which is why we make a great team."

"So you're not going to chuck me aside for a god?"

Kate turned and snuggled into his arms. They wrapped

around her, just tight enough to make her feel secure, but never bound.

"Nope," she said, resting her cheek against his chest. "It's your humanity that I love. Your loyalty, your caring, the way you act out the bedtime stories for the girls. Everything."

"I still can't believe how lucky I am."

She looked up at him. "We're both lucky."

Then she glanced at Caleb and Karnon, who were still bickering. She didn't know what needed to happen next.

Did they go back to their own realm, and Karnon would follow later? She didn't want to interrupt the two powerful gods, especially with Karnon being a stranger. He might have shown a bit of his vulnerability to her, but that didn't mean he was their friend.

Fornwith looked at her and nodded as if sensing her thoughts. "The trees will not save themselves," his voice rang loudly through the clearing.

Caleb looked chagrined. Karnon merely nodded. "Quite correct, old friend. I fear I miss sparring with my cousin more than I realized." He looked at Caleb. "Once you have Morag, send word and I will join you. I can retain more of my energy and power by remaining here until I'm needed." He lifted a hand toward Kate and Logan. "I will accompany you to the portal."

He turned and walked back toward where they'd entered his realm. Each tree he passed lifted its branches up and out of the way of his antlers.

Logan slipped his hand into hers, and they followed Caleb

and Karnon. One piece down in the puzzle to save the trees and stop Connor's plans to weaken Entwine.

Next stop, the Veil.

MICHAEL HEARD BETH'S CAR PULL UP IN FRONT OF THE manor and went out to meet her.

He hadn't been able to stop thinking of their kiss in the alleyway. When she was in his arms, he'd forgotten for a moment that this was all supposed to be casual, temporary. It felt like she had always been there.

Even though he could have told her what he'd found in the Archives when they'd had dinner at the B&B, he didn't want to pull any attention away from what Beth had discovered about her parents.

And he'd wanted another excuse to see her again. Alone.

Beth got out of her car, looking amazing as usual. But when he got closer, he saw the dark circles under her eyes.

"You okay?" he asked.

"Yeah, still processing all the bio dad stuff. Plus I saw Harvey puttering around town."

Michael stiffened. "Why is he still here? You agreed to the blackmail."

"Because he always wants a backup plan and a potential way to sweeten the deal." Beth rubbed her neck, right where the edge of a scar emerged from under her collar. "He enjoys causing pain and messing with your mind."

He unclenched his hands, realizing he'd formed fists. "Is there anything I can do?"

Beth met his gaze and smiled. Its sadness made him want to pound Harvey against the stone wall of their house.

"Distract me?"

"That I can do." He made a sweeping gesture with his arm toward the house. "I've got a lunch of tomato soup and grilled cheese sandwiches awaiting us."

"How very American of you."

Michael smiled. "I love American food. I can't wait to get back there."

Beth nodded. "Me too."

They both stared at each other for a long moment, not saying anything.

When they both left Scotland, anything that was happening between them would end, as well. Michael found himself suddenly having second thoughts about leaving too soon.

He cleared his throat. "I'll fill you in on what I learned from the Archives. Fi's sister, Nora, is going to help."

Beth walked past him toward the house, but then turned back and kissed him on the cheek. "Thank you." Her eyes looked golden amber in the light.

He watched her disappear into the house, trying to ignore the warmth her lips had left behind.

Percy had already set out the grilled cheese and soup in the dining room.

"I wasn't sure what you would be in the mood for, so there's tea and beer." Michael pulled out a chair for her.

Beth sat down. "Usually, I would take you up on the beer, but it would just make me sleepy right now." She rubbed the side of her face. "But I'll take a raincheck on that drink for when I'm back to a hundred percent."

"I'm sorry, it'll still be another day on the DNA results." Michael sat down, too, and poured some Earl Grey into both their cups. He slid the cream toward her.

Beth doctored her tea and took a long sip. "It's okay. I'm feeling good about the results."

"I am, too."

"You are?"

Michael nodded and took a bite of the sandwich. He chewed while he thought of how to explain it. "When I met Harvey, I picked up on what you'd already told me—deceitful, manipulative, and a healthy dose of rage. But there was something deeper. Something he had hidden behind thick armor. It felt old and settled."

Beth put down her soup spoon. "That he wasn't my father?"

"And that he's been playing the lie for years for his own benefit." He dropped a few sugar cubes into his tea and stirred it. "That's my take, but of course, we don't know for sure. I can't read minds, not unless I take control of them."

"Could you find out? Could you control his mind, so we know what's going on in case there is something worse he's hiding?"

A flare of anger heated Michael's cheeks. "Do you hear what you're asking?"

Beth looked a little chagrined but it quickly disappeared. "I know, I know, but you don't understand how dangerous he is."

Michael leaned back in his chair. Just like always, *how can I use Michael?* Or *how far can I run from him?*

It was always those two options.

Beth looked at him for a few moments, not saying anything.

"I feel like I fucked up again, hard, and I didn't intend it," she said finally.

"You did."

Beth scooted her chair closer to him. "What would help fix it? I can say I'm sorry or you can just yell at me for being an ass. I'm up for either option."

He felt his lips curl into a smile before he could stop them. "I feel like you run into this scenario often."

"Yeah, pretty much. It's why I don't have many friends."

She looked down at the table, and then reached over for her grilled cheese and took a big bite. While she chewed, she didn't glance up at him.

He wanted to comfort her, even though she'd been the one asking him to mindfuck someone. He thought he'd figured her out, but each time he did, she switched it up on him.

"You have Sam and Kate as friends."

She shook her head. "They'd be better off without me."

"Well, you are a bit of an acquired taste."

Beth shot him a nasty look, but some of the sadness had left her face.

Goal accomplished.

"I've accepted I'm not everyone's cup of tea."

"Very true. Logan is in the neutral zone, figuring you out."

She gave him a hint of a smile. "The Romulan Neutral Zone?"

He nodded. "But you can count me as your friend, as well as Robert, so that's at least five. That's something."

Regardless of whatever was between them, he was her friend.

Her smile grew, making her eyes spark. "That's definitely something."

Michael tapped the table. "But just to be clear, I will never take control of someone's mind ever again, even if the reasons seem good."

Beth sighed. "I know you told me that before, but Harvey is dangerous. He could be planning something terrible."

Michael shook his head. "To force my way into someone's mind would not only cause physical pain, but I could kill someone. The psyche is an extremely delicate thing."

"Was it really bad when you did it before?"

"How do you know I did it before?"

"You said you wouldn't do it again, so it means you did it at least once already."

He hadn't realized he'd let that slip. Michael looked down the length of the table, not really seeing it. Instead, he saw the past. "It was more than once, but the first time was when I was really young."

"You don't have to say anything more."

Her face looked softer than he'd ever seen before, but there was a fierceness in her eyes that spoke of memories she'd rather forget. Painful memories.

He wanted to tell her. Lord help him, but he realized he

needed to. She might be the only person who would under-stand the darkness that had entered his soul that day.

"I was five the first time it happened. We had a handyman from one of the local families. What we didn't know was that he abused children."

Beth scooted even closer and put a gentle hand on his wrist. He couldn't hear Percy in the kitchen. The only sound was the wind brushing against the windowpanes.

Michael put his other hand over hers, drawing strength from her touch. "Duncan has been very vocal about what he went through, so I know he won't mind if I tell you."

"The handyman attacked him?" Beth asked.

Michael nodded. "Duncan was seven. He loved helping Trent on his fix-it projects. I had been playing here, in the din-ing room. No one else was home except for our butler at the time, and he was in the kitchen making lunch. I suddenly had this feeling that something was wrong. I was still learning my powers at that point."

Beth didn't say anything. She gave him time. She gave him space.

"The feeling came from the basement." Michael found him-self almost whispering. "I went down there." Flashes of what he'd seen exploded in his head. His chest tightened. "I saw Trent holding Duncan down."

Michael struggled for breath as the scene filled his mind. He was so small. Too small to pull Trent off his brother. Duncan cried out, screaming for help.

A trembling began in his hands and made its way through

his body. "I pleaded with him to stop." Hot tears blurred his vision, clearing away the past. "But he wouldn't."

Beth was out of her chair in a flash, pulling him to his feet and into her arms.

"You're safe. It's okay. You're okay."

She rubbed his back and stroked his hair, rocking him slowly back and forth.

He tried to pull away but she yanked him back. She was stronger than he'd expected.

"I got you," she whispered against his shoulder. "I got you."

The will to flee died with those words.

He wound his arms about her waist and just let her hold him.

He was the imperfect doctor who'd spent his adult life trying to balance the scales back in his favor, healing rather than harming.

But no matter how much he did, it never seemed enough.

This was dangerous letting her see him, *really* see him. But he had to finish this out, this terrible story.

After a few moments, he moved back just slightly.

"I had to save Duncan the only way I could. I pushed my will into Trent's mind." He met Beth's gaze. "I made him ram his head against the wall. He lapsed into a coma for a week before he finally woke up. There was brain damage."

Her gaze didn't flinch. No judgment. No condemnation. No horror.

Just understanding and acceptance.

She wiped the tears from his cheeks with her thumbs. "You

were five and you did what you had to do."

"It was still wrong."

"Would you have reached your butler in time?"

"No."

"Any other adults at home?"

"No."

"Were you an abnormally large five-year-old that could take down a grown man?" She raised an eyebrow.

He sniffed. "No."

"I think you were a hero."

"You have a funny definition of hero." He searched her face and again was reminded of how similar they were—the darkness and light constantly warring. But within the tangled shadows, there was still a glimmer of hope.

"My definition of a hero is different because of my damage." Beth smoothed his hair back, her fingers resting warm and firm against his scalp. "Because sometimes, heroes have to take the hit on their soul—the sacrifice so that innocents can be safe. I did that in juvie to save someone." Her gaze became so intense he couldn't look away. "And I'd do it again in a heartbeat."

He kissed her, but it was so different than before. No hot urgency or pent-up lust. Her lips were soft and tender under his. Beth's hands moved to his neck, pulling him in closer.

He felt her heartbeat pound against his chest, and his joined in time.

For a moment, it was as if they were one, and he realized with crystal clarity just how lonely he'd been all these years. Beth understood him like no one else ever had.

If he wasn't careful, this would go from the fun, casual arrangement they'd agreed upon to something deeper. Something that felt like it could be love.

Michael moved from her lips and kissed her cheeks, her eyebrows, and her nose. "Thank you. I don't know if I'll ever shed the horror of what I did that day, but you made it a little easier to bear." He smiled. "Let's finish our soup before it gets cold."

She sat down and flashed him a smile, looking like her old self again. "So tell me about Fi's sister."

"Nora works with dampening stones."

Beth touched his arm. "Wait a second. Should we be talking about this?" She lowered her voice. "With Connor using ghosts as spies?"

"It's okay," Michael replied. "Beatrice has secured this place, too. She has patrols."

"But how would you know if they got overrun or attacked?"

Michael pointed the cuckoo clock on the wall. "Ray will make that go off."

Beth looked pleased. "I didn't realize he could still do his poltergeist mojo, but I feel better now." She lifted a hand toward Michael. "Continue."

He nodded. "We use the dampening stones to mask someone's energy when they use their abilities."

"So they stay off RAVEN's radar."

"We found a reference to the stones in the Archives," Michael continued. "They were used to drain the power of a witch who had been killing members of the town."

Beth perked up. "And you're thinking maybe we can weaken

the necromancer by taking that ghostly essence he's hoarding."

Michael nodded. "I know Sam doesn't want to kill him. This could help make it easier for the Wardens to take him into custody." He took out his phone. "I'll text Nora and tell her we're coming by."

"But what about Connor's spies?"

"I texted Sam right after I asked you to come over. Beatrice sent a team to the Allen's house to secure it. Plus, if Nora works on anything for us, their home needs to be protected anyway."

Excitement glowed on Beth's face. "Good thinking. And I gave Sam something at the library that might help, too. Connor won't know what hits him."

He marveled at how she just rolled with whatever came her way. She was sad when she got there, comforted him when he needed it, and now was excited for taking down Connor.

As complex as he was always accused of being, she might actually be his perfect fit.

He tried to squash that thought, but it kept bobbing up to the surface of his mind.

Even if she were his match, he'd only screw it up. His track record was as bad as Beth's. It was best if they continued as they agreed—light, fun, and then they'd go their separate ways.

He bit into his grilled cheese sandwich, but it wasn't going to fill the hollow space inside at the thought of not seeing her again.

CHAPTER 21

S AM STOOD BY THE B&B'S STAIRCASE, WATCHING THE TWO ghosts, Martin and Rebecca Dean, disappear and returning their waves with a smile on her face. Gone were all the signs of the fire from their skin and clothes. That's how it always happened when the Bargain was fulfilled, when she had helped ghosts with their unfinished business. They were restored to how they had been before death.

The ghostly essence they'd given her as payment buzzed through her body. She felt like she could light up the town square if she tried.

She'd been working on helping the Deans for a few weeks now, but after Beth had bailed on her at the library, she'd finally received the call she'd been waiting on. Their revised will had been found in a cookie jar they'd given to their youngest son.

Now he'll be the one inheriting their fortune as they wanted, and not his older siblings.

Kate had suggested she ask Beth to find the will, but old habits die hard. They'd been estranged for so many years that

Beth wasn't the first one who popped into her mind to go to for help.

Beth would have probably refused. But then again, maybe she wouldn't have? She'd been different at the library earlier. More vulnerable.

Robert had once told her things which had been frayed could be mended, but there was a price. It seemed Beth wasn't the only one who was hesitant about paying it fully. The chance to be hurt again so deeply was daunting.

Sam walked into the study, the woodsy smell from the fireplace greeting her when she crossed the threshold. Robert was squirreled away here with his latest encyclopedia, trying to catch up on what he'd missed over the past few hundred years.

She also found Beatrice and Darrin. They looked like they'd been arguing. Robert had his head bent over the "F" volume of the encyclopedia, sitting on the settee, but she knew he'd tell her later what they'd said.

Beatrice composed herself quickly. "Darrin came as we asked."

Sam nodded. Kate was off to see Karnon and get his agreement to help. Sam needed to do her part and make sure they could find Morag in the Veil, and for that, they needed a Runner.

She closed her eyes and reached out with her gift. No other ghosts were in the B&B except for Beatrice. Both Darrin and Robert gave off a signature of ghostly essence, but it was different from what she picked up from ghosts.

Beatrice huffed. "I've already cleared the perimeter."

Sam opened her eyes and smiled. "It can't hurt to be extra careful."

"I suppose," Beatrice acknowledged.

"Thank you for coming, Darrin," Sam said. "We need your help to go through the Veil and retrieve a specific ghost."

Darrin raised an eyebrow. "I'll need to tell Sloane about this is if I agree. Veil crossings will raise alarm bells in Command."

"Command is where they monitor everything," Beatrice added.

Sam sat down in a chair near Robert. "Understood. Sloane might be the only Warden who will agree to this, so I want her to know. It's to save the trees who have lost their voices."

Darrin's face paled. "So it's true?"

"It is," Robert replied. "We need to heal them, not only for the forest but for the protection of Entwine."

"What could possibly help you beyond the Veil?" Darrin asked.

Sam took a deep breath. "We need Morag." Darrin stiffened. "For just a short time," Sam continued. "We believe it's the one thing that will get Karnon's agreement to help. Caleb needs him to bring the trees back from the brink."

"Do you know who Morag is?" Darrin's words were hushed.

It felt like tiny beads of ice collected on Sam's skin. Caleb had concerns about Morag—and Kate had shared as much— but there was a sheen of fear in Darrin's eyes.

"Is she a god, too?" Sam's words were equally soft in the quiet of the study.

Darrin ran a hand through his hair. "She's got god-blood,

but never ascended. The Wardens have used her in the past for strategic guidance." He paused. "She's very persuasive. To let her out, even for a short time . . ."

"I don't think we have a choice," Sam said. "And Sloane will end up agreeing to our plan because Connor doesn't want us to heal the trees. He's planning to attack Entwine."

Darrin nodded after a long moment. "I will ask her. Connor needs to be captured before he hurts anyone or anything else." The pain on his face was raw when he said his former apprentice's name.

"It must be difficult for you, knowing what Connor has done," Robert said gently. He closed the encyclopedia and put it on the coffee table in front of him.

Sam wondered if Darrin knew the Wardens wanted Connor dead. Most likely he did.

"I keep thinking I messed up somewhere. That I could have done something differently with Connor." The Runner shot Sam a wondering look. "Sloane said you spoke to him?"

"I did, though I didn't know it was him at the time." She put her hands in the pockets of her long duster. "He seems to want to get to know me, or rather for me to know him. He feels a connection."

"Because you're both Siphoners," Darrin said. "It's a rare gift."

"I wonder what his endgame is," Sam said. "Why go to these extremes?"

"I'd like to know that, too," Darrin said. "But we are where we are and there's no going back." He looked at Sam. "If Sloane does agree to all this, do you understand the dangers of going through the Veil, the dangers to you?"

"I've heard something about ghostly essence," Sam admitted. "And that my daggers can help shield me."

"And Kate can stop time," Beatrice added, her chest puffed out in pride. "That should help."

Darrin looked relieved. "Only seasoned necromancers can make the trip usually, but if Kate stops time, you should be fine."

"Can you not retrieve Morag yourself?" Robert asked, concern heavy in his words. "Then Samantha would not have to put herself at risk."

Darrin frowned. "Even without the Warden's locks upon Morag's resting place, any ghost over a millennium old can't be retrieved by a Runner alone."

"Over a . . ." Sam couldn't finish her sentence. The enormity of what she was about to attempt hit her hard. Could she even do this? Darrin said "seasoned necromancers." She'd only been doing this again for a short time, and she still didn't know the extent of her gifts. And what if Kate stopping time wasn't good enough, and the essence was sucked from her body?

Robert stood and walked to her chair, sitting on the arm. He took her hand in his. "We will find another way to satisfy this Karnon if you feel unsure, Samantha."

She looked up into his face. Hadn't she been just marveling about bringing him back to life? True, she had the Universe's help, but she'd felt the power running through her. Her power.

Kate might hesitate, but Beth wouldn't have any doubts.

Sam heard Beth's voice in her mind from when they'd performed their Blood Sister ritual as kids.

I love you, Samantha Eveline Hamilton and Katharine Amanda Peterson. When you need me, I will be your heart, your courage, and your strength. We are sisters in blood.

Sam pulled on some of Beth's courage now. Not through their connection as TOP, but through the friendship that had sustained her as a child. The friendship she finally realized she didn't want to be without any longer, which meant she had to pay the price and open herself up to be hurt.

Regardless of whether or not Beth wanted her back as a friend, it was a leap of faith.

"I'll do it," Sam said. "Kate will help stop time and with Darrin by my side, we'll find Morag and save the trees."

"And protect that damned Threshold," Beatrice said, anger in her tone.

"What would happen if someone got through the Threshold and into Entwine?" Sam asked.

Darrin looked like he wanted to talk but instead turned away.

Beatrice shook her head. "He's Warden-bound not to speak of it, but I'm not. I still don't understand how a group like RAVEN could use ghostly essence, but they keep trying to breach the Threshold." She touched the side of her nose with her finger. "Which tells me they have plans."

What if that energy could be harnessed as a weapon? Or to make someone invincible? Sam's stomach clenched.

"Do you suppose Connor wishes to use ghostly essence for

something nefarious?" Robert asked, his thoughts clearly running in the same direction as Sam's. "Unlike RAVEN, he is perfectly suited for its use or misuse in this case."

Darrin turned around. "Sloane fears this, as well, but no one knows for sure."

Sam glanced at Darrin. "When do you suggest we go through the Veil?"

"Midnight would be ideal," Darrin said. "The Veil is thinnest at that point, which will make our journey a bit easier."

Beatrice nodded. "The patrols are on the hour, every hour, so I'd suggest a few minutes after. Even with Sloane's help, you don't want the other Wardens knowing until it's done."

"Kate should be back shortly with Karnon's agreement." Sam stood. If anyone could get a god to agree to something, it's Kate. "We can plan for tonight. The trees might not be able to hold on for much longer, and we don't want them to lose their voices forever."

Darrin nodded. "If you'll get your daggers, I'll show you how to funnel the ghostly essence into them."

"If you remember, Samantha has done so in the past. At RAVEN," Robert said.

He left off the rest of what had happened at RAVEN when she'd listened to the voices in her daggers and given them the ghostly energy, and they'd knocked out the guard. She had no idea if the voices were the daggers themselves or something more.

The Runner nodded. "Yes, but that was in the heat of the moment, and the energy was used immediately. I can help Sam channel the energy into the daggers for storage—on purpose and not when it's her life at stake."

"I'll grab them." Sam headed out of the study and back to where she'd left her purse by the front door.

Ever since RAVEN, she'd carried her daggers around with her everywhere. But now they had elegant sheaths, so she wasn't always worried about drawing blood when she reached for her wallet.

She took them from her purse, and they vibrated against her palms.

Somehow, they seemed to know what was coming.

And they were eager.

BETH STARED AT THE ALLEN HOUSE THROUGH THE WINDOWS of Michael's car. He'd driven them over there to meet with Nora. She hoped Fi's sister would be able to help them figure out a way to weaken Connor.

Nora had moved back into the Allen home with Fi again. Beth was glad Fi had the extra support with Ken still missing. Even though their father was a messed-up snitch, he was still their father. And Beth knew just how crazy those emotions were when it came to family.

"Anything wrong?" Michael asked. He took the keys from the ignition.

"No, just thinking about fucked up families." She turned to look at him. Damn he was gorgeous.

Even more so since he'd opened up to her at lunch. Could someone get more attractive, really? She'd heard people say that happened when they started to care for someone, but it had never happened to her.

Not until now.

Michael breathed in. "Any word from potential Bio Dad?"

"I think he's giving me some space until I get the DNA results back." She smiled. "You're going to like him."

"*You* barely know him."

She shook her head. "I can't explain it, I just know. And wait until you see him climb trees."

Michael smiled back. "I don't think I've ever seen you impressed by anyone until now, Beth Marshall."

She got out of the car. "Jealous that I don't think you're incredible?"

Beth was thankful he couldn't read minds.

He locked the car and walked around to meet her. "You don't? I'm hurt."

She bumped his shoulder. "You're so full of it."

The front door opened. "Michael!"

The brunette's yell echoed through the still afternoon air. She had the same heart-shaped face as Fi but was a little taller than her sister. And from the smile she flashed at Michael, she's clearly smitten.

"Hey, Nora," Michael managed to get out before she launched into him for a hug.

"It's been too many years," Nora said. She pulled back and looked at him. "But you're still too hot for your own good."

THRESHOLD ✒ 273

Was Michael blushing? He'd never blushed around her, and she hit him with some zingers.

The invisible hackles on Beth's back rose.

Michael kissed Nora's cheek. "It has been too long. You look great."

Beth had to admit that Nora was adorable.

And he'd kissed her.

Okay, it was her cheek, but still . . .

"Are you all right?" Fi asked from the doorway. She walked down the steps slowly, a knowing smile on her face. "You're looking a wee bit sick. We've got a variety of stomach fixes inside."

Could Fi know she'd been getting a bit busy with Michael? Maybe. The kid was pretty intuitive.

Beth forced herself to smile. "I'm fine. Michael just drives too fast."

Michael flashed her a quizzical look, but Beth ignored him. She held out her hand to Nora, anything to get her to stop pawing all over Michael. "I'm Beth Marshall. Nice to meet you."

Nora disentangled herself from Michael and shook her hand. "I *know*. Fi and I watch your show. Between medical school and then interning at various hospitals, I haven't been able to be home much. I appreciate all the time you spend with my sister."

Of course she was going to be nice, too. Figures.

"Said sister is right here," Fi huffed. "You make me sound like a charity case."

Nora looked wounded. "I didn't mean it that way. Honest."

"I'm just teasing." Fi grinned. "You've always been too soft. All heart and no grit."

Her sister gave her a grudging smile. "I forgot how it was to be at home again."

"Wonderful?" Fi asked.

Nora laughed and turned to Beth and Michael. "Come on in. I'll make us a cuppa."

Michael nodded. "I can't wait to hear about your residency."

Beth watched them walk up the steps and into the house.

"It's okay if you're jealous," Fi said. She gathered her hair into a messy bun and stuck a pen in it to hold.

"Who said I'm jealous?"

Fi eyed her hands. "Your knuckles are white, and your shoulders are practically touching your ears."

Beth realized she was right. She relaxed her body with a concerted effort. "Did they date before?"

Fi laughed. "No, but my sister is hoping that now might be her chance."

Beth glanced at the doorway they'd disappeared through. "She is, is she?" Warmth slid through her, carried by determination. If anyone was going to have designs on Michael, it would be Beth.

Fi stepped in front of her, blocking her gaze. "Look, I know I give her a hard time, but you can't kill my sister."

Beth blinked her eyes a few times. "Who said anything about killing her?"

"That look in your eyes did."

Beth usually covered her emotions much better than this,

but with everything that had happened to her in the past week, it was no wonder Fi could read something. Though she'd never kill over love. That would be stupid.

"I don't love him," Beth muttered.

Fi raised both her eyebrows. "Who said anything about love?"

Beth's mind froze. Her easy comebacks retreated, likely laughing all the way. Why had she even brought up the L word at all?

"I figured that's where your mind was going," Beth said, pulling on her acting chops. "But if I'm interested in anything with Michael, it's just some fun." She smiled. "And if we do get a little busy while I'm in Scotland, your sister can have him when I'm done."

And that was the truth, though she tried to ignore how the idea of Michael with someone else stabbed into her chest.

Fi nodded. "Fair enough. Let's get inside." She walked up the steps.

The Allen house was a bunch of small rooms. Pretty typical for the UK. Beth missed her spacious L.A. mansion.

Fi lifted her hand toward Beth. "This way."

She followed her through the hallway and down another narrow one until they reached the kitchen.

The teapot on the stove behind Nora hissed and bubbled. It was a galley-style kitchen with cracked linoleum floors and chipped counters, but here and there were cheerful touches— bright mugs, a Christmas dish towel, and hand-drawn pictures of the forest on the fridge. Emily's work, if Beth wasn't mistaken.

Kate's older daughter had talent in the art department.

Nora gestured toward a tiny table in the corner. "Please, sit down."

Beth joined Michael at the table, slinging her coat around the back of her chair.

"I don't know how much Michael or Fi have told you about what I do," Nora said to Beth.

"Not much. Just that you work on setting up the dampening stones to capture the energy if someone uses their powers."

"That's the gist, yes. The stones themselves are already attuned to storing energy," Nora said. "I just create the pathways within the stones to capture the type of energy someone gives off when using their abilities. And reinforce them so the stones don't burn out right away."

"The one that used to be here burned out from your dad's abilities," Michael said. "How long had that one been in place?"

The tea kettle whistled, and Nora got up to grab it from the stove.

"About five years," Fi answered. "For the most part, Da had kept his gifts in check, but the last few years, with Nora being gone so much . . ."

"And Fi acting out," Nora added.

Fi didn't deny it. "It was a royal brew for disaster." She filled up a red porcelain teapot that said *A cuppa a day keeps the monsters away* on the side.

"I have a feeling RAVEN might have been working on your dad for a while." Michael sat back in his chair. "Even under the strain of you two." He smiled. "It would have taken a lot to make him crack. He is one of the strongest men I've known."

"I've thought the same." Beth glanced at the Allen sisters. "I didn't know your dad, but I've seen long cons, and what happened with him reeks of it. I wouldn't be surprised if RAVEN spent time breaking down your dad's values and moral code."

Harvey had broken many a mark over time.

Nora gripped the counter. "I think it was eating him alive, helping RAVEN, which is why Da almost destroyed this house and everyone in it. If Kate hadn't been here, we'd be standing in a crater. It wasn't like him. I feel . . . like he'd been pushed to his limits."

"And wanted to die before betraying anyone," Beth mused.

Fi opened up a tin of cookies and brought it over to the table. "I still wonder if he'll suddenly show up out of the blue." She looked down. "I hope he does." Her voice was a whisper. "Fucked up or not, he's still my Da."

Nora put her arm around Fi. "I'm here now."

Fi gave her a long hug. "I love you, Doctor Perfect."

Nora squeezed her. "And I love you, Little Miss Nettle."

"Little Miss Nettle?" Beth couldn't help asking. The Doctor Perfect piece she got.

Nora pulled away and kissed Fi's temple. "She's so darn annoying all the time, like a nettle that's gotten caught in your clothes. It's what our Da called her."

Fi wiped her cheeks, smearing a bit of her mascara. "The name fits." She laughed, chasing some of the hollowness from her eyes.

Seeing them together reminded Beth of how she'd been with

Kate and Sam when they were kids. They only had each other to really lean on back then.

"I'm glad you two have each other," Michael said. "Family is important."

Nora gave Michael a watery smile. "Don't I know it. I'd do anything for family." She gave her head a sharp shake. "Okay, enough blubbering about, you've got a necromancer to stop."

Fi rescued the teapot and the mugs from the counter, bringing them back over. "So, you think you can use a stone to weaken him, take his energy?"

Michael nodded. "That's the plan. I don't want Sam to be faced with having to kill him." His eyes darkened. "She'd do it to save everyone else, but then would never forgive herself."

Beth knew he was thinking about what he'd shared with her, about hurting the handyman.

"Can you reconfigure a stone for us, Nora?" Michael asked.

Nora grabbed a cookie from the tin. "I think so. One keyed to ghostly essence." She poured the tea. The heady scent of cinnamon tickled Beth's nose.

"Is there a danger of the stone taking the ghostly essence from Sam or any ghosts nearby?" Michael asked.

Nora loaded up her tea with healthy spoonfuls of sugar. "Not from the ghosts. That's who they are, and the energy is natural to their being. But from Sam, it could affect her. I wouldn't be able to have the stone distinguish between them."

"Don't worry about Sam. As long as she knows she'll feel weak, it'll be fine. Plus, she's got the daggers," Beth said. "She can always load them up with the essence and then pull from it once the rogue necromancer has been sucked dry. She's going to test her daggers out on the upcoming Veil breach."

Nora sat up straight. "The Veil breach?!"

Fi mimicked her posture. "Can I come?"

Michael sipped his tea. "It's a long story, but Sam has to get a ghost who Caleb's cousin wants to see. In return, this cousin will restore the voices of the trees that the necromancer harmed." He looked at Fi. "And no, you can't come."

Fi frowned but Beth didn't disagree with Michael. They already had a number going on the mission.

Nora looked stunned. "Just what have you gotten yourself into, Michael Forbes?"

Michael smiled at Beth. "A kick ass adventure."

Beth smiled back. "Damn straight, skippy. You're rolling with TOP now, and we don't do things the easy way."

"You never do things the easy way, Marshall. Even without TOP."

"Which is why you like hanging out with me." Beth poked his arm.

Michael laughed. "I'm doing it to help Sam with the necromancer."

"Riiiight." Beth raised an eyebrow.

Nora cleared her throat. "Erm, when do you need the stone reconfigured? We have one that hasn't been set up yet in town, so I can use that one."

"As soon as possible," Beth replied, still basking in the sparring with Michael. She would miss that when she went back to L.A. Everyone else was intimidated by her, but not him.

"How long have you two known each other?" Fi asked, pointing in between Michael and Beth.

"Not long," Michael said.

"Just since I arrived in Scotland," Beth added.

"Hmmm," Fi said, then sipped her tea.

Nora asked Michael something about the hospital, and Beth met Fi's gaze. The kid gave her a mischievous smile, no doubt imagining romance between her and Michael where there wasn't any.

Romance existed in Sam's novels, not in Beth's life.

Michael laughed at something Nora said and caught Beth's eye. She smiled back, not knowing what made him laugh. She couldn't help it.

And for the first time, she actually wondered what it would feel like to have a little romance in her life.

CHAPTER 22

SAM NODDED TO ROBERT IN THE KITCHEN. THE COAST WAS clear. No ghosts. She'd gotten into the habit of checking each time everyone was together. Beatrice might keep a close eye on the B&B, but it didn't hurt to be extra safe.

Sam leaned her elbows on the marble kitchen island and watched Kate bustling around the stove, pausing every time she passed Logan to grab a quick kiss. Logan cut up vegetables on the counter. He'd donned one of Kate's aprons and looked at home. Robert was setting the table, but seemed to sense her gaze. He looked over and gave her a smile that sent heat rushing through her.

"I know we're going to talk about the trees and the Veil once Beth and Michael get here," Sam said, "but for a moment, let's pretend we're just two couples getting together for dinner."

She wondered if it could ever be like that. No murders to solve or lives to save.

Kate smiled. "Normal stuff."

Logan nodded. "We can do that." He flashed her a quick

look before returning to the veggie cutting.

"This looks delicious." Robert slid his arm around Sam's waist, and she leaned against him. "I fear I will miss your cooking when Samantha and I leave this place."

Kate shot Sam a sharp look. "You're not leaving anytime soon, right?"

Sam shook her head. "No, but we can't stay here forever, especially if the B&B gets back up and running again. Bronson texted me from London that he's close to hiring a manager."

"I suppose you're right." Kate pulled some rolls from the oven. They smelled heavenly. "But you need to stay nearby, 'kay?"

Robert gave Kate a small bow. "We would not wish to be far from your presence, dear Kate."

Logan slid the cut veggies onto a platter. Then he paused and cocked his head. "I heard a car outside."

It had to be Beth and Michael.

"I wonder if Beth will ever admit she's got feelings for Michael?" Sam asked softly.

Kate nodded. "She's softening up a bit despite her protests. Not gooey yet, but definitely getting a bit mushy. But we'll have to see what Michael's mush level is to be sure."

Robert gave Sam a side squeeze and kissed her temple. "I hope they will give each other a chance before it is too late."

Sam heard a car door slam.

Logan nodded. "Once they leave Scotland, they'll lose their chance." He gazed at Kate, his eyes full of love. "You have to seize the opportunity when you can. It might not come again."

The front door of the B&B opened. But none of the usual bickering. Sam raised an eyebrow toward Kate.

Kate looked worried. "We're in here," she called out. "Dinner's still cooking."

Beth walked in first and took a deep breath. "It smells tasty."

Michael followed her in. They stood so close, side by side, they were almost touching. "You just ate cookies," Michael said.

Beth gave him a soft smile. "But Kate's cooking trumps anything else."

The smile Michael returned was full of affection.

Sam had sensed that something had changed between them when they'd run into MacCallum & Sons after her, but could they have finally admitted their feelings for each other?

Kate wiped her hands on a dish towel and had the biggest shit-eating grin on her face. She'd picked up on what Sam had. Something *was* blossoming with Michael and Beth.

"Hope you brought your appetite," Kate said. "We've got pot roast, veggies and dip, and rolls—freshly made, not store-bought."

"I made them," Logan piped up. "The girls helped."

Michael joined them. "Where are the girls?"

No sign of anything unusual on his face, Sam noted. But Michael could always hide things from her a bit better than Beth could.

"Upstairs," Sam replied. "They're working on a school project, but they'll be down for dinner."

"Was Fi's sister helpful in your queries?" Robert asked.

"Nora is confident she can adjust the dampening stones to collect Connor's ghostly essence, or whatever he's holding inside him," Michael replied.

"Yes, she was *very* helpful," Beth said.

Michael smiled. "She's an old friend."

Beth stole a carrot from the bunch Logan had just cut up and took a bite with gusto.

Sam wanted to look at Kate but didn't want to be too obvious.

"So the stone will drain what Connor has inside him?" Logan asked.

"Yup, and if he tries to whammy anyone, too," Beth added. "Just like it can capture someone's energy from using their gifts."

"What about my ghostly essence?" Sam held up her hands and willed the energy to spark. It came immediately and much faster than before. She almost felt like her body was building pathways, like a secondary bloodstream.

Was that possible? From what Sloane had said, Connor appeared to be the only one she could ask about it. And everyone wanted him dead. Well, not everyone.

Beth tilted her head. "Anything you have in your body, ghostly essence-wise, will be sucked out along with Connor's, according to Nora."

Michael sent Sam a reassuring look. "The weaker we can make Connor, the easier it will be to subdue him so the Wardens can lock him up."

"Makes sense," Sam said. "And I'll put what I can into the

daggers ahead of time. Darrin showed me how to store the essence in them and retrieve it."

Kate peered through the oven door. "Okay, we have about a half hour left, so let's share our info before the girls come down." She gave Robert and Michael a stern look. "And yes, this is the Kitchen Debrief."

Everyone laughed, and any remaining tension was broken apart for the time being.

Claiming her right as the cook of their fine dinner, Kate went first on the debrief.

"Karnon was naked?" Beth asked, leaning in. "Was everything extra value sized?"

Sam wanted to know, too, but remained quiet for Robert's sake. Her curiosity wasn't worth his upset.

Michael sighed. "Is that your main question from her whole story?"

"What?" Beth looked affronted, but her smile ruined it. "How often have you seen a naked god?"

Michael was silent.

"I rest my case." Beth elbowed him.

"I will not answer Beth's question right now." Kate winked at Beth. "But the important thing is that we're good to go. Once Morag is delivered, Karnon will help the trees."

Robert grew serious. "Considering what Imogene told us, Connor might try to stop Karnon."

Kate nodded. "Caleb is setting up wards while the trees are being healed, but we should be on our guard, as well."

Sam took a long sip of her merlot. "Onto my piece."

She filled them in on her talk with Darrin and his help with her daggers.

"Did you hear anything," Kate asked, "from the guardians of the daggers?"

"Isn't that a movie?" Michael asked.

Beth crossed her arms. "Do we really know they're guardians? They could be some evil spirits banished to the daggers, and now Sam let them free with the whole 'summon me' shenanigans at RAVEN."

Sam felt a flicker of anger lick around her heart. "Those shenanigans saved my life—and Robert's and Mackenzie's. And I didn't enjoy hurting that guard. I don't have your killer instincts, Beth."

Beth pursed her lips. "Maybe not, but you didn't hesitate to do what you had to do. It impressed me."

Kate wobbled in her chair. "I'm sorry, did the world just go wonky for a moment? I thought I heard Beth complimenting Sam."

"Can it, Red." Beth's words seemed more automatic than heated. She turned back to Sam. "Though it does seem strange to me that suddenly those things came to life."

"I can't explain it either," Sam admitted. "But I had them locked away for years, so maybe once I had used them with Ray, they woke up or something."

"Have they spoken to you again?" Logan asked.

Beth perked up, no doubt anxious for the answer.

"Not exactly," Sam said. "Though I thought I heard something when Darrin took me through the drill of sending energy into the daggers and then taking it out again."

Beth uncrossed her arms. "Like 'you're all going to die, suckers'?"

Kate shook her head. "Evil creatures never announce stuff like that unless they know nothing can stop them. It gives the good guys a chance."

"The daggers aren't evil. I know this because they were the last things my dad gave me before he died." Sam's voice rose in intensity. "He wouldn't have given me something that could hurt me. He wouldn't."

Her parents had sacrificed everything for her—even their lives.

The warmth of Robert's arm wrapped around her shoulders. "No one is accusing your father of wrongdoing."

"I was just joking," Beth muttered. "Well, mostly joking. I'm just worried because we don't know enough about these daggers. And . . . I don't want you and Red to get yourselves killed."

Hearing the vulnerability in Beth's words, Sam's earlier resolve filled her again. She needed to take the leap. Beth never would do so on her own.

"I don't want anything to happen to you either, Beth." Sam reached over and took Beth's hand. "You're one of my best friends and I was foolish to let that end." Sam tried to swallow, finding her throat suddenly dry. "If you need forgiveness, you have it from me. I hope you'll forgive me, too." She squeezed her hand. "So stop pushing me away. It's not going to work. I'm stubborn like that. I'm the strength of our trio, remember?"

Beth looked way for a long moment but then her gaze locked on Sam. "And I'm the courage."

"And I'm the heart." Kate touched Beth's arm and Sam's shoulder. "About damn time one of you held out a friggin' olive branch."

The energy chain between them clicked into place, more powerful than before. The connection was strong, but also felt lighter, less binding.

"Do you ever get used to seeing that?" Logan asked Robert. "The bond between them?"

Robert shook his head. "Never."

"It's really beautiful," Michael replied.

Beth pulled back. The connection broke.

"See what?" Beth asked, her voice sharp.

Robert scrunched up his brow. "Since I see with Entwine's eyes, there is a shimmering green light hovering above your skin when all three of you touch."

"I don't 'see' anything with my eyes, but I do with my senses," Michael replied. "At the risk of sounding corny, it's love and friendship. Sunshine and puppies, Marshall. Sorry." He shot a look at Beth. "And you've got an extra something around you."

Robert nodded. "I see that, as well. Beth glows like Samantha, but it feels different somehow."

"And what do you see, Logan?" Kate asked.

Logan steepled his fingers. "Like Michael, I don't 'see' it, but my senses tingle."

"Your fae wings," Sam said, flashing a smile at Beth. Beth didn't return it, but she stopped frowning.

Logan nodded. "I'm sensing power. Pure, unbridled power when the three of you touch."

Sam looked at Beth and then Kate. If what they had was spilling over into being sensed by others, their power and connection as TOP was definitely growing.

"Perhaps Beth should accompany you and Kate on your Veil quest?" Robert asked. "In case you need the power of the Triumvirate at your disposal. You never know what might come your way in the farthest reaches of Entwine."

Sam tilted her head at Beth. "You up for a potentially dangerous mission?"

"Do you know me?" Beth snorted.

Kate sighed. "Oh, great. Now I'll have to not only stop time but play referee to these two."

"Can you manage both of them?" Sam asked Robert. "The energy to bring Kate and Beth into Entwine and back?"

Robert nodded, his gaze locking with hers. "I will be fine, and Darrin will also be there to assist. Beth has proven herself a formidable warrior, and I could not ask for a better ally to stand with me in protecting the woman I love."

Beth grinned. "That means a lot coming from you because I know how hung up you are on Sam. I might even say pussy—"

Michael covered Beth's mouth with his hand for a second. Enough to stop her next word. "You need a mute button."

"I've been saying that for years," Kate sighed.

"About the Veil quest," Sam said. "We need to go tonight at midnight."

The timer dinged on the stove. Kate stood. "Well, it's a good thing we're loading up on fuel. Pot roast now. Next stop, the Veil."

Sam felt better. She hadn't realized she'd been worrying about going through the Veil, even with Kate's help. But having Beth there . . . well, when all three of them were together, Sam always felt they were invincible.

And she'd been courageous tonight. Regardless of what happened in the future, regardless of whether or not Beth wanted to still be her friend, Beth now knew how Sam felt. Somehow taking that leap made her feel stronger than ever before.

Sam felt hopeful for the first time that they would get through this. That they'd stop Connor.

BETH WATCHED ROBERT DISAPPEAR WITH KATE INTO Entwine. They were there one minute, and then poof, gone the next, leaving her alone in the study.

She hoped this ghost heist worked because she understood the suffering of the silenced trees. She knew what it was like when you needed to shut down and escape something horrible. No one, no thing, deserved to stay in that kind of prison.

And hopefully healing the trees would mess up Connor's master plan, or at least make him work harder for it. They'd need to weaken him if they could.

Who knew how powerful he was becoming with all that ghostly essence. And she still wasn't sold on the dampening stone being their savior. That would be too easy.

Robert reappeared a moment later. He was breathing heavily and sweating. He looked like he hadn't slept in a few days.

"I don't have to go to Entwine if it's too much," Beth said. She'd rather keep all her fingers and toes. He'd gotten Kate there, and that was the important part.

Robert shook his head. "Just give me a moment."

I can help.

That voice again.

"How can you help?" Beth asked. Robert looked at her quizzically, but she waved her hand at him. "I told Sam about this. I'm hearing a voice. We don't know if it's a ghost."

I'll give Robert a boost. Rev him up so he can take you to Entwine more easily.

"She says she can give you a jolt. Power you up."

Robert studied the space around Beth. "I still see the shapes around you, but the energy is more powerful. Your glow is brighter. Do you trust this voice?"

Beth thought about it. So far all it has done was try to help her or pester her, but there were easier ways to kill her than this. Plus, it had warned her to run from Connor, so it definitely wasn't working for him.

"I think we can trust the voice." She looked at the air around her. "But don't make me regret this."

Laughter. It sounded familiar. *Tell Robert to stand still.*

"Don't move, big guy," Beth said. Robert did as she asked.

Hold out your hands. I'm going to send the energy through you.

"What?"

Beth, trust me. I wouldn't hurt you for anything.

Maybe it was her mom? She didn't have Sam's lie detector skills with ghosts, but it felt like the truth.

"She's going to send the energy through me and into you, Robert."

He looked concerned but simply nodded. "I trust you."

Beth held out her hands toward Robert. "What am I supposed to . . ."

The energy blasted through her before she could finish her sentence. No easing into it, no foreplay, just a surge of pure power.

She saw fragments of the icy lake that always appeared when she used her abilities. They spun through the air and then seemed to shift into position.

The energy rushed down her arms and into her hands, filling them with brilliant orange light. Then it burst out of her fingers, hitting the pieces of ice. They reflected the light into Robert.

He stiffened but held his stance. He didn't seem to be in pain, but something was definitely happening. His eyes blazed orange for a moment before returning to brown.

Robert smiled, almost bouncing on his feet. His cheeks were rosy. He bristled with energy. He bowed slightly toward Beth. "Thank you, mysterious voice, for your assistance. I am ready to depart if you are, Beth." He held out his hand.

"Thanks, voice." She didn't hear a reply this time, but still felt a glimmer of the energy around her. Beth took Robert's hand. "Let's go."

The study disappeared around her and then suddenly, she

was somewhere else. It looked like a train station of sorts. Sam leaned over the side of the railing, looking down at the archways. Kate pointed to one that had dragons carved into the dark stone. They turned toward Robert and Beth.

"What took you so long?" Kate asked.

"We had to juice up Robert a bit," Beth replied.

"We?" Sam asked.

"We don't have time for this," Darrin said, waving them to follow him. "We're trying to keep this on the hush-hush, remember?"

They followed him down a side hallway. Beth looked back over her shoulder at Sam and Robert. "Have you investigated those archways yet, Sam?"

"No, but I want to." Sam looked troubled. "I'd like to understand a bit more about what happens when you pass on."

Beth laughed. "Yeah, like is it your own personal Heaven or Hell, or are you in Gen Pop having to share everything with everyone?"

"Gen Pop?" Kate asked.

"General Population in prison and juvie." Beth shrugged. "Meaning, you're all together. Believe me, it's better than getting special treatment on your own."

Kate gave her a sad look, and Beth knew what was coming—the pity.

"Now I know why you like Los Angeles so much," Kate said. "It reminds you of juvie, crowded and full of criminals."

Beth's mouth dropped open. She closed it after a moment and smiled. "Just for the record, not everyone in juvie is a criminal. You still manage to surprise me, Red."

Kate returned her smile. "You know I am always here for you whenever you need to talk about the crap you went through, but I know what it's like to get those puppy dog eyes." She shook her head slightly. "It was like that for me the first year after Paul died. People mean well, but it made it really hard to move on."

"Sometimes it feels like a century since I was locked up. Other times it feels like it was just yesterday."

But at least every time she saw Sam now, it didn't immediately bring back those painful memories.

Just every other time.

Improvement.

She still wasn't sure how she felt about that whole friendship declaration in the kitchen earlier. That was a lie. She knew how she felt, and it scared her.

More blocks in her wall had come down, battered by the hope that she might recapture what she'd lost with Sam.

The corridor ended with a blue door with a silver square plate in its center. There was no knob.

Darrin took his right index finger and scrolled something on the plate, too fast for Beth to follow. The door clicked and opened, releasing a white mist.

"That's not creepy," Beth whispered.

Darrin turned back to them. "Through here is the entryway to the Veil. The air is full of bits of ghostly essence from those who venture too near it. It'll be hard to see, so stick close." His gaze met Robert's. "You should stay further back. It's dangerous for you to get too close. Though you have blood in your veins, you also have ghostly essence."

The Runner opened the door fully, and then disappeared into the white mist.

Beth ignored Sam and Robert's shocked gazes and grabbed Kate's hand, pulling her inside after Darrin.

Even though Darrin had said the mist was ghostly essence, she still expected it to be like mist—wet and cold. Instead, it was wet and warm, like tears.

Beth couldn't see any walls, just more mist. But in the distance, way in the distance, there was something dark yet pulsing with glowing light. They followed Darrin, who walked toward it.

She'd teased before about aliens, but she sincerely hoped they weren't walking toward a mothership to be whisked away and probed.

Kate's eyes were wide. "Those pulses, it's like a heartbeat."

Shit. It wasn't a ship. It was something that was going to eat them. Beth stopped in her tracks causing Kate to stumble.

Darrin turned and smiled at them. "Don't be afraid. The Veil breathes with the life of Entwine, that's all."

Beth dropped Kate's hand and wiped her own against her jeans. "Who said anyone was scared?"

Sam walked up to stand in between Beth and Kate.

"The Veil keeps the balance." Sam held her hand out toward the glow. "It keeps the ghosts safe on the other side so they can still exist after they've gone through the archways."

"And since when did you learn all this?' Beth asked.

Sam shook her head. "It just came to me right now, into my mind, just like the Rules do."

Darrin began walking again. They followed.

Beth looked down at her feet and found them almost hidden in the whitish mist swirling about. "So, if all the ghosts who have moved on through their archways are behind the Veil, how is Sam going to find the one ghost in the haystack?"

"That is precisely the reason why Darrin is here," Robert replied. "He will help Samantha find Morag."

"How long is it going to take to get to the Veil? Because . . ." Kate stopped speaking. "Wait, we're suddenly here. How is that possible? We've only been walking a few minutes."

Beth found Kate was right. They were in front of the glow, but she couldn't see anything really, not with the mist.

Darrin smiled. "Time and distance work differently in Entwine, in the Rinth, and in other realms, compared to your world."

"Great, time works differently here. What if I can't stop it?" Kate muttered.

"You can," Darrin said. "You're the Oracle."

Kate didn't look convinced.

Beth bumped her arm. "You got this, Red."

"You do," Sam said. "If you weren't really the Oracle, we wouldn't have been able to form TOP. You need three uber-powerful women for the Triumverate."

Beth nodded. "Sam's right, and you know I don't say that very often."

Kate gave them a grudging smile. She patted the pockets of

her long duster. "I do have my Tardis and my Time Baggies."

Beth gazed at Kate, putting on a brave face, willing to do what she could to save the trees, even though she was scared. Unlike Sam, she'd stuck by Beth's side even when Beth tried to push her away. Kate might be the heart of their trio, but she was also one of the bravest people Beth knew.

Darrin faced the glow and flung his arms open. The mist skidded to the left and right as if Darrin had opened up a set of curtains and revealed the Veil.

Beth didn't know what she was expecting. Well, maybe she did. Something along the lines of a semi-opaque wall of light or shadows behind a gauzy window.

But the Veil was made up of the vines she had seen on their way here, the ones that had made up the hallways, but these were smaller and more delicate. And they weren't moving, they were still.

The green strands crisscrossed, reminding Beth of the lattice-design on top of the peach pies Sam's mom had loved making. In between the scalloped lines of crust bubbled juicy peach filling.

Like that filling, there were openings in between the vines. Openings filled with light behind a sparkly membrane of some sort. Beth looked to the left and right, but couldn't see any end to the Veil. Looking up and down revealed the same truth. Whatever this was, it was enormous.

Sam walked closer and peered through one of the openings about the size of a dinner plate. She turned back to Beth and Kate. "There are people in there."

Beth and Kate joined her. Sam was right. Each opening was like a window with scenes playing out in front of them.

Beth saw someone who looked like a Viking taking out a stag. She moved to the next one and it was a mother cuddling her baby in front of a roaring fire. In yet another one, a man was in a back alley getting stabbed.

"Are these memories of the people who passed on?" Beth asked.

Darrin shrugged. "Yes and no. Each person who passes continues on their path, but they bring with them their past. Some get lost in it while others move on." He gazed at Beth with eyes that were too knowing. "It doesn't end with death."

"So it's not sunshine and roses for some," Beth said. "Or fire and brimstone for others."

The Runner smiled. "What lies beyond is for those who travel that road."

Beth crossed her arms. "Typical vague bullshit."

"Where is Morag?" Sam asked.

Darrin closed his eyes and laid one wrist over the other. The silver cuffs he wore flashed, and then settled into a steady silver glow. Beth sensed energy dart out from Darrin's cuffs, reminding her of the cord she saw when she used her gifts.

"You're calling up her window," Beth said.

Kate raised an eyebrow. "Have you been moonlighting with the Runners?"

"It's because she's a Seeker," Darrin replied, eyes still closed. "She senses when others are doing something similar."

The Veil began to move, flowing past them to the right.

Then it moved upward, as if someone were pulling on it.

Kate turned away from the fast-moving lights. "I'm feeling nauseous."

It didn't bother Beth. She followed every move and almost began to anticipate the next.

The Veil finally stopped moving. The vines here looked a bit older. Still vital and alive, but more seasoned, if that was possible.

Darrin pointed to the window of light in front of them. Sam, Beth, and Kate clustered around. There was a woman with long brown hair and a beautiful green dress. Something flashed in the light, like she was wearing jewels. She sat by a lake. Beth had the feeling she was waiting for something.

"You ready?" Beth asked Kate.

Kate nodded. "As ready as I'll ever be."

Darrin wiped his brow. It was obvious the strain of manipulating the Veil was becoming tough on the Runner. He looked at Kate. "Just like we discussed."

Kate nodded. "I stop time out here as soon as you and Sam go inside the Veil, that way I hold the portal-thingy open without you two being crushed alive or being trapped with Morag."

"More like Sam being drained of life," Darrin said. "We wouldn't be crushed. But everything is going to be fine," he quickly added.

Beth grabbed Sam's arm. "Wait just one hot second here. The daggers will protect you, right?"

"They should," Sam said softly, probably so Robert wouldn't hear. He'd stopped further back from the Veil. "But with Kate stopping time, it'll minimize the drain on me."

Beth frowned. "You better not die in there, okay? I am not going to be stuck consoling Robert regardless of his immense skill with the coffee maker. I still don't know how he gets the brew so smooth."

Sam and Kate laughed and, for a moment, the enormity of what they were preparing to do receded just a bit.

Kate tilted her head. "Your mushy bits are showing, Marshall. I see them behind your humor."

Her usual snappy retorts flooded into her mind, but standing in front of the otherworldly Veil with her two best friends robbed them of their fire.

"It's both your faults that I've grown even a little soft," Beth said, looking at Kate, too.

"I won't apologize," Kate said.

"Me neither," Sam added.

How was she going to leave them behind when she moved back to the States?

"Be careful, you two, okay?" Beth said, willing her emotions back under wraps. They needed to stay on task.

Sam nodded to Darrin "Okay, let's do this."

"I'll make the opening as wide as I can." Darrin's cuffs blazed again. The vines stretched slowly and the window became as big as a door. Darrin waved a hand in front of Morag's window. The air shivered and the sparkly membrane disappeared. "I'll handle the lock on the inside." Darrin gripped Sam's shoulder and they walked into the Veil.

Kate had the Tardis pressed close to her mouth. Beth couldn't hear what she was whispering. The wispy bits of ghostly essence in the air began moving in slow motion. The plastic baggie came next from Kate's pocket, but it had an etching of silver sparks around the edges.

She looked toward Beth, but her eyes were completely white. Kate wasn't seeing Beth, she was seeing the Time Stream. Her entire body had the same silver glow as the Time Baggie.

Kate should never doubt herself again. It was apparent she was the friggin' Oracle.

Beth felt a little like she had when they'd all stood in front of the Universe and saved Robert. The real shit was going down.

Robert moved up to stand beside Beth.

"You're too close to the Veil, Robert. It's not safe for . . ." She suddenly couldn't speak. Everything shuddered to a halt. Her mind went blank.

Then something gripped her arm, breaking her out of stasis, and spun her around.

It was a woman.

She recognized her face from the photos Evan had shown her.

It was her mom.

And she wasn't alone.

CHAPTER 23

SAM STEPPED THROUGH THE VEIL WITH DARRIN. THERE was a slight tugging against her skin, as if they'd broken through some seal.

Above them, the sky looked like a normal sky. If Sam didn't know any better, she'd think they were in the living world. A beautiful sunlit meadow stretched in front of her. The woman she'd seen through the Veil window, Morag, sat underneath a tree in the distance.

Sam breathed in the rich scent of the grass carried on a light breeze. Bees buzzed around some wildflowers. It was so peaceful here. She could imagine taking her shoes off and just laying in the grass with Robert. No Connor, no murders, no mayhem.

A wave of dizziness flowed through her, and she wobbled on her feet.

Darrin's hand steadied her. "Use your daggers. The Veil is pulling on the ghostly essence inside your body. Remember, once that's depleted, it will go after your life force."

Sam reached into her purse and pulled out the daggers,

removing them from their sheaths. The iron gleamed in the sunlight, almost sparkling.

She imagined the essence flowing from the daggers and into her, like how she had practiced with Darrin. There was a whisper at the edge of her hearing, but she couldn't make out the words, or if it was just the breeze. Then the blue essence flowed out from her daggers. It licked along her skin, covering her arms, legs, hands, everywhere. It sank into her.

Her vision cleared, and she felt focused. She sheathed the daggers and put them back in her purse. "How long do we have before the essence I just absorbed is depleted?"

"We should have long enough, but let's make this quick if we can." He touched her shoulder. "If I need to, I'll yank you out of here, and we'll forget Morag."

She nodded. "How do we approach her?"

"We tell her what we need, and then it's her choice if she wants to come or not." Darrin hesitated. "Hopefully, her love of Karnon should be enough."

"Have you spoken to her often?"

"Several times," Darrin admitted. "As I mentioned, the Wardens have utilized her for insight. She often sees things others have missed."

They had almost reached the ghost. Morag turned toward them, a book open on her lap. Her long brown hair was held back with a jeweled circlet on her head. The stones in the circlet flashed red and green when she moved. She looked like she had been around Sam's age when she died.

Her large eyes tipped up at the ends, and her gaze had

already narrowed upon Darrin. "What is it this time, Runner? Another war to avert?" The tone was frustration tinged with an undercurrent of eagerness.

"Of sorts," Darrin replied. "Morag, I would like you to meet Samantha Hamilton. Sam, this is Morag."

Morag put her book down on the blanket underneath her, next to a frosted glass of lemonade and a basket of strawberries.

She looked Sam over with a regal stare of a queen. "Ah yes, the necromancer who brought a ghost back to life. How did you manage that feat?"

"I'm not quite sure," Sam admitted. Darrin had said to be honest, and she sensed Morag might spot lies. No need to anger someone who they needed to come with them willingly.

Morag seemed to digest her words and mull them over. Sam tried not to fidget under her scrutiny.

"Who have the Wardens angered this time?" Morag asked, shifting her gaze from Sam to Darrin. The ghost got to her feet.

She was just a smidge shorter than Kate. Her dress was the same color green as the grass underneath them. Jewels were woven throughout the fabric in patterns that looked like butterflies. The jewels were the same red and green as the ones in her circlet, but here and there, what looked like amethysts and sapphires winked in the light as well.

She could have been the picture of a fairy princess if she didn't have that forbidding scowl on her face.

Darrin held up his hands. "We have a necromancer who is not following the Rules," he told her. "He's harmed the trees of Caleb's forest and others nearby."

Understanding dawned in Morag's light eyes. "Endangering Entwine."

Darrin nodded. "We fear he might try to breach the Threshold. If we can heal the trees, that will help in our efforts to stop him."

Morag hadn't looked at Darrin while he spoke. Instead her attention had been on Sam. "You are here because you need my Karnon's help with the trees." There was a brush of affection in her steely tone when she said the god's name.

"We do," Sam replied. "And we've offered to let him see you once again in exchange for his help."

Morag took a few steps closer to Sam. "And what do you offer me?"

"Surely seeing Karnon again is something you would like, too?" Darrin asked.

Morag tilted her head. "Of course, I want to see my love again. But you need my agreement to take me through the Veil. So again I ask, what do you offer me?"

Darrin looked unhappy but resigned. Morag knew she had all the leverage. They needed Karnon, so they needed her.

"What did you have in mind?" Darrin asked.

Morag smiled. The curve of her lips held a dark satisfaction. Sam's stomach dropped.

"Give us some privacy, Runner." Morag's command rang through the air. Darrin flashed Sam a quick apologetic look, but obeyed, retreating back toward the entrance to the Veil.

She looked at Sam. "I want a Bargain with you, necromancer. Not for unfinished business, but for a future favor."

Sam shook her head. "I can't make a Bargain for a future favor without knowing what it is."

"Yet you have promised a Bargain with Imogene without knowing her request."

Sam tried to hide her surprise, but knew she'd failed when Morag's smile grew wider. Sam didn't know how this ghost, sequestered behind the Veil, knew what was happening in the living world, but it didn't bode well.

"I agreed to the *potential* of a Bargain," Sam admitted. "But no terms were set and no Bargain was made." She took a step toward Morag. To show any weakness or hesitation now would be a mistake. "I follow the Rules."

Morag moved even closer, looking up at Sam from underneath thick, dark lashes. "You haven't always followed the rules," she whispered. "In fact, you've broken them for your parents."

Sam's breath caught in her throat. Somehow she'd discovered that Sam had seen her mother. Necromancers weren't allowed to see their family after they died. It was the so-called "price" for the gift of seeing the dead.

And if Morag told the Wardens, Sam didn't know what the consequences could be.

Sam met her gaze. "What do you want me to do?"

"It's a future favor, remember?"

Neither of them looked away, locked in a staring match.

"You can't ask me to kill anyone," Sam said. "That's Rule #11."

Morag's gaze flickered for just an instant, and then she

looked away. Sam had won the staring match. And her gut had been right. Whatever Morag wanted, it wasn't going to be good.

"Fine," Morag replied with a barbed tone.

They needed Karnon for the trees, which meant Sam had to agree. But she was still in charge of the ground rules of the Bargain. Morag wasn't in control when it came to that.

Sam's arms began to tingle, like ants were crawling on her skin. It was the energy she always felt when the Universe knew she was going to agree to a Bargain, even before she said the words.

"What is your need?" Sam asked.

"I require a future favor from you."

Sam nodded. "I will do my best to help you with this future favor. However, I will not harm anyone, living or dead, related to or in any way arising out of said future favor." She paused. "And I will follow the Rules as I see fit. Is this acceptable to your need?"

Rule #5: The ghost must accept the Bargain and seal it.

Morag frowned, but then nodded. "I see I might have underestimated you, necromancer."

Sam took one of her daggers from her purse and unsheathed it. Morag inhaled sharply, the sound harsh in the idyllic meadow.

The iron of the dagger glimmered as it had earlier, sparks running along its surface. It hummed in her hand, seeming to sense Morag.

The whispers she'd heard before were definitely not in the

breeze. They grew frenzied, but she couldn't make out what they were saying.

"Those who have underestimated me haven't fared well," Sam said. With her eyes still on Morag, she sheathed the dagger. She didn't need to see it to know exactly where it was. It was bright in her mind's eye, even with it just holding the barest amount of ghostly essence.

Morag stared at her for a long moment before finally giving Sam a short nod. "I agree to your terms."

Glowing embers of light floated down from the sky. They reminded Sam of glimmering feathers drifting on the wind or pieces of a bonfire blaze. Kate called them fireflies. Whatever they were, they were the Universe's acknowledgement of the Bargain.

She lifted her hands toward them. They hit her skin with a warm rush of light and energy, sinking deep within her—all the way to her bones.

For just a second, she felt something similar to when she'd brought Robert back to life—that connection with something greater—and to everything living and dead. Then it was gone.

The energy rose up through her throat, rushing toward her mouth. "The Bargain is struck."

Her voice, deepened with the power of the Bargain, rumbled through the air.

Morag walked over to her blanket and grabbed her book. Sam now saw the cover. *The Art of War.* "I'm looking forward to working with you, Sam. We're going to have some fun." The last part held danger in its light tone.

Sam watched Morag make her way toward Darrin and the entrance of the Veil.

She couldn't move for a moment. What had she just agreed to?

But there was no going back now. If she didn't keep the Bargain, Sam could die. The risk was worth it, though, if they could stop Connor, maybe even save him in the process.

And also save Entwine.

"HEY, HONEY." BETH'S MOM SMILED, AND SEVERAL TEARS rolled down her face. It was the same voice Beth had heard all along. If she hadn't channeled energy into Robert because of her mom's voice, she might have thought she had been hallucinating all this. But she couldn't deny this was real.

"Mom?" It felt weird to say that to a stranger, but it also felt right.

Her gaze swept over her mom, noting every detail. The brown hair, loose and flowing. The freckles across the bridge of her nose, just like in the picture. She was a bit shorter than Beth, but lean like her. Her brown eyes were filled with tears, making them look almost hazel in the light.

Her mom nodded. "Sorry if I scared you, popping in and out like I did, but I could only get through when I felt your walls weakening."

"I wasn't scared," Beth said. "Freaked out, yes."

Her mom smiled, and it was Beth's smile. Beth felt her eyes

fill, but quickly focused on the line of women standing behind her mom. They were all within arms-length from each other. Beth gave up counting after twenty-five.

They looked familiar.

She turned around and found Robert frozen. Kate was transparent, as if she were in between realms. Morag's window was still wide open.

"How am I seeing you without touching Sammy?" Beth asked. "And why do you have your own personal conga line?"

"You're seeing me right now because I'm pulling energy from the Veil." Her mom took a step forward, and all the other women did the same. "The women behind me are your ancestors."

"You're shitting me."

"I'm not."

Beth walked past her mom to the woman standing behind her. She had black hair shot with gray streaks and dark eyes, and she was close to six feet tall. "And who are you supposed to be?"

The woman scowled. "I'm your grandmother. And we don't have time for mindless chit-chat, girl." She looked at Beth's mom. "Tell her, Melody."

Melody took Beth's hand.

Beth yanked her hand back. "Wait a second. This can't be real. Robert was the only ghost who could touch others. Well, except for Ray but he was a poltergeist." She squinted at her mom. No feeling of danger or malice. "You don't seem like a poltergeist," Beth conceded, "but grandma over there looks like she could rip something apart with just her gaze."

Said grandma smiled and lifted her chin toward Beth. "Glad to see Harvey didn't douse your fire." She sobered. "I didn't think he'd go to the lengths he did. I'm sorry, child."

Anger flooded through Beth. "You saw what he did to me?" She got up close and personal in her grandma's face. Ole Granny didn't flinch or blink.

Damn she was tough.

Beth turned to her mom. "Evan told me you wanted Harvey to adopt me. You knew what he was. Why?"

Her mom shook her head slowly. "Harvey had always been kind to me. I thought he'd treat you the same." Anger seeped into her eyes. "But he hid his cruelty. He fooled me, and for that I'm sorry." Her hands clenched into fists. "If I could kill him for what he's done . . ."

Looks like she got her fire from her mom. She couldn't forgive her. Not yet. Not without knowing more. But she'd admitted her fault. It was a start in the right direction.

Beth pointed at the women behind her mom. "So you're telling me these are all my ancestors. Where are the guys?"

"The Seeker power is matriarchal, through the women of our family," Melody said. "And we're all connected, even after we pass on, because our power comes from the very first of us and continues to build with each generation."

"Wait, so I can do what I do because there's some Neanderthal Seeker way back?" Beth strained to see the rest of the woman, but they disappeared into the mist.

Melody smiled, bringing a glint of amber to her brown eyes.

"Something like that." She cupped Beth's cheek with her hand. "I've dreamt of this day. I just wish I had more time. I can only pull energy from the Veil for so long. We need to tell you about the necromancer."

"Do you know where he is? We need to stop him before he kills anyone else."

Melody shook her head. "Like Sam glows to ghosts, so does he, but he's masking his energy, shielding it somehow. All ghosts have been warned to stay away from him. It's *you* I'm worried about."

"All of TOP is in danger, not just me," Beth said.

"It's bigger than that."

Beth stared at the fear in Melody's face. A chill rubbed against her bones. "What could be worse than TOP being obliterated completely?"

"If he kills you, he'll destroy us all," her grandma gestured to the women behind her, "because we're connected. And the power he'll receive will finally be enough to do what he's wanted since the beginning."

Beth's breath caught in her lungs. They'd been trying to figure out what Connor's game plan was.

"What does he want?"

Melody's face hardened, all worry and fear gone. She lifted her hands and gestured around them. "He wants to breach Entwine."

"We already suspected that, but why?"

Her grandma sighed. "It doesn't matter *why*, girl. If he breaches the Threshold, Entwine will be destroyed."

"The Universe wouldn't allow it." With all that Balance crap being spouted by Sam, Caleb, and Robert, Beth couldn't imagine the Universe putting up with something that cataclysmic happening.

"The Universe needs the help of its agents," Melody replied. "Connor has already thinned their ranks. He'll kill them all if they try to stop him."

"I could give a rat's ass about the Wardens, but what about the ghosts waiting to go through the archways?" Beth asked. "And the ones already behind the Veil?"

Her grandma frowned. "He'll devour all ghostly essence inside Entwine, including the Veil. And I'm afraid that will only be the beginning."

"Can we stop him? Can TOP do it?" Beth looked into Melody's eyes but couldn't read her emotions.

"You can't go anywhere near him. It's too dangerous," Melody said. "We can't see the future, that's not our gift, but as long as Connor doesn't get his hands on you, the others might have a chance to stop him."

Beth wasn't going to back away from the fight, no matter what her ghostly mom said. But she didn't want to argue with her. "Can Sammy kill him with her daggers?"

"If she learns how to access their full power in time." Her grandma lowered her voice and leaned forward. "They were forged for Sam and for her alone."

What? Sam never told her that. Did Sam know?

Her grandma's face and body flickered, like a signal was being lost. And then her mom glitched, too. Beth suddenly had flashbacks to *Star Wars*, but instead of her ancestors begging her for help, they were warning her.

"Wait, I have more questions." Beth went to grab her mom's hands, but there was nothing solid for her to hold onto.

"Don't let him get near you, girl," her grandma warned. "If he does, all is lost. Screw your deal with RAVEN. Put an ocean between you and Connor."

The women in the line behind her mom and grandma grew transparent, and then blew away in wisps similar to the ghostly essence around them. Then Grandma disappeared.

"Don't go, Mom." Beth hugged her arms to herself, knowing she couldn't touch her.

"I'll be close by." Her mom reached a hand toward Beth, her fingers already disappearing into the white mist. "There is so much you don't understand about your gifts."

In another second, she was completely gone. A brush of warm wind rustled through Beth's hair.

Be careful, my darling girl.

Beth stared at where they'd been.

"Are you okay?" Kate asked from behind her.

Beth turned around and found Darrin and Sam staring at her along with Kate. In the distance, a safe distance, Robert stood with a ghost that had to be Morag. Everything must have gone okay with retrieving the incentive for Karnon, but Sam didn't look too happy.

"Nope, not okay." Beth wiped her face with the back of her hand. "I just saw my mom."

Darrin's cuffs flashed. He looked at Sam. "We need to go

now. The Wardens have been alerted. Power was diverted from the Veil."

Beth followed them back to the door and into the halls of Entwine, her mind reeling with what her ancestors had told her. If she stayed out of the fight, she knew they would lose. They were stronger together. Kate and Sammy had pounded that into her head.

But if Beth ended up getting caught by Connor, she'd be responsible for Entwine being destroyed.

She wasn't sure what she was going to do.

CHAPTER 24

BETH GRABBED THE POT FROM THE COFFEE MAKER. SHE needed to tell Kate and Sam about what her mother had shared with her last night—about why it would be "game over" if Connor killed her and absorbed her ghost.

But she didn't want to deal with their reactions. She could already hear their protests.

Coffee first.

She filled up the insulated tumbler that had her TV show's emblem on it—a searchlight—and her name emblazoned in red lettering. She turned to Kate, who was packing up some muffins in the kitchen. "I could have gotten you the swag for free, you know." She held up the tumbler.

Kate smiled. "I like to support my friends."

"Which is why she has several sets of my books and this," Sam added, holding out her own tumbler with a picture of her last romance novel cover. The model did look a lot like Robert. "Can I get some, too?"

Beth took the tumbler from Sam and filled it up. The warm

scent of pumpkin spice wafted in the air.

"Oh, is there anything at Yasmin's shop you need?" Sam asked. "Robert and I are going to talk to her to see if she's had any visions that could help with Connor."

Kate nodded. "Get me some red candles for the holders I recovered from the attic." She handed Sam a baggie filled with mini chocolate chip muffins. "And good idea about Yasmin. She always sees the immediate practical stuff, and something might be connected to Connor."

"Still no visions, Red?" Beth asked.

Kate frowned. "No. You'd think I would have something. It's not like every day you have a necromancer running around killing people."

"Thank heavens," Sam said quietly.

Kate shot her a look. "You know what I mean. This is epic level business."

Time to get this over with. "Speaking of epic level business," Beth said, "there's something I need to tell you before we go off to save the trees. And while the girls are outside playing."

Sam looked serious. "And I need to tell you about what happened when I met Morag."

Kate looked between the two of them. "I'm not going to like what either of you are going to say, am I?"

Both Sam and Beth said "no" at the same time.

"Oh, Lord." Kate went over to her brewing tea. "I'm glad I decided on the extra strong Scottish Breakfast this morning. Who wants to go first?"

Once they found out, they'd try to bench her, but Beth was

already hiding her involvement with RAVEN, and that had weighed on her heavily. This was something she owed them, because if Connor did manage to kill her, they were all royally screwed.

They deserved to know the stakes.

She raised her hand. "I'll go."

Kate brought her tea and the plate of muffins over to the table, and they sat down.

"Remember how I told you last night that there are generations of Marshall women attached to me?" Beth began. Sam and Kate nodded. "Because of that attachment, it means I'll pack an extra large helping of ghostly essence for Connor."

The color drained from Sam's face. "And just how many relatives did you say you had attached to you?"

Beth shrugged. "No idea. I lost count at twenty-five."

Kate frowned. "So you're saying that if he kills you and your ghost, like he did with the others, he'd get everyone in your family line?"

"Yup, everyone attached to me."

Kate leaned back in her chair. "Crap."

Beth took a mini muffin and popped it in her mouth, chewing slowly. She wasn't sure who would say it first, who would tell her she needed to leave, get on a plane, get as far away as she could from Rosebridge and Connor.

Her money was on Kate. She had never stopped caring about Beth, even after some of the shit she had pulled.

"So we'll need to be extra careful, then," Sam finally said. "We should make sure someone is with you at all times, whether it's me, Kate, Logan, Robert, or Michael. Connor might be a necromancer, but he's still a person, just like me, and should be able to be wounded." She gave Beth a serious look. "What I mean is, if he's trying to kill you, one of us can attack him while he's focused on you."

Beth wasn't surprised that Sam didn't get all warm and fuzzy with worry, but there was a ruthless quality to her reasoning she hadn't expected. Maybe she was rubbing off on Sam?

Kate put down her mug. "I agree with Sam. We'll fill everyone in on what's at stake so they know."

Beth shook her head at Kate. "You're not going to knock me out and smuggle me out of the country for my own good?"

Kate laughed. "As if that would work. You'd just be back here trying to help. You forget, I know you, Beth Marshall— *really* know you."

"And you've never been one to back away from a fight," Sam added, smiling. "I know you, too, very well."

All the ammunition she'd prepared to fight the battle fell away. She looked at each of them. They'd all changed since she arrived in Scotland a short while ago. They'd grown. And she realized she'd underestimated both of them in her expectations.

They did know her like no one else really did, because they all had seen each other at their most vulnerable during a time when nothing could be hidden. She still remembered the night they did their Blood Sister Ritual, when they were just scared kids proclaiming to the Universe that they'd always be family.

Somewhere along the way, they'd stopped counting on each other, but things were shifting. She'd felt it for some time now.

Beth rubbed the scar on her thumb from that night of the ritual. "I'm bummed you two are so understanding about this. I was kinda hoping for a fight."

"You'll have your fight when we face Connor together," Sam said, the smile gone from her face. "I have a feeling it's going to take all of us to stop him, even if the dampening stone works to deplete his power."

Beth took both their hands. "We're the Triumverate of Pain in the Ass. We don't give up."

They both laughed, which is what she'd hoped for. Sammy was the one who had always rallied them with her unshakable belief they would triumph, even as kids. Doubt was not allowed.

"So what's your bad news?" Beth asked Sam. She sat back in her chair and took another sip of coffee.

Sam wrapped her hands around her tumbler. "I had to agree to a future favor to get Morag to come with me."

Beth knew both Caleb and Darrin had said that Morag was formidable, so she wasn't surprised she'd want something. "What kind of favor?"

"No clue, but I laid out the ground rules."

Kate nodded. "Good. Though I bet she'll worm her way around those."

"She'll definitely try," Sam said. "I have no doubt of that." She shook her head slowly. "I couldn't get a good read on her."

"Did she pass your ghostly lie detector test?" Beth asked.

"She did, but then again, she didn't tell me much that revealed anything of value." Sam looked at them. "I'm just worried she'll ask me to do something awful." Her words were soft.

Sam wasn't like Beth, comfortable in the gray areas of life when it came to choices. And Beth didn't want to see her change. Not in that way.

Beth would bear the soul damage for all of them if she could.

Another brick trembled and fell from her wall.

"When she does ask you," Beth said, "we'll be there to help you through it."

Kate shot her a surprised look. "Oh *we* will, will we? Are you sticking around after all?"

Beth smiled. "I'm a Zoom call away, and I have my own private jet, so I can be here in a jiffy if you need me."

Sam smiled back at her, the haunted look gone from her eyes. "Thanks, Beth."

"This feels a bit like the old times," Kate said, looking at both of them. "When we were kids."

It did.

And even though it still scared Beth, because she might lose this again, this feeling, she found she might just want to fight for it this time.

BETH'S BREATH PLUMED IN THE FRIGID MORNING AIR. THEY'D gathered where Alison had been murdered, where the first trees had lost their voice. She hoped the deal with Karnon had been worth what Sam had promised to Morag.

She looked at the silenced trees. Their bark had grayed, almost losing all its color. They hadn't had many leaves to begin with, but now they were just towering skeletons against the blue sky, limbs bare and frail.

Beth hoped they weren't too late.

Karnon and Vivian stood by the trees, along with Emily and Patty. Kate had been right that Karnon was gorgeous, though he didn't look extra-large like she had described him. He just seemed like a tall man, albeit with incredible antlers. They must kill his back.

"Where's Morag?" Beth whispered to Kate, who stood beside her.

With her eggplant-colored wool coat, Kate's hair looked even more red than usual. She pointed to one of the healthy trees next to the silenced ones. "You know Caleb always likes to make an entrance."

As if on cue, Caleb walked out from behind the tree with Morag.

She was still in that brilliant green dress encrusted with jewels, but she'd bound her brown hair in a long braid.

Kate began walking over toward them and Beth followed.

"Morag has been delivered to you, as promised," Caleb announced, giving Karnon a deep bow and a flourish of hands.

Karnon froze for a moment, his eyes only on Morag. "And in exchange, I will heal the silenced trees."

There was a soft pop of sound. Beth had the feeling some clerk of Entwine was recording the agreement.

"My love," Morag said, holding her hand out toward

Karnon. Her tone was gentle.

Karnon immediately rushed to her side, taking her hand, and holding it against his cheek. "My love," he echoed back. His words were heavy, yet bursting with joy at the same time.

"How is she touching him?" Beth asked in a whisper. "She's a ghost."

Kate tilted her head toward Karnon. "He's a god, like Caleb, so they can control who can touch them or who they can touch—ghost or not."

Based on the heat in their eyes, Beth surmised there would be a lot of touching between them tonight.

"When I am done here," Karnon said to Morag, "we will retreat to my lands until the necromancer retrieves you."

Morag ran her fingers along his antlers, and Karnon shuddered. "I look forward to our reunion. We have much to share." Her gaze moved from Karnon and lit upon Kate's daughters. "And who are these two beauties?"

"These are my daughters, Emily and Patty," Kate said. She moved in close. Beth knew she'd be ready to scoop up the girls to safety if Morag so much as looked at them funny.

Vivian moved to stand with Kate, flanking the girls. "And they are *all* under my protection." The grass blackened in a semi-circle in front of Vivian and Kate.

If Kate had any lingering doubts about Vivian's intentions when it came to the girls, they should be put to rest right then and there. Beth saw Morag get the message, as well. A hint of respect glinted in the ghost's eyes.

"Hi, Miss Morag," Patty said, and then gave her a bow so

low, Beth was surprised she didn't fall over. "Mr. Karnon has told us all about you."

Emily glanced at the blackened grass, and then gave Morag a considered look. "The crows say you're not a very nice person."

A flash of something dark slid across Morag's face. She glared at the crows in the nearby trees. They cawed loudly and took flight in a flurry of feathers. Vivian took a step toward her and the semi-circle of blackness widened. The tension in the clearing was palpable, like a trap about to be sprung.

Kate glanced at Beth and raised her eyebrows. Beth would answer her plea, though typically she wasn't the one to diffuse situations. She usually lit the match.

"The crows are right, Emily," Beth said, walking slowly over to the girls. "What they say is true of all grown-ups. We're rarely all good or all bad. Or all nice or all mean. We've all made decisions we might regret."

"I know I have made mistakes in the past," Karnon said, his eyes on Morag. His buttery voice seemed to warm the very air. "Ones which I would rectify if I could."

Light returned to Morag's face. She smiled at Karnon and lifted her chin toward Beth. "As have I."

The tension level suddenly dropped from a fifteen to a one.

Caleb and Vivian both looked surprised by Morag's admission. Vivian recovered first. She glanced at Kate and Beth. "If you can step back, please. The trees are sensitive, and we don't want to overwhelm them when they come back." She flicked a look at Morag. "And you, as well."

Morag didn't argue. She just turned to Karnon and though

neither of them said anything, Beth felt some energy buzz between them in the air. With a satisfied smile, Morag walked over to a tree stump in the distance, and she sat down.

Kate gave the girls a hug, and Beth high-fived them. Then they moved further away as Vivian instructed.

Beth whispered to Kate. "You're welcome."

Kate grinned at her. "Look at you, the peacemaker. Sam isn't going to believe it."

Beth frowned at her but couldn't hold it against Kate's glee. "Do you know how all of this is going to work?"

"Emily told me that Patty will help find the trees' spirits, their souls," Kate said. "Then Vivian and Caleb will connect with them. Karnon will do his thing, which I'm not sure what that is, and then Emily will remind them where they belong."

"I'm glad Caleb has protections set up against Connor," Beth said, "just in case he tried to show up today."

She looked around the forest, listening to the soft shooshing of the wind in the trees, the leaves, and the grass. The cool air felt clean and fresh in her lungs.

"I've got to admit," Beth said, "I'm going to miss this place. And Logan, and Robert, and you, and Sam. Hell, I'll even miss Vivian, who still gives me the heebie-jeebies."

"Even Michael?" Kate asked with mischief in her voice.

Beth smiled. "Even him."

"You can stay at the B&B as long as you like." Kate kept her gaze on Emily and Patty. "After you film the Scottish episodes, there's London and France and lots of other places that aren't too far away. And Rosebridge can be your home base."

"Looking out for my business interests, are you?"

"You know exactly what I'm looking out for—our friendship. I just tried to cover it up enough so that you could justify staying." Kate gave her a side look.

"I can't stay."

They stood in silence for a bit. Only the sound of the girls' chatter and Caleb's patient voice broke the morning air.

"Why?" Kate asked.

"I just can't. Let it alone, Red."

"No." Kate turned to her, and Beth had never seen her more serious. She lowered her voice. "We might die facing Connor. The time for petty bullshit has past. I've even made legal arrangements for Aggie and Stu to have custody of the girls if something happens to me."

Fear seized Beth's heart. "You're not going to die, Kate. I won't let that happen."

Kate shook her head. "No one can promise that. Now why can't you stay? Tell me the real reason."

Beth stared at her for a few moments. Kate was right. None of them might come out of this alive.

"As long as Harvey and Gloria are around, everyone around me is in danger," Beth said finally. "I had an exit strategy all worked out, which would have kept everyone safe. But then they got out of prison early. If I stay here, they could get more interested in you, Sam, Robert, or even all of Rosebridge."

"You're worried about Rosebridge?"

Beth shrugged. "What can I say? It's grown on me. There are a lot of innocent people who live here, and I wouldn't sic

Harvey and Gloria on them. Not when I can easily leave."

Kate smiled. "I knew there'd been a shift."

"What shift?"

"You're opening up, admitting you care about someone other than yourself."

Beth bristled. "I've told you before that I love you and the girls."

"But that's safe, that's easy," Kate said. "You know I'll never stop loving you and neither will the girls. We're not going to hurt you."

"You're not making sense." Beth looked over at the girls. They were listening to Vivian's instructions intently.

"Admit you care about Robert, Logan, Sam, Fi, Michael . . ." Kate paused. "Should I go on?"

Beth looked back at her. "I just told you that I wanted to protect them. Isn't that enough?" She glanced at her tracker. "Look, I promised to meet up with Michael about the DNA results. I should go."

A semi-truth. He hadn't told her he had the results yet, but it would help her escape from Kate's prodding.

Beth turned to leave but Kate grabbed her arm.

"Tell me one thing before you go," Kate said.

Beth turned back around slowly. "What?"

"If you *never* admit you care for someone," Kate said, "will it hurt *any less* if something happens to them, or will it hurt *more*?"

Beth felt transfixed by the love in Kate's eyes. Kate had been right. It was a safe bet to love her, but to tell someone else—to tell them that she really cared without wrapping it up in a joke?

I've got you, my girl.

Her mom's voice was a soothing balm in her ear. Beth couldn't feel her arms, but she felt her love just the same.

She closed her eyes, basking in that feeling.

You're safe.

Images flooded her mind. Aggie standing up to Harvey, Fi hugging her after knife practice, and Ethyl sharing a croissant with Beth after the bakery closed and telling her about her breast cancer returning.

And Sam. Too many memories, good and bad. But just like with Kate, Beth would die for her. For any of them. No hesitation.

And . . . and the way Michael had felt in her arms, trembling after sharing what he'd gone through as a child. She was too afraid to think about how she might really feel about him.

But they'd all made their way through the cracks in her wall—the cracks Kate had started all those years ago.

The entire row of top bricks leapt from Beth's wall, the motion bringing with it a lightness, even a sense of freedom.

The wall still remained, but she could breathe, just a little.

"You made your point," Beth grumbled, opening her eyes. "And my mom piped in, too."

Kate grabbed her in a hug, and Beth hugged her back. "I'll get that wall down inside you," Kate said into her shoulder. "I know it."

Beth pulled back. "You only get one brick out of my wall per month, Red. Them's the rules. Don't be trying for more."

She wasn't about to tell Kate she'd gotten a whole row this time.

"One brick a day."

"One a week."

"Done."

"Shit." Beth shook her head. "How the hell did I get into a bargaining match over my bricks? You're a pain in my ass."

"We've already established that I'm a much-needed pain in your ass." Kate hit her arm. "But you're right, Harvey and Gloria are psycho scary. Once this necromancer business is handled, we'll put our heads together on a solution."

"*Now*, Patty," Vivian said, drawing Beth's attention back to the trees. Patty put her arms around one of the injured trees. Vivian joined her by the tree. She held out her hands, palms up. Her eyes began to glow, and the tree limbs shuddered.

"I have you," Vivian said, her voice smooth and calm. "Do not worry. You are safe."

Her words echoed what Beth had heard from her mom. Just like her, the trees needed to be reassured.

Karnon stepped closer to Vivian. His antlers began to glow, the gold and bronze flowing together as if they had melted into liquid. He placed a hand against the tree. "Take of my essence," Karnon intoned. "Forget not what you witnessed, but let it make you stronger. Bone to branch, skin to bark, blood to sap. Breathe in what I give freely and be restored."

The blackness at the tip of one of his antlers spread down further, and a wash of pain flooded his face. "Call them, Caleb," Karnon said softly.

Caleb touched one of the branches. "Come back to us my

friends, my family. Fill the earth and sky with your beauty and wisdom." He looked at Emily and nodded.

Emily lifted her hands up to the sky and began a song filled with caws, hoots, and something that reminded Beth of the sound of wind rushing through feathers.

Emily yanked off her hat, letting her red hair be free, looking every bit like a wild thing of the forest.

The owls and crows joined in her song. The sunlight blazed bright, almost blinding.

Then the light dissolved back to a normal glow.

Beth took off her sunglasses, not believing her eyes. The tree's bark was rich brown again. Fresh leaves flooded its limbs. The crows and owls took flight, their cries sounding joyful in the bright sunshine.

The girls waved at them, and Kate gave them a big thumbs up. They started on the next tree, but then Patty froze in mid-hug, arms wrapped around the trunk.

Tears streaked her face. "They're calling for help. The trees are calling."

Vivian touched her hand, and all life appeared to drain from the forest goddess' face. "The Necromancer has struck again."

"Where?" Beth demanded.

Vivian met her gaze. "The old cemetery in Rosebridge, at the edge of the forest."

"You stay here, Red," Beth said. "Finish helping the trees. I'll call Logan and Sam."

"But you shouldn't go anywhere alone," Kate protested. "If Connor catches you . . ."

Beth shook her head. "We don't have a choice. We can't leave any of the trees in danger."

Kate looked like she wanted to argue, but in the end she nodded. "Go. Be careful."

Beth hugged her quickly, and then turned to run back to the B&B.

She prayed they wouldn't be too late.

CHAPTER 25

BETH STOPPED RUNNING WHEN SHE REACHED THE GARDEN outside the B&B. The fragrance of Kate's roses filled her lungs.

She called Logan, who picked up immediately.

"There's been another attack," she said, a little out of breath. At least all her training at RAVEN had kept her cardio up.

"Where?"

"The old cemetery in Rosebridge."

"Are they still alive?"

"We don't know." She paused. "The trees are calling for help."

"On my way."

"We'll meet you there."

She texted Michael. Sam was next.

Then the hairs on her arms rose. She was being watched.

Beth looked around, and then finally spotted Harvey by the iron trellis near the shed.

She let out a sigh of relief, not because she was happy to see

Harvey, but at least it wasn't Connor. She thought seriously about sprinting around the side to avoid him, but he'd seen her, and she didn't want to overtly piss him off, not when he could still take things to Defcon One.

Beth sauntered over to him, not sure how much he'd heard of her phone call to Logan. If she acted impatient, he'd dig, so she had to play it cool. She didn't want him knowing about a rogue necromancer on the prowl. He'd only try to figure a way to leverage Connor for his own means, and that was a combination she didn't want to see happen.

"What are you doing here?" she asked, once she was in range. "My first payment already went through."

The breeze wafted through his hair. "It did, thank you." He smiled, but it was like a paper mask over the ugliness that she knew was underneath. "I was just concerned about the serial killer I've been hearing so much of around town." His voice lowered. "How the killer has been targeting people with abilities, which made me worry about you."

Holy crap. How did he know that? It's not like a hint of any connection had been in the papers.

Beth crossed her arms. "I know you're only concerned with my well-being because it would affect future blackmail payments."

Harvey tried to look crushed but didn't manage it. He wasn't as good on mimicking the deeper emotions. "It hurts me you would think that," he said. "We might not be close any longer, but I'm still your father."

She dropped her arms and sighed. "Look, I don't have time

to argue over the tatters of what's left of our relationship. I'm late for an appointment." She filled her face with the usual animosity and frustration Harvey was used to. It could be dangerous to let him know she knew he might not be her real father. "Was there anything else?"

Harvey studied her for a moment. "Only that I've discovered there is an organization right outside of Rosebridge who recruits people with special gifts. It's called RAVEN."

There was no way she was going to hide her flinch, so she gave into it. "How in hell do you know about them?"

He smiled and this time it made his eyes gleam, reminding her of a Disney villain hatching a plan. "I have my ways, daughter." Smooth voice. That was never good.

Beth needed to join Logan and the others. The quickest way out was to push this to a head.

Harvey enjoyed riling her up, so she kept her voice calm and bored. "Let me guess, once you found out who they were, you tried to sell me to them for a tidy profit."

He barely frowned but she caught it. "I would never *sell* you, Tiffany. I merely offered your services for a sizable finder's fee—and a hefty consultant's salary for you, of course."

Beth tilted her head. "So why am I not in their custody . . . I mean, their *employ*?"

"They weren't interested." He shook his head. "I was quite shocked. It's not like you hide your abilities with your TV show. They had the proof they needed that your gifts were real." He gazed at her intently. "There must be another reason."

If she tried to lie, he might get a whiff of it and keep digging.

Best to give him some truth. "Sam, Kate, and I went up against RAVEN a little while ago," she said. "We went into their facility and rescued some people being held against their will. We know about them, warts and all, and have made provisions if we suddenly disappear."

Approval warmed Harvey's face. "Smart move. I see you picked up a few tricks from me after all."

"Just a few." Beth walked past him, knowing he would follow . . . and he did. She didn't worry about giving him her back any longer. If he tried anything, she'd cut him down.

"Could you give me a lift into town?" he asked. "At least if that's where you're headed."

"I'm not giving you a lift anywhere." She kept walking around the side of the B&B to where her car was parked.

"I suppose I could wait until Kate and the girls come back. I didn't really get a chance to meet her daughters."

Beth reached her car and then turned around. "I'll take you into town." She moved closer until they were within inches of each other. "But I'll warn you, as you so kindly warned me, if anything happens to those girls, it won't be me you need to worry about. Kate's boyfriend is the Detective Chief Constable here. The girls aren't the low-hanging fruit you're so fond of."

She saw the thoughts racing behind his eyes and knew he was calculating the odds. She doubted he'd try something against the girls—he'd been too obvious with his taunts—but it was apparent they'd been a potential part of one of his schemes.

Hopefully Logan would be enough of a deterrent. She didn't want to give away just how powerful they were becoming as

TOP. RAVEN might have turned Harvey down, but there could be other interested parties, especially if word of the Triumvirate got out.

Harvey walked over to the passenger side of Beth's car. He placed a well-manicured hand on the hood. "Your warning is unnecessary. I would never harm those girls. You always did have an overactive imagination."

She got into the car. "When are you headed back to the States?" The engine roared to life, and she headed down the long driveway to the road.

"Not for a bit," he replied. "There could be more opportunities for me to explore here." He laughed, the sound rough against her skin. It was the same laugh she'd heard before the torture would begin in their root cellar.

Beth clenched the steering wheel more tightly. She'd been right about Harvey scoping other angles with RAVEN, but what else could he be after?

SAM PULLED UP OUTSIDE THE CEMETERY WITH ROBERT. Logan was still five minutes behind them with paramedics. There had been an accident on the main road, and he'd just gotten around it, according to his text.

They got out of her car, and Sam looked at Robert. "Go."

He took off his ring and disappeared. She knew he could get to the victim the fastest.

If they were still alive, Robert was their best chance. And she could follow his essence wherever he went.

Sam moved her purse around to her back and took off at a run toward the cemetery entrance. The signature of Robert's essence guided her—a thin blue trail with flecks of gold on the edges. She'd discovered all ghostly essence was a blue color to her, but each ghost added something different, something that was specific to them.

Wait. There was another trail leading in the opposite direction. This one was blood red with bits of what looked like ash swirling around it.

The small of her back burned where her purse rested against her jacket. She skidded to a halt and opened her bag. Bright blue light blazed from within. The daggers were glowing around their hilts, but starting to burn bright, as well, was the Moldavite tree Beth had given her. Its green glow wove around the blue. It was definitely drawn to the residual essence the daggers still held, but it didn't appear to be altering the glow or affecting it.

She still didn't know what the Moldavite did, but it was obvious from her daggers that there was something dangerous at the end of that red trail.

Connor.

She looked to her left. Even though she couldn't see Robert, she knew he'd be with the victim. If they were still alive, he'd protect them. If they were dead, then Sam's presence wouldn't matter anyway. Connor would have obliterated their ghostly essence already.

Could that be the ash swirling within the red? The remnants

of ghosts? Her stomach clenched. He had to be stopped.

She grabbed the daggers out of their sheaths and set off to the right, following the red trail to Connor.

Sam didn't dare run, for it would make too much noise, though he might already know she was coming.

She kept low, moving around the gravestones, being careful to not step on any graves. The ghosts hated that.

Hey, daggers. I might need your help again.

Her inner plea met with silence.

She slipped around a rusted bench.

I don't know how we're supposed to work together. I'll be facing a dangerous necromancer in about a minute. If you don't want me to die, I need your help.

The daggers' light flickered. Someone was listening at least.

The red trail grew wider, thicker. She was getting close. A fog swirled around her, chilling the sweat on her skin. Had Connor somehow conjured this up?

Sam inched around the walls of a large crypt, the stone chipped and worn, though the dragons carved into the top looked untouched.

"I'm glad you found me, Sam."

Her heart nearly burst from her chest. She whirled around, daggers out, and found Connor leaning against one of the nearby headstones.

The fog cleared slightly, as if disturbed by the presence of the two necromancers.

He looked like how Robert described him: slim, sandy brown hair, barely out of his teens. She couldn't see the color of his eyes because they were tearing. In fact, tears were running down his face.

And then she realized she'd seen him at Yasmin's shop. Yasmin had given him a reading.

It wouldn't have been a coincidence, him being at her shop. She prayed to the Universe that Yasmin was okay.

He coughed into the sleeve of his jacket.

"What did you do to Yasmin?"

"She's fine." He coughed again, and then fished a tissue out of his pocket to wipe his eyes. "Your friend hit me with some pepper spray."

Relief flooded through her. "So you failed then?"

Connor gave her a watery smile. "It wasn't my intent to kill her. I merely drained but a fraction of her life force to knock her out. I knew the trees would send a message." He gave her an approving look. "You found a way to heal them. I'm impressed."

The sound of a twig breaking cut through the air. Sam flinched and turned toward the noise.

Two men emerged from the retreating fog. They were both in black and heavily armed with guns, but they didn't have them drawn.

They didn't look like RAVEN.

Connor motioned for them to fall back. "Don't mind my bodyguards. They'll make sure we aren't bothered by anyone living. And I've masked our necromancer signature energy, so the Wardens won't find us either."

His bodyguards nodded and disappeared back into the mist.

The heat from the Moldavite in her purse still warmed her back. Beth said it was something used to disrupt energy. Maybe it was already burning holes in whatever masking Connor had done, which is why it began to glow as soon as she entered the cemetery.

Sam moved to the right slightly, so the crypt wall was at her back. She'd only seen two men, but that didn't mean he didn't have more lurking about.

"What are you talking about, our necromancer signature energy?"

"You don't know how to block your energy signature yet?" Connor asked. "I can teach you. That way the Wardens can't track you and ghosts can't see your glow." He smiled. "There is so much I can tell you, so much you don't know."

She desperately wanted the answers he might be able to give, but that could come later, after he was locked up.

"Why did you want me here, Connor? To kill me?" She crouched slightly, grounding herself. Her daggers had stopped glowing. Probably not a good sign.

Connor eyed them. "I was wondering what those were."

"Something I hope I don't have to use." Her words were low in her throat. "Now, why do you want me here?"

He met her gaze. "I didn't mean to kill Allie. I only wanted to talk to her."

Her lie detector was green. Connor had enough ghostly essence within him that it should be reliable still.

"Her father is a Warden," Connor continued. "I'd hoped she could convince him to intervene on my behalf."

"To call off the Warden hit squad hunting you?" And any necromancers, per Sloane.

Connor shook his head and wiped his eyes again. They were less red now, and Sam could see that one of his eyes was blue, the other brown. Again as Robert described. He must have masked his appearance at Yasmin's shop.

"Not exactly. I was just there to talk, but Allie had heard what I was doing to ghosts and overreacted." He looked up at the sky. The sun was trying to break through the fog. "She was going to summon the Wardens, and I couldn't allow that. I just meant to silence her, not kill her."

"And John in the RAVEN forest? Another accident?"

A flash of anger raced across Connor's face, suddenly making him look much older and much more dangerous. "He saw me with Alison and followed me." Connor laughed, but it held an edge of the anger she had seen on his face. "He thought he could take me out, bring me to justice. He was a fool."

John had died trying to do the right thing. It made his death even worse for her to bear.

Her hands were sweaty, but she couldn't wipe them without putting down a dagger. They might not want to share any magic blasts of essence with her, but they were still sharp and still weapons.

"And destroying ghosts? That can't be an accident or self-defense," Sam said. "Let me guess, you were putting them out of their eternal misery."

She took a step closer. He might be able to hurt her from a distance, but she needed to get in close to use her daggers.

Hopefully she wouldn't have to, but her gut was telling her otherwise.

Connor looked down at his hands. "You don't understand how alike we are, Sam. You've felt the rush of the Brigh, the ghostly essence. I know you have."

She had. When all the ghosts who had owed her for their Bargains over the years had paid up, it was indescribable. She'd almost forgotten about saving Robert, she got so caught up in the rush.

Connor didn't seem bothered by her lack of response. "At first, I did it to help the ghosts who came to me for release." Connor lifted his head and gazed at Sam. "Some didn't want to move on, and they couldn't continue to pay the tariffs charged by the Wardens for space in Entwine."

Tariffs?

"You said at first?"

A spark of hunger gleamed in his eyes. "Ghosts have already had a chance at life. It wasn't like I was truly killing them. They're not really alive. And Brigh is a taste of immortality, of power."

He brought some red essence to his fingertips, and the hunger in his eyes grew to something that looked a lot like obsession.

She'd felt the pull of essence even after that night of saving Robert, but hadn't succumbed like Connor did.

"You're hooked on it, aren't you?"

He smiled. "It's better than any drug, and it isn't harmful. I heal almost instantly." He took a step toward her. "And there's an endless supply." His words were breathy.

Yup, he was hooked.

"Power of any kind is not worth destroying souls." Sam didn't keep the snarl out of her voice.

He shrugged. "Sometimes the ends truly do justify the means."

A breeze brushed Sam's hair against her cheeks. "Always spoken by someone doing something unforgivable. Tell me, have you killed someone, someone alive, with the intent of their death?"

After a long moment, he nodded. "But I didn't kill Yasmin, even though I could have. And I left Imogene intact, for you."

Sam shook her head. "We're not keeping score on your murders, Connor. Leaving a few alive doesn't outweigh all the destruction you've caused."

Connor shook his head. "You see everything so black and white, don't you? No wonder why you've never given in and embraced the Brigh within you."

"When it comes to murder, I do see things in black and white." She took another step closer. Almost there. "But I'm willing to hear the rest of your story, argue for a lighter sentence."

He laughed, but it had a dark cutting quality on the edges, like swirling razor blades. "Lighter sentence? The only outcome for me, according to the Wardens, is death. In fact, didn't they send you on a mission to do just that?"

"I refused," she said, and he looked pleased.

"I knew you'd see through the Wardens' plans."

She raised an eyebrow. "What are you talking about?"

"We're both a danger to the Wardens, Sam. Once they're done with me, they'll come for you. You can hold onto ghostly essence, and you're becoming even more powerful now that you formed the Triumvirate. It's only a matter of time before their fear wins out." He took a step forward. "That's why I reached out to you. Together, we'd be unstoppable." His voice brimmed with conviction.

Could the Wardens turn on her, too? He believed what he was saying, if her lie detector was truly accurate with him.

"We'd be unstoppable at what?" Sam asked. "Why are you doing all this?"

Connor looked down for a moment and took a deep breath. "I want to see my parents." His words were small, but they hit Sam immediately, as if he'd shouted them. "I need to say good-bye. To explain. To make them understand. I didn't mean for things to happen the way they did."

As necromancers, they were prevented from seeing loved ones who'd passed on.

Though she'd managed to see her mom just once, she still hadn't been able to reach her father. She was suddenly back in the burning car, hearing him urge her to get out and save herself. She shook her head hard, dispelling the image. Now wasn't the time to lose focus.

Connor clenched his fists. "They wouldn't be able to deny us if we joined forces. We could see our parents again, Sam. Don't you want that, too?"

The pain in his voice was the same pain she'd felt for years after her parents had died. Her throat tightened, holding in tears.

"I get it. And you're right," she finally replied. "Not being able to see our parents is unfair, unjust, and unthinkable. If you give yourself up, we can talk to the Wardens together. See if there is any way around the Rules."

His face softened. "They won't listen to words, Sam. You know that. You've seen what the Universe is capable of when it wants its way."

She wasn't sure what he was alluding to, but it was becoming clear she wasn't going to convince him to give himself up.

"I can't let you leave here, Connor." She gripped her daggers more tightly.

"You won't win if you go against me." He lifted his hands, and where Sam's had sparked with ghostly essence, his burned so bright, she had to squint against the red glare. "Those daggers are no match against me, no weapon is." He looked disappointed in her.

"I disagree." Sam took that final step closer. "I'm part of the Triumvirate of Pluthar. You're right that my abilities have grown. And *these* are no ordinary daggers."

Anytime now, daggers.

She didn't like bluffing, but to show weakness could embolden him to attack.

There was no answer from the daggers, but her purse grew even hotter against the small of her back. Was the Moldavite tree doing something?

The air grew heavy. A ghost was materializing.

Connor's face held disbelief. "How did a ghost find us? I'm masking our signatures." He scanned the area quickly, and then his eyes settled on Sam. "Your bag is glowing green."

"Is it?" She didn't turn to look, keeping her gaze on Connor.

"I don't know what you've done, Sam, but I can't take any chances." Connor lifted his hands. They still blazed with red essence. "I can't let the ghost tell the Wardens where I am."

Sam reached out with her senses. There, by the statue of Gabriel. The ghost would materialize in a few moments.

And they'd have no chance against Connor.

She lunged at him, slicing into his right shoulder and forearm with her daggers. They were only shallow cuts. She wanted to distract him, not seriously injure him. He grabbed one of her wrists. It felt like her flesh burned. She kneed him in the groin. Connor grunted, bending over and releasing her.

"Run!" Sam shouted at the ghost. She could just see the shape in her periphery.

Where he'd gripped her, the red essence still clung to her skin, the burning fading into numbness every place it touched.

Fear rushed through her, and she realized it came from Connor's red essence. It had to be the dread that others felt.

She quickly constructed her internal barriers she used to block ghostly emotions. It worked. She was clearheaded again, but it hadn't stopped the numbness.

"Attacking me was a waste." Connor straightened. The red essence in his hands flowed to his wounds. They closed before her eyes. "I told you, I can heal myself."

Sam struggled to keep hold of the dagger in her left hand.

She couldn't feel anything in her fingers. The red essence began to climb up her arm. She willed the essence she had in her body to the surface. It battled for a moment, but the red devoured it. She'd loaded most of the ghostly essence into her daggers and used it up last night in the Veil.

The essence had made it to her neck, circling it, burning everywhere it touched. She cried out, tears filling her eyes. She was going to die, and no one was coming to save her. Not this time. No Beth. No Kate.

"Don't you hurt her!" a voice shouted.

God no, the ghost who had materialized was Beatrice.

Connor lifted his hands up toward Beatrice. Sam rushed over to stand in his way. He moved to the right, and Sam followed, blocking him from Beatrice.

"You would risk your life against me for a *ghost*?" Confusion lit in his eyes.

"I would risk my life for anyone in danger, living or dead," she choked out, and then her throat closed up before she could ask Beatrice to tell Robert she loved him. Everything was going numb. Something moved beyond Connor's shoulder. She thought it was one of his mercenaries, but then she recognized his brown cardigan. He'd been wearing it the night he died in the burning car.

Her dad.

He smiled at her, pride in his eyes.

Then she blinked, and he was gone.

She. Is. Worthy.

The voices of the daggers spoke in unison, in perfect harmony. It was beautiful. Her daggers drew all the red ghostly essence into themselves, from the surface of her skin to what had managed to penetrate inside her. They blazed bright blue, heating in her hands. Feeling spiked back through her arms, her shoulders, her neck.

Beatrice was suddenly by Sam's side. "And don't be thinking of trying anything funny on me, boy. I'm protected." She tapped a glowing leaf pinned to her maid's uniform.

Frustration reddened Connor's face. "I would have taken my Brigh back and healed you, Sam."

Beatrice crossed her arms. "Mighty convenient to say that now that Sam bested your attack."

Connor frowned at Beatrice. "You've called the Wardens, haven't you?"

Beatrice just lifted her chin and gave him a regal stare.

If her daggers ate up the red essence inside her, maybe they could weaken Connor? And with the Wardens coming, they could end all this now.

"Sorry about this," Sam said. She grabbed his left arm and thrust her dagger into it.

He jerked back but she held on.

No red essence came into the wound. There was nothing at all on his arm.

Connor looked disappointed in her. "I can control the Brigh. I've pulled it away from my arm, away from your dagger. You can't drain me."

He was right. She couldn't drain him if he knew it was coming. The dampening stone would be their only hope to weaken him. Sam released him, pulling back her dagger. "It's over, Connor. The Wardens are coming."

"It's not over," Connor said. "But it can be. You still have the power to stop all this, Sam."

"I told you, I'm not joining you against the Wardens."

Connor shook his head. "There's another way. Deliver Beth to me, and you have my word all the killing will end. With all that essence, I'll be able to breach Entwine and cross the Veil." He closed his eyes. "I'll see my parents. I won't need to harm anyone else."

"Not happening," Sam said, wondering how the hell he knew about Beth's lineage.

The air grew thick again. The Wardens must finally have come. No. It was two ghosts.

Sam opened her mouth in warning, but Connor smiled.

"They're with me." He reached out his hands, and the red essence flowed to the ghosts. It didn't seem to hurt them. It looked more like the connection of a circuit. Their essence flowed and twined with his.

"If you hurt them—"

"I won't. They work for me." The ghosts didn't look happy, but neither refuted his words. Connor met her gaze. "I know you aren't close with Beth. Think of it as a sacrifice for the greater good. A way to save all these ghosts you love so much."

"You're sick." Sam wanted to strike him again to hold him there, but she wasn't sure if her daggers would save her once more.

Connor's eyes widened. "The Wardens are coming. I have to

go. Bring Beth to the Threshold in three days' time at midnight, or I will come and find her myself. And I will not be responsible for who gets hurt in the process."

Before she could say anything, he disappeared, along with the ghosts.

Into Entwine.

"Did you recognize those ghosts?" Sam asked Beatrice.

"No, but I fear he'll kill them to wrap up any loose ends." Beatrice looked grim.

Energy shifted in the air. It didn't feel like when ghosts materialized, but it was similar. It had to be the Wardens, finally.

Beatrice leaned in closer. "We're not giving him Beth, are we? Kate loves her dearly, and she actually reminds me a wee bit of myself."

Sam gave her a quick smile. "No, we're not giving him Beth. But now we know where to find him in three days' time. And we'll be ready."

She still wouldn't kill Connor, but he needed to be stopped somehow.

It was time for a strategy session with Caleb, Sloane, and everyone involved.

CHAPTER 26

Beth turned to Jensen. "I'm not going in there." She lifted her chin toward the MRI machine in one of the RAVEN labs. She'd rather face down Connor with his deadly red essence than go into that tight little tube of metal, even if they blazed it full of light.

And she needed to get to Michael's place for the DNA results. They'd finally come in. And it was the excuse she gave Sam as to why she couldn't stick around and chat about Connor's demands. Which was partially true, but she hated this charade. She'd have to come clean with everyone soon.

"It's entirely safe," Dr. Robert Carmichael said. He pushed his glasses up further on his nose. "We just want to measure your readings while you're using your gifts."

Even though she knew Bob was one of the good guys—he'd helped them during the RAVEN rescue—this wasn't going to happen.

"Can't we do a CT scan, Bob?" she asked.

At least that was an open donut. She stared at the MRI machine. She'd be confined, locked in. Memories jabbed into her mind of the root cellar and of what Harvey and Gloria had done to her.

The pain. The screaming. The blood.

Jensen touched her arm, startling her from her thoughts. "Look, it's okay. We can push this off to another time." There was concern coloring his words.

She looked at her reflection in the mirrored wall. No wonder. Her skin was sweaty, and her eyes looked haunted. Nothing that a trip down her twisted memory lane wouldn't cause.

"What's your angle?" she asked Jensen. "Is there something worse you'll subject me to if I refuse?" She wouldn't put it past RAVEN to do a bait and switch on her.

Jensen looked at her like she'd lost her mind. "I know you hate RAVEN, but don't paint everyone with the same brush. I didn't peg you for being so close-minded."

Beth narrowed her eyes. "But you'll get in trouble with the General if this test doesn't happen."

"I'll explain that you need more time." Jensen nodded to the doctor. "I'll take the heat."

He seemed genuine, which didn't make sense. "Why are you doing this?"

"You saved over two hundred lives last week when we stopped that arms dealer," Jensen said. "The least I can do is buy you some time with the General. Give me the form, Doc. I'll sign off on the delay."

The door to the lab opened and the General walked in. "No need." He nodded to Bob, who looked like he wanted to fade back into the wall. "We'll put off the tests until Ms. Marshall feels up to it, under my orders."

"Absolutely," the doctor said. "Just let me know when you're ready, Beth."

The General smiled at Beth, and her alarm bells began clanging. "Let's chat in my office, shall we?" The General turned around and headed toward the door, not waiting to see if she complied.

Jensen looked worried, but gave Beth a reassuring nod.

She walked through the lab door, catching up to Ollie's dad. Though she tried to fight it, she couldn't prevent the trickle of fear sliding against her nerves. Harvey was a psychopath she knew. The General was a wild card.

He led her to his office, performed the usual security protocols, and then held the door for her to enter. Wasn't this when people scream at their screens, shouting at the dumb girl not to go into the lair of the killer?

"There's nothing for you to fear. I can assure you, Beth, if I might call you Beth, that if I wanted to lock you up, I would have done so already."

Beth met his gaze. "You can call me Beth as long as I can call you James."

He gave her a slight nod.

She walked through the door, scanning quickly left to right for an ambush. Unless the old suits of armor were housing someone, she was safe.

The rest of the office was typical—boring desk, file cabinets the color of dried mud, and a shelf filled with awards and plaques. Maybe he'd won first place in the Best Efforts for World Domination competition.

"So James, what did you want to chat about?' Beth leaned against one of the cabinets. She wasn't going to sit.

He mirrored her stance, leaning back against the side of his desk, facing her. "I wanted to thank you personally for your service."

"Said service is at a cost. I'm not here willingly."

He smiled, which made him look even scarier. "I disagree. You are here willingly. You were the one who agreed to our deal. No one held a gun to your head."

"Not a literal one, but you would have killed me and my friends or kidnapped us if I hadn't struck the deal."

James studied her. "It's interesting your choice of word, 'friends.' For the longest time you didn't have any, at least none we could leverage."

"You've been monitoring me." It wasn't a question. She knew they must have been, at least since her television show came out. "How long?"

James gestured to the chairs in front of his desk. "Please sit." He walked over and sat in one of the chairs himself. "Look, no instant restraints, no poison, no bomb."

She frowned. "Well, of course it wouldn't be in *your* chair."

He got up and sat in the other chair. Again, no booby traps.

"So this is going to be a long conversation then?" Beth eyed the door before finally sitting.

"Considering we've barely spoken," he said, "yes, it will indeed be a longer conversation. And as for your question, we've been monitoring you for the past five years."

"My show has been on for seven."

"True, but we thought you were a fraud initially." James leaned forward, a glint in his eye. "But once you started finding things that were at least a century in age, I knew what you were."

"A Seeker."

"They're very rare, you know."

Now was the chance for her to get a little something out of this *tête-à-tête*.

"Have you run into another Seeker before?"

She was curious if he'd lie about her mother.

James nodded. "Long ago. In fact, she was here at this facility."

Beth tilted her head. "As a prisoner and guinea pig, no doubt."

"Both for a time," James conceded, "but she eventually did work with us on several missions of her own free will."

"What happened to her?" She doubted he'd be truthful, but she had to ask.

"You seem very interested in this stranger." His words were light but weighted in suspicion.

Beth nodded. "I am. I've never heard of anyone who can do what I do, and believe me, I've searched. Neither of my parents have abilities. I had to learn what I could do on my own." She leaned back in her chair. "If there's someone out there who can help fill in the gaps for me about my gifts, you bet I want to know about them, and what happened to them."

All truth, which was the safest bet when dealing with the Sociopath-in-Charge.

James relaxed, his shoulders easing back. "I'm sorry to tell you this, but she died."

Beth snorted. "Of course, you killed her. What happened? You couldn't replicate her gifts, and she wouldn't play nice?"

A flash of anger lit within his brown eyes. "I would have never killed her."

His declaration rang true to Beth. He wasn't faking the faint thread of pain that echoed in his face. Wait a second. Had the General been sweet on her mom?

She tried not to make a face.

"Sorry if I hit a sore spot. It's just that usually you do kill people, so it wasn't a stretch, given what I've seen."

James recovered quickly, back behind his mask. "Fair point. I've done what I've had to over the years because I believe in our mission. But the other Seeker escaped. She died of natural causes—an aneurysm in her brain."

There was only a slight tremor in his voice, barely detectable unless you were listening for it. Whatever he'd felt toward her mom, there was affection wrapped up in all the usual RAVEN bullshit.

"And I'm guessing I was right that you couldn't replicate her gifts, which is why you needed me."

"It is definitely perplexing." James leaned forward. "No matter what we tried, we couldn't even scratch the surface."

Because Beth knew what he didn't. The power wasn't hers alone, or her mom's. It was from the matriarchal line. If you didn't have the bloodline, you were out of luck.

"Why didn't you snatch me up once I got on your radar?"

James shrugged. "As you know, a Seeker has to use their gifts willingly. So we would have needed leverage on you, and there wasn't any. You hated your parents, there were no real boyfriends or girlfriends that you cared about, and there were no close friends. You severed those ties years ago, or so we thought until recently."

She didn't bother to argue. She wouldn't have made the deal if she didn't care about her friends.

"So why not use Sam and Kate as leverage?"

James glanced at the ceiling for a moment. "Let's just say we didn't want to attract unwanted attention, given their roles."

"I get it," she said. "I wouldn't want to go up against the Universe either. Or Time itself."

"We had to approach the problem from another direction."

"Your leverage problem with me?"

"Yes. Duncan was a double prize for us. He had powers we could use, and Kate cared for him." A sour look filled his face. "Logan slipped through our grasp initially. He didn't test positive for any powers, but I have my suspicions."

"He's a damn good DCC, that's his superpower." With fae wings, potentially, whatever that really meant.

"Be that as it may, both men would have leveraged Kate, which in turn would have pressured you. But in the end, there was no need. Your failed rescue attempt was the perfect opportunity to secure you to our side."

Beth crossed her arms. "Failed? We whooped your ass."

"Inside the facility maybe, but you wouldn't have made it off the grounds."

Again, he was right. They all knew they'd been let go, no matter how much Beth had tried to hide it.

"Why are you doing the villain monologue bit? Do you need a gold star for your efforts? Or is there some diabolical master plan, and you're leading up to a big reveal?"

James laughed, but it sounded rehearsed, like he'd watched someone else do it and mimicked them. "Nothing of the sort. I just wanted us to get to know each other a bit better. And to also impress upon you that we will always be a step ahead of any plans you have."

"And what kind of *plans* do you think I have?"

"The rogue necromancer."

Beth controlled her reaction. "If you know anything about him, you know we're outgunned."

"But that doesn't mean you aren't going to try."

"Why do you care? RAVEN doesn't mess with necromancers."

James' right eye twitched. "We usually don't. However, Seekers don't come around every day. I would hate to lose such a valuable asset. He's not only killing people, but also consuming their souls."

Made sense they wanted to protect her so they could continue using her, but he was hiding something.

"I don't have a soul," she replied. "Well, at least not one that would be worth eating. I'd make him sick."

"Don't surrender to him, Beth. I know about the offer he

made to Sam." A glimmer of fear washed over his face so fast, she thought she might have imagined it. And there was real concern in his voice. What was going on?

She didn't bother asking him how he knew about what Connor had proposed to Sam. He'd proved he was a step ahead.

"Are you locking me up?"

He took a long moment to answer. "No."

"Then I'll meet with whomever I want." She stood.

James stood as well. "Those you trust may let you down."

"Your concern would be touching if it wasn't selfish. You remind me so much of Harvey. By the way, he told me you turned down his offer."

James frowned. "If he becomes a problem for you, we can get rid of him."

The idea of RAVEN killing Harvey filled her with an instant sense of relief, but she wasn't sure if she was at that point yet. If Harvey took her money and disappeared, it would be less black on her soul, and she knew Sam would be proud of her. Not that it should matter what Sam thought.

Beth zipped up her leather jacket. "I'll keep that in mind. Are we done here?"

He nodded. "Remember, this is a two-way street, Beth, our agreement. If you need RAVEN's help, for anything, we're here."

She snorted. "I've already been paying for this agreement of ours. I don't want to owe you anything further."

"You wouldn't."

She stared at him. Was he offering up RAVEN's resources to

her for free? "Why are we really talking, James?"

"You remind me of her." His words hung in the air for a moment, the edges dripping with something that sounded like regret. "I wouldn't want you to die, not when I, and RAVEN, could prevent it."

"That makes two of us." She turned her back to him and headed out of his office.

She didn't have to ask who the "her" was. He was obviously talking about her mother. Did he know Melody was her mother, or was he just reminiscing?

Two-way street.

Such a crock. Like she'd ever trust RAVEN to be on their side for anything, especially without wanting something in return.

MICHAEL BALANCED THE BROWNIES, CUPS, AND POT OF tea carefully on the tray, concentrating on not jostling them with his stride down the hallway to where Beth waited in the sitting room.

She'd seemed preoccupied when she showed up to get the DNA results. He wondered if she was still worried about Yasmin. He'd checked on her earlier at the hospital, and she was still a little weak, but otherwise okay.

Yasmin had used pepper spray on Connor when he'd attacked her. It wasn't legal in Scotland, but her Uncle Stu had connections. Michael didn't buy Connor's assertions that the attack on Yasmin was all a ploy to get Sam's attention. Yasmin's vision that she'd need pepper spray had saved her.

He stopped at the entrance to the sitting room, watching Beth in front of the fire, her hands stretched toward the warmth. For just a moment, he imagined how it would be to share a home with her. Curling up in front of the fireplace, shutting the world away.

Michael shook his head, trying to dispel the image. This was just casual, nothing more. They'd both agreed to it.

"Are you going to stand there all afternoon?" Beth asked, still facing the fire.

"How . . ."

"I've got excellent hearing, and you're breathing a bit heavy." She turned around and gave him a side-smile. The firelight made her brown eyes gleam. "Please tell me you brought chocolate."

"Brownies. My mother's special recipe." And guaranteed to make anyone feel better. He knew this for a fact.

Beth met him halfway and cleared a spot on the coffee table in front of the settee. He set down the tray.

She grabbed a brownie from the plate and bit into it. Her eyes fluttered closed. "Holy shit, these might be the best brownies I've ever had. Breathe a word of this to Kate, and you're dead."

Michael sat on the settee and grabbed a brownie for himself. "Your secrets are safe with me."

Beth joined him. "Good. I'd hate to have to kill you."

"That would be problematic, especially since you'd like my family to help you against Connor." Michael checked the teapot. Almost ready. "Of course, Lennox wouldn't care, but the rest would be a bit put out if I died."

Beth nodded. "True, true. I guess you're safe for now." She tilted her head. "Where *is* your family?"

Michael broke apart the brownie, putting one half on a plate. "Mother and Father are at the McKinneys' for afternoon tea, while Duncan is helping Glenna move into the flat she's snagged with MacKenzie. Lennox is looking at new weaponry for the Manor's defenses, and the servants are enjoying a day off."

"So we're alone?" Beth waggled her eyebrows up and down. "Was that on purpose, Forbes?"

He smiled. "Mayyybeee. But I'm cool with just hanging out." He held up his cup. "And drinking tea."

He'd originally planned to take advantage of the empty house to explore more of what this arrangement might be between them, but his gut told him she needed a friend more than a lover right now.

"You're being awful accommodating." Her words held a teasing quality.

"I can be a lot of things, Beth. Layers, remember?" he teased back.

She took another bite of brownie, and they sat in silence for a few moments.

"Do you want to tell me what's bothering you?" he asked finally. "Maybe I can help."

"How do you know something is bothering me?"

No snark or bite to her words, just curiosity. She also didn't ask if he'd used his abilities to sense her emotions.

Progress.

He checked the tea. Perfect. "Just something in your eyes." He poured tea into her cup and doctored it the way she liked it. "You've had a lot of crap to deal with lately." He put her cup on a small saucer and handed it to her.

Her eyes widened slightly. "You're really okay with just sitting here and talking?"

He shrugged. "I think you need it. Am I wrong?"

"No." She shook her head slowly. "I'm just not used to guys wanting to talk. They usually just want to know what I look like naked."

"Oh, I definitely want to know what you look like naked." He grinned and poured out some tea for himself.

She laughed, and some of the darkness in her eyes washed away. "Well, that's good," she said, "because I want to see how you look naked, too."

He held up his cup. "Let's drink to that."

"To eventually seeing each other naked." She laughed again and clinked her teacup to his. She met his gaze. "Thank you."

"For what?"

"For making me feel a little better."

She sounded grateful, and all he'd done was offer to listen. It reminded him again of how fragile she was on the inside. Maybe how fragile they both were behind their walls. It would be nice to not have to worry, to let someone see you—darkness and all.

He held out his hand. She stared at it for a moment before

finally taking it. It felt natural to hold her hand, like he'd already done it a million times.

"You're welcome. And I meant what I said. Maybe I can help with whatever you're struggling with."

She rubbed her thumb against the top of his hand, sending flashes of warmth through him. "Where to start?" Beth asked. "I've had an extra helping added to my usual shit show."

He thought about when he would talk to his patients, guiding them through difficult decisions. It always helped to remember the positive when everything seemed overwhelming.

"Tell me about something good that has happened to you in the last two days," he said. "Tell me that first."

Beth looked down at their hands. "Well, this is pretty good. And what happened in the alleyway before we were interrupted."

He smiled. "What else?"

She took a quick breath. "I saw my mom, my real mom." She looked up and met his gaze. "She showed up when we were getting Morag from behind the Veil. Turns out I'm attached to all the women in my family line."

Michael's mind spun with questions. How was that possible? How did it affect her gifts? How had she even seen a ghost?

But he realized there was only one answer that really mattered to him right now, because it might help Beth.

"How did it feel . . . seeing your mom?"

"It was amazing." Her voice was almost a whisper. She blinked her eyes quickly. "I felt her love for me. I've never felt that before from Harvey or from Gloria—to know that I'm really loved. But that's where part of the crap comes in."

"How bad is it?"

"Sam didn't tell you everything about what happened with Connor," Beth said.

"What do you mean?"

"I asked her not to tell you because I wanted to tell you myself."

The heaviness in her voice sent stabs of fear through him. "What is it, Beth?"

She met his gaze and her eyes shone with unshed tears. "He's demanded me as a sacrifice. Somehow, he's found out that I'm attached to my ancestors, all their ghosts. If he kills me and absorbs my essence, he gets theirs, too. It could be enough for him to break into Entwine and rip apart the Veil."

The urge to sweep her from the manor and get her far away from Rosebridge—from Connor, from danger—rushed through him. He couldn't deny the worry and fear tightening his chest. Whatever this was between them, it wasn't casual to him. Not by a long shot.

"Any chance I can take you on an impromptu Hawaiian holiday?"

She smiled but shook her head. "The old me would have run at the first sign of trouble, but not now. I can't leave Sam and Kate to fight Connor alone." She paused and her eyes unfocused slightly, as if she were somewhere else. "They might be the only two people who really know me. I'm just realizing that now when it might be too late."

"I want to get to know you." The words were out of his

mouth before he'd realized it, but he didn't regret them. He'd spoken the truth.

"I'm messed up." She squeezed his hand. "You don't need my emotional drama."

"I'm messed up, too." He lifted her hand and kissed her knuckles, feeling her tremble slightly. "You've only heard a small piece of my emotional drama."

She slowly pulled her hand from his. "Does Nora know about your past?" The question had a casual air, but Michael didn't miss the interest in her gaze.

Was Beth a little jealous?

Michael shook his head. "Not really, and definitely not what I shared with you a few days ago. I haven't told anyone about that outside of my family."

A pleased look flashed quickly across her face. "Why haven't you told her?"

"Because we're not that close."

"She's excellent girlfriend material."

"You think so?" Michael asked. "We do both love medicine."

She frowned. "And it's obvious she wants something serious with you."

He couldn't tell if she was testing him or trying to convince herself, again, why anything serious between them wouldn't work.

"I don't know," he said. "I've never felt that spark with her."

"I know that spark quite well," she said.

Had her cheeks just flushed?

If this was just a physical attraction, he'd know what to do.

But he was falling for her, which meant he was in uncharted territory.

He needed to play it light, keep to what they'd agreed to until she realized just how incredible they might be together.

"I thought you might," he said. "In fact, I think you're sparking hard for Stu, though I wouldn't act on that. Aggie would probably kill you."

Beth almost spit out her tea back into her cup. "You're ridiculous."

"I am, huh?"

"You are. Just admit, you're sparking for me."

There was an openness in her face he hadn't seen before. Maybe she finally sensed there was something deeper between them now. Or maybe he was just hoping. Either way, he'd continue to play it casual until she changed things.

He turned toward her. "I don't know what you're talking about."

"Oh, you don't?" She cupped his cheek.

His gaze dipped to her lips. "I'm only sparking for the brownies right now."

"Fuck the brownies," Beth growled in a low whisper and pulled him to her.

Her lips met his in a bruising kiss.

She pushed him back on the settee and their momentum tumbled them onto the coffee table, sending tea and brownies flying.

CHAPTER 27

BETH LOOKED AT THE BROWNIE AND TEA CARNAGE ON THE coffee table and on the floor.

"Oops. Are you okay?" She helped Michael sit back up.

Michael rubbed his shoulder. "That coffee table is hard." He gave her a smile. "If I knew you were going to grab me, I would have moved things out of the way."

She frowned at him. "Maybe it's a sign we shouldn't be doing this."

"You don't believe in signs. You make your own way in the Universe. You're no one's puppet and all that."

"Have you been talking with Sam?"

"No. I might not know everything about you, but I do know that."

She still glowed inside, just a little, that he'd admitted he wanted to know her better. Again, something no other man had ever said . . . or attempted.

"Have I ruined the mood, getting you bruised against the coffee table?" she asked. She poked at his chest with her finger.

"Not exactly the romantic interlude you were probably planning."

His smile grew wider, and her heart began to beat faster. Damn, he was hot. "I didn't have anything specific planned," he admitted. "When it comes to you, I've found plans don't work."

"Is that a bad thing?"

Why did she just ask that? It didn't matter. This was short-term.

He scooted closer on the settee. "Nope, I kinda like it. I tend to be a planner. You make me let loose."

She moved closer, too. "So you'd be okay if I slammed you up against the wall and had my way with you?"

He frowned just a bit. "There are too many pictures hanging there that my mother adores. Knowing us, we'd break them."

"You're right, we would." She didn't keep the regret from her voice. It would be fun to have some wall action. It had been too long.

Michael stood. "In front of the fireplace it is." He scooped her up in his arms. "We shouldn't cause too much property damage there."

She savored the feeling of lightness in his arms. He was strong. She couldn't wait to get him into a pair of leather handcuffs the next time they got busy.

Michael's gaze had turned tender. She couldn't breathe for a moment. He wasn't trying to make this anything more than casual, was he?

No, she was just letting fear sneak in again. Even if she

wavered a bit now and then when she was with him, it was best this way. No strings, and no one's heart getting broken.

"I'm glad we agreed not to let this get serious," she said.

Something passed across his face looking suspiciously like disappointment.

He shrugged. "If it was serious, then you'd have to deal with my crazy family, and I'm not that cruel."

She grinned. "Thank you for sparing me."

He walked over to the fireplace and gently placed her on her feet, his face in shadow. "I've been thinking about this, about you and me, for quite some time now."

His voice was low and filled with promise. Desire sparked through her body in sharp bursts.

"I wanted to take you right outside of the police station that first time you did your hoodoo voodoo with your gifts," she admitted.

He looked surprised. "But you were grilling me that day, giving me the third degree."

"I'm . . . complicated."

He laughed and it was a full, rolling, belly laugh. The fire's glow warmed his blond hair and sent dancing shadows across his face.

He placed his hands on her hips. "For me, it was when you came to see my house for the first time."

"You mean when your brother, Duncan, was a dick."

He nodded. "And when I saw how his words hurt you, saw the woman underneath the armor, that's when I was hooked."

She put her hands against his chest, resting her palms on

hard muscles she'd hoped to see soon. Oh screw it, she wanted to see them now. She moved her hands down and lifted his shirt up. He obliged, raising his arms so she could get it off easily. Her hands went back to his incredible chest. Did all Scottish men have killer abs and asses? She'd been missing out.

She kissed one pec and then the other. He inhaled quickly, and she smiled. "In my fantasies, we've christened every place I've seen in your house."

He took one of her hands and kissed each finger. "Even the shoe bench by the front door? It's tiny."

She wobbled, her knees shaky. It felt like he kissed not just her fingers, but everything. "Especially that bench. It has the padded seat after all. Sam might like having sex in the forest, but I need more comfort."

He laughed again, and she snuggled into his chest, wrapping her arms around him, wanting to feel that laughter rumble through her.

She pulled back and kissed him softly on the lips. "I'm glad we're finally doing this."

"Me, too." It felt as if he wanted to say something more, but instead he just kissed her.

Her hands wound in his hair. He picked her up again. She wrapped her legs around him. The kiss deepened, his tongue sliding against hers—slowly, firmly.

Michael lowered her slightly to rub against his body, and she felt how ready he was. She wrapped her legs around him tighter, drowning in the feel of him between her legs.

Her head fell back, and he kissed her neck, nibbling and

biting her skin. Then he knelt slightly, laying her back on the plush rug in front of the fireplace.

She rolled, legs still wrapped around him and pinned him underneath her. Now it was her turn to kiss his neck, down to his collarbone. And to his nipples. She licked one in lazy circles, then moved to the other, then back again.

Beth ran her tongue down his chest to his bellybutton, and his soft moans became faster, bringing a smile to her face. She unbuttoned his pants and slid the zipper down slowly.

She looked up at him and found he'd propped himself up on his elbows, eyes latched onto her every move.

Her fingers slid under his boxer briefs and then along his length. His breath was a quick hiss. She gripped him and pulled slowly toward her, then back again. He bucked, hips rising up from the floor.

The plea was clear, and she was happy to oblige.

She shimmied his pants down, and he kicked them off. Next came his boxer briefs. They were the same blue of his eyes.

She looked up and down his entire body. "Wowza. You're gorgeous."

He laughed softly, then sat up and cupped her cheek, kissing her. "You're the gorgeous one."

She raised an eyebrow. "You haven't even seen me naked yet."

"That's not what makes you gorgeous to me."

He wasn't lying. She saw it in his face. Her heart pounded in her chest.

She needed to get this back on track, back to casual. "I

wasn't finished, doctor." She pushed him back down again and then took him into her mouth.

"*Beth.*" He moaned her name.

She licked down his length, hands cupping his balls, then up again. She took him inside her mouth as far as he would go, her right hand moving to grip him at the base. He bucked again beneath her, and she moved faster and faster.

A trembling vibrated through his legs, and she pulled back. She didn't want to push things too far just yet. The afternoon was young, and she needed all that hardness inside her.

She gave one last swirl of her tongue around his tip and sat back.

"Since I've seen you naked, it's only fair I reciprocate." Beth unbuttoned her top.

Michael sat up again, his gaze followed her movements. Her top slid back onto the rug. Next came her bra. She'd worn one of burgundy lace. It made her skin gleam next to it.

"And it's my turn to taste you like I promised I would." His words sent spirals of heat through her that had nothing to do with the fire.

She got to her feet and slid her pants off slowly, along with her panties. She crooked a finger at him. "Show me."

Michael went to his knees in front of her, hands gripping her hips. He kissed up the inside of her right thigh, slowly. She swayed on her feet, captivated by the feel of his mouth on her skin. Then he moved to her left thigh. His lips were soft but so very hot, almost burning her skin.

He rose higher. Her hands tangled in his hair, then his

tongue slid into her wetness. "Fuck yeah," she moaned. Thankfully his hands on her hips kept her steady.

She pushed his hair out of the way so she could watch his mouth against her, his tongue flicking, sliding, pushing. She moved one of her hands up to her breast, pinching her nipple in time with his tongue.

"Yes," she urged. "Fast, then slow."

He instantly obliged. Her orgasm began to build, a white hot nova in the midst of a dark, starry night.

She wanted him inside her now.

"Do you have any condoms?" Her words were broken by pants. She put her hands on his shoulders and pushed him back gently.

"In my room."

"Mine are closer." Beth went to her purse and took out a handful of packets. "I've got Ultra Thin in a variety of sizes and widths." She walked back over to him. "But I'm thinking the Extra Large will work."

He gave her a look she couldn't read. "Do you carry a condom stash wherever you go?"

Her usual reply would have been something silly or noncommittal. Sex was sex.

But she wanted to tell him the truth.

"No." She ripped open the packet. "I bought these specifically for you." She sat on the floor beside him and eased the condom down his length. Beth didn't look at him, focusing on the task at hand.

He lifted her chin with his finger. "Good." He looked

pleased, and she couldn't help but smile back at him.

"Looks like I made the right choice." She glanced back at the condom fitting perfectly.

"You did," he replied. She had a sense he might be talking about more than just the fit.

Hope swirled inside her, but she pushed it down, trying desperately to focus on the physical. That she could control.

Beth straddled him, guiding him inside her. His hands went to her waist. She moved up and down, slowly at first, enjoying the feel of her nipples rubbing against his chest.

That pleasure turned into sharp jabs of need.

His mouth found hers while their bodies found a rhythm. The sound of flesh on flesh intoxicated her. She pulled back from their kiss, her eyes meeting his. In front of her, the doctor was gone, the playful pain in the ass had disappeared, leaving just a man who looked as vulnerable as she felt.

No, not just a man. He was someone who had somehow wormed his way into her heart. She couldn't deny it any longer.

"Whatever you do, don't stop, Michael." She didn't recognize her voice. It sounded raw.

"I won't, Beth," he said. "I won't stop."

She finally understood all that shit Sam had spouted in her books about dissolving into someone.

They were one. Together.

Moving in a frenzied dance.

Sweat-soaked skin sliding against each other.

Faster and faster. Building and building.

Beth's orgasm ripped through her, arcing her body back.

Michael followed, burying his face into her chest. She wrapped her arms around him, holding him. He did the same, his grip not faltering on the web of scars she knew he felt on her back.

Their harsh breathing competed with the crackling of the flames in the fireplace. Beth didn't want to move, didn't want this to end. She'd had a taste of what it could be like being with someone she cared about. It was better than she could have ever imagined, but it was also frightening, because she now had something more to lose.

She was falling for Michael.

Crap, crap, and double crap.

Fuck those brownies.

Sam looked around the pub and found Kate and Logan in a back corner. The Wet Whistle was the only pub in Rosebridge, which meant it would be busy, even in the late afternoon. And no one would be paying much attention to them. It was a good place for a meeting with a Warden.

It had been Sloane's suggestion. They needed to figure out next steps with Connor and find out if Sloane could help.

Sam slipped off her jacket, already warm. "Come on," she said to Robert.

Fiddle music played from the speakers as she led him back through the tables, the floor sticky under her boots. Sam tugged on his arm whenever someone's outfit made Robert stop in his tracks. He still couldn't get used to so much skin being shown, But at least she'd finally disabused him of trying to give his coat away to cover someone up.

Logan stood and gave her a hug and a healthy handshake to Robert. "We ordered for you," he half shouted in Sam's ear.

Kate pointed to the pints in the center of the table next to a heaping bowl of chips with dipping sauces. Sam's stomach grumbled. She'd missed lunch to meet with Nora, Fi's sister. She'd needed to test out the dampening stones to make sure the ghostly essence in her daggers wouldn't be siphoned when they used them on Connor.

"Everything go okay with Nora?" Kate asked, not having to shout. She could use what she called her "big girl voice" on command.

Sam gave a thumbs up. "We're good to go."

"I do not understand how we will be able to hear Sloane once she arrives," Robert almost yelled. "I can barely hear myself speak."

"Thankfully, I can help with that." Sloane's voice cut through a suddenly quiet pub. Sam looked around. Everyone else was still speaking, but Sam couldn't hear them. Or the music.

When she looked back at the table, Sloane was seated next to Logan. The deep crimson jacket she wore had the same Celtic symbols she had in her earrings, woven in silver.

"Where's Beth?" Sloane asked.

Logan just stared at Sloane, no doubt processing how she'd suddenly appeared at their table.

"She's getting her DNA results from Michael," Sam said.

Sloane nodded. "I'm glad that finally got sorted out. I was forbidden to say anything—rules and all that." She turned to Logan with a smile. "Hello there. I've heard a lot about you."

Logan smiled back, finding his voice again. "I hope it was all good."

"It was." Sloane picked up one of the pints. Suddenly, there were five. "Even from Vivian, and she's a tough one to please." She gestured to the people in the pub around them. "Don't worry, they won't see anything unusual. And no one can hear what we're saying, including ghosts. We don't need Connor's spies in the mix."

"That's a relief. Beatrice is keeping close watch on the B&B, the Allen's house, and Michael's place." Sam slid some chips onto a plate, along with some of the dipping sauces. Though they looked like French fries, they were so much tastier. After a few swallows, she felt her energy returning.

Kate leaned around Logan to look at Sloane. "I know you helped me at the end, but are you pissed at me for what went down at RAVEN?"

The Warden took a sip of her pint and made a pleased noise. "You mean when you defied my wishes and manipulated Time to save everyone? With the odds completely against you? And I had to bring your dead husband into the mix in order to save you?"

Kate fidgeted in her seat. "Yes, for that."

"I'm not upset." Sloane reached over and touched her arm briefly. "I didn't trust in your abilities, and that was my mistake. You're more powerful than I realized. Of course, Caleb enjoyed reminding me that he'd never doubted you for an instant."

Kate brightened. "I've figured out how to stop Time, too, with my Time Baggies."

Sloane's eyebrows rose slowly. "You know you don't need anything but yourself to stop Time, right?"

"That's what Vivian said, too," Kate admitted. "But I need training wheels for a bit. I'm still learning, you know."

Logan kissed her cheek. "You're incredible, training wheels or not."

Sloane's smile grew wider. "I'm glad she chose you. We had bets going between you and Duncan. Of course, I won."

Logan began to sputter, and Sam knew she needed to get things back on track, back to the reason why they were there.

"I was surprised you wanted to meet here," Sam said.

Sloane looked down at her pint. "I needed a breather from Entwine. There was an incident . . ."

"Who was hurt?" Concern filled Robert's eyes.

"Several Wardens. Connor drew them out. It was a trap."

Fear clawed its way up into Sam's chest. "Are they dead?"

"Two died. Three more were hurt."

Logan's gaze hardened. "If we don't stop him, he'll just keep on killing. And he's even worse than my brother, Graham. He's destroying souls."

"You won't get much support from the Wardens when you go up against Connor, I'm afraid." Sloane wiped her mouth with a napkin. "We need the surviving Wardens within Entwine for contingency plans."

"And that includes you?" Sam asked.

Sloane shook her head. "No. I'll stand with you."

Robert looked upset. "You are needed in Entwine. And you are our only true ally among the Wardens."

Sloane gave him an approving look. "Always thinking a few steps ahead, Robert. I love that about you. But to be honest, if Connor makes it into Entwine, we might not be able to save everyone in time. If I can, I need to help you stop him before he can breach the Threshold."

Sam tilted her head. "I wanted to ask you about that. I saw two ghosts help Connor escape into Entwine from the cemetery. So why would him getting into Entwine via the Threshold be any different?"

"What he did to escape us was a brief jump right at the edges. Any longer, and Entwine would eject him because we've revoked his access." Sloane's empty glass refilled on its own. "But if he gets Beth's family essence, he'll be able to not only force his way in, but stay."

Robert took a sip of his pint. "Why not allow him to see his parents so he does not have to breach the Veil in order to do so?"

"Here we go with the Rules again," Kate said under her breath.

"We can't let him see his parents," Sloane replied, giving Kate the eye, "because his parents don't want to see him."

"What?" Sam shook her head. "I don't understand."

Sloane stared at Sam. "Everything is about choice. We couldn't force you to be a necromancer. A ghost can't force you to take a Bargain. Anyone in Entwine and beyond the Veil has a choice, too. If they don't want to see someone living, they don't have to."

"Is she telling the truth?" Robert asked.

"She is." Sam's lie detector was green. "But why wouldn't they want to see him?"

"Not everyone had great parents like you, Sam," Kate said.

The Warden chewed on a few chips in silence. "Kate's right. And sometimes the wrong choices are made out of fear. Remember when I said Connor was damaged?"

"Yes," Sam replied.

"Damaged how?" Logan asked.

"He killed his sister," the Warden said.

Kate looked sick. "By accident?"

Sloane shrugged. "No one knows for sure, but his parents blamed him and put him in a home for troubled kids."

"I bet that made things worse," Logan said.

Sam remembered what Connor had said in the cemetery and why he wanted to see his parents. "I think he regrets what he did."

"That's why I wanted to give him a chance." The Warden traced circles on the chipped wooden table. "I know what it's like to be ostracized from those you care about, even when you apologize for something you did."

"Which is why you selected him to train to be a Runner with Darrin after his parents died," Robert said.

Sloane nodded. "The other Wardens wanted to offer him the Necromancer agreement because we had no other candidates. I advocated for the Runner position in order to try to hold them at bay until Sam came to her senses."

Though she didn't agree with Connor's methods, Sam understood the desire to see those you loved again. But it was more than that.

"Connor is addicted to essence." She took a swallow of beer while she saw her words sink in. "He wants more and mentioned having an unlimited supply."

"I suspected he was hooked on it," Sloane said.

Logan's jaw clenched. "Which means he won't give it up."

"And we should expect he knows we're planning something." Kate dipped a chip in some hot mustard. "Even if he believes we might give Beth up, you're technically aligned with the Wardens now that you re-upped you contract."

"Which means we need a game plan," Sam said. "What can you offer by way of firepower, Sloane?"

The Warden smiled and this time it was her usual grin full of mischief. "I can't hold onto essence like you and Connor can, but I know how to use it. I can provide a distraction for whatever your big play is." A look of concern washed over Sloane's face. "You do have a big play, don't you?"

Sam leaned in closer and lowered her voice, even though she knew no one could hear them. "We're going to use a dampening stone to siphon the ghostly essence he's harboring. That will hopefully make him weak enough for us to take him into custody. I tried doing that with my daggers, but he can move the essence within his body. The dampening stone will take it all, and the element of surprise should give us the advantage."

Robert leaned back in his chair. "It appears time to rally the troops to our cause and seek the best plan of attack."

"Way ahead of you, Robert." Kate slid more chips onto her plate. "We're having a big planning party tonight at the B&B after dinner. Michael's family will be there, along with Vivian and Caleb."

Robert nodded toward Sloane. "Of course, you would be most welcome at our war council tonight."

The Warden stood. "I need to get back to Entwine, but Darrin can fill me in. He'll get me the info."

Sam stood, too. "Thanks for helping us, and for giving a non-lethal option a chance."

"You're my favorite," Sloane said. "What can I say?" She turned as if she were going to walk away from their table but was suddenly gone.

The sound of the pub rushed back in with a roar.

Sam hoped Nora's stone would work. If it didn't, they were screwed.

CHAPTER 28

"WE REALLY SHOULD GET UP AND PUT ON MORE clothes," Beth said. She stretched, and then snuggled right back into Michael's chest. He'd put his briefs back on, but thankfully he'd left his chest bare. She'd done the same.

Lying there, half-naked with Michael, she could almost forget her messed up life. How she needed to protect Michael from her fake parents and somehow defeat a crazy necromancer. She felt almost normal for the first time in her life. Could she get there permanently? Real relationships, mundane drama, maybe even love before she was sixty?

That tiny bud of hope that had been growing since coming to Scotland scored a heavy blow against her wall. Several more bricks went down.

But there were still many more to go.

At least the DNA results had confirmed what she'd hoped. Michael had shared them with her after they'd come up for air. Harvey and Gloria were not her parents. Hallelujah.

"We probably *should* grab the rest of our clothes." Michael kissed her forehead. "Who knows which of my family is going to come home first."

"Would they be shocked?"

"Probably not." Michael turned slightly and met her gaze. "I think everyone has been expecting us to hook up."

Beth sat up, enjoying the fire's heat on her back. "Seriously though, regardless of my teasing earlier, you have a pretty incredible family. Your mom would move mountains for you, and Glenna believes in love so much, she can't wait until you find some."

Michael sat up, too. "Yeah, good luck with that."

Beth ignored the pang she felt at his words. It was ridiculous really. It's not like she had any luck in the love department either.

"Duncan has come around since RAVEN, and even your dad seems to be warming up." She smiled. "You probably don't notice it, but every time he looks at you when you're not looking, there's pride in his eyes."

Michael stared into the fire. "I hated most of my family for a long time, and they deserved some of it. But I realize now, and after therapy, that I hated myself more."

"Because of what you did to Trent and to Lennox?"

His gaze shot to hers, eyes widening. "How did you know about Lennox?"

Beth shrugged. "Once you told me that Lennox needed to believe your gifts were weak, and that you owed him, I knew there was something deeper that happened." She scooted over to sit next to him. "Was it really bad?"

Michael slipped an arm around her waist. "It was."

Even if they couldn't have a future romantically, they were still friends. "Did you want to tell me what happened?"

He exhaled. She just waited.

"Lennox has a fear of water." Michael's voice was soft. "He's never learned to swim because of that fear. I made him . . ." He seemed unable to form more words.

Beth turned to him. Pain rippled across his face and settled in his eyes. "It's okay. You can tell me."

"I made Lennox jump into a nearby lake when he was fifteen," Michael said. "I took over his mind, and I forced him."

"There had to be a good reason."

"Why do you sound so sure?"

"Because I know you, and you don't do horrible things just 'cause." The words came easily, and they were the truth. She did know him, because he was a lot like her. And she always had a reason for her actions.

He looked disgusted with himself. "We'd argued in the forest, and he'd pushed me. I fell back over a fallen tree limb and broke my arm." He paused. "Looking back on it as I got older, I don't think he meant to hurt me. It was an accident."

"But at the time you were angry. You wanted revenge." Beth understood the need for revenge. She'd moved past it with Sammy, but one day, Harvey and Gloria would pay.

"I did want revenge."

"How old were you?

"Nine." His voice grew small.

Beth touched his cheek. "It's understandable that you acted

out. You were just a kid. I've known kids who've done way worse." Memories from juvie swarmed in her mind, but she locked them away quickly.

Michael leaned into her hand. "He was upset because he thought I'd made his girlfriend break up with him with my abilities."

"Did you?"

"No. Maybe? I don't know," Michael said. "I might have. I couldn't control my powers all the time. Lennox snapped when I couldn't deny for certain."

"Did he apologize?"

"To my parents, but not to me." Michael took her hand and kissed the palm. "I was so angry. There'd always been pressure on me to keep the peace, to keep things calm, but never a time I could actually be upset."

She squeezed his hand. "That's a lot of crap building up inside you."

"He kept needling me, pushing me, making my life as miserable as his was." Michael looked down. "I still remember forcing him into the water, then standing on the dock and watching him struggle."

"But you saved him in the end, didn't you?"

He looked at her. "Someone else could have saved him. Why would you think I did?"

"Because you're not a monster. Take it from me, I know monsters."

His face softened. "I'm so sorry you do."

"We can't change the past." She turned to look into the fire.

"And now, at least I know I'm not biologically screwed up at an anatomical level, though I have done some pretty awful things in my life."

"We've all done awful things to varying degrees, but the fact you listened and helped me let a little of my pain go." He kissed her shoulder. "That you saved Sam and Kate from Graham." Another kiss. "That you rescued all those people from RAVEN, that's the real Beth Marshall." This time a nip of her skin.

She looked back at him. "Are you angling for another round, stud?"

She half-hoped he was. Anything to stay here with him, feeling like this.

Michael shook his head. "No, I just like touching you."

"Even my scars?" The last word came out a bit too high.

Dammit. Men had seen her scars many times, and she didn't care what they thought, but this was the first time she'd been with someone she had feelings for.

It was different.

Michael's hand moved to her back, tracing the ridges of scar tissue from the belt Harvey had used to beat her raw. Feeling such a gentle touch where terrifying memories remained threatened tears. She blinked them back.

"I make scars in my line of work." He held her gaze. "To me, they're are a sign of strength, of survival, of healing. I think you're the most courageous woman I've ever met."

"I wasn't courageous as a kid." A tear escaped her attempts and rolled down her cheek, hot and wet.

"Do you want to tell me?"

He waited while her inner voices argued.

It's okay to let it out.

Wait, that wasn't her internal voice. That was her mom.

Beth looked around the room.

Let him help you as you helped him.

"Are you okay?" Michael asked.

Beth nodded. "Just ghosts of both the present and the past."

Hearing her mom's voice calmed her, steadied her. Maybe it was time to tell someone—someone who also had demons.

He took his hand from her back and wiped the tears from her cheek. "You don't have to tell me if you don't want to."

"I want to." And she did. She didn't want to tarnish the light both Sam and Kate had inside them, but Michael's was shadowed like hers. He could take it.

She took a deep breath. "I don't remember everything from my childhood. There are missing chunks from my memory." And that missing time scared her more than she admitted.

He nodded. "That's common when there's extreme trauma."

Her nose caught phantom whiffs of marjoram conjured from that time. The memories clawed their way up from the dark hole she'd banished them to, dripping acid as they rose.

Beth twined her fingers together, finding it hard to breathe. "They put me in the root cellar when I didn't do what they wanted, when I fought them."

He didn't say anything. He just waited again.

"Ever since they'd realized what I could do, they used me," Beth said. "At first it was fun, a game, but when I got older, I realized they were stealing. And hurting people."

"When you refused they punished you," Michael said.

Beth nodded. "They didn't mind when I lied or broke the rules as long as it didn't affect them. They actually praised that type of behavior."

"What did they have you steal?"

"Cash was what they wanted most. It was less traceable than jewelry or other goods." Her palms slicked with sweat. She wiped them on the rug. "Other times it was information. Journals, computers, photos. Anything they could use for leverage."

"So they were always blackmailers."

"Among other things." Beth's chest tightened. "I didn't realize until much later that they were running a theft ring in New York. A full-scale operation. The blackmail material bought them cops and officials, which is why they were never caught."

Michael frowned. "But you were tossed into juvie because some of their crimes were pinned on you. How did that happen if they owned the cops?"

"They wanted it to happen," Beth whispered. She'd never said her fears out loud. "It's the only thing that makes sense."

"Do they hate you that much?"

Beth nodded. "Harvey does. He's never come out and said it, but I know it." The scars on her back itched with remembered fire. She fought not to touch them. "Gloria didn't care one way or another. If I was useful, things were good. If I wasn't, then she didn't care if Harvey beat me."

Michael's eyes hardened. "Cold."

Beth snorted. "She could teach ice a thing or two. At least I always saw Harvey coming. Gloria was always more dangerous.

She was the one who decided I should be put in the root cellar as punishment when I began disobeying them."

"And Sam and Kate know nothing of this?"

"Just the broad strokes, what I really couldn't hide from them at the time. And I don't want them knowing anything of what I'm telling you now. Got it?"

He nodded. "Everything we've said here stays between us."

She didn't doubt his promise. She trusted him. And he joined a small handful of people she did.

It was time to get some of the poison out, to share some of the pain. She didn't need to hear her mom's voice to feel her approval.

"They used to put me in a small closet in the root cellar. There was just barely enough room for me to stand up." A shiver ran through her body.

Michael squeezed her hands. "It's okay. I got you."

The memories jostled in her head, eager for their freedom. Bloody snapshots of horrific moments. They finally settled on the dark door that led into the root cellar.

"Harvey would beat me first, usually with his old belt. It had a large silver buckle that would leave bruises the size of a lemon." She couldn't get enough air in. "Then after I was good and bloody, they'd let the flies in through a small opening in the door."

Michael stiffened. "Flies?"

"Black flies. The blood drew them. They would bite me, attack me, over and over." She hadn't told anyone this. Ever. Her voice became a harsh whisper. "I would scream and bang myself against the walls, the door, trying to get out."

The horror on Michael's face brought the rest of her tears up and over in a warm rush down her cheeks. He didn't say anything, he just pulled her onto his lap and hugged her tightly. She clung to him with everything she had.

"I tried to refuse them." Each word was hard-won over the sobs squeezing her body, strong enough to bruise her ribs. "But it hurt so much. Eventually I would have to give in, to steal for them again." She hadn't let herself cry like that in years. It felt like she was crumbling, with Michael's arms being the only thing holding her together.

Michael rocked her back and forth, stroking her hair, and murmuring against her temple. She couldn't make out exactly what he was saying, but it sounded like, "We'll stop them. We won't let them hurt anyone we love."

It wasn't "It's okay, you'll be fine," or any of the other silly platitudes that people tried to throw her way when she told them the bare minimum of what she'd gone through. Some of the pain eased away on a ribbon of darkness, pulling more tears from her in its wake.

Beth didn't know how long they sat there, but once the tears finally stopped, she pulled back slightly and looked at Michael. "Didn't think you'd get a blubbering mess on your hands, did you? I'm definitely not camera ready now."

Michael grabbed his shirt and handed it to her. "Robert told me that a gentleman always has a handkerchief ready for a lady. I'm afraid this will have to do."

Beth blew her nose into it a few times. Then she rubbed

under her eyes and winced at the black mascara on the cloth. "Well, I'm definitely no lady."

Michael kissed her cheek. "You're a warrior, and I'd take that over a lady any day."

She blew her nose again. "I mean, I know the sex was amazing, but still . . ."

He laughed. "We're going to get through this, Beth. We'll stop the necromancer and keep your fake family from hurting anyone." He moved her off his lap and got to his feet, helping her up.

She raised an eyebrow. "You're suddenly optimistic."

Michael grabbed her bra and top and handed them to her. "Maybe it's because I have something now that I don't want to lose." His gaze met hers for a moment, and then he busied himself with the teacups and tray.

Her heart skipped a beat. She'd thought the same exact thing earlier. Could he be falling for her, too?

Beth got dressed and found her shoes. The sure-fire way to stop Connor from breaching Entwine would be for her to kill herself before he could do it. If she were dead, he couldn't pull on her family's powers to get souped-up. She'd thought about killing herself before, but not since juvie.

A few months back, there wouldn't have been anything or anyone worth dying for. Now, there was.

She watched Michael balance the tray in his hands.

But the reasons that would make her want to sacrifice her life to save everyone were the same reasons she wanted to live.

She had people she loved and who loved her, too.

And if there was even a sliver of a chance for Michael and her, she suddenly realized she wanted it.

M ICHAEL LOOKED AROUND THE B&B'S KITCHEN, surprised everyone could fit for their planning session, though it was still definitely crowded.

Vivian kept snatching up the different cookies and sweets that Kate had put out on the marble kitchen island. Some she ended up nibbling on, but a few she squirreled away in her satchel.

He'd asked Kate how Caleb and Vivian could be at the B&B since it wasn't the forest. She'd told him the B&B sat upon forest grounds and still held the roots of trees underneath that were connected. And there was something about her being an anchor that changed things, too. She wasn't clear on that part.

He watched his father pepper Vivian with questions, no doubt for their Archives. She answered some and ignored others with a smile.

Michael was relieved she was in a good mood. His father was just barely healing from his last injury. Even though Vivian was on their side now, he knew it could change in an instant. There was something wild and uncertain about her.

Caleb sat with Emily and Patty, regaling them with some adventure. Kate kept a watchful eye, along with Logan. Several times, Michael caught Kate giving Caleb signals over the girls' heads. Most likely telling him to minimize gory details.

Duncan leaned against the fridge, chatting with Sam, Robert, and Darrin. There didn't seem to be any awkwardness between him and Kate, thankfully.

Glenna and Mackenzie talked in whispers by the Chore Board—when they weren't stealing kisses. Mackenzie still had a hollow look about her, most likely fostered from being held prisoner by her father for so many years, but she smiled more easily the more time she spent with his sister.

His mother, Jean, looked over the girls' artwork on the wall with Beth. Every now and again, Beth would catch his eye, and he had to restrain himself from scooping her up and running off somewhere. He was both turned on and worried about what their afternoon together really meant. Is this what it was like when you loved someone?

Had he just thought love?

What did he know about love? He'd never been in love before. Maybe it was just a really strong affection with some lust thrown in. He rubbed his face. Who was he kidding? He couldn't seem to muster up the elusive Dr. Forbes, even if his life depended on it. He was in deep.

"Sorry I'm late." Nora's voice startled him out of his inner bashings. She looked tired. Dark circles left half-moons under her eyes. He imagined trying to keep up with rounds at the hospital and reconfiguring the dampening stone had been taking its toll.

He took the duffel from her shoulder and put it next to an empty chair at their table. "Go ahead and sit. Let me get you a cup of coffee and a slice of Kate's apple cobbler."

On his way to the treats, he almost got bowled over by the girls making a beeline for Vivian.

Emily reached her first. "Miss Vivian, I felt the life force of the forest for the first time today."

Patty arched an eyebrow. "But she still can't talk to trees."

"I can talk to the owls and crows."

Patty opened her mouth but Vivian held up her hand and both girls instantly grew quiet. "You both helped save the trees and will both become protectors of the forest in your own time," the goddess said. "Each gift is important and given by the Universe with care."

Kate joined them. "Miss Vivian is absolutely right. But now we need to start our planning session, which means you two have to go to bed."

The girls started grumbling. Beth walked over to them and leaned down. "You two need to guard the home base here and help Stu and Aggie while we're in the forest tomorrow, which means you need to get your rest."

"But I want to come," Patty said. "The trees might need me."

Emily placed her hands on her hips. "And I want to help protect Mom in the fight."

Michael put Nora's coffee and cobbler on the kitchen island. He crouched until he was close to their eye level. "I know for a fact that if you two were in the forest, your mom, Auntie Beth, and all of us would be so distracted, we wouldn't be paying attention to the battle." The girls looked undecided but were obviously moved by Michael's argument.

Emily gazed up at Beth. "I'll agree if you promise to teach me how to throw a shuriken."

"Ahhh, a bargain is in the brewing," Caleb said softly. "Well done, Emily."

Beth ignored him. "I agree, as long as your mom is okay with it."

Kate nodded. "But they have to be ones that aren't so sharp, and I need to be there."

Beth nodded. Then Emily held out her hand to Beth, and they shook on it.

Michael thought about what might sway Patty. "And if you agree to stay here at the B&B, I'll read you the stories about the history of the forest from our Family Archives."

"Really?" Patty asked. Her entire face lit up.

Michael nodded.

"I agree," Patty declared, rising up on her tippy-toes.

Staring at Patty's happy smile, Michael felt a pull he hadn't felt before. Being a father was always something he knew he "should" do, but suddenly, he felt he might *want* to do it—with the right person.

He didn't look at Beth. He didn't want her to see anything in his eyes that might spook her.

The girls didn't give another argument. They just walked calmly through the kitchen and then pelted up the stairs amid squeals of laughter.

"Those two are something else," Michael said to Kate.

She smiled. "Don't I know it. I'm so lucky." She raised her voice. "If everyone can take a seat, we'll lay out what we know and how best to handle our meeting with Connor tomorrow night."

Sam looked past Kate toward the back door. "Beatrice confirmed again that the B&B is free of other ghosts. We're safe to talk without Connor's spies."

Michael sat back down and handed the coffee and cobbler to Nora. She immediately dove in, as if she hadn't eaten in ages.

"Where's Fi?" Michael asked. "We invited her."

Nora shrugged. "Your guess is as good as mine. She ran off all excited about another lead on our Da's whereabouts." Worry clouded her gaze. "I just hope she's not too disappointed if it doesn't pan out."

Duncan squeezed her shoulder. "I'm sure she'll be fine. She's stubborn. She's not going to give up until she finds out, one way or another."

Nora nodded and seemed about to say something else, but turned around when Caleb began speaking.

"I will defend the forest during the battle," he said, "and protect the trees."

"I can kill, Connor, correct?" Vivian asked. Her voice sounded casual, as if she were asking if she could have another cookie.

Sam's face hardened. "Not unless there is no other choice."

Vivian frowned, and the tulips in the center of her table began to wilt.

"But you can rough him up," Beth offered. "Wear him down." The forest goddess brightened, and the tulips shot up straight and tall again.

"Something's not sitting right with me about Connor's

demand to meet at the Threshold," Michael said. "He knows we have Caleb and Vivian on our side."

"I've been worried about the same thing," Logan admitted. "Connor has been ahead of us the entire way. He'd stack the deck in his favor, just like any criminal. What aren't we seeing?"

No one said anything.

Sam spoke up. "Until we figure out what we might be missing, we've got to keep moving forward with our plan. With the reconfigured dampening stone from Nora, we'll siphon his ghostly essence, and then he'll be just like anyone else, which means we can capture him without killing him." She smiled at Nora. "Did you want to share what you've done with the stone?"

Nora looked around the room, suddenly seeming shy. Michael was surprised. True, they were in the presence of Caleb and Vivian, but Nora never had any issues with confidence.

"Is there something wrong with the stone?" Michael asked.

Nora shook her head immediately. "No, nothing like that." She got to her feet slowly and looked around the room. "The stone is ready. I reconfigured it to pull energy rather than just absorb it."

Caleb tilted his chin toward her. "That's quite a feat, lass. Those stones are persnickety at best."

Michael smiled. "Nora has always had a way with the stones. Her work has saved our town for many years."

Nora's face flushed. "But we don't know if it'll really work against Connor. Sam mentioned that the ghostly essence he holds is different." She gazed down at Michael, looking more worried than he'd ever seen before. "Maybe we should scrap the idea."

Beth shook her head. "Don't doubt yourself, Nora. Sam said it worked on her when you did the test run earlier." Beth's voice softened. "It's going to be okay."

Nora opened her mouth, and then closed it again. Finally, she nodded and sat down, busying herself with her cobbler.

Something was definitely bothering her. Michael promised himself he'd reach out, see where he could help once this was behind them—provided they survived this.

"I'm afraid the stone won't be enough." The voice came from the direction of the back door.

Everyone flinched or started except for the two gods.

A man stood there, dressed in black, looking much like a ninja. He had dark hair, was a little over six feet tall, and his eyes were just like Beth's, brown and brooding.

Beth walked over to him. "Evan, uh, Dad, uh . . . what should I call you?" She danced from foot-to-foot, as if she wanted to hug him, but then didn't. Her two sides—harsh and hopeful—were warring with each other.

Evan smiled. "Whatever you choose." Then he sobered and looked at the gathering. "I needed to warn you. Connor is gathering an army of mercenaries."

"In Rosebridge?" Logan asked

Evan nodded. "Yes, and in the surrounding towns. I've got contacts in the area who I tasked with keeping tabs on any influx of foreigners."

"Most likely he'll use them as pawns against Caleb, Vivian,

and any of us with abilities," Michael said. He looked at Beth, his chest too tight. "Then during the chaos, he'll try to kill Beth and breach the Threshold. We can't let that happen."

He felt his mother's gaze on him. Had she heard something in his voice?

"I can't ask my constables to fight." Logan sounded regretful.

Sam glanced at Beth. "Can you get your mercenary buddies from L.A. here in time?"

Beth shook her head. "No, but I might have a solution." She looked determined, but nervous.

"You are not thinking what I suspect you're thinking, are you?" her dad said, disapproval heavy on his face.

"Cool it, Dad." She waved a hand at him. "It's potentially my funeral either way. I'd rather go out with guns blazing."

"I have a bad feeling about this," Kate whispered loudly.

"We can use RAVEN to fight Connor's army." Beth's words sat suspended in the air for a few moments. "I can convince them to help us."

Then all hell broke loose.

CHAPTER 29

Beth held up her hands. "Let me explain." No one was listening to her. No one except for Michael. His gaze locked with hers for a moment, and all the chaos became a dull roar in her head. He should be mad. He should feel betrayed.

But all she saw in his eyes was understanding.

He made his way to her and grabbed her hand. She hadn't realized she'd felt unsteady until that moment. Suddenly, she had regained her strength, and it wasn't from his abilities.

It was because he was Michael.

It was because she was falling in love with him.

She didn't even bother trying to deny it anymore. What was the point? She was probably going to die tomorrow.

"We are not making a deal with RAVEN." Duncan's voice was like steel, cutting through everything. He looked ill, no doubt reliving his capture by RAVEN, and their escape just last month. Everyone else fell silent.

"I understand," Beth said. "I do. I hate RAVEN with every fiber of my being. They use people with abilities. They are evil."

"To even consider this option is a mistake," her dad muttered under his breath.

"RAVEN isn't suddenly going to help us," Kate said.

Sam studied Beth. "What's really going on here?"

Beth took a deep breath. "I've been working with RAVEN since after the attack."

"I knew you were bad news." Anger flooded Lennox's face. "When are they coming to raid our town? Or are they doing that now while we're all distracted here?"

Michael's parents got up. So did Duncan. Beth had to save this somehow before they lost everyone.

"They can't raid your town." Beth's words were strong and sure. The Forbeses stopped.

Michael looked at her. "It's why we made it out of RAVEN alive, isn't it?" He squeezed her hand. "You made a horrible deal to keep us safe."

"I did. It's kept you safe, and Kate, Sam, the girls, Logan, Fi . . . anyone I chose." She took a deep breath and looked at his parents. "Including your entire town. They know." She looked at Nora. "I'm sorry, but your dad told them about Benning Brook and all the gifted people who live there."

Nora shook her head slowly, despair filling her face.

Beth's voice shook. "I couldn't let RAVEN take anyone else, even if it meant I had to work for them."

Sam and Kate were immediately on their feet and at Beth's side in an instant, pulling her into a hug.

"I'm sorry," was all Beth could manage.

Kate pulled back first, her face stern. "Don't you *ever* pull something like that again without telling us."

"We're TOP now," Sam said. "We've got your back." She squeezed Beth's shoulder. "You can trust us, Beth. You can."

"So how does this deal with RAVEN get them as your private army?" Lennox asked, the distaste bitter in his tone.

For once, she welcomed him being an ass. It gave her something else to focus on. She couldn't look at the love on the faces of her friends for a moment longer.

"The General told me RAVEN was at my disposal," Beth said. "He's worried about me meeting with the necromancer. I'm sure he'd agree to sending in his troops."

"You can't trust him," her dad said. "He's the one who held your mother prisoner."

"I don't," Beth replied. "He's already told me I might be betrayed. I think it's his way of letting me know he'll be after something else, even if he helps me."

Caleb leaned forward in his chair. "They want to get a closer look at the Threshold. We've always managed to hold them back, but if we invite him in . . ."

"He'll case the joint," Kate interjected.

"We'll keep the General out," Beth said. "Just RAVEN operatives."

Caleb looked like he was considering her words.

Michael held up his hand. "All in favor of using RAVEN as our own pawns against Connor to give us a fighting chance of getting out of this alive, raise your hands."

Mackenzie raised her hand. "I don't like working with RAVEN, but as long as my dad isn't there, I vote we use them.

I hate to admit it, but their operatives are the best."

Kate and Sam also raised their hands. Everyone else slowly followed suit until it was down to Lennox, Duncan, and Vivian.

"Am I allowed to kill RAVEN operatives?" Vivian asked.

Kate patted her arm. "No, but you can kill Connor's cronies if they try anything."

Vivian smiled, and then raised her hand. She glanced at Lennox, but he crossed his arms and remained silent. The tulips on her table wilted again.

Beth shot a look at Kate. She'd already told her what Michael had shared about getting Lennox's agreement, about his respect for Kate.

Kate walked up to Lennox. "I know this sucks, I don't like it either, but I need you if I have any hope of surviving. I want to come home to my kids, Lennox. Please."

Lennox looked at her for a long moment, and then nodded.

Duncan stood. "I'm sorry, I can't agree to using RAVEN, so I'm excusing myself from this battle." He walked out of the kitchen.

Beth ran after him and caught him by the door. "Working with RAVEN was the only way to get us out of the facility," Beth said. "You were in bad shape. It was your best shot to live."

"Don't use me as an excuse."

"I'm not. I didn't mean it like that."

He rubbed his knuckles against his beard. "I'm not angry with you, Beth, but I can't fight alongside them." He lowered his voice. "You know they probably killed Ken, and as soon as your deal with them isn't fruitful, they'll destroy our town."

There was nothing she could say to that. He was right. RAVEN could be capable of anything.

She watched him open the front door and leave. The cold chill left in his wake circled her like an icy tornado. She'd thought she'd be able to get intel on how to take down RAVEN by working with them and then they'd all be free. But now they needed RAVEN to stand a chance against Connor's army.

Enemy of my enemy shit.

She looked back at the kitchen. Michael had surprised her. In front of everyone, he'd taken her hand and given her support. She wasn't used to having someone to lean on. Someone who knew exactly who she was and didn't care, who didn't run.

They needed to win against Connor somehow.

Like Michael, she now had even more to fight for, and her dark future had a glimmer of light in the shape of a tall, blonde, pain-in-the-ass Viking.

THE FOREST WAS QUIET. MOONLIGHT LIT EVERY BRANCH IN an eerie glow.

"Why does this feel like the start of a horror movie?" Beth said softly to Sam. "Any moment, zombies are going to attack."

"Brains," Michael groaned behind her.

Beth jumped, and then turned around to hit him on his chest. "Don't scare me like that." He didn't apologize, just smiled, and in that smile, Beth was suddenly back in the Forbes Manor, naked in front of the fire. How could she be horny when she was about to face death, a.k.a. Connor?

"I see you're wearing the gauntlet you used at RAVEN," Beth said.

Michael nodded and hit the button, activating the electrical charge. "This way I can still help, even if I won't kill anyone."

She snuck in a quick kiss on his cheek. "See, you're definitely one of the good guys."

"Is everyone here?" Sam asked, giving them an approving look.

Beth held up a finger, then another, counting off their team. "You, me, Kate, Michael, Lennox, Glenna, Mackenzie, Caleb, Vivian, Logan, Robert, and Nora." She scanned the group again. "I don't see Sloane yet, but I'm sure she'll turn up."

Caleb had just finished marking each RAVEN operative, along with their team, with something that was supposed to let them know who was who in the dark. That way Vivian wouldn't spear the wrong person with those nasty roots of hers.

In theory.

James had readily agreed to send Beth his troops, but he'd been pissed when she didn't allow him to be one of them. There was no way she wanted him to get near the Threshold. Intel from his operatives was one thing, but his direct involvement was non-negotiable. He reluctantly agreed, but sent Jensen in his place. That was his non-negotiable.

Caleb lifted his staff, and then plunged it into the ground. "Let the Universe guide our vision and our purpose. The forest protects. The forest endures. The forest triumphs."

Kate began to glow, as if someone had traced an outline around her made of moonlight. Beth looked at her hands. They had the same outline as Kate. Everyone did.

"We're not going to be glow lights to the enemy, are we?" Beth asked.

Vivian walked over to them. Gone were the dresses she seemed to favor. Tonight, she wore black leggings, a black shirt, and a black skintight jacket. Her dark hair was held back in a tie made of vines. Only her pale face reflected any color in the moonlight. She shook her head. "My father's work is for our eyes only."

"And he's protected the ghosts, too," Sam said. "Beatrice and the others will be immune to Connor's attacks on essence." She eyed Caleb who didn't look the least bit taxed after all his work. She lowered her voice. "He's definitely more powerful now than when we first met him."

The tricolor rings in Vivian's eyes began to swirl. "I've noticed this as well, and wondered at the meaning."

"For now, I'm grateful," Michael said. "We need all the help and firepower we can muster."

"My owls report that Connor and his army approach," Vivian said. "No guns have been sighted. Probably because they need you alive, Beth. We'll let them enter the forest and allow them to get into position, so they feel comfortable." She smiled, revealing teeth that looked sharper than Beth remembered. "Then we'll attack."

"Speaking of the attack," Kate said. "What about the trees

seeing all the potential death that could happen tonight? Will they be okay?"

Vivian nodded. "Before he left for his own lands, Karnon and my father set up protections for the trees against what they will witness tonight. An emotional shield of sorts. They will weather this battle without being silenced."

Michael called Nora over. The kid still looked like crap, like she hadn't slept at all last night, even though she was protected at the B&B, but Beth knew she was probably still reeling from her admission about her dad revealing their town to RAVEN.

That and Fi still being incommunicado, adding to Nora's stress. Beth had texted Fi too, but had just received an *I'm close to finding my Da* text. She hoped she wasn't finding his dead body. Maybe she'd ask James when this was over, now that they were more buddy buddy. He'd probably lie, but she might pick up a clue to help Fi.

"Come," Caleb said. "It's time to journey to the Threshold."

"It's time to journey to the Threshold," Beth repeated, imitating a movie announcer's voice. Kate bent over in giggles while Sam's lips twitched. Caleb merely raised an eyebrow and led them further into the forest.

Beth knew it was nerves giving everyone the giggles, but it still felt good, especially since there wouldn't be much to laugh at once Connor and his mercenaries arrived.

In only a short distance, they walked out through the trees into a large clearing. In front of them, to the left, was an old tree stump the width of an elephant.

They followed Caleb toward something sparking moonlight

in the distance. Along the right, the forest crept in closer with dense trees. To the left, there was a pile of old fallen trees.

Now that they were closer, Beth realized the glowing thing was actually a gate of sorts. On either side of it rose a tree, towering into the sky.

The gate itself was two or three times Beth's height and made of some metal, though it shone as if it had captured the moonlight within it. The gate's design was of two trees, the metal swirling together as if they were in an embrace. Their roots were beautiful, echoing the curved pattern in the main design, but the branches they raised toward the sky were jagged.

Almost like a warning.

It was beautiful and creepy at the same time.

The edges of the gates looked like they grew into the trees on either side, and their silver bled into the trees, sending shining rivers of light through their dark bark.

The light pulsed, as if it were a heartbeat.

Obviously, the Threshold to Entwine.

Caleb pointed to a line of oaks on the right. "Nora, hide over there until Connor is close enough."

Jensen motioned to two of his operatives. They joined her in hiding.

"How did you get the General to agree to all this?" Jensen asked.

Beth checked her shurikens and knife. "It's on a need-to-know basis, and you know what I'm going to say next."

She expected him to do the usual frown and walk away, but instead he looked worried. "Be careful."

Beth laughed. "Afraid your Golden Goose is going to be killed? The General already hit me up with that one."

Jensen shook his head. "You don't realize how many lives we've been able to save because of your gifts. I know RAVEN's methods might be harsh, but we've done a lot of good."

Beth wasn't sure if she believed him, but Jensen did seem earnest.

"If the kidnapping and experimentation stopped, you might be able to convince me."

He lowered his voice. "If you knew what we were up against, you might think differently. Try not to get killed, Marshall." He gave her a quick nod, the old Jensen back firmly in place, and then walked off.

"Buddy of yours?" Lennox asked. Not a trace of snark in his tone. Now that they were here, Lennox seemed to have accepted the fact they were out of options. RAVEN was in the mix whether he liked it or not.

"Handler. He usually runs me through the operations piece when I'm seeking something for them." She sighed. "I miss having my gun."

Lennox nodded. "Me, too. But with close quarters like this, we're more likely to hit someone we don't intend to."

"Vivian mentioned that Connor's crew doesn't have guns either. They don't want to destroy this ticket into Entwine." She tapped her chest.

Evan joined them. "Everyone else is in position," he said. "Sam and Kate will stay here with you to lure Connor in so Nora can use the dampening stone."

Lennox left to take his position to the left of the Threshold, behind some tall pines.

"Where will you be?" Beth asked.

"Around." Evan smiled. "I'm not going to let anything happen to you, especially now that you know who I am."

Beth grabbed his arm. "Can you keep extra watch on Michael?"

Evan grinned. "Sure. Any particular reason?"

"None that I'm willing to share just yet."

He pulled her into a hug. "I'm happy for you."

Beth hugged him back for a second longer, and then released him. "Let's not celebrate yet. It's new."

Evan just gave her a wink and disappeared into the shadows. He needed to teach her his ninja ways when this was all over.

A yell split the air.

Beth whirled around and saw one of the RAVEN operatives flying back through the air, away from the Threshold. He hit the ground and didn't move.

Jensen ran over and checked his pulse. Then he motioned to two of his men. They took the fallen operative and dragged him behind the trees where Nora hid.

Beth walked over to Sam and Kate, who stood to the left of the entrance to Entwine. She'd figured the Threshold would be protected, but it clearly packed some serious firepower.

"What happened?" Beth asked.

Sam looked grim. "I think he was trying to get in or something. I saw him touch the Threshold, and then get flung back through the air."

Kate looked at Beth. "Could you tell if he died?"

Beth shrugged. "I couldn't tell. Jensen removed him, but he could have done that to make sure Connor wasn't tipped off by having a dead body in the field." Beth lifted her chin toward Sam. "How's it coming with your dagger convo?"

Sam made a face. "They're not talking, but I did help three more ghosts this morning, so at least I was able to charge the daggers back up with essence."

"Remember that Nora's dampening stone is going to make you feel weak," Beth reminded her.

Sam nodded and then sparked some ghostly essence on the tip of her nose. "Guess I better have fun with it quick." The spark moved to the top of her head, like a mini firework display going off.

Beth laughed. "Is that new?"

Sam laughed with her. "I'm practicing."

"Hey, you two," Kate said. "Remember we're the Triumvirate of Problem-Solving. We will get through this. Together."

The hopeful look on her face darkened.

And then Beth felt it, too.

The same thing she'd felt in the forest by RAVEN.

Dread.

As if it were a physical thing, coming closer, devouring everything in its path.

Connor emerged from the tree line where they'd entered the clearing, followed by a troop of mercenaries.

CHAPTER 30

B ETH KNEW WHAT TO EXPECT BASED ON SAM AND ROBERT'S description, but she still couldn't believe a kid was doing all this.

Okay, he was maybe twenty years old, but he was still a kid to her.

He stopped about fifty feet away.

"I admit," Connor said to Sam. "I wasn't quite sure you were going to bring her."

Sam fisted her hands, no doubt wanting to take out her daggers, but they were trying to lull Connor into thinking they were doing what he wanted. "You didn't give me much of a choice. You threatened to kill everyone in your path."

They needed him to come closer, so Nora didn't have to come out from her concealment and put herself in danger.

"So, you're the necromancer I've heard so much about," Beth said. "I'm surprised you're going to these lengths to see your parents, especially after what you did."

Connor took several strides forward. Even with some distance still, she saw the anger on his face. "You don't know anything about me."

Beth pursed her lips. "Oh, but I do. See, the Wardens are a pretty chatty bunch, and we heard you killed your sister. Did you kill your parents, too?"

He walked closer. "They died in a house fire. And what happened with my sister was an accident."

"Sure, whatever you say." Beth turned around, looking at the Threshold. "I admit, the entrance to Entwine appears formidable, but given all the essence you must have oozing out of your pores, I'm not sure why you need my mojo."

She didn't hear his footsteps in the grass, but when the hairs on her neck stood up at attention, she knew he was near.

"You're either very brave or very foolish to turn your back on me."

Beth shrugged. "What does it matter? You're going to kill me anyway."

"I could make it relatively painless."

He held all the cards, or so he thought. Why would he make that offer?

Beth turned around fully. "There's something you need from me besides my death, isn't there?"

Connor was close enough now. Nora should be able to start draining him with the dampening stone. Beth flicked a quick look to Sam. Sam shook her head. She must not be feeling anything yet.

"There *is* something I'd like you to do." Connor wavered on his feet a bit, and then recovered.

Maybe Nora was finally doing her thing? "Do tell," Beth said.

"If you don't fight me, if you give in willingly, I can absorb your essence, including your ancestors' essence, quickly after you die."

Out of the corner of her eye, she saw Sam stagger.

"And if I don't give in?"

Connor frowned. "Then it will take longer. And that means more people could die trying to stop me."

Kate disappeared into the trees toward Nora's hiding place, no doubt to make sure everything was going according to plan. Beth needed to stretch this out a bit.

"I'm curious," Beth said. "How did you even find out about the Seeker line and how it works? RAVEN doesn't know, and I just barely found out myself."

She'd been wondering this since Connor had made his demand for her to be sacrificed.

"I had some inside knowledge from a very helpful source." Connor lifted his hand. "You can show yourself now, Harvey. I'm sure your daughter would like to say a few words to you before she dies."

There was movement in the ranks of Connor's mercenaries, and Harvey emerged.

Even at a distance, Beth recognized his gloating smile.

Anger burned up through her. She slipped a shuriken from her satchel, palming it. She needed to draw him out to get a clearer shot.

"I knew you hated me, Harvey, but I thought you got off

on torture. If I'm dead, you lose any chance of making my life miserable."

Harvey shrugged. "Once I discovered that Evan was here, I knew you'd connect with your mother, your real mother, and become too powerful for me to manipulate. Worse, you might kill me."

Beth tilted her head. "I'm glad we're done with *that* part of the lie."

"It was useful for a while." Harvey's smile grew nasty. "But now I get the pleasure of not only seeing you die, but also knowing my sister and my mother will be destroyed. The Seeker line will be destroyed. *Forever.*" The satisfaction in his voice turned Beth's stomach.

Connor shook his head, looking dazed. Good. Nora's stone was working. Beth risked a quick glance at Sam. She looked pale and drawn, but was still standing.

"Why do you hate the family line so much?" Beth asked. She walked toward Harvey. "If I'm going to die because of that hatred, I'd like to know why."

Harvey stepped out a bit further, though he was still flanked by two of Connor's mercenaries.

"The Seeker line doesn't care about any male offspring," Harvey said. "We can't carry on the family line. I suppose I should be grateful to your grandmother that she didn't kill me at birth. That's usually what happens."

For a moment, Beth saw the real Harvey. His face contorted in pain, in hurt, over what had happened in the past.

"Did they torture you?" She couldn't help asking.

Harvey nodded. "Not by means that left any physical mark. I just didn't exist to them. Sometimes they'd even forget to feed me." He took a breath. "Until your mother came along. She took care of me. But I knew it wasn't out of love. It was out of pity." He laughed, the sound was dark. "And now they'll all know that I was their undoing."

Beth finally understood why Harvey was the way he was. It didn't make it right, and it didn't justify what he'd done, but it explained why he despised her so. She was a reminder of how he'd been considered without value, a throwaway, by his family.

She realized there had still been a part of her that felt she'd done something to earn his wrath, but she hadn't. It was all his damage, his issues.

Several more bricks in her wall crumbled to the ground.

"Thank you," Beth said to Harvey.

Then she flung her shuriken and hit her mark, his stomach.

Harvey cried out and clutched his belly, blood covering his hands.

She'd need to kill him tonight, if she didn't end up dead first, but for now, she'd give him some pain.

Several mercenaries rushed forward toward Beth, but Connor suddenly went down on his knees, right in their path, his hands gripping the grass. "I'm not feeling . . . something is happening . . ." He lifted his hand, and red essence wafted from it, lifting up into the air, as if caught on the wind.

Beth could kiss Nora right now. It was working.

Then Connor lifted his head and gave Beth a broad grin. "Wait a second. False alarm." He got to his feet quickly. "But your friend on the other hand." He pointed at Sam.

Beth turned and found Sam on the ground, Robert by her side.

Nora burst out of her hiding place—behind the line of oak trees—with the dampening stone in her hands. Kate was hot on her heels. Kate tried to grab the glowing dampening stone but pulled back, as if it were hot.

"I'm so sorry, Beth," Nora said. "I had no choice."

Kate tackled her, and the stone fell free, the glow dying.

Connor shook his head. "The plan was for the stone to finish Sam off. But don't blame Nora. I kidnapped her sister. If Nora hadn't reconfigured the stone to drain only Sam dry, I would have killed Fi."

"You're a sick fuck, you know that?"

Connor ignored Beth, his gaze moving to where Robert had gathered Sam up in his arms. Beth slipped her Kershaw knife free.

"I really liked Sam, but if she won't join me, I can't have another necromancer around who can store Brigh like I can. I promise I'll make it quick." Connor lifted his hands toward Sam, red essence swirling from his fingertips.

Beth slashed at Connor's thigh, cutting deep.

He grunted in pain, and the red essence from Connor's hands missed Sam and Robert, landing instead on one of his own mercenaries. The man's tortured screams cut through the air.

Robert disappeared with Sam. One minute they were there, and the next they were gone. Beth hoped she was still alive.

Connor's eyes glowed red, and the essence swirled around his thigh, healing it.

The time for subterfuge was over. They were in serious trouble.

"Attack!" Beth screamed.

CHAPTER 31

SAM HEARD VOICES SHOUTING AROUND HER. SHE COULDN'T open her eyes. She remembered standing at the clearing near the Threshold and feeling weak.

The dampening stone appeared to be working on Connor, too, but then . . .

A warm hand touched her cheek.

"Samantha, can you hear me?" It was Robert. She tried to speak, but nothing came out.

"Her daggers shielded her, expelling essence to be absorbed by the dampening stone," said a voice she recognized. It was Sloane.

"That shifty little bastard, kidnapping poor Fi to force Nora's hand. I'd like to give him a piece of my mind and a fist or two."

Beatrice.

Sam's eyes fluttered open. She realized Robert was holding her. "What's happening?" she managed to croak.

She looked around. Beatrice stood in front of her, along with other ghosts she recognized—Ellie, Wendy, Monica, and

Amber, the victims of Graham. Ray, Kate's old poltergeist, was there too.

She wasn't dying again, was she?

Sloane came closer. The Warden looked grim. "You're in Entwine. Robert got you here just in time. The dampening stone was reconfigured to take your own essence and energy from you, not just the ghostly essence."

"Nora betrayed us," Robert said softly.

Now it made sense. She'd been braced to feel the ghostly energy leaving her, but no wonder why she'd collapsed.

Sam tried to sit up. "I have to go back. Beth. Kate. They need me."

Sloane shook her head. "We have to rebuild your life force first."

"You mean the ghostly essence she once held?" Robert asked. "Perhaps the daggers could refuel her."

"If Sam had enough of her own life force, she could use the essence in the daggers to do just that," Sloane said. "But she's almost depleted."

Then a look came over Sloane's face, as if she'd just thought of something. She motioned to Ray, who rushed over. Sloane whispered into his ear. Ray nodded, and then disappeared.

"One of the other necromancers is coming to assist," Sloane said. "He'll direct the energy from the ghosts."

"We're going to give you everything we can, lass," Beatrice said.

Ellie, along with Graham's other victims, waved at Sam.

Beatrice gestured behind them. "We even called in some

reinforcements. Everyone was happy to help." Sam couldn't make out their faces, but there were rows and rows of ghosts lined up. More than the number of ghosts she'd saved.

They were there—for her.

Ghosts who had saved her from Graham, and now they were saving her again.

The living, the dead—everything was truly connected. She remembered the moment when the Universe had shown her just this. She'd been so foolish to give up her gift all those years ago.

Regardless of the deal she'd made with the Universe to bring Robert back to life, she realized she wanted this now with her whole heart. Being a necromancer, helping ghosts, repairing the lives of the living . . . this was what she was meant to do.

Tears filled Sam's eyes. "Thank you."

Beatrice smiled. "We'll get you back on your feet in no time, so you can kick Connor's ass."

"We need to kill him. He's too powerful," Sloane said. She didn't look happy about it. "I'm afraid he can't be saved."

Sam wanted to argue, but she'd seen the delight in his eyes when he'd taunted Beth. Plus, he'd tried to kill her.

Sloane waved her hand toward someone to approach. "Sam, this is Akiro. He'll get the energy back into your system and configured correctly."

The man was a bit taller than Sloane. He was slender, but Sam had the sense of muscles underneath his dark blue tunic. As for age, he looked both young and ancient at the same time.

Akiro took her hand. His grip was strong, but not crushing.

"I'm sorry we're meeting under these dire circumstances."

"Are you a necromancer?"

He nodded. "If you survive this night, we have much to talk about." Akiro nodded to Beatrice. "Begin."

Blue ghostly essence flowed to Beatrice from the other ghosts, collecting around her. Beatrice thrust her hands toward Akiro, and the energy jumped through the air, latching onto him, traveling down his shoulders to his arms, his wrists, and then his hands. "And I'm deeply sorry about this."

"About what?" Sam asked.

His eyes softened. "About the pain. And this is just the beginning."

The blue essence jumped from his hand to Sam's. Sharp knives of agony sliced through her, stabbing into her veins and exploding them. Her body felt as if it disintegrated, only held together by Robert's arms around her.

She screamed, the sound long and ragged.

"Hold on, Samantha," Robert whispered.

Tears ran down her face. Everything ached. She wanted it to stop. She wanted to give up.

But Kate needed her.

Beth needed her.

Entwine needed her.

Accepting being a necromancer meant accepting it all.

Sam sucked in a quick breath and braced for the next round of torture.

She would get back and save her friends.

And Entwine.

KATE SCRAMBLED BACK TO HER FEET. CHAOS HAD EXPLODED around her, with RAVEN bursting from their hiding places to take on Connor's cronies.

"Get up," she told Nora.

The girl looked like she was in shock. Kate pulled her to her feet. Logan rushed over, and together they half-dragged her behind the trees and out of the way. The fighting was in the field. No one had come for them yet.

They got Nora to a tree, so she had her back up against something solid.

Nora kept shaking her head and repeating, "I'm so sorry."

"I'll keep watch," Logan said, eyes scanning for any signs of attack.

"Nora, I need you to focus," Kate said.

Nora ignored her, caught in a loop.

Kate shook her.

Nothing.

Well, she'd never slapped anyone before, but there was always a first time.

Kate slapped her across the face, just hard enough to break her out of it. Nora rubbed her cheek and looked at Kate, as if seeing her for the first time.

"Can the dampening stone be salvaged? Can you use it to drain Connor's life force?"

Nora shook her head quickly. "No. It's full of Sam's. There's no more room."

"Can Connor get to that energy to power up?" The last thing they needed was Connor flying even higher on Sam's life force.

"No." The frantic bunny look was finally fading from her eyes. "It's configured to take energy, not give it. He wouldn't be able to do anything."

At least there was that.

"Listen, he should have your sister close," Kate said. Because he was probably planning to kill her as soon as he was done with Entwine. But she didn't need to scare Nora even more. "Go find Fi."

"You're letting me go?" Nora looked unsure. "I might have killed Sam."

Kate shook her head. "You were under duress. I get it. But don't show your face around my B&B for a while. If we make it through this, that is."

"Thank you," Nora whispered. She hugged Kate quickly, and then ran around the edge of the fighting.

"That was nice of you," Logan said.

Kate shrugged. "Well, we've all done stupid things for those we love." He snorted, and she wagged a finger at him. "Don't you bring up RAVEN."

"My lips are sealed."

"Okay, what's the status of everyone?" she asked.

"Mackenzie and Glenna were coming in from the back. Vivian and Caleb were going to take on the stragglers at the edges. Michael and Lennox were right behind me when Beth yelled to attack. I had to find you first to make sure you were okay." He looked a little sheepish. "That wasn't part of the plan."

"Neither was Sam almost dying." Kate moved closer to the trees and peeked through at the battle. "Hopefully Robert got her away okay."

"I'm sure he did," Logan said. "So, what are you planning next? Stopping Time or trying to see the near future?"

Kate wasn't sure what would help more. Stopping time on a larger scale wasn't something she was sure she could do. And it still wouldn't siphon away Connor's energy.

"Let's try the near future." It wasn't something she could do on command, but she hoped that being in Caleb's forest and being so close to the Threshold would help. She crouched and dug through the hard soil until she reached more warmth underneath.

"Come on, near future," she murmured. She closed her eyes, focusing on the roots, the forest, the energy around her.

A surge of power washed underneath her fingers. She knew instantly that someone had died on the field, and their blood had been sacrificed to the forest. She prayed it wasn't someone she knew and found she even hoped RAVEN would be victorious. Strange bedfellows did war make.

Icy pinpricks jabbed into her fingers, still deep within the soil. Wait a second. No, this couldn't be a vision. She'd be incapacitated and helpless. She tried to pull her hands away, but it was as if the land held her in place.

The chill crept higher, into her chest, freezing her lungs. Before she could struggle again, the vision cloaked her in ice.

The oak trees folded in upon themselves, sliding away like pieces of a Broadway set. She found herself in the center of the field, RAVEN and Connor's mercenaries frozen in battle.

"I'm glad you're finally here," said a woman's voice from behind her.

Kate turned around to find a woman dressed in all white. Her hair was long and silver, but shot through with ribbons of steel gray. Careworn lines in her face didn't take away from her beauty.

"Who are you?" Kate asked.

The woman smiled. "I am the Threshold."

CHAPTER 32

BETH DUCKED, AND CONNOR'S ARM MISSED HER. THERE was no way she wanted to be touched by that nasty red stuff. Pieces of black, like flaked skin, swam within the red. Maybe it was pieces of his soul, if he still had one.

She needed to get clear of him before he sucked her dry.

Three of his mercenaries blocked her dash toward the center of the field. Beth sliced one in the stomach. He fell quickly. She dropped to the ground and opened up the femoral artery of the second mercenary with an upward strike. The last one had the drop on her, but then he stiffened, clutching his throat, blood gushing over his fingers.

Jensen pushed him to the ground and wiped off his blade. "The General wants you to come with me, now."

"I'm sure he does, but I'm not leaving my friends."

"We have a way to keep you safe from Connor."

Jensen pulled her back and out of the way of a sword.

"Let me guess, locking me away and using me as a lab rat." She dove down to the ground again, using her knife to slice through the Achilles of her attacker. His screams were sharp and bright. Sam would be proud of her. So far, she hadn't killed anyone.

The air shifted behind her. She rolled away. Connor's hands gripped the air where she'd been. Jensen rushed forward and managed to catch Connor's arm, slicing through his shoulder, almost to the bone. Connor winced, but almost immediately, red essence flooded the wound, healing it.

"Get out of here, Jensen," Beth urged, but it was too late. Connor caught him by the throat with one hand, and the red essence flowed from him to Jensen.

Beth couldn't move. She watched Jensen flail around, as if he had been set on fire. His frantic gaze met hers, and she couldn't breathe.

There was no way to help him, to stop what was happening, but she wouldn't let his sacrifice be in vain. She moved back slowly away from Connor, stepping over bodies. The last thing she wanted to do was trip and make it easy on Connor.

He stalked forward, following her.

Jensen rammed into him, ablaze with essence.

They fell to the ground.

Jensen screamed, and the sound cut through Beth, plowing through her wall inside, splitting it in two. Then he stopped moving. Connor hadn't just killed him, he'd destroyed his soul.

Like a trained dog, the red essence fled from Jensen and back up Connor's arm.

"You're worse than RAVEN." She took another step backwards. "And that means a lot coming from me."

"You can end this all if you just let me touch you," he said.

"Creepy much?" She kept moving backwards, toward the main fighting.

"Once I have your energy, I'll breach the Threshold, and no one else has to die."

"Not buying it."

Connor lunged at her, and a huge root exploded from the ground in between them.

"Run!" Vivian yelled. The forest goddess stood a few feet away, arms lifted toward the full moon. Her eyes glowed, tri-color rings circling. As if caught on a breeze, her hair lifted and flowed away from her, sparking with pieces of moonlight. Owls burst from the trees and flooded the skies in sharp flashes of cream and white. They dove, attacking Connor's troops.

Beth ran, dodging roots and vines. Some were coated in blood, while others dragged their victims into the ground.

She came up against a wall of roots, blocking passage. She couldn't get through.

"This way." Evan jumped over the top of the roots. "Back to the Threshold." Blood coated the left side of his face. It didn't look like his own.

"You really are a Scottish Spiderman," Beth said. "You need to teach me how to jump like that."

"If we make it out alive, I'll teach you everything I know."

They dodged and weaved around more roots.

Beth risked a glance back and found Connor trying to reach Vivian, but Caleb had appeared in between them. "You will not lay a hand on my daughter." The runes in his staff glowed so bright, she had to squint against the glare. He thrust the staff at Connor, and the necromancer flew back, through the air, away from the Threshold.

Beth stopped. "Did they get him?"

Her dad stopped, too. "No, but they bought us some time to make a stand." He pulled on her arm. "Come on."

They made it to the Threshold. Vivian's roots and vines didn't seem active here. Her dad scanned the darkness. Here and there were flashes showing them who was still part of their team and still fighting.

"How did you know we'd be safe from Vivian's plant friends here?"

"This close to the Threshold, there would be a danger she'd damage the structure itself. She wouldn't chance it."

Beth moved until she had one of the trees flanking the Threshold at her back. Evan did the same.

She couldn't believe she'd finally found him, and this might be the quickest reunion ever.

"I'm going to call you Dad, if that's okay?"

He smiled. "I'd like that."

There was so much she wanted to ask him. So much she wanted to know about her mom. So much to tell him about her life.

A prick against her neck startled her attention back. Someone was holding a blade to her throat. The harsh breathing in her ear told her who it was. The air reeked of garlic.

Harvey.

CHAPTER 33

MICHAEL SLAMMED HIS GAUNTLET INTO THE SIDE OF THE mercenary's head, sending a fast blast of electricity into his temple. The mercenary dropped quickly.

Glenna burst through the darkness in front of him, her face and shirt caked with dirt, as if she'd been crawling through mud. "They're using tranq darts. One of them took down Mackenzie before she could do anything. I stashed her somewhere safe, but she'll be out for a while."

The battle around them began to move toward the Threshold. Lennox sent another mercenary screaming into the night with every bit of metal on his body burning. A RAVEN operative ran by them, then turned and flung a knife, piercing his opponent in the eye.

"Have you seen Beth?" Michael asked. He'd been searching for her since she'd called the attack, but couldn't find her.

"No." Glenna fell to the ground and grabbed one of the mercenaries by the calf, sending a bolt of electricity through him. "I'm almost out." Exhaustion dimmed the light in her eyes. "I don't have a way to recharge unless I take what's left in your gauntlet, and it might not be enough."

"You should go home," Michael said. "Get Duncan's help to come and get Mackenzie."

"But I can still fight," she protested.

Lennox shook his head. "Michael is right. Without your powers, it's not safe for you here." His face softened. "And this way we won't worry."

She hugged them both quickly, and then disappeared into the night. Being small had its advantages.

Michael turned back to Lennox. "We should make our way to the Threshold. That's where—"

Out of the corner of his eye, he saw something flash through the darkness. A tranq dart headed for Lennox. Michael threw himself in its path. The needle point pierced his shoulder easily. Michael fell to the ground, hand already reaching to pull the dart out.

Lennox rushed forward, hands outstretched toward the enemy. The mercenary's night vision goggles began to smoke around the metal edges. He screamed, clawing at his face. The smell of burnt flesh clogged the air. Lennox knocked the tranq gun from the mercenary's hand and melted it with his mind.

He turned to Michael. "Are you okay?"

Michael nodded. He hadn't used his abilities to heal himself since he'd been a kid. He always felt he should be using it for others, but he needed to be awake and alive to help Beth. In his mind's eye, he tore apart the chemical compounds in the dart's payload that was starting to surge through his system.

Lennox helped him to his feet. "I forgot you could do that."

Michael shook his head a few times, dispelling the last bit of toxin. "Healing?"

"Yeah." Lennox's face clouded. "I only remember the bad stuff."

Beth's words floated back to Michael. "We were both just kids." He took a deep breath. They might die tonight, and Michael didn't want to let this to remain unsaid any longer. "I forgive you for breaking my arm, and for making my life hell growing up." Surprise flitted through Lennox's eyes. "And I'm sorry, for the hundredth time, for what I put you through."

"Having your mind violated isn't something easily forgiven." Lennox's words didn't have their usual bite.

"I've vowed never to do it again, never to hurt someone like that again."

Lennox stared at him for another moment. He looked like he wanted to say something more, but instead bent to strip the mercenary of his weapons.

Michael helped him. "I've got to find Beth."

"You've got it bad for her, don't you?" Again, no usual derision in his tone, just a question.

Michael scanned the darkened field. Everyone had passed them by on the way to the Threshold. The sharp copper scent of blood reached his nose.

"I do," he admitted.

"Is it love?" Lennox attached the mercenary's knife belt with its sheath around his waist.

"I don't know. I've never been in love before."

"Is she the first thing you think about when you wake up and the last thing you think about before you fall asleep? Does she make you want to be a better person?"

He looked at Lennox, wondering where this was all coming from. Was his brother in love?

"Yes to all of the above." Michael tightened the gauntlet on his arm.

Lennox laughed and clapped him on the shoulder. "You're in trouble then. Come on, let's go find Beth before she gets herself killed."

They'd made it about a hundred feet when the skies filled with owls—spots of creamy white against the dark night sky. Roots burst free from the ground around them, taking out two mercenaries who had been sneaking up from behind. "It's Vivian." Lennox's voice held something that Michael had never heard before.

Admiration.

Michael scanned the field for any sign of Beth. He finally found her after a few moments.

She was at the Threshold.

Was that her fake dad behind her?

If Connor hadn't killed her yet, Harvey would.

Adrenaline pounded through his system.

"Come on," Michael said and grabbed Lennox's arm.

They took off at a run.

Michael only hoped they'd reach her in time.

"Excuse me, what?" Kate asked the woman whose smile brightened, glowing like the twisting branches of the gates she stood near.

"You can call me Gwen. 'The Threshold' is too formal." Gwen's face grew serious and she placed her hand against one of the trees flanking the gates. "It's been a least two decades since the last breach attempt, but this one actually has a chance of succeeding."

"How are you in my vision?" Kate didn't know what was going on, but her visions never included chatting with some magical creature. Maybe she was hallucinating, and this wasn't a vision? But she'd felt the telltale coldness.

"I hijacked your vision," Gwen admitted. "I know Time quite well. He owed me a favor."

Time was really an entity. Kate's mind spun.

Gwen stood in front of the gates to Entwine. "As the Triumverate of Pluthar, you can access the energies of Entwine together. But the connection must be pure, which is why very few TOPs, as you call it, survive."

Great. The deck always seemed stacked against them.

"A pure connection?"

"A true sisterhood."

That wasn't happening anytime soon. Sam had just recently opened up, but Beth wasn't there yet.

"We're going to fail at stopping Connor, aren't we?"

Gwen gave her a look she couldn't easily read, but it wasn't good. "I can't tell you the outcome as it's still in flux, but you will need the power of Entwine to survive—for *all* of us to survive—this night." Gwen shook her head slowly. "I told Sloane this was a long shot."

"This was Sloane's idea?"

Gwen nodded.

Kate rubbed her temples, already throbbing with a headache. "Okay, for argument's sake, let's say we've got a true sisterhood connection. How do we call on the energy of Entwine?"

Gwen walked over to her. "This will help." She touched Kate's forehead, and the headache magically disappeared. But in its place was knowledge. Suddenly everything cleared away in her mind. She knew what they had to do to stop Connor.

"Good luck, Oracle. We're counting on TOP."

Gwen removed her hand, and Kate felt herself hurtling back. Back into her body.

Logan lay beside her, staring at her.

"Hey, I have to tell you of the crazy vision/not vision I just had."

Then she saw the blood seeping from his neck and covering his chest.

His eyes didn't move.

No. It couldn't be.

She reached out a trembling hand to touch his face, and a shadow loomed over her.

"He's dead," the mercenary said. He wiped his bloody blade on Logan's shoulder. Then he grabbed her wrist and pulled her to her feet. "But Connor wants you alive."

Logan grabbed his ankle and jerked him back. The mercenary fell to the ground. Logan got to his feet and rushed the man, but then froze. The tip of a blade came out of Logan's back.

"No!" Kate screamed and ran to him.

The mercenary pulled his blade out, and Kate managed to catch Logan before he fell.

"I'm sorry," Logan choked out, blood spilling over his lips.

She rocked him back and forth. "It's okay. You're going to be okay."

Logan's hand reached her face. She felt the blood slick on her cheek from his fingers. It was so warm against her cool skin.

"I love you." His whisper caught at the end.

Her tears fell on his cheeks, smearing the blood. "I love you, too."

This couldn't be happening, shouldn't be happening.

His eyes looked past her. "Please. Don't let me die."

Then his eyes closed, and his hand fell from her cheek.

Kate plunged a hand into the dirt. "Rewind!" she shouted. "Let me fix this! Let me stop this!"

Nothing happened. No surge of energy.

"Help me!" she screamed to the forest, digging her hand deeper into the dirt. If she could just reach the energy she could kickstart his heart, heal his wounds, do something, *anything*.

But she couldn't feel a thing. Like the entire forest was silent. Connor had done something to it.

The smell of smoke hit her nose. The forest was on fire,

which shouldn't be possible from what Caleb had told her.

"Connor's waiting." The mercenary grabbed her shoulder, pulling her back.

Logan's body fell from her lap to the ground.

Her grief transformed into rage. It roared through her body. She spun around and faced Logan's killer. "Connor can wait," she growled, thrusting her hand against his chest, letting her rage spill free.

The mercenary's eyes widened, and he staggered back.

Before her eyes, his face grew sunken, and then wizened. His body looked as if the flesh had been sucked away under his clothes. His hair grew gray, then silver, then fell out.

He made choking sounds, reaching for her.

Then he shuddered, eyes growing white. Then he finally dissolved into a pile of dust and bones.

A part of her knew she should be shocked. She'd just killed someone with a power she didn't understand. Somehow, she'd sped up time for him and him alone.

But when she looked at Logan's body, it was a part easily quieted and a voice easily silenced.

Her rage demanded payment.

She picked up the mercenary's sword, wiped the blade against his tattered clothing, and headed off to find Connor.

CHAPTER 34

BETH TRIED NOT TO FLINCH, ALREADY FEELING THE WARM trickle of blood trail down to her collarbone. Evan had disappeared.

"Isn't Connor going to be upset you're endangering his ticket into Entwine?"

Harvey grabbed her right arm, pulling her back to him. "I'm making sure you die tonight. If Connor returns in time, he can have you, but if not . . ." He took in a ragged breath.

"Stomach wounds are a bitch, aren't they?" She hoped she'd nicked an internal organ with her earlier attack. Beth slid her left hand down her waist, trying to reach her satchel. It was closer than her knife sheath. If she could get a shuriken free, she'd plant it in Harvey's face. "Where is wonder boy, anyway?"

"Those gods you have on retainer are keeping him occupied, but soon they'll be busy trying to save their precious trees."

"They might kill him." Her fingers reached the lip of her satchel.

"Not unless they can take away all the power he's amassed,"

Harvey said, his breath tickling her ear. "I know you're back there, Evan."

Harvey turned, pulling Beth with him to face the darkness by the side of one of the trees. "Come out and throw your weapons down, or I'll kill her right now."

Evan walked forward, peeling away from the shadows as if he'd been a part of them. He placed his knives on the ground.

Beth's fingers dug into her satchel, touching the metal of her favorite shuriken.

"You won't win," Evan said.

Harvey laughed. "And what are you basing that on?"

"My daughter." Evan smiled at Beth, and it was filled with something Beth had always yearned for from her parents, but never received.

Pride and belief.

Beth pulled the shuriken free. She pushed herself forward and to the side, tearing herself from Harvey's grip. His knife sliced through the skin on her neck, but it was a shallow cut.

She spun and threw the shuriken in the overhand throw Ollie had taught her. The metal flew through the air and sank deep into his cheek. She'd been aiming for his eyes.

He grunted in pain and pulled the shuriken from his cheek. Blood poured from the wound, seeping down his neck. Evan slammed into Harvey, taking him down. Beth grabbed her knife but her dad already had Harvey trussed up, hands tied behind his back.

Evan looked past her, alarm on his face. "Is that Kate?"

Beth turned and saw Kate walking from the tree line where

Nora had originally been hiding. Was that a sword in her hand?

Kate's face was bloodied, shirt torn, eyes completely white.

A mercenary was coming in hot from her right.

"Kate, watch out!" Beth yelled and ran toward her friend.

Kate's gaze flicked toward the attacker, and she squeezed her hand into a fist. The man exploded into dust.

Beth skidded to a halt.

Holy crap.

The wind picked up, bringing the acrid scent of smoke. Beth saw an orange blaze in the distance. How was that possible? Caleb had told them the forest was protected against anything but natural disasters.

But Harvey had just hinted at the forest being in danger.

Connor walked out from behind the trees to Beth's right. "Your friends are strong adversaries, but I finally gave them something more important to stop than me."

The thought of all those trees being hurt, dying, cut a hole in Beth's gut. She knew they felt everything.

She'd make sure Connor did, too.

"I'm not going to be sad when I kill you." Beth gripped her knife and grounded her stance.

"Get in line." Kate had made it to her.

Beth almost didn't recognize her voice. It was rough, like she'd been screaming.

Kate fisted her hand, staring at Connor. Beth saw shimmering light arc through the air toward him from Kate, but immediately a shield of red essence blocked anything Kate was throwing at him.

It looked like he wasn't going to go poof into dust.

Kate moved in closer, swinging her sword at him with both hands.

Beth reached out to grab her back. Kate would get herself killed.

But Evan's arms wrapped around her waist, and he pulled her off her feet. He dragged her back toward the Threshold, but she broke free.

"I have to help, Kate." Beth tried to run past him but he blocked her.

"You have to escape," Evan urged. "He'll destroy you and gain Entwine."

He spun her around and pushed her toward the Threshold and Harvey, but Harvey was no longer tied up and no longer in the distance at the gates to Entwine. He was right in front of her.

As if in slow motion, Beth watched him thrust his knife at her heart.

She couldn't move.

CHAPTER 35

SAM GOT TO HER FEET SLOWLY WITH THE HELP OF ROBERT and Akiro.

She felt better than she had before, as if she were filled with powerful warm light.

The necromancer held out his hand and closed his eyes. "You're strong. Your life force is already replicating on its own." He opened his eyes, a look of surprise in them. "More quickly than I've ever seen before."

Sam thought about those new pathways she'd felt from the ghostly essence. Maybe they helped with her own energy, too?

"Good, you're ready." Sloane walked over. "We need to get back to the Threshold to end this." Her face was grim, resigned.

"Wait," a voice said from behind Sloane.

Sloane turned around, and Sam saw a young girl, maybe Emily's age. She had short brown hair to her shoulders and was dressed in jeans and a t-shirt.

"You shouldn't be here," Sloane said to the girl, her words short and clipped. "I'll have a Runner take you back."

The girl shook her head. "I need to talk to Sam." Her voice was firm. "I'm not leaving until I do."

"This isn't the time—"

"I want to hear what she has to say," Sam said, interrupting Sloane. She didn't know who the girl was, but something told her to listen.

Approval shone in Akiro's eyes. "The necromancer has accepted the request. You cannot interfere, Sloane."

Rule #35: A Warden cannot prevent a necromancer from speaking to any ghost.

The Rule floated into Sam's mind, and it was one she hadn't known before. She looked forward to studying with Akiro if she made it through this alive.

The girl came forward to stand in front of Sam. "My name is Megan. I'm Connor's sister."

Sam immediately wanted to know if Connor had really killed her, but it was always best to let the ghost lead the conversation, even when there was no Bargain involved. "Why do you want to speak to me?"

Megan held out her hands to Sam. "Connor needs help, not a death sentence. If you can get him off the ghostly essence, you can save him. I know you can."

Before she'd met Connor in the cemetery, Sam would have agreed right away with Megan's plea, but addicted to essence or not, Connor enjoyed killing. Save him? Sam wasn't so sure that was possible, but that didn't mean they couldn't lock him up first and then try.

Sloane shook her head. "After what he did to you, Megan, I

can't believe you're asking us to spare his life."

"He didn't mean to kill me," Megan said. "He didn't know the strength of his siphoning ability. But my death did change him." She frowned, looking much older than her years. "And my parents didn't help either. If you call someone a monster, a *freak* for long enough, why believe anything different?"

Sam's parents had been supportive, but she'd been called a freak, and worse, by the other kids when she'd been growing up. So had Beth and Kate.

"I know what that's like," Sam said. "I can imagine how Connor must have felt, facing everything alone."

Akiro's lips tightened. "You would forgive him for all the blood on his hands?"

"No," Sam replied. "He still needs to answer for what he's done, but if it's possible, he should do so free of the essence and its hold upon him."

The other necromancer tilted his head. "He would suffer more if he was able to feel remorse without the essence influencing him. Good point." That wasn't what Sam had been going for, but if it saved Connor's life, so be it.

Sloane looked grim. "I'm sorry, Megan, but Connor has grown too dangerous." She lifted a hand, and two Runners appeared next to Megan on either side of the girl.

Megan's gaze latched onto Sam. "You have to help him, please." Tears streamed down her face. "He's my family."

And then she was gone, along with the Runners. They disappeared without a sound.

Sam knew what it was like to be helpless while your family

was in danger, and like Sam, Megan might have to watch while they died in front of her.

"If there is a chance to end this without killing him, promise me you'll take it?" Sam asked.

Sloane's hands clenched and unclenched. "You don't have to kill him yourself, Sam. I will." Sloane didn't look happy with her decision, but resolve showed in her eyes "We need to leave, now."

But Sloane had told her that the Wardens couldn't kill Connor on their own. There was something Sloane wasn't telling them.

Robert took his ring from his pocket and looked at Sam. He knew, as did Sloane, that Sam would return to the Threshold. She really had no choice. Not only was Entwine in the danger, but also the lives of her friends.

But the pain in Megan's face, the sob in her voice, remained with Sam.

"Just remember, you didn't give up on me," Sam said to Sloane. "Even when I turned my back on my gifts." She held the Warden's gaze. "Even when I put the *entire Balance* in jeopardy, you kept fighting for me. I'm beginning to trust you, to believe in you. Prove to me that I'm not wrong about who you really are."

Sloane turned away from Sam before she could read her face. "Now, Robert."

Sam put her hand on Robert's shoulder, and he slid the ring back on his finger. In a flash of light and noise, they were suddenly back in the forest. The battle raging around them.

Michael and Lennox made their way to the fallen trees near the Threshold. They would get some cover while they figured out the next steps.

By the time they'd made it through the battle, Harvey had been tied up and taken care of. Michael felt like he could suddenly breathe again, though he wasn't sure what Kate was doing, striding across the field with a sword.

"She's going to kill Connor," Lennox whispered. "I saw it in her at RAVEN. When push comes to shove, she'll protect her own."

Michael smelled smoke on the breeze. The woods were on fire. "We need to help her, help Beth." Michael stood.

The rest happened so quickly. Evan grappling with Beth. Connor grabbing a sword and fighting Kate. Harvey, suddenly free of his bonds, running toward Beth. He'd reach Beth before Michael could get there, and shouting a warning would only distract her from the real danger.

There was one thing Michael could do, but it would mean breaking a vow.

Lennox followed his gaze. "Do it, brother. You have to."

"You can't mean . . ."

"I do. Save the woman you love."

Harvey's knife gleamed in the moonlight.

Beth turned and froze.

Michael reached out with his gifts and latched onto Harvey's mind. He dove deep, through the filth, the crimes, and the pain. It didn't take much to control Harvey, especially with all his focus on killing Beth.

"Your back is bloody," Michael said, his voice low. "Your chest, too. Wounds the size of a belt buckle. So painful."

Harvey hunched over, as if he'd been struck. Then his hands went to his chest, knife dropping from his grip. He looked at his fingers as if they had something on them. Michael knew what he saw.

Blood.

"Here come the flies." Michael let the image he had pictured from Beth's story fill his mind. Black flies, buzzing, biting.

Harvey cried out and began batting the air and his body. He stumbled further backwards, as if he could escape them.

"There's only one thing to do." Michael pictured him slamming his body, his head, against one of the trees next to the Threshold, like Beth had done against the wood of the root cellar door.

Harvey turned and ran full speed at the tree, slamming into it. Then again. And again.

Each time, more blood. Each time going back for more, until he crumpled to the ground.

Michael felt the last breath leave Harvey's body.

Then the darkness reached up and swallowed Michael whole.

CHAPTER 36

BETH STARED AT HARVEY'S BATTERED BODY. SHE CHECKED his pulse. He was dead.

The way he'd been acting and screaming about the flies, she knew it could mean only one thing.

Michael had used his abilities on him.

To save her.

The sound of metal clanging drew her attention back toward Connor. Was Kate really sword fighting?

No. It was Robert. Sam was back and running toward Kate who was on the ground, battling the red essence. She had a shield of white around her, matching her eyes, but it was starting to flicker.

Beth turned to run toward Kate, but a yell split through the air. It sounded like Lennox.

"Help!"

She saw him carrying Michael around the fallen trees. Michael was limp in his brother's arms.

He couldn't be dead. Was he dead?

Sam would have to save Kate on her own.

Beth ran for Lennox and Michael, leaping over bodies, skirting around open holes in the ground. She took off her jacket and helped Lennox place Michael on the ground. "What happened?"

"He took control of Harvey's mind. I don't know what he saw, but it sounded terrible from what Michael was saying."

She searched Michael's pale face. His eyes were open, but unfocused. "He's not . . ."

"No, he's still alive." Lennox looked frightened, an emotion she wasn't used to seeing on his face. "I think what he did hurt him, too."

"Michael," she called softly. She touched his face, even kissed him gently, but nothing. It was like he had gone somewhere. "I don't know what to do. I don't know how to help."

You can seek more than objects.

Her mom's voice wafted into her ears.

"What are you talking about?"

Lennox looked at her like she was crazy.

"It's my dead mom, okay. She might be able to help."

Your head guides you to objects and to things people have lost, but your heart will guide you to emotions, even to secrets that are being hidden. You must open your heart.

The thought of doing something like that would have sent her boarding the next plane home just a few weeks ago, but Sam and Kate had been wearing her down.

And then Michael had snuck by her defenses. If he died now and she could have saved him, she'd never forgive herself.

It was worth whatever the cost. "Show me."

She felt a whisper of touch on her back, like fingers.

Let us in.

Fear spiked through her, trying to build up her crumbling walls. Let ghosts in? It was ugly inside. They wouldn't like what they saw. They'd judge her. They'd try to change her.

The touch moved to her cheek.

You'll need us to help Michael. We need to be joined.

Beth gazed at Michael's face, at those eyes that sparked with laughter and mischief, at the lines on his face, which came at great cost.

He'd do the same for her. She knew it in her bones.

"I'm going to try to save him," she told Lennox. "I don't know what it will take or how long, but try to stop Connor from killing me until I can help Michael, okay?"

Lennox stood, determination blazing on his face. "He'll have to kill me first."

Evan joined them, knife out. "And me as well."

"Thanks, Dad." Beth's voice cracked.

Lennox touched her arm. "Go save my brother. And tell him." He paused, swallowing. "Tell him I forgive him."

Beth widened the split in her walls left by Jensen's death.

"Come on in," she whispered.

SAM LOOKED AROUND QUICKLY AND TOOK HER DAGGERS OUT from their sheaths. She found Beth, along with Evan and

Harvey, near the Threshold, and she spied Michael and Lennox behind a fallen tree.

The Warden looked at her watch. "It's been almost a day for you inside Entwine, but less than an hour has passed here."

A flash of red hair caught her eye. Kate was on a collision course with Connor.

"Can you get me close to Connor through Entwine?" Sam asked Robert, and he nodded.

"What are you going to do?" she asked Sloane. The Warden couldn't kill Connor outright if he was still powered up.

Sloane smiled. "I may not be able to take the ghostly essence from him, but I can manipulate what he has inside and make it painful, keep him distracted while Kate tells you the plan."

The Warden slipped away.

Plan? What plan? It had to be what Sloane had been hiding—a way to kill Connor.

"Kate has reached Connor," Robert said. He took off his ring and grabbed Sam's arm.

They ran through Entwine, the forest a gauzy outline around them, until they were right behind Connor.

They burst free from Entwine. Connor spun around, as if he somehow sensed them. Probably the essence warned him.

"I thought you were dead." Connor tried to grab her arm but she blocked him with a dagger.

"Over here!" Kate yelled. Red essence licked along a milky white shield around her. There was a sharp hissing sound. The essence was eating its way through Kate's shield.

Her attention diverted, Sam saw Connor's blade coming,

but she wouldn't be able to block it in time.

A flash of silver filled her vision, and Connor's blade met another's with a sharp clang of metal. "Go save Kate," Robert said, parrying another of Connor's blows with his sword. "Leave him to me."

He slashed at Connor, opening up a red line across his chest.

Sam rushed to Kate. She ran her daggers all over Kate's shield until every last ounce of essence had been sucked away.

And just in time, too. The shield dissolved into glowing bits of light, just like she'd seen Kate conjure in the yew tunnel when they'd first gone to meet Vivian.

Kate looked dazed. "I don't know where that shield came from. I should be dead." Then her face crumpled. "But Logan is dead. He's dead, Sam."

It felt as if someone scooped out Sam's heart, leaving a hollow space behind. Logan was dead? Kate had finally opened herself back up to love, and weeks later, her world had been smashed yet again.

"It's not fair." Sam pulled her into her arms and squeezed her. "I'm so sorry, Kate."

Kate's sobs shuddered against Sam's chest.

Sam suddenly realized the only sounds of battle she heard were Robert and Connor in their swordfight. She risked a quick glance back at them.

Robert held his own against the necromancer, popping in and out of Entwine to strike, never letting Connor's essence touch him.

Suddenly Connor stiffened and hunched over.

"You've been a bad boy, Connor." Sloane had appeared behind him.

She flicked her hand back.

Pain rippled across Connor's face. "How?"

Sloane's gaze hardened in the flickering moonlight above.

"Every necromancer has a special gift. This was mine."

The Warden had been a necromancer?

Sloane looked at Kate. "Tell her what Gwen put inside your head." She winced. "Sorry. I can't hold him forever, so you're going to have to hurry."

Kate wiped her eyes with the back of her hand, leaving blood and dirt on her face. She still looked devastated but determined.

"Gwen is the Threshold," Kate shared. "She told me how we can use the power of the Triumvirate to open the Threshold gates, so Entwine can take back all the essence Connor is holding onto and return it to its rightful place." Kate flashed a look at Sloane. "She said it was your idea."

Sloane nodded. "What Connor had done to you, Sam, reminded me of an old story of a former Triumvirate of Pluthar. They created a vacuum, so Entwine could call back the energy that originated from that realm—like a large dampening stone—which we could use on Connor."

"You'll fail," Connor gritted out through clenched teeth. "The Brigh is embedded within my very cells, my very bones. Entwine will not be able to take it back."

Sloane frowned at Connor and put up another hand. Connor twisted, falling to the ground.

"Will it hurt the ghosts?" Robert asked.

"The ghosts will be fine. That essence is where it's supposed to be." She eyed Sam's daggers. "And anything you have in there will be protected."

"So what do we have to do, Kate? Blood sacrifices? Surrender our souls?" Sam wouldn't be surprised by anything at this point.

Kate looked worried. "We have to be a true sisterhood to make the ritual work. Fully trusting and open. Otherwise, we all die."

And she stood corrected. She *was* surprised. And worried.

"It's not going to work. Beth isn't fully open yet," Sam said.

"I know," Kate agreed.

Sloane hunched a bit and then straightened. "I think he's pulling more energy from the ghosts he controls in Entwine. You better hurry and get Beth."

"She's sitting over there," Kate pointed.

They ran over to her and found Lennox and Evan standing guard with Michael's body on the ground.

"He's in a catatonic state," Lennox said when they got close enough. "He had to use his abilities to stop Harvey from killing Beth."

"Beth," Sam said. "We've got to perform a ritual to stop Connor."

She didn't move a muscle. No snarky remark either.

"She's gone after him." Evan nodded. "To save him."

Sam turned and watched Sloane struggling to hold Connor.

If Beth didn't return soon, they were all dead.

And Entwine would be lost.

CHAPTER 37

BETH FOUND HERSELF IN UTTER DARKNESS. "WE'RE HERE, Beth," her mom's voice sounded from nearby. A light began to glow, causing the darkness to scatter, scuttling into the distance.

Her mom came into view first, as if she'd swallowed the moon. Her entire body glowed. She stood just a few feet away. Next to her was Beth's grandmother, then her great-gran, and each one after, spiraling around her in a glowing circle.

Yet the circle wasn't big enough.

Even more of her ancestors faded off into the distance, their glow like the tail of a comet.

Her grandmother waved a hand at Beth. "I have to set the record straight, first, about Harvey's accusations."

Beth's mom looked frustrated. "Now is not the time, Mom."

"It is the time. Beth needs to understand that I didn't starve him or had any plans to kill him." Her grandmother looked angry. "Was I the best mother? No, I could have been better, but Harvey was always one for the drama." She looked at Beth, and her face softened just a little. "I didn't want you thinking the worst of me."

Beth hadn't realized how Harvey's words had bothered her until now. How she'd been worried she had indeed come from a damaged line. "Thanks, Gran," Beth said. "He was usually full of shit, but it's good to get the truth."

"Take my hands," her mom instructed.

Beth did so immediately. The time for hesitation was over. She needed to know how to save Michael. She looked into her mom's face, seeing echoes of her own. How had she ever thought Gloria was her mother?

"You had no reason to question it," her mom said and then smiled. "Sorry, but we can all hear your thoughts because we're in our sacred place, where all Seekers first find their gifts and guidance."

"You've heard my inner thoughts before," Beth said.

Her mom smiled. "True, but only some of the time."

"How come you never reached out to me before I came to Scotland?" Beth knew she had to concentrate on Michael, but she needed to know.

Her mom frowned. "I tried, many times, but I couldn't connect with you. Too many bricks in your wall.

"I needed them to survive."

"I know. I was the same way once RAVEN took me, but Evan was the one who finally broke through."

"Michael's been pummeling down my walls, too," Beth said. "I need to save him, Mom."

Her mom nodded. "He's retreating further and further

away," she said, "which is why we have to act fast."

Beth squeezed her hands, afraid she'd suddenly disappear. "If I survive all this, will I still be able to hear you? See you?"

"We'll be here," her grandmother piped up, "ready to finally give you the training you'll need. It's about damn time, too. You've been doing it all wrong."

Her great-gran smiled. "And you'll need to have babies soon, dear. We're counting on you to keep the family line going."

The old Beth would have sparred with her grandmother and protested against her great-gran's assertions of children, but then she looked along the line at all the members of her family. All Seekers. All just like her. All she felt was belonging.

Finally.

Beth took a deep breath. "Okay, let's get this mind dive on the road. Ask me to find Michael, though I've never been able to find a person before."

"You don't need anyone to ask you to find things or people," her mom said. "That's something Harvey shackled you with. Something he could use to control you, so you wouldn't realize you could do it all on your own."

Her grandmother crossed her arms. "I told you. Doing it all wrong."

Her mom frowned at the comment but ignored her. "Just like objects, you'll find emotions, secrets, and memories all have their own energetic vibration. That's what Seekers pick up on. You match with the vibration you're seeking."

"And that's when the frozen lake forms?'

"Everyone has their own method. Mine was a window."

"Mine was a book," her grandmother added.

Her mom continued, "However, it's a bit tricky when you're trying to connect with something that's not physical."

"Like emotions or memories," Beth said.

"Exactly. So it helps when you know the person."

Her great-gran brightened. "That's why many of us were spies. We would infiltrate the enemy, get close to them, and then bam! We'd discover all their secrets and win the day."

Beth couldn't wait to have more time to grill these women about what she could accomplish, but she had to keep focused on Michael.

"I know Michael pretty well, and also some of his memories. We, ah, got close recently. You didn't watch all that, did you?"

Her mom gave her a naughty grin.

"Okay, we're going to have to set some ground rules on peeping ghosts in the future."

"Spoilsport," her grandmother muttered.

"Michael used one of your memories to kill Harvey," her mom said. "How would he have felt after he did something like that?"

Beth didn't hesitate. "Awful, full of loathing, angry at himself for breaking his vow."

"Did he share any memories with you where he felt that same way?" her mom asked.

"The one where he almost killed Lennox."

"There's a good chance he's retreated there." her mom said. "Think of that memory and what he told you."

Beth did as she asked. Michael had mentioned there was a

dock, a lake, and it had been summertime in Scotland.

Beth was so used to someone else asking her to find something. What if she couldn't do this? What if it didn't work?

Her mom squeezed her hands. "Think of who he is and why you care for him. Connect with that feeling."

Beth let out a long breath and thought of yesterday. Her silly grab at him, the rumble of laughter traveling from his skin to hers, the way the fire caught the strawberry blonde strands in his hair, the look in his eyes when she told him not to stop.

Michael.

He was a warm ribbon of gold in her mind. Butterscotch smoothness with a whisky undertone. She wrapped him around her, holding tight.

The frozen lake formed in front of her.

"Good, Beth," her mom said. "Now think of that memory he shared with you, and follow that feeling." Her mom let go of her hands.

The dock. Summer. Lennox shouting for help from the water. The golden ribbon jerked forward, hitting the icy surface, then going through it.

Beth hung on. Pictures, like snapshots, whirred by her. The Forbes Manor. A baby. Michael's dad. A picture of all the boys. The ribbon unwound from her body, hurtling her through the chaos of memories, and then landing on her ass next to a lake.

"Who are you?" the boy asked her. He looked around nine or ten.

She'd found Michael.

CHAPTER 38

BETH STOOD UP. WAIT A SECOND. WHY WASN'T SHE LOOKING down at Michael from her height?

He was a kid.

And she was . . . ?

She looked at her hands. Small, cracked nails from clawing at the root cellar door.

Oh God. She was a kid again, too.

"Who are you?" Young Michael repeated.

"I'm Beth." Even her voice sounded like it had all those years ago. A bit on the fragile side, though she'd tried to hide it.

She studied him for a moment. He had the same blond hair, though it was longer, down to his chin. His face was rounder. Not the chiseled cheekbones he had now.

He was taller than she was, but just a smidge. He was wearing jeans, a blue t-shirt, and an old flannel that looked too big for him.

But his eyes were the same. Piercing and shifting blue, depending on his mood. Right now, they were cloudy and assessing. The breeze sent Michael's hair in front of his face. He pushed it back.

"You're not supposed to be here," he said.

"Neither are you." She grabbed his arm. "We need to go right now. You have to wake up."

Hopefully before Connor slaughtered them both.

Michael pulled his arm from her grip. "I'm not going anywhere. I belong here." The resignation in his voice contained an element of heartbreak.

There was movement near the dock. It was Michael and Lennox. Lennox was around fifteen or sixteen and had a dazed look on his face.

Oh, no. This was the actual memory. And they were going to watch it happen.

Lennox stopped right at the edge of the dock. He seemed to be coming out of whatever mind control Michael had him under. He saw the water in front of him, and fear whitened his face.

Memory Michael squeezed his eyes shut and thrust out his hand. "You want to dive into the water. You're boiling and need to cool off."

Lennox's face went slack again. He didn't hesitate any longer. He jumped off the dock and into the water.

And began flailing.

Going under.

"I wanted to kill him," Young Michael whispered to her, watching himself on the dock.

"We've all felt that way. And Lennox is a dick."

Michael looked startled, and then smiled. "He is a dick."
Then he sobered. "But I shouldn't have done it."

They watched Memory Michael dive into the lake, swimming with excellent form out to Lennox. It was obvious he'd always loved swimming. He grabbed Lennox and pulled him back to the dock. They both held onto the wooden planks, breathing heavy and hard. Then Lennox pulled himself up onto the dock. He walked away from Michael, never looking back.

"Things were never the same between us." Michael's voice lowered. "I hurt him."

The memory reset. Memory Michael and Lennox walked to the dock.

Beth stood in front of Young Michael, blocking his view of the memory. "Lennox was the one who told me to save you."

Michael shook his head. "No, that can't be right."

"He told me to give you a message. He forgives you."

"I don't believe you." Michael moved around her to watch the memory.

Beth spun him back around. "You need to stop this pity party and get back to the real world."

"No!" He wriggled free of her grip and ran toward the dock.

She sprinted after him and caught him. They fell to the ground.

"You have to come back." He struggled again, and she held him down. They were roughly the same weight, but she knew how to pin someone. One of Harvey's lessons.

"I belong here!"

"No, you don't!"

"I do." Tears streamed down Michael's face. "I did it again, Beth!" he yelled. "I hurt someone again! I promised I wouldn't, and I did it! I killed someone. I *killed* someone!"

She stopped trying to hold him down. She, instead, pulled him up to his feet and into her arms. "You did it to save me."

His entire body shook in her embrace. "I could kill again. What if I kill again?"

"If you do, there will be a reason for it. You're a good person, Michael Forbes. I know you are."

He quieted and pulled back slightly to look into her face. "How do you know I am?"

She wiped the tears from his cheeks with her thumb. "Because I . . ."

The words became strangled in her throat. Once she said them, they couldn't be unsaid, which meant he could hurt her, *really* hurt her.

But she knew him, that wasn't a lie. And Michael could hurt her. Hell, she could hurt him, too. But he wouldn't do it out of spite or hatred or malice.

Beth stared into his eyes, bright blue with tears. "Because I love you, Michael Forbes. The good, the bad, the darkness, the light. It scares the shit out of me, but I love you."

In the blink of an eye, Michael was the Michael she knew. The kid was gone.

The memory froze.

She was back to her usual self, too.

"You really love me?" he asked.

She punched him in the chest. "Always the ego with you.

What do you want? Should I get a tattoo declaring my love for you?"

He smiled, and her heart began to race. "Maybe we should get matching tattoos, because I love you, too, Beth Pain-in-the-Ass Marshall."

She just stared at him for a moment. Had he really said he loved her?

"Hey, you're the pain in the ass, not me, Forbes."

"Shut up."

He pulled her close and kissed her. The last of the bricks in her wall didn't just fall, they exploded.

And then she was back.

No longer in Michael's arms.

Cold dark night. Smoke in the air. Lennox and Evan standing guard.

Michael blinked his eyes open, and Lennox helped him up. Then he pulled him into a crushing hug.

Sam and Kate rushed forward.

"Come on, we have to get to the Threshold," Sam urged, pulling on Beth's arm.

"We have ten minutes to save everyone," Kate added.

"Make that five!" Sloane shouted. "Hurry!"

"So it's the usual, we're in deep shit," Beth said.

"Yup," they both replied.

Without any more words, they turned and ran toward the Threshold.

CHAPTER 39

THEY REACHED THE THRESHOLD, STEPPING OVER THE bloody mess that was Harvey.

Beth realized for the first time in her life that if they survived this night, she'd be able to stay here with Sam and Kate. She didn't have to disappear. Gloria was still a threat, but she'd lost her main partner, and that was something.

And Beth wasn't afraid any more to let Kate and Sam in—all the way in.

The gate glowed in the moonlight, the trees and roots etched in silver. Beth risked a glance toward the trees in the distance. There was no more orange glow. Caleb and Vivian had put out the fire.

"Okay, what's the plan, Red?"

Beth turned and looked at Kate closely for the first time since she'd gone after Connor with a sword. Blood still caked part of her face, but it had been broken apart by tear tracks.

Where was Logan?

Sam caught her eye and shook her head slightly.

Beth got the hint. Save the world now, grieve later.

Kate took each of their hands. "We have to all join together in front of the Threshold. Gwen gave me the words to perform the ritual."

Beth didn't ask who Gwen was. It didn't matter.

"There's a catch," Sam said.

Out of the corner of her eye, Beth saw Sloane stagger. "Spill it. We're running out of time."

Kate looked worried. "We have to be fully joined as a sisterhood, meaning opening up and trusting. All of us."

Beth nodded. "Piece of cake."

Sam looked at her as if she was crazy. "What happened when you saved Michael?"

Beth grinned. "I'm in love, bitches. So, buckle up and prepare to be smothered in it."

A tiny smile on Kate's lips lightened some of the darkness on her face. Sam just laughed. Full on with snorts. Beth pulled them both into a hug. Screw the hand-holding shit.

The power flared immediately between them. From Kate, the energy was weak and filled with pain. Beth felt the loss of Logan as if she'd experienced it herself. Tears filled her eyes.

Beth poured love into that connection, filling in the broken bits and frayed pieces. "I've got you, Red. You're going to be okay."

And from Sam the power was strong, but rigid, unyielding. Since her parents had died, Sam had only had herself to count on. Beth knew that feeling well, but they weren't alone. They had each other. She understood that now.

Beth poured love into that connection with Sam, softening it, opening it up to acceptance. "I've got your back, Sam. And I forgive you for everything."

Sam looked at her with surprise, and tears glistened in her eyes. And yet Beth still had more love, more light within her. The connection between them blazed stronger and brighter than ever before.

It rushed through Beth, filling her up. She still had pockets of darkness, she always would. But as long as there was light, the darkness wouldn't consume her.

They stared at each other, and for a moment the Threshold, the forest, the battle, everything disappeared.

Rather than the chain she'd always felt when they'd joined, it was now something living, something growing that connected them.

Kate's eyes blazed bright white. The pain was still on her face, but so was her incredible spirit. Beth couldn't ask for a more faithful friend.

Sam's eyes swirled with storms, black and white jostling together with bits of lightening scattered throughout. The strength Beth had originally despised—but secretly coveted—was tempered by understanding. Beth couldn't ask for a more resilient friend.

She knew her own eyes would be black, except for a wider rim of white around the edges. The white representing the light and spirit of her family, her ancestors.

The energy between them flared, embers of light breaking free and swirling in the air like stars.

"Repeat after me, but when we get to the last line, we have to say it together three times," Kate instructed.

Kate chanted the words. Beth and Sam repeated them.

"*What has been stolen*
now will be found.
Darkness devoured,
lightness unbound.
Calling home to be one
with the Universe once more.
Part of Entwine.
The Balance restored."

Kate nodded to them, and they repeated it together.

"*Part of Entwine. The Balance restored.*
Part of Ent—"

Sloane flew through the air, hitting the tree to the right of the Threshold, cutting them off.

The Warden slid to the ground in a heap.

Connor appeared behind Sam and reached for Beth. "It's over," he said and tried to pull Beth out of their embrace.

Red essence flared over Beth's shoulder and onto her back. It felt as if her skin were being ripped off, piece by piece, but she'd faced worse as a child.

She didn't know Connor well, but she knew of the pain that came with a family who didn't love you. Feeling like you had to fight for every scrap of love you could, and it still wasn't enough.

"Show me his fear," she hissed.

No sooner had she said the words than the frozen lake

appeared and a gray ribbon wrapped around her. Pain, sorrow, murder. Her mouth tasted of ashes. The ribbon yanked her forward, hitting the frozen surface hard, almost cracking it. And then she was through. The darkness of his mind grasped at her, clawing, trying to pull her under, but the ribbon led her unerringly to a shivering pocket of green light.

Unlike Michael's memory, this was a chaotic mix of past, present, and what appeared to be future. A young girl's body, and a boy that looked like Connor standing over her, tears streaming down his face. Connor shouting to the skies at his parents' gravesite. The red essence sliding into his mind, twisting it, until he wasn't sure where either of them began. The Veil standing strong against his attempts to tear it down. After everything he had sacrificed, he was failing.

She needed him to feel this—to feel all his fear—so much that it would derail his attack long enough for them to repeat those final words.

For the first time ever, she could call on family. Beth thought of her mom, and she was suddenly back with all the Seekers. She staggered and went down on her knees. The red essence was sinking into her. Soon she wouldn't be able to hold on.

Her mother rushed to her. "What do you need?"

"Can you help me take something I've found and release it into his mind?" She held out her hand and summoned what she'd seen. A green glowing ball hovered over her palm.

Her grandmother huffed. "Of course, we can." She shouted down the line. "Ladies, let's show Beth how it's done."

A blaze of green, matching the ball in her hand, flared

through the line of women, surging toward her great-gran, her grandmother, through her mom, and then it hit her in full force.

She willed herself back into Connor's mind and poured the energy into the sphere holding the fear she'd seen. It shook, trembled, and then blew up, coating everything in sickly shades of green.

Pain ripped through her. She fought to hold on. The gray ribbon fluttered near Beth. She grabbed onto it with everything she had and was back in her body.

Beth sagged in their arms. Everything had gone numb. She couldn't speak, only a croak escaped her lips. Connor fell back, letting Beth go, his eyes wide.

"Hold on, Beth," Sam urged. Her dagger blazed bright blue as she held it flat against Beth's shoulder. The red essence fled from Beth's body, running toward Sam's blade. Beth gasped a deep breath and then another.

Connor rushed them again, this time reaching for Sam.

"Stop!" Kate yelled, and Connor froze.

She looked a bit dazed. "I guess I really don't need the Time Baggies after all."

She nodded to Beth and Sam.

Their voices rose again, together.

Part of Entwine. The Balance restored.

Part of Entwine. The Balance restored.

Part of Entwine. The Balance restored.

The Threshold gates blew open.

Connor stumbled back, freed from whatever hold Kate had

on him. A brilliant blue light flooded out and swarmed over Connor. The red essence rose up through his skin. He screamed and screamed, sounding like his very being was being ripped apart. He tried to run, but he fell to the ground.

Essence poured out of his nose, his mouth, and his eyes, bringing blood with it. Every bit of essence that rose into the light turned blue. The black flecks disappeared, as if they were being burned away.

His cries choked off, and he went limp. The blue light disappeared back through the Threshold gates, and they closed with a resounding *clank*.

Movement caught Beth's eye. Sloane was back up on her feet, bloody but moving fast. She disappeared, and then reappeared next to Connor.

Beth hadn't even seen her pull her knife out, but it was in Sloane's hand, flashing down toward Connor.

"*No!*" Sam yelled and ran toward them.

The knife hit the ground so hard, Beth felt the vibration underneath her feet. It had missed Connor completely.

Sam stopped in her tracks.

Sloane snapped her fingers, and Darrin appeared, along with three extremely burly dudes. Did the Wardens have muscle on their payroll?

Darrin handed her something that flashed silver in the moonlight, like a rope, but thicker. They tied it around Connor.

Sloane nodded her head toward Sam, and then the Warden and her team disappeared back into Entwine with Connor.

"What just happened?" Kate asked.

Sam turned and walked back to them, a smile on her face. "Sloane is someone I can trust."

Beth rubbed her eyes, feeling like she could sleep for days. "As long as we never see Connor again, I'm good."

Then there was movement past Sam's shoulder that perked her up. Vivian approached, along with Caleb, and there was someone with them.

Beth smiled and elbowed Kate.

"Hey, Pip. Look over there."

Kate followed her gaze.

Her face blazed with happiness. "Logan!" she shouted.

Beth had never seen her run so fast. She took Logan down to the ground with one leap.

Vivian joined them by the Threshold.

"Did you save him?" Sam asked Vivian.

The forest goddess nodded. "He called to me on the edge of death. A moment later, and I wouldn't have been able to help him. I owed him a boon, you see."

Beth grabbed Vivian into a hug. The goddess hesitated for a moment and then hugged her back.

"Thank you," Beth whispered.

"It was my pleasure." Vivian released her. "I'm quite fond of Kate, too. And her girls would never forgive me if I had a chance to save Mr. Logan and didn't." She smiled, and then walked back toward Caleb, passing Robert on the way.

Robert swept Sam away in a whirl reminiscent of Sam's romance novels, and the usual PDA began.

Beth wobbled on her feet. Whatever she'd done to Connor had taken its toll on her.

Then strong arms scooped her up. "Saving the world again, I see," Michael said.

"Uh-huh. And I saved you, too."

"Very true. I guess I owe you now."

She traced the edge of his lip. "I can think of several ways you can pay me back, once I've got my strength back that is."

He waggled his eyebrows at her. "Shall I bring the brownies?"

She nodded. "And I'll bring the restraints." Beth grabbed his shirt and pulled him down for a kiss.

She'd been yearning for a family, for a sisterhood, and for love, but believed she was too damaged to be worthy of any of them.

Plot twist, she'd managed all three, which meant someone had screwed up in the karmic wheel. Or maybe something was going to happen to mess up her life again.

But for now—for now—she was going to bask in something she'd never felt, something she had never hoped to feel.

Joy.

CHAPTER 40

"DID YOU ORDER UP THE WEATHER, RED?" BETH ASKED. "Is that one of your new Timey Wimey powers?"

They sat on the back patio area of the B&B, basking in the sunshine on an unseasonably warm day for this time of year.

Now that the Threshold battle was behind them by at least a week, Beth felt some of her worry relax. She kept on expecting either Harvey or Connor—or both—to do the villain-pop-back-up-trick, à la *Friday the 13th*.

Kate shook her head. "I still need to work on some of those Timey Wimey powers. I'm going to figure out how to get hold of Time and get some questions answered."

"Like how you aged someone to death?" Sam asked. She passed bottles of beer to Beth and Kate. "I think you called it 'dusting them?'"

"It was really gross," Kate admitted. "Like Indiana-Jones-and-the-Ark gross."

"Hey, maybe you can use that to ripen avocados." Beth dipped a chip into some salsa.

Kate nodded. "I should try that. Then if I disingrate a few, it's no big deal."

Beth leaned back, closing her eyes, enjoying the warmth of the sun. "I could almost be back in L.A."

"After you film your episodes next month, are you planning on going back to the States?" Sam asked. "Because I hope you say no and stay."

Beth opened her eyes. "So you want me around?"

They all had been doing a bit of a tip-toe dance since the battle. For a moment, when they'd all been joined, they'd seen each other's souls. Nothing could be the same after that. And she had forgiven Sam, finally.

Kate dolloped some guacamole on her plate. "Of course, we *both* want you around. Don't tell me you're going back to your old loner ways?"

Beth shook her head. "But I'm still getting used to all this." She gestured around their circle.

"You can still be your usual bitch," Sam said. "But we'll now know that it comes from a place of caring."

Kate laughed. "Who knew you had that much love inside you?" Then she sobered. "When you hit me with it, well . . . it really helped, because I thought I'd lost Logan."

Beth clinked her bottle with Kate. "Who knew Vivian would come through in the clutch. I think you owe her a *lot* of treats."

"Don't worry," Kate said. "I've already planned a trek to her tree. Logan is going to help bring all the goodies to her. And the girls have drawn a picture of Saint Vivian, halo and all."

Sam almost spit out her chip.

"How's the forest doing?" Beth asked.

Kate leaned back in her chair. "Better. The Wardens were able to repair the enchantment on the forest that Connor broke, and Nora is making amends. She's volunteered, with Fi, to help Caleb plant new trees to replace those lost."

"Speaking of Wardens, Sloane is still recovering." Sam looked worried. "She was weakened by trying to stop Connor when he attacked her."

"At least she's still alive." Beth ran her fingers over the condensation on her bottle. "Jensen and I weren't buddies, but he saved me from Connor and paid an awful price."

The image of his eyes before he died kept floating into her mind. She hadn't been able to shake the guilt.

"I don't like that you're still working for RAVEN." Kate had her mom-chiding tone at full blast.

Beth shrugged. "They lost almost all their local operatives in the battle. I feel responsible for them, and especially for Jensen. But I was able to negotiate a better work schedule at least. I've got to start filming some new episodes soon."

Sam grabbed more chips. "And staying tight with RAVEN allows you to still gather intel to potentially take them down."

"Exactly," Beth said. "Hey, you could put a black ops shadowy group in your next book. The brooding soldier falls in love with the prisoner he's responsible for."

Sam tilted her head. "You mean your mom and dad's love story?"

Beth nodded. "Evan had to take care of some business, whatever that is, but he's promised we'll have a long debrief soon." She winked. "And he knows I can verify everything with my ghost mom, so no lying."

"While we're on the subject of love stories," Kate gave Beth a knowing look. "A little birdy told me Michael might be transferring to the local hospital."

Beth tried not to smile but couldn't help it. "Glenna can't keep her mouth shut."

Sam poked her arm. "And you were just doing the whole 'do you want me to stay' act. Sheesh. If he's staying, you're definitely staying."

"True," Beth admitted. "He's too good in the sack to leave."

Kate laughed. "Our little Beth wasn't lying. She's in lurrrrvvvv."

"She is." Sam put a hand to her chest. "We raised her right after all."

"Shut up, you two." Beth brandished her fists toward both of them.

"Michael and Beth, sitting in a tree," Kate sang, "K.I.S.S.I.N.G."

"It's Sam who likes to get busy in trees," Beth fired back.

"And Kate likes sheds," Sam said.

They all convulsed into laughter and chip throwing.

Beth realized now that letting down her inner walls, calling off the guards, and being able to just *be* wasn't like dying at all. It was what living—truly living—was all about.

Having people in your life who loved you for who you were—the good and the damaged.

She wasn't naive enough, though, to believe the Universe

was done with them yet. There would be more challenges, especially now that their powers were evolving.

But for the first time, they would face whatever was thrown at them together, truly together.

As TOP.

As friends.

And most importantly of all . . . as sisters.

I love you,
Samantha Eveline Hamilton,
Katharine Amanda Peterson,
Tiffany Beth Marshall.
When you need me, I will be
your strength,
your heart,
your courage.
We are sisters in blood.

ACKNOWLEDGEMENTS

Thank you to all the readers who have helped this trilogy to succeed!

I appreciate everyone who shared my posts on social media, who recommended my books to their family and friends, who spent the time to review my books on Amazon and Goodreads.

Those reviews have meant so much! I love hearing what moved you, what surprised you, and what made you keep reading.

And your reviews have helped others take a chance on my books not only online, but at in-person events too.

I have many people to thank. Though I may write alone, I haven't had to walk this path alone.

These books wouldn't have been possible without the excellent eye and guidance of my dear friend, Jessica Petersen. As my editor, she knows the world of Entwine almost as well as I do. And because of that, she knows instantly what my voice is and understands the complexity within these characters. She's also the cover design artist, and as many of you have shared with me, these covers are truly magical. I'm blessed to have you in my life, Jess!

Cherry Weiner was the first agent who took a chance on me. We started working together with my first book, but we couldn't get it sold. When we had to part ways due to the shifting of her work focus, she remained a strong supporter of my books. Getting an agent the way I did (I'll have to share the story again sometime) provided me a boost of confidence, and I carried that with me all the way. Thanks for all your support, Cherry!

My critique group has kept me sane and on track through all the ups and downs of a writer's life. We'll have our twentieth anniversary in a few years. So hard to believe it's been that long. I'm lucky to have them in my life, along with their unwavering belief that I could succeed. Thank you so much for being there!

If you're a writer and you don't have a critique group, form one. Now.

Special thanks go out to my family. My niece and nephew, Mary Kate and Charlie, are such huge cheerleaders of mine. They never doubted I would publish my books, even when cancer kept trying to knock me down. I love you both so much!!

My sister, Kim, has been there every step of the way—from book launches, to NYC trips, to holding up copies of Entwine in the MET. The Shearer sisters are always embarking on fun adventures! I love you, Kim. Thanks for being a wonderful big sis!

My brother, John, recently told me that all my hard work was paying off. He understands how difficult it is to juggle multiple careers and passions. But he also knows what it's like to pursue your dreams. And you can't let anything stop you. Love ya, John! By the way, I'll always be younger than you!!

To my friends, both new and old, you ROCK!! I don't know how I got so lucky to have so many people rooting for me, helping me, really "seeing" me for who I am and loving me all the way.

And through it all, Karen Weir (formally Hodge for all our high-school buddies out there) has been there. I remember when I used to make up stories during class and dream of seeing them in print someday. Thank you for being one of my first listeners and also an important beta reader for the entire trilogy. I did it, Kare!! I made my dreams happen. Love you!

My furry editors and snuggle cats, Cleo and Feta, have watched over me throughout. With Cleo approaching nineteen, I give her laptime whenever she wants it. Even when it interferes with writing time. Hey, she's ninety in cat years, so she deserves the extra cuddles. Especially for nursing me through my cancer battles. And Feta is simply Feta. Crazy, silly, and loving, all wrapped up in fuzzy soft body. Hugs and love to you both, always and forever!

Finally to leiomyosarcoma, my super rare cancer, it's time to acknowledge you here. I had a tumor-naming contest when it first appeared in 2005. My nephew won, naming it Bob. While I would like to be done with Bob and his buddies—it's been four times now—I have to acknowledge the role they played. Cancer gave me the kick in the butt I needed to stop wasting time and start truly living life. Thank you, and don't let the door hit you on the way out. Haha!

It was a longer stretch between *Raven* and *Threshold*, and I appreciate the patience and love you've had for me during this journey.

Threshold was extra important because I know so many of you can identify with having emotional scars and damage. Even if you didn't go through what Beth did, we have all had challenges that make us close off our hearts, even for just a little while.

And as this was the finale of the trilogy, I wanted to make sure I did justice to this incredible friendship between Sam, Kate, and Beth. Since they are all aspects of myself that I have brought together inside me, joined together internally if you will, I needed to make sure that what happens at the end of *Threshold* was satisfying to my readers as well.

We are all flawed and complicated beings, but we deserve to be seen and to be loved.

Until my next book—my next adventure with you, dear readers—know that you are valued and appreciated. And never, ever, dim your shine. Glow brightly and inspire others to do the same.

Much love to you all!

$\mathcal{A}$BOUT THE $\mathcal{A}$UTHOR

A NEW YORK TRANSPLANT, TRACEY SHEARER NOW CALLS the Pacific Northwest her home—a land teeming with ghosts, writers, and coffee shops.

The loss of both her parents and her own battles with cancer fuel her love of stories that explore how important our connections to each other are. And through her work as a mentor and coach, Tracey enjoys helping other writers realize their dreams.

Under the close supervision of her two rescue kitties, Cleo and Feta, Tracey is expanding her award-winning short story, "The Potential", into a novel. You can find her on Twitter and IG at @TraceyLShearer and at traceyshearer.com. You can also join her Motivated Magic Writing Group on Facebook for writing tips, trainings, motivation, and inspiration.

Made in the USA
Las Vegas, NV
06 December 2022

61369170R00289